# BRAIN DEAD

ALSO BY EILEEN DREYER

*Bad Medicine*

*Nothing Personal*

*If Looks Could Kill*

*A Man to Die For*

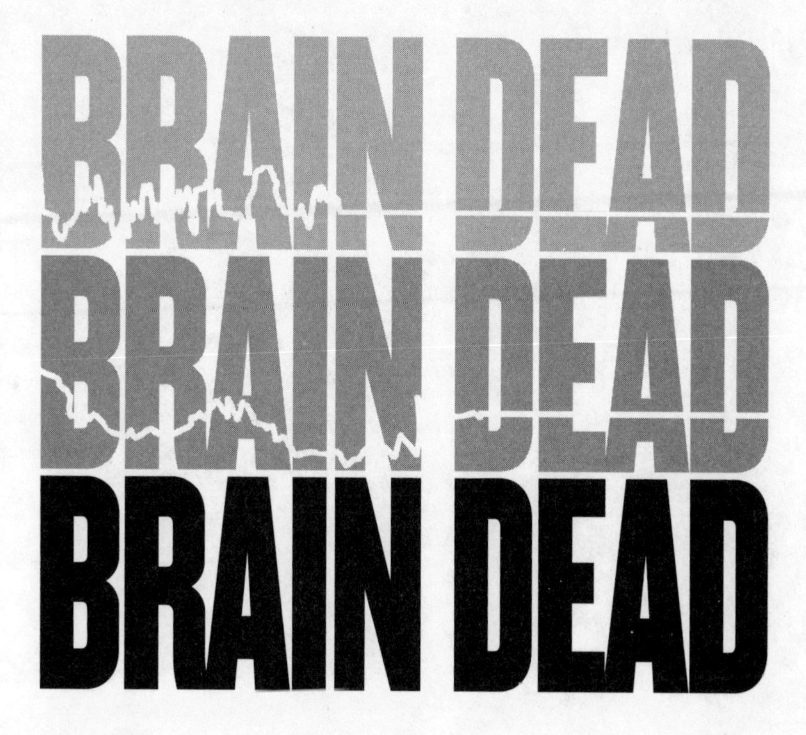


# EILEEN DREYER

HarperCollins*Publishers*

HarperCollins books may be purchased for educational, business, or sales promotional use. For information please write: Special Markets Department, HarperCollins Publishers, Inc., 10 East 53rd Street, New York, NY 10022.

FIRST EDITION

*Designed by Ruth Lee*

ISBN 0-06-101095-2

I have had the rare privilege to know some singular, rare Irish characters in my life: Grandpa Dunne; Uncle Bill; both Uncle Eddies; Uncle Tom; Uncle Joe; Pa Quinn; Uncle Fal; Uncle Jimmy; Chris King, who taught me the forbidden verses of Irish songs; Sean O'Driscoll in his enchanted castle; and my mother, Dode Dunne Helm, whom I will always remember laughing. When each of you left, the world lost a little magic we'll never see again. I hope you don't mind that I've woven bits of you into the warp and weave of Joe Leary.

*The lions of the hills are gone.*

It is always with the best intentions that the worst work is done.

—Oscar Wilde, "Intentions," 1891

A final note about geography. Neither Puckett nor Puckett County exist. With apologies to Washington, Missouri, which I blithely moved down the river a ways, I squeezed in Puckett to provide me with a county without an adequate coroner's system that close to St. Louis. Hope you guys don't mind.

# ACKNOWLEDGMENTS

ACKNOWLEDGMENTS
ACKNOWLEDGMENTS

ONCE AGAIN, I WOULD LIKE TO THANK THE PEOPLE WHO GAVE so graciously of their time and talent to help me with this book:

Dr. Mary Case and Mary Fran Ernst of the St. Louis County Medical Examiner's Office; John Maguire of the *St. Louis Post-Dispatch*; Virginia Lynch and the International Association of Forensic Nurses; everyone at the Alzheimer Association of St. Louis, especially Joan McKinnick; Harvey Kerr of USC-Los Angeles County Medical Center; Betty Jordan of the Chicago Police Department; Steffie Walker, dear friend and spokesperson for her people; John Podolak of the St. Louis Police Department and his wife, Michelle, for proofreading; and, of course, to the best editor in the business, Carolyn Marino, who makes me work so hard.

The mistakes, as usual, are mine—or, if you'd like, dramatic license.

My thanks also to the Divas for support above and beyond the call, especially Tami Hoag for dealing with all this first and Karyn Witmer-Gow for judicious butt-kicking. And, of course, Rick and the kids for putting up with endless Chinese and much-too-enthusiastic discussions about the effects of arson.

# PROLOGUE

The angel of death came at dawn. It wasn't the usual time for the angel to make its appearance; the old man knew that. He was familiar with the breed. He'd seen them hover in the fetid midnight of a jungle, heard their sly rustle at 3 A.M. in the alleys that crooked away from taxi stands like spider legs in the cold night air. He'd fought off a few and given one or two a knowing nod. He'd danced one step ahead of them for some seventy-eight years, and he wasn't in the mood to let this one catch up with him now.

Especially not here.

It was too clean here, too impersonal. The old man wanted to meet this angel on his feet, head up, eyes wide open, in the kind of place he'd always fought his fights. He wanted the chance to beat it back just one more time before giving in to the inevitable.

Go gentle, my ass, he thought, curling his bent, broken fingers into fists beyond the wrist straps that made him impotent and old.

"My name is Butch Cleveland," he rasped with a voice ruined by beer, cigarettes, and parade grounds. "United States Marine Corps. Serial number 3124456. And that's all you're getting from me, you son of a bitch."

"I'm sorry," the angel said, bending over him.

It shouldn't be at dawn, Butch thought, squirming to get away when there was, ultimately, no place to go. Not when the sun finally showed up. Death belongs in the night, deep in the dark hours of dreams and terrors, when sappers break the fences and two-dollar fares carry automatics. The dawn brings redemption. The sun means promise. Hope. Another night overcome.

"Not now," was all he could say, trembling.

"Shift's over," the angel told him.

He was crying now, ashamed of the tears and the trembling and his own terror. "I'm not going."

"Nothing you can do."

But there was. He fought the angel. He fought the pain. And, when it came to it, he fought the drug that had been injected into his IV for ten hours, more than anyone but a bull sergeant who had survived Tarawa and North Market could have withstood.

The angel of death walked back out of Butch Cleveland's room as the sun topped the low hills outside. Butch Cleveland, the angel knew, would now be obliging and die. Nobody could withstand that much Digoxin. Not even Butch. And when Butch did die, nobody would notice, because Butch was old and senile and sick.

The angel carefully recapped the used syringe and pushed the evidence into a bright-red contaminated supply box. Then, ever on the alert for the whisper of nursing shoes along the quiet hallway, the angel slipped back into the doorway of Butch's room to make certain of the results.

The angel believed in work well done, and Butch's death would be that. Just like the others. Just like the ones to come. After all this time, the angel knew how to do the job.

Ah, there it was. A gurgle. A gasp. A heartbeat of silence in the sterile, white-walled room. Smiling with quiet anticipation, the angel stepped from the shadows in order to see Butch Cleveland's eyes flutter to emptiness.

Butch Cleveland's eyes were wide open. His face was brick-red, his arms shaking against the restraints. The acrid stench of loosened bowels already permeated the air. Butch caught sight of the angel, haloed by the rising sun, and spat all the way across the room in a final act of defiance.

"*Semper fi*, you cocksucker!"

But no one in this place noticed an old man's scream. Butch Cleveland thrashed and choked in a dying seizure that lasted ten full minutes, and no one came. Only the angel, who watched with avid attention until the old man twitched into final, wide-eyed silence. Then, sighing with perfect satisfaction, the angel walked out to deal with the rest of the day.

IF A PERSON'S EX-HUSBAND HAD TO COME INTO THE ER WHERE she worked, she'd probably want him to come in looking just like Billy Mayfield: pea green, sweating like a pig, and puking up sock lint.

Billy was even considerate enough to show up about eleven on a Sunday morning in October. That way, not only could his ex-wife enjoy his near-operatic distress, so could her coworkers.

The ER at Memorial Medical Center wasn't usually busy, because Puckett, Missouri, wasn't usually a busy place. Tucked along the southern bank of the Missouri River about ninety miles west of the Gateway Arch in St. Louis, the town consisted mostly of a bedroom community that balanced its economy on farming, river traffic, and the encroaching St. Louis suburbs.

Memorial Medical Center especially wasn't a busy place on Sunday morning, when the greater percentage of the town was still in church. Therefore the only problems occupying the staff of the emergency department were a brace of abdominal pains and a mother who needed her ten-year-old cured of his flu by the big hockey game the next day.

There was one dead body in room five, but he didn't demand

much attention. He certainly didn't press the Call button or complain about the wait. A perfect guest with all the time in the world, which was a good thing, because his nurse had been waiting at least two hours for the coroner to call back so she could stamp Mr. Cleveland's morgue pass.

That was the bad news. The good news was that Butch Cleveland was Timmie Leary-Parker's only patient, which meant she could waste a little time on a phone call to her daughter.

"You ready for Mass, Meghan?" she asked, cleaning her stethoscope with an alcohol wipe as she talked. She was perched on a charting desk with her feet on a chair, the crumbs from her breakfast bagel still caught in her lab coat pockets.

"I already went, Mom," the six-year-old informed her in arch tones. "Grandda and I have been singing."

Timmie stopped rubbing. She heard the whoop of a siren in the ambulance entrance, but chose to ignore it. "Singing what?"

" 'Spar-Strangled Banner.' "

" 'Star-Spangled Banner,' " Timmie corrected in relief, knowing just what other tunes her father could have been sharing. "You watching baseball?"

"The Astros. Renfield doesn't like the Astros. He wants the Dodgers. We haven't seen the Dodgers since we left home."

Timmie smiled. "Renfield's a lizard, hon. Lizards don't get to vote."

"He is *not* a lizard. He's a Jackson's chameleon. And he lives here, too, now."

"Well, find a show on flies and grasshoppers, and we'll tape it for him, okay? California grasshoppers."

Timmie was rewarded by a bright giggle and another "Mo-o-om," which, for a six-year-old girl, said everything.

"Hee-e-e-elp me-e-e-e-e!"

Timmie looked up. The ambulance had evidently arrived, carrying what sounded for all the world like that little girl in *The Exorcist*. Definitely new business. Somebody else's, Timmie fervently hoped. Whoever it was was making retching noises, which Timmie hated more than anything but drunks and lawyers.

"Whoa, what's that?" Dr. Barbara Adkins demanded as she sauntered over with her lunch Mountain Dew in hand.

Timmie considered the hoarse wails that echoed off the tiled walls like reverb at a rock concert. "Hangover," she said.

"What hangover?" Meghan demanded in Timmie's ear.

"Nah," Barb said, dropping into one of the other chairs and draining half the can in one gulp. "Childbirth."

"Hog caller with a kidney stone," Timmie countered.

"Mo-o-om," Meghan intoned with marginal patience. "You were talking to *me*?"

Timmie focused on her daughter. "Yes, I was, baby. In fact, I was just about to ask you if you had your room cleaned, so you can go to the horse show with me this afternoon."

"After I write Daddy, for when he finds us."

"We're not lost, honey," Timmie reminded her. She didn't add that it was Meghan's dad who was lost, or that given enough time he'd remember to look for them. Probably any minute now, considering how badly Timmie's week was already going.

"He-e-e-e-e-el-p . . ."

"If I'm any judge of tonal qualities," Barb observed laconically as she lobbed her empty can toward the trash, "he's in room three. Wonder who's gonna get him?"

"New patient, room three," the intercom promptly announced. "Timmie Leary-Parker, room three."

The can hit the bucket with a clang for a three-pointer and Timmie sighed. "Of course."

Two years ago, Timmie had been married to an up-and-coming Los Angeles lawyer, mother of a beautiful preschooler, and employed as forensic and trauma nurse at the busiest gun-and-knife club in the country. Now she was divorced from a cocaine addict, her daughter was best friends with a reptile, and her career was reduced to puke patrol in a stop-and-go ER outside St. Louis. Was life wonderful or what?

"Okay," she capitulated. "Will somebody put out yet another call to the coroner about Mr. Cleveland? I know he's dead, but that doesn't mean he should have to put up with all that noise. In the meantime, as soon as I get off the phone with Meghan, I guess I'll be in doing the spew samba."

"The flu?" Timmie demanded of the EMTs ten minutes later as she hugged the far wall of room three in an effort to escape the pungent aromas emanating from the unwashed, unshaven, middle-aged man who moaned and twisted on her cart. "*That's* all this is?"

"No . . ." her patient managed between belly-rumbling groans. "I'm dyin' here . . . can't even . . . feel my fingers and toes . . . "

As much air as he was sucking in to replace his lost stomach contents, Timmie wasn't in the least surprised. "How long have you been sick?" she yelled loudly enough to be heard.

Behind her, the door opened and a tech leaned in. "Didn't you hear your page?" he demanded of her. "Phone."

Timmie was busy tossing the EMTs a fresh barf bucket and trying to climb into some kind of protective gown. "I'll call back," she said without turning around.

"It's your baby-sitter," he insisted. "Says it's urgent."

Timmie yanked on gloves. "Geez, I just talked to Meghan. She couldn't have had her problem then? Ask if it involves blood, smoke, or a badge. If not, it'll wait."

The door shushed closed just as her patient swung back into his favorite refrain of "Help me . . . "

"You're new," the EMT said to her. "Aren't you?"

Timmie smiled and forbore telling him that she wasn't new at all. Just back. Like the proverbial bad penny. Or Freddy Krueger. "Just moved from California. Want to tell me about my patient?"

"California?"

The EMT actually looked a little disappointed. Probably expected something more exotic from a California transplant with a guy's name. Timmie had short-cropped dark-brown hair, Irish skin, and blue eyes. Short, unpolished nails, standard-issue maroon scrubs and lab coat, and unimaginative white running shoes. Timmie thought of flashing the guy her tattoo to make him feel better, but decided this wasn't the time or the place. Nor was he the man she wanted to drop her pants for.

"And you came here?" he asked, incredulous.

Timmie grinned. "And I came here. To hear all about my patient."

The EMT snapped to attention. "Claims he's been sick about a week," he offered, clamping the patient's sweaty hands around the basin and beating a hasty retreat to the sink. "Definite double bucket, from the looks of his trailer."

"Timmie Leary-Parker, coroner, line two," the secretary droned over the paging system. "Timmie Leary-Parker."

Yanking her stethoscope from around her neck, Timmie headed for ground zero. "Of course he calls me now," she said to no one in particular. "Well, he can just wait a minute."

"Leary?" her patient demanded on a moan, his watery red eyes rolling Timmie's way. "You? Any relation to Joe?"

Timmie should have been more surprised. "Yep."

He flashed a sudden smile. "How is he?"

"Fine. Just fine."

Her patient nodded, lowered his head back into the bucket. "Good. He's somethin', Joe is . . ." He paused for another spectacular eruption, which didn't do Timmie's stomach any good. She wrapped the blood pressure cuff around his arm anyway.

"What's your name?" she asked.

"Is Ellen here?" the patient whined instead, his voice echoing inside the bucket. "She workin'?"

"Ellen?" Timmie asked.

"His name's Mayfield," the EMT said. "Billy Mayfield."

"Ellen Mayfield," Billy whined some more. "She works here. She's my wife."

"*Was* his wife," came the delighted announcement from the once-again-open doorway. "Hey there, Billy. Thought that was you in here singin' the porcelain psalm. How's it hangin'?"

Timmie turned again to find not Billy's ex, Ellen, but Barb Adkins, dessert soda in hand, grin on her wide, homely face.

Not standing, actually. Slouching, eyes half closed, head to the side. Barb was deceptively lazy-looking, slumping down so that her massive size seemed less a threat, her equally impressive brain less intimidating. Barb was an inch over six feet and a couple of pounds shy of two-fifty, all solid. She'd worked her way through med school as a bouncer up at the clubs on Laclede's Landing in St. Louis, and kept the ER's noisier patients in line just by standing over them.

"It's not hangin'," another voice offered behind her. "More like flyin'."

"Launching."

"Hurling."

Timmie had been mistaken. It wasn't just Barb leaning in the doorway, but damn near the entire membership of the SSS. The Suckered Sister Sorority, as they called themselves at moments of diminished self-respect. Divorce detritus. Left-behinds who shared stories and beer on Friday and intricate revenge plots any other time. Eight members, all told, including one male who demanded equal time and a lab tech who was still trying to make that all-important choice between divorce and murder.

And the gang was almost all here to share Ellen Mayfield's finest moment since the judge had awarded her full custody of the kids and the house. All, that is, except Ellen.

"Nice to see you guys," Timmie greeted them, her attention caught by Billy's blood pressure, which was low for all the energy he was expending. "You want to come in here and do this?"

Several heads shook emphatically. "Uh-uh."

"We're just the Greek chorus," Barb assured her.

"State's witnesses," somebody else agreed. "For the appropriate documentation of punishment."

"Get the fuck outta here!" Billy growled, his sagging cheeks gray and twitching beneath small, close-set eyes.

"Barb can't get out of here," Timmie said with a cherubic smile. "She's the doctor who's going to treat you."

"Oh, shit." Billy moaned.

Barb stepped on in, still beaming brightly. "Something you seem to be uncomfortably familiar with today, huh, Billy?"

"Timmie, Mr. Van Adder on line two," the paging system droned overhead. "Mr. Van Adder, the coroner, who says he's not going to wait a minute longer?"

All heads raised. Timmie gave in and peeled off a glove. "Somebody at least get lab for Billy so I can clear Mr. Cleveland, okay? And make sure you get liver enzymes. Maybe it's the ambience in here, but he looks a weensy bit yellow to me."

"Yellow's the perfect color for him, ya ask me," Barb offered equably.

Billy shut his eyes like a man before a firing squad. Timmie tossed her gloves and squeezed past the crowd in the doorway.

The work lane was a lot quieter and smelled better. A couple of supply techs were restocking carts along one arc of the circle that made up the ER's work area, and the pediatrician stood chatting on the phone by the X-ray view box. No disasters, no showdowns, no scrambling police or screaming families. Timmie wasn't sure how long she was going to be able to stand all this peace-and-quiet shit before she lost her mind.

"What's so funny?" the secretary asked on his way by.

"Life," she said. "Don't you think life is funny?"

"Not really. But then, give me a ticket to the Mayfield-Mayfield rematch in room three, and I may change my mind."

Timmie grinned as she plopped herself down at the desk and scanned the chart of Butch Cleveland, whom she'd helped pronounce dead no more than three hours ago. The family had already been notified, the funeral home attendants were drinking nurse's lounge coffee, and Timmie had had the old man wrapped and tagged for at least two hours. The only thing missing was the okay from the coroner to release the body to the Price Health Systems research lab, to which it had been donated. Timmie pulled a pen from behind her ear and punched the blinking button to line one.

"Hey, there, Mr. Van Adder," she greeted the coroner. "This is Timmie Leary-Parker, coming to you live from Memorial."

Which is more than we can say for that little old man, would have been the answer from the guys back in L.A. Mr. Van Adder had much more style.

"Timmie?" he barked. "What the hell kind of name is that?"

Oh good, Timmie thought. And here she'd been worried that

she might not have any confrontation left in her life now that she was divorced and home from the street wars.

"It's a silly-ass kind of name, Mr. Van Adder," she assured him, absently clicking away at her pen. "But I'm stuck with it. So why don't we just talk about Mr. Cleveland, who's been lying in my room for the better part of the morning? It's not that I don't enjoy his company, but I think he wants to get on with things."

"I have other priorities," Van Adder snapped.

Like rotating tires and draining oil pans. The Puckett County coroner was also the owner of Mike's Mobil, not to mention the Van Adder Private Ambulance and Towing Service.

"Wait," he said suddenly. "Leary, you said your name was."

"Leary-Parker," she amended, as if it would do any good.

He ignored her, just as she knew he would. "You wouldn't be Joe Leary's girl, would you?"

"Yes, sir."

"No kiddin'. Well, why didn't you say so in the first place? How the hell is he?"

"He's fine. Just fine."

"Good." Van Adder chuckled with real pleasure. "He's somethin', your daddy, ya know that? Made me like *poetry*, for God's sake. Named you for some sports guy, didn't he?"

"Yes, sir."

Another laugh, hearty and knowing. "That's right. Who else but Joe? Now, he from Restcrest?"

It took a second for Timmie to jump gears back to little Mr. Cleveland, who waited so quietly in room five.

"Restcrest. Yes, sir."

Restcrest being the unimaginatively named Alzheimer's care unit that shared a parking lot and administrative staff with Memorial Medical Center.

"Let him go, then."

Timmie found herself momentarily speechless. "Don't you want to know anything about him?" she asked.

Van Adder huffed impatiently. "What exactly should I know?

He's old, he's batty as a brick, and he's dead. Lucky for his family, don't you think?"

Timmie did think, but that had nothing to do with it. "Are all the coroner's calls this easy?"

"Why not? I don't get paid more for the complicated ones."

Timmie's astonished laugh sounded more like a bark. "You've got to be kidding."

Van Adder graced her with a moment of cold silence. "You got a problem, Miss Leary?"

Oh yeah, she had a problem. No more than one county away in almost any direction, calls like this were being handled by excellent death investigation systems that ranked right up there with and far above the one she'd grown used to in Los Angeles. And here she was stuck with Goober from Mayberry.

Taking a calming second to rub the bridge of her nose, Timmie briefly considered letting Mr. Van Adder know that as a forensic nurse she knew better than to accept a half-assed response from any coroner. She ditched the idea just about as fast. She knew all about Mr. Van Adder. She'd been apprised about just what kinds of odds she'd be facing when she was hired on at Memorial to help modernize its ER. She just hadn't thought she'd have such a hard time keeping her mouth shut about it.

"It's your ballpark," she finally acquiesced ungracefully.

"Something you might want to remember," Van Adder snapped. "You could have let them take the body an hour ago. Old Man Cleveland's been sick a hundred years, he's been dead a couple hours, and he's going right to that big lab in St. Louis to have his brain chopped. It's part of the Restcrest admission requirements, or didn't they tell you that?"

"They told me."

"Then is that all?"

Timmie looked at all the information she'd garnered as a matter of long-respected practice and bit her tongue. "Guess so."

"Good. You give my best to your daddy, now."

Timmie hung up the phone, wondering just what was going to happen when she had to call the coroner with a death he *should* investigate. Then, because she had no choice, she signed off on Mr. Cleveland's file and let him go.

"Okay," she said, closing the chart. "He's ready."

"Dr. Raymond been here yet?" the secretary asked.

Timmie sighed. "Oh yeah, I forgot. Call him, will you?"

She'd forgotten on purpose. She wasn't ready to see Alex Raymond yet. Alex Raymond had risen from town gentry to COO of the Neurological Research Group, which administered Restcrest. Alex was also the hero of some fifteen-year-old adolescent fantasies not quite ready to be put to rest and the answer to a need not yet ready to be acknowledged.

"The Holy Man has been beeped," the secretary announced.

Timmie's head came up. "You don't like him?"

The secretary snorted. "Just a little too perfect for me, you know? What other nursing home administrator makes you wait to ship bodies until he can say good-bye? Say good-bye to what, protoplasm? Please. He'd have a more meaningful discussion with his name tag."

Timmie found that she was grinning again. Yep, sounded like the Alex Raymond she remembered. "Well, let me know. Other than him, Mr. Cleveland's ready to roll."

"Don't listen to him," Timmie heard from behind her. "Dr. Raymond really does care about his little old people."

Timmie turned to find Ellen Mayfield perching herself on the desk, alongside Mr. Cleveland's chart. Alone, Timmie noted with a little surprise. Lately, she'd been traveling mostly in a pair with another SSS devotee, Cindy Dunn. Timmie made herself a bet on how long it would take for Cindy to show up.

"So I've heard," Timmie allowed. "Why aren't you in room three enjoying the wages of sin?"

Ellen's smile was too nice, especially on a face still muddy with the leftover bruises from Billy's latest attempt to win back his place in the bosom of his family. "I figured I'd let Barb soften him up a little first. He's really sick?"

"Like a dog. He either got bad beer or good gin."

Ellen nodded with a fleeting smile. "I guess it would be ugly to say I hope his liver's finally giving out."

Heck, her voice was even too nice. Sucked out all that perfectly good self-righteous indignation that made a statement like that so worthwhile. But then, Ellen never seemed to have the energy for indignation. A wide-faced, gently plump forty-year-old with tired eyes, olive skin, and flat black hair, she smiled as if it were an effort and meant every kind word she said.

"I don't think it's ugly at all," Timmie assured her. "In fact, I was just having the same fantasies about the coroner."

Ellen just smiled. "Tucker Van Adder? Oh, don't mind him. You just keep forgetting this isn't Los Angeles."

Which meant that if Ellen wasn't going to dis her husband, she certainly wasn't going to dis the coroner. And that if Ellen had been less thoughtful, she would have suggested Timmie respect the status quo more than she obviously had since arriving.

"Ellen, there you are," Barb called from across the hall.

Timmie leaned around to see the physician shambling their way, weighted down with clipboards and trailing EKG tracings like a comet's tail. Dancing attendance, finally, was Cindy Dunn, whose smile was even more avid than Barb's.

"This, Ellen Mayfield," she crowed, "is the day you've dreamed of."

The self-proclaimed SSS Auxiliary by dint of her widowhood, which she likened to divorce without the alimony, Cindy was as pale as Ellen was dark, a bone-thin, sallow, dishwater blond with a taste for sequins and studs and hair that was moussed into a cockatoo's crest. Cindy wasn't a particularly good nurse, but she was slavishly devoted to her friends in the SSS, especially Ellen, who pardoned her small sins and enjoyed her bad jokes.

"Okay," Barb announced, pulling away the pen Timmie was still clicking. "For Billy I prescribe IVs, high colonics, and a fire hose. I'll leave it up to you to decide where to put what."

"Barb, stop," Ellen demurred. "He could really be sick."

"After that," Barb continued with a mad gleam in her eye, "we'll admit him so we can really start to torture him."

"Now, honey," Ellen objected. "You really mean all he needs is Compazine and fluids so he can stop vomiting, don't you?"

Timmie winced.

Barb went on four-point alert. "You're in serious jeopardy of losing your SSS secret decoder ring," she warned.

"Let me do it," Cindy offered, bouncing like Tigger. "As long as I can put on gloves before inserting the hose."

"No thanks, hon," Ellen said, a hand up. "I have trouble enough with him without you-all helpin' me out."

"Wuss," Barb accused easily.

"Traitor," Cindy echoed.

"Just make sure you wait to give him the Compazine until after he's signed his child support payment," Timmie advised, and finally got Ellen to really smile.

Watching Ellen head down the hall, the three women shook their heads. Timmie grabbed her pen back and updated her notes.

"She really is too nice for her own good," Barb despaired.

"No kidding," Cindy retorted with a sad shake of her head. "I ask you. Compassion and empathy. What kind of reaction is that to the best news of the month?"

Barb patted Cindy's Wal-Mart-ringed hand. "I promise to be much more appreciative when you tell me my ex is down there hawking up his liver, okay?"

Cindy's smile was conspiratorial. "I'll see what I can do."

They all laughed.

"Now that's what I like to hear," a soft baritone announced from the doorway.

Timmie wasn't sure whether to hide or run. Her wait was over. Alex Raymond was here. And looking like every one of her very old daydreams, too. He strode down the hall in hunting jacket, jodhpurs, and boots, tailored to perfection, disheveled enough to be real. Golden hair, golden eyes, golden boy. Six feet of perfectly honed male who hadn't changed all that much from his twelfth birthday, when his parents had given him his first thoroughbred jumper.

"Hi, Dr. Raymond," Cindy cooed, coming right to attention like a cheerleader at halftime. "Thanks for coming."

To be taken any way he wanted it. He took it without offense, his answering smile sweet and genuine. Also nothing new. Watching him effortlessly skirt Cindy's come-on, Timmie felt twenty-year-old hero worship fight to rear its ugly head and quashed it with a vengeance. Leave it to Alex to end up even more beautiful than she'd remembered. And just as nice.

"Well, I was on the way in when I got the page. You're all coming out to the benefit horse show after work, aren't you?"

Cindy damn near did the dance of joy. "You bet we are."

Alex had noticed Timmie, and she could see him trying to dredge up a name. "It's for a good cause," he said, as if to her.

"Yeah," Barb agreed. "Our jobs. If you and Restcrest look good, the rest of the hospital looks good. And if we look good, we have a better chance of staying gainfully employed."

Alex's smile brightened appreciably. "I can't do what I do without you. That's what I want the patrons to see. The uninterrupted care we provide for our Alzheimer's patients."

"Bring a couple of them along," Timmie suggested dryly. "Cute ones, with bows in their hair."

She guessed she'd expected a fight. She got another smile and felt like a heel. "Oh, they'll be there on the fringes, where nobody can hurt them," he said. "But people with the kind of money we need don't want to be confused by reality. So we'll give them you guys instead . . ." Suddenly, he snapped his fingers, confusion disappearing. "Timmie Leary, my God! I almost didn't recognize you. How long you been back?"

She didn't bother to correct him. "About five weeks."

"How's your dad?"

"Fine. Just fine."

"Wonderful! Then you'll come? And bring Joe." His ever-smiling eyes glinted with wry amusement. "Can't hurt the Neurological Research Group to be associated with Joe Leary."

Timmie almost answered. Almost gave herself away in front of everyone. Thankfully, Cindy saved her.

"She'll be there," Cindy said for her, inching a little closer to Alex. "So will I. I'll be happy to help at the scoring table again this year. It's the closest I get to showing anymore."

For the first time, Alex Raymond didn't look perfectly at ease. "Oh, I'm not sure this year, Cindy. They've brought a professional group along for that. Check with them, okay?"

Cindy's glow died. "Sure. I just thought I could help."

"You will, just by being there . . . well," he said, raking a hand through his perfect hair. "I do need to get back. Is Mr. Cleveland here?"

Timmie picked up the chart, prepared to discuss Van Adder.

"Uh, excuse me . . . please . . . "

Heads turned. Alex froze, his mouth open. Timmie took one look at the middle-aged man weaving on his feet at the door from triage and dropped Mr. Cleveland's chart. The man was waxen and sweaty and wide-eyed, his hand to his chest.

"Oh, Jesus," Timmie murmured, already on the run.

"Pulmonary embolism?" Barb asked, hot on Timmie's heels.

"Gunshot," Timmie corrected just as the man began to fold. Her adrenaline kicked in like afterburners, and Timmie covered the last five feet almost in a leap to catch him as he went down. Folding him right over her shoulder in a fireman's lift, she headed for an empty room. She'd finally caught sight of the blood, right there beneath the man's splayed fingers.

"Somebody get a chest tray!" she yelled instinctively.

"Chest tray, hell!" Barb retorted. "Call the helicopter!"

"Repeat after me," Timmie conceded, staggering into the sole trauma room and dropping the man on the cart. "You are not in L.A. anymore. You are not in L.A."

"Mr. Cleveland!" Alex called from the doorway. "Anything I need to know?"

"No!" Timmie answered, her fingers palpating a carotid pulse, her eyes focused on the ragged little hole in the middle of the white T-shirt. "Already been released. No questions, although the coroner might have been more interested, if you ask me."

"Thanks!" he called and headed out, knowing better than to interfere where he wasn't qualified.

"I'm . . . sorry," the patient was apologizing, mouth round and quivering like a fish caught out of water, eyes wider, lips already ashen. Timmie yanked over the crash cart and dialed up the oxygen. The tech broke out the space suits and tossed around goggles while another nurse scrabbled for IV catheters and Cindy dithered by the door, screaming for lab and X ray.

"Get him in shock trousers!" Barb yelled. "Sir, can you tell me who shot you?"

"My son. He . . . he was so . . . angry . . ."

Timmie's stomach hit her knees. She saw the gunpowder soot at the edge of that hole, the scrapes on the man's fingers, and she yanked out her scissors. She instinctively catalogued the pallor, the panting, grunting breaths the man was taking, the sheen of sweat on his skin.

"It's gonna be okay," Timmie assured the man in her patented small-kids-and-terrified-animals tone.

As quickly as she could, she half-rolled him to find that there was no exit wound. Low-velocity bullet, which meant it could have visited any number of organs before giving up. No gaping hole, though. No completely vaporized organs. Bad news and good. He was crashing fast, but not so fast they couldn't get him as far as a level one trauma center, which Memorial definitely wasn't.

"He has breath sounds," Barb said, her voice a little panicky. "I never would have guessed gunshot. How'd you know?"

"I never would have guessed pulmonary embolism," Timmie said with a manic grin as she cut his shirt up the side, as far away as she could from the evidence. "Never saw that many. Paul, find a couple of lunch bags, okay? Nobody touch his clothes but me."

"Lunch bags?" the tech demanded, hands full of catheter trays and IV bags. "I don't think he's hyperventilating here."

"To cover his hands. For evidence. This is Prosecutionville. Start the IVs higher in his arms, and Barb, for God's sake, don't put any tubes through that hole."

Cindy made trumpet noises as she fumbled with the trauma flow sheets she was attempting to fill out. "Timmie Leary, forensic nurse to the rescue!"

"Consider this on-the-job training, kids," Timmie offered as she worked. "The police will be grateful."

"He needs to be CAT-scanned," Barb said.

"I don't think we have time," Timmie assured her. "See if there's a hole we can plug with a finger till we get him to a real hospital. You find it, I'll do the ride along." Then she took a breath and made a wild stab. "Check his descending aorta."

Barb stopped dead, shot a look at the man's face, his eyes that couldn't quite focus anymore. "You serious?"

"You're a surgeon," Timmie retorted, hooking an IV line to the number-fourteen catheter she'd inserted just south of the man's elbow. "You're supposed to live for shit like that."

Barb took another look at the pallor, the panting breaths, the blood pressure machine that was reading an unsteady seventy diastolic pressure and closed her eyes. Then she asked for a blade and an ETA for the helicopter.

"Jesus!" she whispered five minutes later, wrist-deep in the man's torso, blood spattering her shoes. "You're right."

"Transport's landing," the secretary called from the door. "The Big House is notified and standing by, chest doc on line three to talk to you, Barb. Timmie, will you *please* call your baby-sitter back? She yelled at me this time."

With Barb's finger in the hole, the patient's pressure started to click up. The flow of blood from the chest eased, and the crew slowed its pace from frantic to steady.

"You sure you want to go?" Barb asked. "It's a long ride."

"I'd love to," Timmie said. "Anything rather than deal with a baby-sitter who can't manage one active six-year-old and her pet."

"It's not about your daughter," the secretary said. "Didn't I tell you? It's about your father."

Timmie pushed her goggles into place and reached alongside Barb's wrist. "That settles it. Send me in, Coach."

Timmie heard the doors open outside and feet stutter down the hall. God, she loved this. It was what kept her at L.A. County–USC, longer than she should have stayed. It was what had sent her beating leather to every trauma center in the St. Louis bistate area. It was what had finally put her here at Memorial's tiny dog-and-pony show instead of a more sedate floor job. Most days she couldn't manage a child, an ex-husband, and a lizard. She certainly couldn't manage a father. But she could manage this. And sometimes that was enough.

The transport team swept into the room in their blue jumpsuits and attitudes, and Timmie did her best not to laugh out loud with delight.

Timmie didn't make it back to Memorial until almost three, when she hopped a ride with one of the investigating officers from Puckett, who was returning to arrest a twelve-year-old named Clifford Ellis for shooting his father.

Timmie felt sated and content. Real action in an unlikely place with a not-bad outcome. She'd been able to get Mr. Ellis to surgery. She'd surprised the cops with her gift of viable evidence. She was a hero. She was Traumawoman, who could see through chest walls and diagnose faster than a speeding bullet. Florence Nightingale with clusters. Even though she still had to unscramble the mess her baby-sitter had dropped in her lap, she'd done a good day's work, and she felt like celebrating.

Which was why it took her so long to realize just what was wrong when she walked into the ER.

"Why are you still here?" she asked the silent little group clumped together on the secondhand brown plaid chairs in the nurse's lounge when they should have been scrambling to get out the door to see horses over at the county park.

It was Barb who looked up, her face oddly blank. "He's dead," she said.

Timmie's stomach dropped. "He can't be," she protested. "They swore he was doing okay. I mean, it didn't take much over an hour to get back out here."

But Barb was shaking her head. "Not Mr. Ellis," she said. "Billy."

Timmie forgot to breathe. "Billy who?" she asked inanely.

Ellen lifted her discolored plump little face that was now tear-streaked. "My Billy. An hour ago. He just . . . crashed. From the flu. The goddamn flu."

Timmie ended up on a straight chair. What had the supernurse missed? What had Florence ignored in her prejudice against that overweight, unpleasant man?

"Well," she said before thinking, "at least Van Adder can't sign this one off without asking questions."

"He already did," Barb said.

"What?"

But it was Ellen who answered. "Van Adder said that since Billy had a history of high blood pressure and alcoholism, what could we expect? The mortuary picked him up half an hour ago."

Timmie opened her mouth to say something and realized she couldn't think of a thing to say. She could understand a hospital like Memorial dropping the ball like this. But she couldn't abide the idea that Tucker Van Adder had. He wasn't just sloppy or lazy, he was criminally incompetent.

"Then we'd better do something about it," Timmie decided. "There's something going on here that isn't right."

Timmie might have felt better about her call to action if she hadn't caught sight of Ellen's reaction. Billy Mayfield's ex-wife didn't look as if she agreed. In fact, she looked appalled. Which made Timmie wonder what the hell else she'd missed.

DANIEL MURPHY STOOD AT THE EDGE OF THE CROWD THAT spilled across Sweeney Park and wondered what the hell he was doing here. He knew he'd asked for just this kind of assignment, but Jesus. Show jumping. Just what a reporter who'd covered everything from Vietnam to Oklahoma City needed on his résumé. Just what he wanted to do on a spanking clean October afternoon when crime ran rampant in the cities and scandal waited to be exposed.

Probably the crux of the problem. It was just what he wanted to do.

Nothing.

No struggle for the masses, no deciphering the deeper truths for the great unwashed. No harried deadlines or living out of a duffel bag or coming to grips with the fact that most people didn't want or deserve the truth anyway.

The problem was, of course, that the minute his new editor had recognized his name, she had decided that with him as their brand-new reporter, the revamped *Puckett Independent* would, like, seek truth and justice in the far suburbs of St. Louis. Murphy kept telling her that it was the duty of junior woodchucks fresh out of journalism school to seek truth and justice. He just wanted a paycheck to fund his well-deserved wallow in oblivion. Sherilee Carter listened with predictable skepticism.

Which was why Sherilee had sent him to the Neurological Research Center Charity Horse Show. She didn't want him to just collect names of attendees for the features page. She wanted him to meet the new Memorial CEO, who would be attending to cheer on his shiny new medical stars. His name was Paul Landry, and Sherilee didn't trust him. It was up to Murphy to find out why.

The site was nice anyway. A wide, protected meadow spread across the bluffs above the Missouri River, out at the western edge of Puckett. Sweeping, manicured lawns, mature trees, and impressive vistas of the huge river that swept by below.

Today the lawns had been transformed into an outdoor ring bristling with flags and edged by rows of imported cars. A huge yellow-and-white-striped tent along one side kept the sun off linen-covered tables and a well-stocked bar, and back by the trees pampered horses were being led in tight circles by pampered humans. Even more overindulged patricians gathered by tent and rail to watch a new horse and rider enter the ring.

As for Paul Landry, he was right where Murphy expected him to be. Comfortably situated by the thousand-dollar tables, smile firmly in place, hand out to the rich and comfortable, who had become fair donation game when they'd decided to develop Puckett as the newest white-flight alternative to St. Louis.

Murphy already knew what was wrong with the new CEO. He'd caught it the minute Landry had compared the running of a small community hospital with an evac unit in Chu Lai.

"Good grief, no," Landry had said in his professionally cultured tenor. "I didn't work there. I was treated there. What they did really made an impression on this underage marine back in seventy-two. It made me want to do the same with my life. Give a little back, you know?"

Landry was small, tight, precise, and professional, with meticulously trimmed hair and a tailor-perfect Hart Schaffner & Marx suit. He was also black. And not light black. Deep, shiny, almost blue-black, standing out in the sleekly white crowd like a raisin in a bowl of milk.

Murphy didn't think that was what had inspired Sherilee's mistrust, though. It was the fact that Landry was a hired gun in a small town. Landry had also just fired Sherilee's best friend's father from the hospital board of directors.

"Great people here," Landry continued, sipping at something amber over rocks. "But we still have a lot of work to do before the hospital can effectively compete in this market."

Already trying to decide what he'd end up bartering from his editor for the information, Murphy turned his attention to the much more agreeable task of watching women ride horses.

"Have you met our Dr. Raymond yet, Mr. Murphy?" an aggressively cultured voice asked beside him.

Murphy didn't turn from where he was contemplating the smooth, sleek haunches of the jumper . . . the one on top. Murphy took a swig of tap water and lusted for Jack Black and sighed. Nice form. He'd give her an eight on the Murphy Scale.

"No, I haven't," he admitted to the overefficient hospital vice president and public relations maven who had her hand poised just above his jacket sleeve.

"Well, we're in luck," Mary Jane Arlington chirped, now tapping with nothing but the tips of her perfectly manicured nails, her blond pageboy stirring not a hair in the afternoon breeze. "He's right here by the bar. Wouldn't you like a quote?"

No, Murphy wanted to say. I want to stand behind the fence and fantasize about sleek, athletic women with tight little asses and powerful thighs. But the lithe brunette on the big gray trotted out of the ring to be replaced by a guy who looked like he bathed in cologne and held his fork upside down. Murphy finished off his water as if it were a chaser and balanced the glass on top of the cigarette butt he'd already left in the flowers.

"Sure. Let's go see Dr. Raymond."

Mary Jane Arlington made it a point to ignore the flowerpot. She also didn't touch Murphy's elbow again as she led the way through the crowd. Probably afraid to come that close to tweed old enough to have grandfathered the pattern she was wearing. Not to mention the fact that Murphy's jeans weren't stone-washed or boot-cut. Just old, like his jacket. Like him.

Dr. Raymond, it transpired, was standing by the fence alternately watching the latest horse and giving ear to a passing stream of well-wishers. A tall, slim man with great posture and the kind of hair that glowed in the sun, he was in standard jodhpurs and boots, black velvet helmet dangling from the hand that wasn't holding the champagne. Dr. Raymond had been the third person over the jumps, the first with a no-fault round.

"Dr. Raymond," Mary Jane trilled, one hand skimming an inch from Murphy's jacket sleeve. "This is Dan Murphy. He's here to cover the horse show and very much wanted to meet you."

The perfectly golden head turned, eyes crinkled with genial goodwill, long-fingered hand out for a shake.

"Daniel Murphy," Mary Jane finished, "Dr. Alex Raymond, the administrator of Restcrest Place Retirement Center, and cofounder of the Neurological Research Group."

Murphy took hold of the hand, surprised by the quick strength and calluses.

"*The* Daniel Murphy?" the doctor was asking, eyes all wide.

Murphy did his best to not walk away. "The only one I know."

The doctor shook his haloed head. "No, really. This is a real treat for me. I've been reading your stuff since I was in grade school. You've been wounded in three wars and spit on by a First Lady."

Murphy should have felt more gracious. It was just that he'd been vaguely hoping that Puckett was enough of a backwater that his name wouldn't mean anything. He also could have lived a long time without that coy little reference to grade school.

"She didn't really spit," he said. "It was more an overzealous show of contempt. Besides, I couldn't blame her. Her husband was a nice guy."

"He was a crook."

Murphy shrugged. "What's your point?"

The handsome doctor laughed. Murphy thought he should

have at least waited until one of them had said something original.

"But what are you doing here?" the doctor asked, making the day perfect.

"Trying my damnedest to retire."

The doctor laughed again. "Well, we're thrilled to have you here. You like horses?"

"Nope. I like old ladies."

A nod, a quick look to the far end of the tent, where the organizers had thought to exhibit some of the victims who benefited from all this largesse. Crumpled, confused, wheelchair-bound forms with bright bows in their sparse gray hair, they looked like the specters of what everyone could expect for their futures if they didn't contribute generously to Dr. Raymond's worthy cause.

As for Dr. Raymond himself, he smiled. "Me, too." And damn if he didn't sound sincere. "My mother was diagnosed with Alzheimer's at fifty-two. She never even got the chance to recognize her grandchildren."

Yeah, and Murphy's mother was in one of the wheelchairs. He knew the drill. "I've been hearing a lot about your work."

"My partner actually does most of the real research. Peter Davies. He can tell you more about the effects of Alzheimer's on the brain than anybody in the U.S. If you'd like I can get you a tour through his lab up at Price University Hospital. He'd be here now, but he's preparing a paper on a discovery he's made about the progression of plaque development in midstage Alzheimer's." Getting a blank reaction, the doctor grinned. "Quite riveting stuff, actually."

Murphy forced a smile. "I'm sure. What about you?"

"I'm on the people end. Intervention, therapy, family support. I doubt you can appreciate what an opportunity we've been given by Price University. Within the next five years, we'll become the primary Alzheimer's research unit in the country."

Considering the fact that Alzheimer's was going to be the top medical moneymaker of the twenty-first century, Murphy figured it wasn't such a stunning leap for the university to make.

"Dr. Raymond trained at Harvard and Case Western," Ms. Arlington cut in, obviously unhappy with the lack of adulation. "And he came home to Puckett to practice. That says something."

That said Dr. Raymond liked small ponds.

"You make it sound like I took up the cloth, Mary Jane," the doctor protested. "I'm just taking advantage of a perfect opportunity."

"Must work," Murphy said, patting his pockets for his cigarettes. "You have a waiting list and planning approval to double your size."

"People want their loved ones to have the best care. And they want to stop a terrible disease."

Perfect answer for sound bite or print. The doctor had been practicing in front of a mirror.

"There's somebody else here I think you might like to meet," Raymond said, taking hold of the elbow Mary Jane had been so loath to touch. "Paul Landry, the new CEO of Memorial? He's been a heck of a help in redesigning and supporting Restcrest. You know we share a parking lot . . ."

Raymond turned to get Landry's attention. Landry looked like he'd been waiting to give it. Both men, polar light and dark, neared like twin stars set to circle, and Murphy, one hand still in a pocket pulling out cigarettes, was forced to follow. A good thing, it turned out. If he hadn't turned just then, he would have been too late.

It was no more than a twitch in the well-behaved crowd. An odd blur on its perfect features. Murphy saw the movement beyond Raymond, saw the glitter of something powerful in the eyes of a man as he moved. Bad, he thought as old instincts kicked in. This is bad. He was hurtling at Raymond even before he saw the first glint of the gun.

"Get down!" he yelled.

"Look out!" a woman echoed. "Gun!"

Murphy pushed with both hands, hard enough to send Raymond reeling into Landry. The three of them slammed to the ground just as the pistol cracked overhead.

Murphy managed to keep watching as he hit the ground. Raymond's boot dug into his ribs, and Landry was yelling in outrage. Murphy saw the gun swing up toward the sky, recognized it as a midsize automatic. He saw a puff of smoke as it snapped again. He couldn't hear it, because the announcer was praising a second perfect round, and people were clapping. People closer were turning, crying out, stumbling. One person got hold of the man, had hands on the wrists that tried to lower the gun again.

The woman who had yelled. A small brunette, too small to control the guy, who should have been able to outreach her. Her feet barely touched the ground as she hung on to those thick wrists. She also had big eyes that flashed steel as she kneed the shooter right in the balls.

She got the gun. The shooter broke free and ran. Scrambling to help, Murphy damn near got his hands on the guy, but Raymond tried to get up and tripped him. People surged forward, away. The small woman with the big eyes lifted the gun above her head, where it wouldn't hurt anyone, and looked around for help. By the time Murphy could get over to her, the shooter had disappeared.

"Are you all right?" a dozen people asked.

"What happened?"

"Get that gun from her."

One towering woman, who looked as if she'd taken a wrong turn from *Gulliver's Travels*, laughed. "What is it with you and guns?" she was demanding, lifting the gun from the brunette's hands.

The brunette grinned as if she'd just skied a hard run. "I do always seem to be at the center of the party, don't I?"

Then she just walked away.

"You pushed me," Landry accused from beneath Murphy.

Still only as far as his knees, Murphy looked down to see Landry sprawled on the grass, already trying to smooth perfect hair. Sherilee would never leave him alone, now. "You're welcome," he said anyway, and gave the CEO a hand up.

* * *

It all eventually sorted itself out. A couple of police showed up, took the gun, got descriptions. Murphy remembered a white male, about six feet, with sparse, light hair and middle-aged lines diminishing once-handsome features. Nice clothes, but nothing that stood out. Murphy remembered the man's rage and wondered just who the lucky recipient was supposed to have been.

The brunette with the big eyes, who had eventually returned holding tightly to a miniaturized version of herself, remembered much the same, had responded to the same instincts as Murphy.

Murphy wasn't surprised. She didn't remind him of any of the other locals. She was twitchy in a big-streets kind of way, like she was always hearing a warning shot whistle over her head. Hell, her nostrils were even wide, as if she smelled smoke and it turned her on. Murphy had spent too much energy drowning out, shooting up, and snorting away that very reaction to mistake it.

"You did that kind of thing much in Los Angeles, did you?" Dr. Raymond asked her as he settled a glass of champagne in her hand. Fifteen feet away, a new horse was making the rounds, the audience just a little more restive as it watched, the sphere of violence neatly closed over with polite behavior, like restitching a rent in a good coat.

"Nah," she said, not bothering to taste her drink as she wrapped her arms around the little girl. "That's what we had med students for."

Bingo, Murphy thought, shaking his head as a second glass was offered to him. Los Angeles.

Everybody laughed. Mary Jane Arlington, who probably wouldn't have laughed, had decamped with the police to make sure their continued presence didn't disturb the crowd. Paul Landry had gone with her, probably seeking unmussed clothes.

The woman with the quick reflexes had evidently been at the show with her daughter and two friends, the laughing behemoth and one other woman, a forgettable Appalachian blond who dressed like the child of Loretta Lynn and Michael Jackson and sucked down complimentary champagne like Gatorade.

"I heard the shots," the Appalachian blond was saying for about the fourth time, her polished, multiringed fingers fluttering, her eyes wet and wide. "And I thought . . . I thought . . ."

Several people patted her on the shoulder. She nodded as if accepting it as her right.

"I just couldn't have gone through it again," she said, sotto voce.

"Well, thanks to Daniel and Timmie here, everything turned out all right," Raymond assured them all.

Murphy wondered if it had occurred to anybody but him that so far not one of them had said anything about *why* Timmie and Daniel had had to save them all from gunshots. It had occurred to Timmie, he thought. He could see it in the lift of one dark eyebrow as she watched the people around her sip their champagne.

"Timmie?" Murphy asked.

"Timothy, actually," she corrected him with a flat look that betrayed a certain amused challenge.

Timothy was about five three, clad in short corduroy, long leather boots, and about four sets of earrings. Looking, even with sedate brunette hair, decidedly unlocal. Looking even less like a horse person.

"Interesting name," Murphy offered. Especially on that aggressively feminine face.

"Oh, I'm sorry," Dr. Raymond apologized. "I didn't even introduce you two. Dan Murphy, this is Timmie—"

"No, no," the big woman behind her urged. "Let Timmie."

Everybody grinned all around, already knowing the joke. Ms. Timothy didn't seem nearly as delighted.

"He doesn't care—" she attempted to say.

"Leary!" the woman jumped in, damn near six and a half feet of enthusiasm. "Her name's Timothy Leary!"

"Timothy Leary-Parker," the victim amended, even as everybody else laughed.

"You weren't—"

"Good God, no. My father wouldn't have known Timothy Leary if he'd bitten him in the butt. I was named for a Cardinals catcher."

Said with a certain perverse pride. It almost got the first smile of the day out of Murphy. "Timmie McCarver," he said with a nod. "Of course. And your daughter?"

She smiled with real pleasure. "Escaped the same fate. This is Meghan," she announced with an affectionate buss to the top of the girl's head.

The girl gave him a gap-toothed grin. "Hey."

Murphy nodded. "Hey."

That seemed to stretch Meghan's patience too far. "Mom," she asked, tilting her head way back. "Can I stand by the fence? Please?"

Timmie gave her another quick hug and pushed her off, watching her all the way.

"And this is Dr. Barbara Adkins," Raymond continued, indicating Timmie's large friend. Mousy hair, mousy skin, thick features, sumo grip. Murphy bet the drunks didn't bother her much. He shook hands and came away sore.

"And Cindy Dunn," Raymond continued. Cindy Dunn was the escapee from the Western Trekkiwear store who had reacted so strongly to the shooting. She certainly brightened up with the introduction, her hair damn near quivering as she shook hands.

"Say something nice about the hospital," Raymond asked the women. "Dan here is with the *St. Louis Post-Dispatch*."

Ah, the price of anonymity. "The *Independent*," Murphy corrected, and survived the reassessment in the doctor's eyes.

"Memorial has a great emergency department," Dr. Barbara Adkins offered, not noticing the pause. "Even better now that Timmie has returned from the wilderness bearing new medical miracles. You should have seen the guy we turfed up to the big house this morning with Timmie's fingers in his chest. It was like playing in the major leagues. And now she's taken on the coroner. I can't wait."

"Problems?" Murphy asked out of habit.

Timmie Leary gave a snort that sounded like a horse with a cold. "Nothing a new coroner won't fix. Last I heard, even assholes don't die from the flu. I'm on a mission to make sure it doesn't get by him again."

"You sure that's wise?" Raymond asked her, brow creased perfectly. "Tucker isn't the kind of man who enjoys being questioned. And he usually does the job all right."

"Wise has never been a behavioral directive of mine," she assured him, twirling her still-full champagne glass in a small hand. "On the other hand, I'm real fond of 'correct,' and there wasn't anything correct about releasing Billy Mayfield today."

"Billy Mayfield?" Raymond asked. "Ellen's husband?"

There ensued a brief discussion on fellow nurses, alcoholic husbands, and inexplicable deaths that Murphy mostly didn't care to follow.

"One of the reasons I was hired was to question the status quo," Timmie finished it all by saying. "Well, I think this time questions aren't enough. I say, when in doubt, act."

"That kind of attitude will get you fired," Cindy Dunn warned with more mirth than caution.

Dr. Atkins looked far less amused. "That kind of attitude damn near got you shot."

Timmie waved an unconcerned hand. "Don't be silly. I've had more guns waved at me than Clint Eastwood. No harm done."

"But this isn't L.A.," Cindy retorted. "And you have more to worry about here, you know? Like your *family*?"

Said with no tact and heavy meaning. For a little woman, Timmie Leary had quite a glare on her. She leveled one on the blond and shut her right up. "Thank you, Cindy. We'll talk later."

Cindy pouted. "It *is* why you came," was all she said.

Standing there at the edge of the group, Murphy felt like a Peeping Tom. Kind of like old times, except he didn't enjoy it anymore. Especially the look on Timmie's face, which made him think she'd just been squeezed into opening up private doors in a public place.

Must be the lack of alcohol. Or cocaine. Or tricyclics. As the man had said, what a lousy time to give up caffeine. Watching for uncomfortable reactions just wasn't fun anymore, especially when he had nothing left to use them on.

Obviously just as uncomfortable with the taut silence,

Raymond cleared his throat. “Come to think of it,” he said, “Timmie could probably give you a great story, Dan. Her father is one of Puckett’s great characters. Isn’t he, Timmie?”

Maybe Murphy was the only one who noticed that she tightened up even further. “He is.”

“I still find myself singing one of his songs when I’m working,” Raymond continued blithely. “What a voice. Do you sing too, Timmie?”

“No, I sure don’t.”

Murphy watched the conversation switch gears like a Volkswagen with a bad clutch and wondered. But heck, he was still wondering who’d try and shoot up a horse show. It was a cinch nobody was interested in talking about it, and that usually meant there was a story here. If anybody had the energy to find one.

“Your father’s a musician?” Murphy asked instead.

“No,” Timmie said. “An Irishman.”

“ ‘I will arise and go now,’ ” Barbara Atkins inexplicably intoned with a soft smile.

“ ‘And go to Innisfree,’ ” everybody but Timmie answered like a litany, and then smiled.

“It’s ‘The Lake Isle of Innisfree,’” the big doctor explained. “From Yeats. Timmie’s dad taught me.”

“It’s his favorite poem,” Raymond enthused with a huge smile. “Just ask him. He’ll recite it at the drop of a hat.”

Barbara laughed. “Heck, he’d throw down the hat, just to get the chance.”

And everybody stood there sipping champagne and watching another horse canter around the ring and contemplating Irish poets. Except for Timmie Leary. She clutched her full glass like a weapon and frowned. And Murphy. Unaccountably, he found himself thinking about the fact that the most interesting statements this afternoon had remained unspoken.

Later that evening, after all the horses had been put back in their trailers and the beautiful people had climbed into their gleaming imports, Murphy sat in his living room that overlooked a weed-populated driveway and tried hard to drum up enthusiasm about what he was writing. He made it to "Saturday afternoon saw a gathering of . . ." before he faltered at the challenge of exactly what to call that crowd today. Sycophants? Leeches?

He hadn't minded the medical crew. Funny how after they'd been pointed out, he'd been able to spot them in the crowd, like clover in the corn. A little more solid, a little less dressed, a lot less self-involved than anyone else. Certainly more real than their shiny star, who had ended up walking away with the trophy in one hand and a profit of eighty thousand in the other.

Murphy thought about that. Thought about the exposé Sherilee expected on Paul Landry, who wasn't really bad, just hungry. Thought about Alex Raymond, with his bright eyes and devoted following and indisputable good cause, and found himself itching with a faint flutter of old prejudices. A reporter's prejudices.

It must have been all that perfect hair. Murphy didn't trust perfect hair. Or it could have been that middle-class-looking guy going postal on a perfect afternoon and nobody having the decency to at least ask why. When the phone rang, Murphy was sitting there wishing he could wash away his tedium with a couple of fingers of something neat and wondering what the hell he was supposed to get out of all this.

"Mr. Murphy?" The voice was hushed, urgent.

"Oh, no, you don't," Murphy automatically protested, recognizing with deadly certainty just what the tone of voice meant. "I'm not doing exposés anymore. I don't care what company is polluting what river or who the mayor's sleeping with. Call somebody who cares."

"Then you don't want to know what's going on at Memorial?"

"Memorial?" He looked at his computer screen, where his words about Memorial should already have been glowing, both literally and figuratively. "No, I'm sure I don't."

He should have hung up. Curiosity was a hell of a lot tougher to cure than altruism, though. Not to mention the inexhaustible urge to knock down white knights, which had gotten him into this profession in the first place.

"Nobody wants to know what they're doing. Nobody cares."

He shook his head. Lit a cigarette one-handed. "Add me to the list."

"You're not from here. You can tell the truth."

"I don't want to tell the truth."

"They're killing people, Mr. Murphy. Ask Timmie Leary. And hurry. She doesn't know it, but she's in danger, too."

"What do you mean?" Murphy demanded.

But his caller had already hung up.

Son of a bitch. Son of a goddamn bitch. His palms were itching. He hated it when his palms itched. It meant he was about to do something stupid. And he couldn't think of anything that would be more stupid than figuring out what was behind that phone call, or what Timothy Leary-Parker had to do with it.

He was still cursing five minutes later when he picked the phone back up and dialed.

"YOU REALLY DON'T WANT TO KNOW WHY HE DID IT?" TIMMIE asked. Leaning against the railing on Timmie's porch, Cindy shook her head emphatically. "I don't even want to know who he was."

Timmy made it all the way down the steps onto her sidewalk before faltering to a stop. Cindy remained behind on the porch, a wooden baseball bat balanced on her right shoulder.

"You're kidding," Timmie said, squinting up at her. "Right?"

Cindy assumed a look that reminded Timmie of Mary Lincoln thinking of the theater. "I didn't sleep all night," she said in a small voice. "I'm not going to sleep again tonight. It's one of the reasons I came over. I just can't . . . after being that close to a shooting, I can't sit home and think about Johnny."

Timmie did her level best not to scowl. She should have expected this. She could always tell Cindy's state of mind by how high her hair was teased, and today it was no more than an inch off her scalp. A sure predictor of gloom.

Well, Timmie just wasn't in the mood for it. It was too nice an afternoon, and she already had enough on her plate to begin with. Behind her on the lawn, Meghan sat crouched over the corpses of summer flowers, and beyond the front door of the house Timmie could hear the muted notes of "Take Me Out to the Ballgame." She was out of money and out of time and out of baby-sitting recommendations, and now it was somehow her fault that some idiot had decided to shoot up a horse show and remind Cindy that her husband was dead. Just the way to set off to work.

"I'm sorry," Timmie inevitably said. "I didn't mean to hurt you. But for God's sake, Billy's dead and Alex almost got shot. Shouldn't at least one person in this town ask why?"

"So you've volunteered for the job."

Timmie blinked, bemused. "Well, why not?"

"You're not in Los Angeles anymore. I mean, you escaped."

Timmie took a second to consider the tidy riot of mums ringing the tall redbrick Victorian house that now belonged to her. She noted the last green of her grass, the translucent strawberry blonde of the sugar maple tree to her right, the deepening garnet of the oak to her left. She saw the streets that transected close by, quiet, tree-laden lanes with graciously preserved homes lined up like prim aunts in dated finery.

This one had been her grandfather's, and his mother's before him. Great-grandmother Leary, an immigrant who'd stepped off the boat the day before her seventeenth birthday to find a better place in a new world. From what Timmie could see from where she stood, it certainly looked as if she'd succeeded.

"I guess it's a matter of semantics," Timmie finally admitted. "I don't think of it as escaping."

Cindy shook her head. "The difference between the two of us, I guess. Johnny was killed in the Chicago Loop, and I never want to see a big city again as long as I live."

"And I think this town needs a serious dose of big city."

Cindy sighed. "Which means you're going to play *Cagney and Lacey.*"

"Nah. *Quincy*. If Alex won't talk to me, maybe I'll get Billy to talk to me. I can at least check his file when I'm at work."

"I don't baby-sit for free," Cindy reminded her. "Not even if you're kicked out of your job for a worthy cause."

Timmie tried a big "what the hell" smile. "Aw, heck, what's life without a little challenge?"

"I'll keep my calendar open just in case."

Timmie looked up to see that Cindy wasn't joking. Immature she might be. A less-than-stellar ER nurse. But she did try so hard. "Thanks, Cindy. I mean it. You're a lifesaver."

"I'm happy to do it," she said. "But only if you call Alex."

"Yeah. I will." She wouldn't. She still couldn't afford it. "And put the bat back. It's my favorite one."

Cindy pointed the Louisville slugger at Meghan. "Not until that creature's behind bars."

Timmie grinned and joined her daughter, who did, indeed, have a three-horned, goggle-eyed beast wrapped around her neck.

"Renfield isn't a creature," Timmie defended him anyway, even as he swiveled one scaly eye her way like the ball turret on the bottom of a B–24. "He's family."

"He looks like an extra from *Godzilla*."

"He probably was. But he won't bother you unless you're a fly." Bending over her daughter, Timmie petted the chameleon and tousled Meghan's hair. "Behave while I'm gone, both of you."

Meghan's face fell noticeably. "What about Patty's?" she asked, her voice teetering between plea and challenge.

Timmie crouched right down to eye level. "We'll go ride ponies at Patty's tomorrow."

"Tomorrow's Billy's funeral," Cindy reminded her. "You told Ellen you'd go."

Timmie kept her attention on her daughter. "We'll go the minute we get back from the funeral. I promise."

Plea sank straight into mutiny. "You promised yesterday. And the day before that. I'm getting tired of promises."

Timmie swept a lock of near-black hair off her daughter's high forehead and forbore swearing. "Nothin' I can do about it, Megs. You know that."

"It's the only reason I came here," Meghan reminded her tartly. "Since there isn't a beach."

You came here because your father jacked us around enough

that we had noplace else to go, Timmie amended silently. Not something she chose to share with a six-year-old, however.

"Enough," Timmie commanded, even knowing why she was getting the grief. "I'll see you when I get home. Please behave for Cindy until I can find another baby-sitter."

Meghan refused to face her mother. "Yes, ma'am."

Dropping one last kiss on her daughter's forehead, Timmie resettled her nursing bag on her shoulder and turned down the street for her walk to the hospital.

"Don't forget to stop by the pharmacy on the way home," Cindy called in farewell.

Timmie just lifted a hand in answer and walked on.

The day was a beaut, all high, sharp sky and gem-colored trees. Just enough of a chill in the air for Timmie to have broken out her jacket. Leaves crunched underfoot and jack-o'-lanterns waited to be lit on front porches. The image of small-town America. The fantasy Timmie had kept with her when the streets of Los Angeles had gotten too mean. Small kids on bikes and parents raking lawns and waving hello to passersby. Sidewalks and yard sales and night sounds that didn't include the constant whine of helicopters.

On one side of her, a Mercedes purred to a stop at the sign. Two kids on skateboards in baggies and ball caps swerved right for her on the sidewalk. Weeds poked through the mat of zoysia old Mr. Bauer had once maintained with a nail clipper, and spray paint on his milk-can mailbox betrayed the gestation of a local gang.

Puckett in the nineties. A pretty, Civil War–born town rediscovered by the wealthy white-flighters of St. Louis, a Missouri River port that had supported a blue-collar trade for generations, a dying transportation hub that saw boards go up over factories and train stations become curio shops. The place Timmie had avoided like the plague for as many years as she'd been able.

Timmie might have loved it here, if it just hadn't been here. If she could have come fresh and of her own accord. It hadn't happened that way, though, so she did the best she could. Today, that meant turning her attention to the new granite-and-glass hospital four blocks ahead that shouldered its way into all the gentle red brick like an ill-mannered twentieth-century trespasser.

Without even realizing it, Timmie began walking faster. Anxious for work, where nothing mattered but her skill, her reflexes, and her sense of humor. Where, in this small town in mid-America, the load would be light and the crises manageable.

Silly her, she should have known better. Especially since she seemed to be the one always screwing up those perfect shifts.

She got her first surprise when she walked into the nurses' lounge to put her things away.

"Well, I give up," she said, staring stupidly at her locker. Between the time she'd left work the day before and gotten in this afternoon, it had somehow sprouted all manner of bouquets, cards, and balloons, bearing congratulatory messages.

"What, you don't like being a shrine?" Mattie Wilson spoke up from the next locker.

Timmie pulled off one small bunch of blue and white chrysanthemums with a card that read "It's a miracle!"

"A shrine?" she asked. "What for?"

"Word around here's how you saved the great white doc from hollow-point poisoning."

Timmie opened the locker door and rained chrysanthemum petals on to the tile floor. "All I did was dance with a tall, sweaty guy. Kind of like high school mixers."

Mattie laughed. "You went to a tough school, girl."

"Well, I was usually the one with the gun, anyway. . . . Oh, look, this one's obviously from my date."

Considering the amount of personal property that regularly disappeared from lockers, Timmie shouldn't have been surprised that somebody had managed to get yet another bouquet inside hers.

Only these flowers were black. And dead. And the card was sealed. Timmie had a feeling this note didn't say congrats.

Mattie gave a low whistle. "Maybe you wanna get that gun back, girl."

Timmie spent a couple of seconds standing there before picking up the brittle flowers. "I bet somebody wants me to open this card, huh?"

Mattie slammed her own locker shut and shrugged into her massive lab coat, which covered what she referred to as her colonel butt. As in, "The colonel and his damned chicken built this butt." Mattie was as short as Timmie and as wide as Barb, with café au lait skin, tilted amber eyes, and buzzed hair. One of the few blacks on the ER staff, Mattie made Timmie feel much more at home in this preternaturally white town.

"I's you," Mattie advised, "I'd throw that trash where it belongs."

"And not know what's inside?" Timmie still hadn't quite gotten around to opening it, however.

Mattie considered her for a minute, hand on hip. "You do have a long nose, don't you?"

Timmie grinned. "I keep getting asked that question. Yeah, okay, shoot me. I'm curious. As opposed to every other soul in this town, I might say." She waved the card at her friend. "Am I the only one asking questions here?"

"You the only one gettin' dead flowers."

"But, Mattie, if everybody's so happy I saved Dr. Raymond, why doesn't anybody try and figure out who from? I mean, that was a gun out there yesterday. Even in my old 'hood that got a mention in the coffee conversation and a couple questions from the five-oh. Especially if the guy who was saved inspired bouquets."

Mattie's laugh could be heard out on Front Street. "You serious? Girl, that wasn't Raymond that boy was after. It was Landry. You spent time out in the real world. You really think this town gonna chase after a nice middle-class white boy just 'cause he pissed some uppity black brother stole his job?"

"Landry?" Timmie asked. "Really? You know who did it?"

Mattie shrugged. "I know the brother fired more'n a few good, solid citizens hereabouts. And I know the only reason you gettin' flowers for cropping that shooter is 'cause Raymond mighta got shot 'stead of a nigger. That card probably says you shouldn't'a bothered, the nigger deserved it."

"Is he?" Timmie asked, knowing Mattie would understand.

"A nigger? Oh, yeah, girl. He jus' wear good suits, is all. Now, throw that card away and let's go do us some sick people."

Timmie did throw the flowers in the trash. The card she kept, though, stuffing it in her pocket as she walked onto the hall.

It took two hours to score Billy Mayfield's records. By then Timmie had taken care of, among other things, five flu victims, two cheerleaders involved in a senseless cartwheel accident, and a kid with a Jujube up his nose. She was definitely ready for lunch. The only thing standing in her way was the triage nurse who stood dead center in the hallway with a chart in each hand.

"Choose," he challenged.

"Hey!" the prize behind curtain number one yelled. "Hey, goddamn it! Do you know who I am?"

Catching the unmistakable roux of Jack Black and Giorgio perfume, Timmie pegged the lady long before she was officially introduced.

"Lillian Carlson," the triage nurse specified. "Wife of Puckett General Bank president Edward Carlson, charter member of the TipaFew luncheon club, and holder, evidently, of half a dozen pieces of lingerie she forgot to pay for from Dawn's Designs. Dawn pressed charges, and Lillian complained of whiplash."

"Whiplash."

"From falling off the display counter."

"Hey!" Mrs. Carlson was yelling as she swung a lovely maroon silk bra like a lariat over her salon-blond head. "Hey, damn it! I'm hurtin' in here! Somebody out there call me a nurse!"

"If I call her a nurse," Timmie asked, "does that mean she has to call me a drunk?"

"She lookin' for you, girl," Mattie informed her.

"Not me," Timmie assured her, hands up so she couldn't land the chart. "Drunks don't like me. Especially friends of Jack."

More truthfully, Timmie didn't like drunks. And bourbon

drunks were much, much worse. Timmie detested bourbon drunks. She couldn't so much as smell the stuff without wanting to vomit.

"In that case, it's curtain number two," the triage nurse said with a smile, which was when Timmie heard what she should have all along, wafting over from room three like an evil miasma.

"Help! . . . Help! . . . Help!"

"Oh, no." She moaned, recognizing the sound. High, quavering, relentless.

"Mrs. Clara Winterborn," Mattie announced with a grin, her head tilted as if she were identifying a rare birdcall.

"Help! . . . Help! . . . Help!"

Timmie's stomach hit her knees. "She's a frequent flier, isn't she?"

"Memorial Med Center's Gold Ambassador Club."

Timmie grabbed the chart. "You guys set me up."

"It's hell being a hero," Mattie assured her and laughed as she walked off into Mrs. Carlson's room.

"I don't suppose there's a third option, is there?" Timmie all but begged.

"Being pulled to rehab for the shift," the triage nurse offered with a nasty grin. "They're short and we're not."

"That's obscene."

"No, it's not. Being pulled to Restcrest is obscene."

Timmie gave in with little grace. "I'm playing this game under protest."

Nobody listened. She turned around and trudged toward her penance.

*Mrs. Clara Winterborn*, the chart read. *Eighty-nine years. Complaint: fever of unknown origin. Address*, *Golden Grove Nursing Home*. Timmie sighed and stepped into the room, to be assailed by the stench of old urine and new bedsores. A brace of nervous, almost identically fidgety women in their sixties hovered at the head of the cart, evidently unable to do more than groom the few tufts of white hair left on the head of the creature in the bed.

A bird. A tiny, frail, bent bird. Mouth open, eyes wide and

empty, body curled in on itself, wrapped in blue Chux, tied in place with Posey and wrist restraints, propped into frozen position with half a dozen pillows. The North American *Gomerus decripidus*, Timmie heard her first nursing supervisor intone in her head. More frequently referred to as the Common Gomer, the moniker being an acronym for Get Out of My Emergency Room. Those patients who seemed to break down faster than old Fords, never got better, and used up all of medicine's time, talent, and tenuous empathy on their decaying, brain-absent bodies. The worst nightmare in medicine.

"The nurse is here, Mother!" one of the women screamed in the creature's ear. "Everything will be all right now!"

"Help! . . . Help! . . . Help!"

"She has a fever," the other said. "Golden Grove should have called us sooner. They know how anxious we get when Mother is ill."

The old woman had bedsores and contractures and about as much meat on her brittle little bones as a picked-over Thanksgiving carcass. Timmie spent a frantic moment searching the record for some kind of signed stop-treatment form. She didn't find one. She wished she were surprised.

"How long has she been . . . ill?" she asked.

Another quick smile and pat. "Mother's been at Golden Grove about ten years since her first stroke, haven't you, Mother? I think we're in here about once every other month. We know some of the nurses so well, we send them birthday presents."

Timmie turned away with the excuse of getting out gloves, blood tubes, and thermometer. What she was really doing was hiding her rage. Her blind, flashing frustration at these two very nice, very sincere women who spent their waking hours torturing their mother because they loved her.

Not only that, they tortured her in a place that shouldn't even be allowed to elicit confessions from Inquisition prisoners, much less treat helpless old ladies. If Mrs. Winterborn had been a cat, the ASPCA would already have had Golden Grove up on charges of cruelty to animals for the kind of care they gave her.

"Hello, Mrs. Winterborn!" Timmie yelled close to her ear without getting any response. "What's the matter?"

"Help! . . . Help! . . . Help!"

"Timmie Leary, to the desk," Ron intoned over the PA, as if she weren't four feet and a curtain away.

"What?" she called out as she wrapped a blood pressure cuff around that wasted arm.

It was Barb who stuck her head in the door. "The chief wants you. Something about Billy Mayfield's chart?"

Great. Another complication. Timmy noted a pressure of 110/56, probably high for old Mrs. Winterborn, and nodded. "In a minute. You know the Winterborns, Barb?"

"Of course she does," one sister said with delight. "I hope you liked the cookies, Dr. Adkins."

Timmie ignored the exchange to finish her quick evaluation, which produced a catheter bag full of foul-smelling, cloudy urine, atrial fibrillation on the monitor, and a definite rattle over the left chest. A couple of tubes of blood later, she traded places with Barb and prepared to face her supervisor.

"Timmie Leary, line one," Ron intoned over the PA.

Timmie stopped long enough to wash her hands before heading for the phone, all the while praying it wasn't a new problem. "Timmie Leary-Parker," she said in a rush.

Nothing.

"Hello?"

Empty space.

"Ron?" she asked, hanging up. "That wasn't Cindy, was it?"

The secretary looked up from where he was reading *GQ*. "Cindy?"

"She's baby-sitting for me tonight."

"Not unless she's taking testosterone, honey. That was a man."

Timmie spent a blank moment staring at the phone, her stomach doing a sudden dive. "A man. And he asked for me?"

"By name. He wasn't there?"

She shook her head, now decidedly unhappy. "It better not be who I think it was."

Ron forgot his *GQ*. "Mad stalker?"

"Worthless ex-husband. He calls again, get a name, okay?"

"Is it worth getting his phone number, too?"

Timmie finally laughed. "He doesn't do guys. He doesn't even do girls. He does intimidation." She did everything but shake herself off. "And on that happy note, I'm off to see Angie."

Ron rolled his very expressive eyes. "I'll pray for you."

"Help! Help! Help!" Mrs. Winterborn screamed.

"And, Ron," Timmie said on her way by. "Have Barb help that woman."

Angie McFadden had an office on the other side of the waiting room, where she couldn't be bothered by noise from the ER she allegedly supervised. Timmie knocked on the pressboard door to what had once been a supply closet and stepped in to find not just Angie waiting for her, but a middle-aged man as well. The mystery guest was in his fifties, balding, with a salt-and-pepper beard and the pocked, pasty skin of a career smoker. He wore a Mobile work shirt with "Tucker" sewn in script over the left pocket, and passed the time fondling an unlit cigarette.

"You wanted me?" Timmie asked her supervisor.

Not in any sense of the word, she was sure. Angie had all but hissed at Timmie from the minute it had been suggested she'd make a lovely addition to her staff. Not a thing had improved in the three weeks Timmie had worked there.

"Mr. Van Adder came in today to look at William Mayfield's chart," she said, swinging a little in her seat. "Then he heard *you* had it."

Timmie considered the sour look on her supervisor's flushed face and decided it wasn't a good day to piss at fences.

"As a matter of fact, I do," she admitted easily. "I wanted to make sure I didn't miss anything when he was here. After all, how many forty-four-year-olds die of the flu, ya know?"

Angie squinted as if trying to assess Timmie's hidden agenda. "And all that noise about the coroner?"

Since Timmie had just remembered that Tucker was the coroner's first name, she figured it would be unwise to do anything but keep smiling. "You mean about the fact that I couldn't understand why he didn't question a death like that?" she asked. Van Adder darkened noticeably, and Timmie said agreeably, "Aw, heck, what do I know?"

So she wasn't immune to temptation. Besides, she wanted to know why Mr. Van Adder had shown up at the hospital for the chart of somebody he'd turfed off his jurisdiction like a fourth-down football.

Van Adder glared. "*You're* Joe's daughter?"

She smiled evenly. "Yes, sir."

One of the backroom boys, she diagnosed. The late-nighters, who always had some town function or benevolent meeting as a cover for the hours spent in smoky, beer-fogged rooms.

His scowl deepened. "I'm Tucker Van Adder."

Timmie nodded. "Yes, sir, I know."

He shook his head. "And you think you can teach me my job, little girl? That right?"

Timmie came so close to telling him off her tongue bled. This guy was an asshole. He was also a local power broker. Not to mention, evidently, close personal friends with her easily threatened supervisor.

Timmie was outspoken. She wasn't an idiot. "I was just a little perplexed, sir. It seemed so unusual."

"Find anything?" Van Adder asked with no little sarcasm.

Considering the fact that she hadn't even cracked the chart, Timmie figured she could be pretty honest. "Not a thing."

"Well, give it to me," Angie demanded. "You don't have any right to it. And Mr. Van Adder wants to review it."

"It's in my locker," Timmie lied blithely. "If I can finish my patient, I'll bring it right out to you."

"Give the patient to somebody else. And clean up all those flowers. I don't think they're funny, either."

"Okay."

And then, before she got into real trouble, she walked out.

Timmie got back to the hall and did a quick check on her patients, who were in various stages of the ER holding pattern. Mrs. Winterborn was waiting to go to X ray, the cheerleaders were still in X ray, and the man with the flu was getting IVs. Which meant Timmie had ten minutes to sneak off with Billy's chart.

She didn't go far, just the empty trauma room, where she knew nobody'd bother her. She scanned the chart once, quickly, then reread every lab result, every path report, every X-ray finding as carefully as she could, looking for some kind of anomaly that would account for what had happened.

What she found was nothing.

No arrhythmias, no toxic levels of anything. No liver failure, no heart failure, no kidney disease. Out-of-whack electrolytes, but nothing that wouldn't be expected from somebody with the two-bucket flu. Nothing, certainly, that should have killed a healthy man that fast.

It should have made her feel better. She hadn't screwed up, at least not in something obvious. Instead, it made her feel more unsettled. Especially considering the fact that the coroner was sitting in Angie's office waiting for that very chart to close it out once and for all.

"Help! . . . Help . . . He—"

Timmie lifted her head at the change in that old voice.

"Fuck! Call a code!"

She left the chart on the table and ran. Barb's voice she couldn't mistake anywhere.

"Code blue, emergency room three. Code blue, emergency room three."

"Do something!" the sisters were screaming as Timmie slammed into the room to find Mrs. Winterborn frozen in position with that last quavering "help" stuck halfway down her throat, her eyes bugged, her skin mottling. Barb was at the cart cranking up the defibrillator, and footsteps and equipment already thundered through the halls. And all Timmie could do was stand flat-footed in the middle of the room wondering just how she could maneuver those old ladies out so she could screw up a code.

"Mother! Oh, God, save her!"

"Are you sure?" Timmie asked, even knowing the answer.

Barb turned with paddles in her hands. "Do you spawn disaster?" she demanded.

"Do something!" the sisters screamed, now harmonizing like bad opera.

Shit, Timmie thought to herself. Shit and double shit and triple shit. "Don't let Mr. Van Adder leave!" she yelled out to the desk and ran for an airway.

They didn't need Mr. Van Adder after all. Gomers never die, the old hospital adage went. And since Mrs. Winterborn's picture would have been beside the term "gomer" in a medical dictionary, neither did she. She survived her fifteenth cardiac arrest to be hooked up to the latest machinery in the unit where her daughters could happily hover, and Timmie handed over Billy's chart, worked the rest of her shift in a funk, and walked home.

The house looked quiet from the outside. Lights spilled like warm milk over the carefully tended lawn, and trees nodded in a small breeze. Inviting. Comforting. Peaceful.

Maybe in some other house. Timmie looked up at hers and faltered to a halt at the edge of her yard. She damn near turned around and went back and volunteered for another shift, even knowing that Meghan waited for her.

As predictably as drunks on New Year's, the depression smacked into her like a high wall at sixty. A lot of good escaping does, she thought, just staring. Just wishing the place into atoms and herself and Meghan back on the beach at high tide. Her mother had been right after all. Whatever you're escaping just waits for you in the dark. Well, it was dark, and it was waiting for her.

Finally dredging up the energy, Timmie pulled out her keys and walked on up to the porch, her shoes squidging on the cement and the trees rustling overhead. She heard Jack Buck's voice drift out from the back as she slid her key into the lock and remembered the pharmacy stop she was supposed to have made.

She could go now. Sneak back out and not be seen. Keep on walking until she got to the river and follow it south, moving on until nobody knew her. Nobody needed her. Nobody closed in on her and weighed her down and picked her apart like a leftover roast.

That made her think of Mrs. Winterborn, up in the unit bound and gagged by machinery and her daughters, and she felt guilty. So she headed in to check on things before escaping to get the prescription for Haldol, which she knew wasn't right, either.

"Hi, honey, I'm home," she called as she shoved open the front door.

The outside of her grandmother's house was picture perfect, because it had been her father's joy to work in the dirt. The inside hadn't mattered as much. Not only that, Timmie's grandmother had abhorred throwing things away, which meant that Timmie had inherited a nine-room storage facility. Newspapers, magazines, books, bank statements, catalogues. Anything and everything. In fifty years nothing had been thrown away, and it all remained to create the fire hazard of the century, teetering on unstable furniture, crammed into dusty corners, stacked to twelve-foot ceilings in places. In the five weeks she'd been home, Timmie had managed to clear a path through four of the rooms, and enough space in the living room to take a good swing with a bat at the Nerf ball hanging by a rope from the light fixture. Everything else was going to have to wait until she could afford to rent a Dumpster.

Cindy poked her head out of the kitchen and smiled. "Boy, am I glad you're home. It's been a real long night. I'm afraid I didn't duck quick enough. It's okay, though, I've been putting ice on it. And I don't think Meghan likes me. She kept threatening me with that lizard."

Would a lizard be considered a weapon? Timmie wondered, fighting a renewed urge to turn around. Could Cindy put Meghan up on charges of assault with a deadly reptile? "I forgot to go to the pharmacy," she said. "Mind waiting till I get back?"

"Of course not." Cindy's smile would have done a martyr proud. "Do you have money for it? I got a hundred from the riverboat last week I still haven't spent."

"No, that's okay. I have it."

Skirting her way past an end table teetering in TV dinner trays and bolts of polyester material, Timmie worked her way past the kitchen to where announcer Jack Buck was still enthusing about the newly reorganized Cardinal team that was playing the Cubs.

"It's a beautiful afternoon at Wrigley Field," he assured the fans from the TV that flickered in the back bedroom.

The set was an old black and white hooked up to the latest in VCRs. It was the only furniture in the room except for a sagging single bed that now held a medical frame and a sunflower quilt, a battered end table, and a ragged, stuffing-sprung old armchair that had once been blue. The chair sat foursquare before the TV like the captain's chair on the *Enterprise*, behind which walls of debris loomed in the shadows. But the man in the chair didn't notice. His eyes were on the grainy action on the TV.

He was a tower of a man, all broad, knobby shoulders and thick white hair and high, wide cheekbones. Piercing blue eyes had faded to rheumy uncertainty, and gnarled, powerful hands were splayed on the arms of the chair as he gave what attention he had to the game and muttered to himself.

"This was the only way I could keep him quiet," Cindy apologized. "He kept trying to leave, but he wouldn't tell me where he was trying to get to."

Timmie crouched down by the side of the chair and laid her small hands on his wide, bony leg. "He can't remember," she admitted. Then she smiled and patted those fleshless knees. "Hi, Daddy."

The soft, distant blue eyes flickered and wandered her way for a minute.

"How's the game?" she asked, patting him. Patting his hand and his knee and readjusting the Posey vest that held him to his favorite chair as if just the physical contact could bring him back to her.

"I have to go now," he said, picking at the frayed material under his fingers. "I have to . . ."

"Everybody says hi," Timmie said, patting the shoulders that had lifted her above all those crowds to see St. Patrick's Day floats and home run victory laps.

"Did you call Dr. Raymond?" Cindy asked from behind her.

Timmie patted a couple of more times without effect. She'd already lost her father again to the game. "I can't afford to."

"There aren't a hell of a lot more homes in town you can try," Cindy reminded her. "He's been kicked out of three. And you know you can't go on with him here. You should have asked at the horse show, like you meant to."

"I know." Timmie thought about that poor, blighted thing tonight, and then about the little man Alex Raymond had made a special trip to say good-bye to. She felt as if she were being gut-kicked, and she was getting pretty damn tired of it. So she stood up.

"I'm going to the pharmacy," she said and walked back out.

Timmie didn't even remember walking to the pharmacy. She couldn't seem to get past the urge to escape. She'd worked so hard her whole life to pretend it all didn't matter, and then she walked back into that house and the lie fell apart. And she wanted to run.

Like that had worked out all that well the last time.

"Have you talked to your father's doctor about all these medications?" the pharmacist asked as he finished typing up the label.

The only twenty-four-hour pharmacy in town, and they had to have a guy with a conscience on.

"Yes," Timmie said quite truthfully as she paced the gray-speckled linoleum floor and looked out the windows into the night. "But I can't change things until I can get him placed again."

She was snowing her father, just to keep him under control. Just like the nursing homes had done each time he'd woken up enough to try to leave and succeeded in breaking at least one jaw in the attempt.

The pharmacist shook his head. "If he's sure."

The doctor? Timmie thought. He's an asshole. So had the one been before him. She couldn't afford a better one, though. Not yet. Not until she began to get just an inch or two ahead of the financial disaster her divorce had made of her life.

"Your dad used to come in here every day on his walks," the pharmacist said with that same soft smile everybody used when talking about her dad. "Never knew a body who loved to share words and music like your dad."

He scribbled, and Timmie, much too familiar with the eulogy, fidgeted. She checked out another window to discover that Mike's Mobile sat kitty-corner out the back. Tucked into the shadows that lurked between that lot and the pharmacy's was a maroon Chevy pickup truck with PUCKETT COUNTY CORONER emblazoned on the door in the same lettering as Tucker over that shirt pocket.

"Every time I fill one of these," the pharmacist was saying behind her, "I think of that poem your dad used to love to quote. You know, 'The lions of the hills are gone.' I feel the same about him. That when he goes . . . well, you know. Was that 'Innisfree' he was quoting? He really did love that one."

"No," Timmie said, turning only halfway toward him. "'Deirdre's Lament for the Sons of Usnach.'"

"That's right. He used to recite the whole thing. Real pretty it was. Real sad. I just remember that first line. 'The lions of the hill are gone.'"

"Uh-huh."

> The lions of the hill are gone,
> And I am left alone—alone—
> Dig the grave both wide and deep,
> For I am sick, and fain would sleep.

Just what she needed tonight, seeing that old man toothless and tied to his chair. Just what she wanted to carry out of this pharmacy with her along with the drugs that would keep him prisoner even beyond the confusion that crippled him.

She turned back to the window out of instinct. She stayed, watching out of surprise.

The coroner's truck was rocking.

There weren't any tremors beneath the pharmacy floor, so Timmie doubted sincerely they were having an earthquake. Not only that, the truck windows were fogged. Not fogged enough, however, that she didn't recognize body parts when she saw them.

Good lord, she thought with a surprised grin. The coroner seemed to be examining a body. She could tell he was thorough, because the legs that were pressed up against the window were quite naked. And his hand was very busy.

"Twenty dollars," the pharmacist announced behind her.

Timmie was so preoccupied that she just reached into her scrub pocket and pulled out the first thing she came to. She almost handed the pharmacist her card. The mysterious card from her locker, which she'd forgotten all about.

Oh, good, she thought, staring at it with dark humor. Another distraction. It was sure better than thinking about why she was here. Or why anybody would allow themselves to be caught naked in a coroner's truck with Tucker Van Adder.

Digging back into her pocket, she finally came up with change. "Here," she said, handing it over.

The pharmacist left her alone, and she ripped open the envelope, prepared to be entertained by somebody's outrage at her attempt to save a black man.

She wasn't entertained. She was confused. In fact, she was angry.

The note was on plain paper, the printing old-fashioned cut-out magazine letters. As for the message, it lacked originality.

STOP NOW BEFORE YOU GET HURT

Stop what? Saving black guys? Grabbing guns?

For God's sake, Timmie thought in disgust. Like I don't have anything better to do than put up with this crap.

She should have tossed the card. She didn't. She must have stood there for a full five minutes, tapping it against her hand and watching out the window and wondering just who was threatened enough by her actions that they'd feel compelled to communicate with her.

She didn't, in the end, find illumination. She did get the privilege of seeing Van Adder's date step out of the truck. Timmie was so preoccupied, though, that she made it all the way out the door before it dawned on her just who it was she'd seen.

"Oh, shit," she said, coming to a dead stop out on the dark, blowing street. "What the hell do I do about *that?*"

MURPHY WAS NOT A JOY-RUNNER. AFTER DOING IT DAMN NEAR every day of his life since his fifteenth birthday, he didn't really believe those assholes who said they got out there and ran ten miles because they loved it. He did it because he figured that if he lived through it at the crack of fucking dawn, the rest of the day couldn't possibly get worse.

It had been a hell of a lot easier to do when he'd lived in L.A. First of all, he'd been younger. He'd run on much newer legs and pinker lungs. Second, L.A. didn't have winter. Not really. Murphy hated winter. He hated dark skies and leafless trees and the way the air never seemed to dry out. It didn't matter that it was only halfway through October. It was cold and it was wet, and Murphy knew it could only get worse.

"Morning, Mr. Murphy," one of his neighbors greeted him as she bent in an old bathrobe at the end of her sidewalk to get her morning paper.

Panting and gasping his way back up Maple Street, Murphy couldn't manage more than a nod and a wave. Not only was it wet here, it was hilly. Why hadn't anybody told him how hilly Missouri was? How the hell could it keep flooding if it had so many goddamn hills?

"You got company this morning," the woman let him know.

Murphy lifted a hand again and kept slogging uphill toward the place he rented from Sherilee. Great. Company. He never managed constructive thought until he made it back into the kitchen and downed his first quart or two of coffee. There was no one on earth he wanted to talk to until that was accomplished.

Then he reached the pillored, redbrick Victorian that commanded the top of the hill and turned into the driveway. There, sitting nose to ass with his old Porsche, was a shiny new Puckett police car.

*That* kind of company. Shit. Murphy stopped right there and wheezed.

The officer in question was just turning back down the stairs from the apartment Murphy had over Sherilee's garage. A skinny guy with slick brown hair, big "do-me-baby" eyes, and the hyper-military gait that was so favored by certain suburban cops, he walked with one hand firmly wrapped around his utility belt, as if he were balancing himself with it.

A cop who liked female civilians much better than male civilians, Murphy guessed from the tight fit of the black-on-black uniform. But only if they were sitting on his lap in a bar or on his face in the backseat of a squad car.

Murphy lurched back into motion. "Can I help you?" he asked, heading onto the grass.

The policeman didn't bother to change his pace. "You Daniel Murphy?"

"Yep."

"I'd like to talk to you."

A master of the obvious, too. Murphy wiped the sweat from his face and walked over to the stairs as the cop hit the bottom step. "Well, then, come on up. I have coffee on, Officer . . ."

"Adkins." He didn't bother to hold out a hand or ease his judgmental expression as he and Murphy changed places on the steps. "I'd prefer you come to the station."

Not an invitation. A heavy-handed command.

Attempted intimidation at six-thirty in the morning. Murphy wondered what he'd stirred up. "No thanks," he said, climbing the steps. "Unless you have a warrant in your hand, I'm going to get some coffee and a shower. And I've never found that police stations do either very well."

The inside of Murphy's apartment was nothing inspiring. Murphy wasn't into inspiring these days. He was into uninvolved. Uninteresting. Unstressful. He had two rooms and a john, all painted white with curtains that looked like old Handi Wipes. The furniture consisted of castoffs from Sherilee's main house, a mishmash of chintz and Southwestern that had washed up from the high tides of her various attempts at redecoration.

Murphy had supplied the artwork, two pen-and-ink sketches he hauled around with him, one of the American Bar in Bangkok, the other of his two daughters, who lived with their mother in New York. Other than that, he had a good stereo, a bad television, and a state-of-the-art laptop he rarely opened anymore.

"I can offer black coffee or black coffee," he said, pulling NYPD mugs from the white metal cabinets and filling them from a saucepan. "Drawback of living alone. I don't plan for company."

Adkins was still bristling. "Black's fine."

"Sit down. God knows, I have to. I'm gettin' too fuckin' old for the kind of hills you got around here."

Standing at parade rest by the door, Adkins didn't seem to be able to let go of his belt long enough to accept the mug. A real problem, Murphy figured. With all the macho cop shit he had clipped to the thing, it must weigh a good twenty pounds. If Adkins let go, his pants might damn well hit his ankles.

He'd brought a brown manila envelope in with him. Smiling like a waitress looking for tips, Murphy directed the mug toward the hand that held the envelope in an effort to help Adkins make the decision.

"You were at the horse show," Adkins said as he let go of his belt for the cup without noticeable disaster. "You saw the shooting?"

Setting down his own mug on the overcarved and underused Colonial kitchen table that never held more than old bills and new catalogues, Murphy nodded. "In living color."

He took a second to shrug out of his old Marine Corps sweatshirt and toss it toward the bedroom before pulling out one of the chairs and dropping down. His T-shirt was soaked, and he smelled like a wet horse. But if the good Officer Adkins wanted to talk to him, that was what he got.

"I'm looking into the incident," Adkins said, not moving.

Murphy pulled over a half-finished pack of cigarettes and shook one out. "About time somebody did."

Lighting his first of the day, he sucked in enough tar and nicotine to clear all the clean air out his lungs and waited for the cop to make his move.

Murphy had asked a couple of questions around town the day before, the "Why would somebody try and shoot Dr. Raymond?" variety, just for the article he'd prepared on the benefit. The reaction he'd gotten had been polite bemusement. Nobody knew. Certainly nobody would hurt Alex Raymond. Nobody would jeopardize the hospital, which was the county's biggest employer, the area's civic pride, the drum major in the town's parade of progress.

But, oddly enough, no one had shown outrage. Not even the fat, garrulous old fart named Bub something who was the town's chief detective. The only person even slightly distressed by Murphy's questions had been the little lady at Vital Statistics. Murphy had stopped by to check the figures on local death rates. The poor little woman manning the desk had reacted as if Murphy had asked the name of every underage virgin in town.

And now Officer Adkins was here to threaten him. Murphy sucked at his nicotine and sipped at his coffee and waited. As for Adkins, he finally gave in and settled into the other chair with more noise than a cavalry horse stopping from a dead run.

"You guys find anything out about it?" Murphy asked.

"The investigation is proceeding."

Well, that line hadn't changed since Jack Webb. It still meant they hadn't learned anything. After yesterday, Murphy wasn't surprised.

"I wanted to see if you might have remembered anything else about the shooting," Adkins said, pulling out a suspiciously clean notebook and flipping pages. "Any little thing, even something you might not have considered important."

Taking another hit of nicotine, Murphy shook his head. "Nope."

Adkins squinted hard, his jaw working. "You've been thinking about it?"

"Hard not to."

"You've been asking questions around town."

"Only to finish the piece I'd started on the benefit. The horses got two hundred words, the shooter got fifty. I think that's about fair, don't you?"

"You think this is all pretty funny, do you?"

Murphy shrugged. "At least I have some kind of reaction. I haven't heard anybody else in town even mention it."

"And you don't have anything else you want to tell me."

Murphy was thoroughly enjoying the officer's consternation. "No. Have you talked to that nurse who was there? Timmie Leary?"

"No. Why?"

"I just saw the guy. She damn near shared tonsils with him."

"And you don't have any thoughts about the incident at all?"

"Well, I'll tell you one thing," he said, balancing his coffee mug on his stomach as he leaned back even farther to stretch his feet out on the table. "I'm glad I'm not a conspiracy theorist. A good conspiracy theorist would figure that since nobody in town wants to talk about what happened, something nefarious must be going on you're all afraid of being found out."

Adkins twitched and then straightened, obviously going back to intimidation as an interview tool. "And you?" he asked. "Are you a conspiracy theorist?"

Murphy gave him wide eyes. "Me? Oh yeah, sure. I think Elvis was behind Kennedy's assassination and that the United Nations is going to invade Utah by reading the road signs backward." He shook his head. "Conspiracy theories are too exhausting, Officer. And that's not what I came to this town looking for."

"What *did* you come here for?"

Murphy lit a second cigarette from his first. "You want the truth? Peace and quiet. I was looking for a little R and R. Be a hell of a lot easier to do without people shooting at me, though. And then, on top of that, I hear the most disturbing thing yesterday. Can you believe it? I was told that the death rate has been skyrocketing around here . . . well, increasing, anyway. It's way up from last year." Murphy paused for another sip of coffee. "You got any ideas on why that's happening, Officer Adkins?"

Murphy knew damn well he was going to regret dicking around with this guy. But he'd never been able to resist the temptation to turn the tables on a bad interrogator. And Adkins was a bad interrogator.

So Murphy flashed him a big smile. "More coffee?"

Adkins sat so stiffly he damn near snapped the handle off the mug. His left eye was twitching, pulling at the acne scars on his cheeks so that they seemed to breathe. Murphy, knowing perfectly well where this was going, just sat back and watched.

Akdins fidgeted. He doodled as if he were writing down thoughts. He glared. And finally, just as Murphy knew he would, he edged up to his purpose with the hesitation of a man asking for his first paid blow job.

"You want to tell me why you're really here?" Adkins asked. "Award-winning guy like you?"

So there it was. It wasn't what Murphy had seen that had the officer here. It was what Murphy might have found out. Murphy and his reputation Sherilee so loved to trumpet around. Murphy and his goddamned, world-famous Pulitzer Prizes.

It didn't seem to matter to anybody that the last of those prizes was at least ten years old. Pulitzers, it seemed, were forever. Kind of like diamonds. Or herpes.

There was something going on in this town. Adkins knew it and Murphy knew it. And whatever it was, it almost certainly revolved around one of three things. Money or power. Money *and* power. Money and power and sex. Whatever it was, the people protecting it didn't want Murphy to find out. And Murphy wasn't going to be able to convince them that he didn't, either.

"Why am I here?" he asked, grinding out his second cigarette. "Got noplace else to go. I burned my bridges at real newspapers a long time ago, but newspapers are the only thing I do. So when I got out of lockup this time, I accepted Sherilee's invitation to write about wine festivals and river towns."

"Lockup?"

"Rehab. Drying out. Straightening up. I am a twelve-step poster child who just wants to write about garden clubs and not be bothered by anybody."

"Then why all the questions?"

Murphy grinned like a co-conspirator. "How long you been a cop, Adkins?"

"Ten years."

Murphy nodded. "After you retire, how long do you think it'll take for you to stop checking plates and scanning crowds?" He threw off one of his more self-effacing smiles. "I'm not out of the habit yet."

Adkins teetered for a long time before falling for the reassurance. Finally he set the coffee cup down and lifted the manila envelope. "Could you tell me if you recognize any of these people, sir?"

Murphy put his feet down and righted his chair. "Happy to."

Adkins pulled out five photos. Black-and-white professional head shots, like for corporate advertising. White, upscale, silver-streaked middle-aged men. Respectable-looking. Forceful. Composed. Out of work, Murphy figured, and wondered which one of them was the father of Sherilee's best friend.

"Nope," he finally said, considering each of them. "I'm afraid not. I don't suppose you want to tell me who they are."

"I'm sorry," Adkins said. "No."

"Yeah, that's what I thought."

Gathering the photos back up, Adkins took a moment to consider Murphy in silence. "Since you don't want to be bothered anyway, I guess it's safe to assume that you won't be pursuing this matter on your own."

"Not likely. Sherilee has me on a pretty tight schedule. I'd be happy to help with a composite if you want, though."

Adkins nodded, and creaked and jingled his way to his feet. "Thank you for your time. And please call me if you remember anything. Anything at all."

Murphy followed him up, hearing his own creaks much too loudly. "I certainly will. And good luck. Puckett's too nice a town for problems like this."

He held out his hand. Adkins took it, but only so he could rotate the grip to get his hand on top. That kind of cop. Murphy let him. He might as well let him think he was big dog. God knows Murphy wasn't going to convince Adkins that he didn't want to know what had Adkins so nervous. What, evidently, had the town fathers so nervous. What they were so anxious to protect that they'd sent Adkins out here with veiled threats and questions.

"Yeah. Well, call me if you need anything."

"I will."

"And remember," Adkins advised portentously as he once again took hold of his utility belt. "Leave the questions to us."

Murphy wanted to laugh. "Don't worry," he said with a big, choirboy smile. "I will."

Two hours later Murphy walked into the office Sherilee Carter had decorated like a quick trip to the Journalism Hall of Fame and blithely broke his word.

"It wasn't your friend's father who tried to shoot up the horse show," he told her as he leaned over to steal a handful of M&M's from the souvenir mug she kept from *All the President's Men*. Murphy couldn't help but think of how many people that damn movie had gotten into trouble. People who had gone into the business with visions of Woodward and Bernstein dancing in their heads.

And then, even worse, Sherilee had arrayed a whole rogue's

gallery on the wall behind her head. Signed photos of David Halberstam, Peter Arnett, Neil Sheehan, Pete Hamill, watching him every time he came in the office like the ghosts of Christmas past.

Murphy's own photo had stayed on the wall only as long as it had taken him to walk in the door that first day. Even so, coupled with Sherilee's unbridled enthusiasm, the office still had the effect of making Murphy feel as if he were looking at pictures of himself in bell-bottoms and an Afro.

Although, come to think of it, in the good old days he had never once worked for an editor who came to the office in a baby-doll dress and pink bow barrettes. But when your father is the third-generation owner of the town paper, Murphy figured you could wear what you damn well pleased.

"How do you know?" Sherilee demanded, swinging around in her daddy's five-hundred-dollar brown leather chair, her short, chubby legs not quite reaching the floor.

Murphy waggled a finger at her. "Ah-ah-ah-ah, wrong answer. Your next statement was supposed to be, 'What makes you think I'd suspect my friend's father?' "

Sherilee blushed. "Okay . . . so what makes you think I'd suspect my friend's father?"

"Because you haven't talked about the shooting any more than anybody else in this town, which means you're terrified you know who did it. He didn't."

"So how do you know?"

"Adkins showed me pictures. I'd bet a month's salary it wasn't him."

"You don't know what he looks like."

"Middle-aged, well-groomed, hair going tastefully silver. Lumped in a group of four other, very similar men who all looked like they worked together as, maybe, hospital administrators."

Her grin was knowing. "Boy, you *are* as good as they say. Okay, if he didn't do it, who did?"

Murphy shrugged and settled a hip on her desk. "I half-expected you to know already, since everybody in town talks to you. Somebody had to recognize him."

"Not necessarily," she said. "The crowd that attends horse shows isn't really the old-timers. And from what I heard, most everybody out there was, like, watching the horse. So what do you do next?"

Murphy ignored every familiar face that smiled benignly at him from the wall and stood back up. "Nothing. Just thought I'd let you know."

That brought Sherilee right to her feet, which, behind the massive mahogany desk she'd also inherited from her father, made her look like she was playing grown-up. "I think not, Murphy! I mean, this is, like, our first big, breaking story together!"

"It's gonna have to break on its own, Sherilee. You didn't hire me to do hard news. You hired me for the dry-goods section, so dry goods is where I'm gonna stay."

She was sneering now. "And do what, considering we have a murderer loose in town?"

"An *attempted* murderer. And who knows? He might already have had second thoughts, been to confession and been absolved without our help. Nobody wants to know about it, and I don't either. I'd rather talk to that guy who seems to make everybody sing."

"Tony Bennett?"

"The guy whose daughter grabbed the gun."

"Joe Leary." Just like everybody else he'd talked to, the minute Sherilee mentioned the name, she smiled. "That's right. It was Timmie out there, wasn't it? Boy, I'll tell you. Coulda knocked me over when I saw her again. Does she look different or what?"

He'd been about to walk out the door. Sherilee's answer stopped him all over again. It seemed he was meant to get answers he hadn't asked for today, whether he liked it or not.

"Considering I don't know different from what, I can't say, Sherilee. Did you know her when she grew up here?"

"Well, she was older than me, but yeah, at least until she moved with her mom to St. Louis after the divorce. But Timmie always had, like, a new hair color, and I'm not talkin' like red or yellow. Green. Orange. Blue. Funny she should get conservative in L.A., huh?"

"Go figure. Any idea why she moved home?"

Sherilee's eyes opened a little more. "Sounds to me like you're more interested in Timmie than her dad, Murphy. This couldn't be love, could it? Like, two strangers in a strange land kind of thing?"

Murphy stiffened like a shot. "Bite your tongue, little girl."

"Well," Sherilee hedged, her expression unusually coy. "Since you swear you're not working on a real story, it's the only reason I can think of that you're asking so much about her. It couldn't have anything to do with the shooting you two shared up close and personal or the fact that for some reason you asked Betty McPherson over at Vital Statistics for death records."

"I'm trying to plan out my golden years," he assured her. "I'd hate to settle in a town with a short life expectancy. Didn't help much, though, since old Betty protected those records like her virginity."

"Oh, Murphy, you're so bogus."

"Don't call me bogus, Sherilee. Anything but bogus."

She grinned like the kid she still was. "How 'bout a lying sack of shit?"

Murphy actually smiled at her. "Nice sibilance, excellent descriptive quality. I give it a seven. Don't break out in a rash. I'm really not interested. I just happened to see a gun and had the police ask me about it."

Suddenly her eyes damn near glowed. "And you don't know a thing about people dying . . . "

"Absolutely not."

"So then I guess you don't care that besides lifesaving, Timmie Leary has chosen threatening the coroner as another of her extracurricular activities."

"I heard about that. From the lady herself. It's just readjustment from life in the big city. She'll get over it."

"How about the fact that the guy she threatened him over is, like, being buried this morning."

"May he rest in peace."

"Or that any witnesses, or maybe . . . *perpetrators* might be hovering in the vicinity big-time."

"I hope they bring raincoats."

"Like his ex-wife, whom he used to beat like a rented mule until she divorced him ten months before his suspicious death."

Murphy found himself slowing to a halt right at the door. "Might be worth going just to see if she spits on his grave."

# FIVE

AT LEAST SHE WAS WEARING BLACK," BARB PHILOSOPHIZED LATER that morning when Timmie broke the news to the SSS about just who she'd seen step out of Van Adder's van the night before. "After all, she is in mourning."

"She's not in mourning," Cindy objected, leaning up from the backseat. "I mean, who the hell would mourn for Billy Mayfield?"

Timmie, Barb, and Mattie answered in unison. "Ellen."

They were, in fact, all technically in mourning for Billy. They were at least in his funeral procession, all decked out in their Sunday best and squeezed into Barb's new Volvo as she negotiated the meandering lanes of Puckett's second-class cemetery to where Billy was going to have his ashes cemented into a wall. They'd already sat through an interminable ceremony at the funeral home, and only had to lay the deceased to rest before heading to their favorite watering hole for debriefing.

Barb had spent the funeral making cracks about Billy's family. Mattie had prayed. Timmie had been preoccupied by the question of just how long Ellen had been sneaking off to Tucker's truck and whether it had anything to do with Tucker's attitude toward Billy's unfortunate demise. She also couldn't help but wonder if it had something to do with those dead roses she'd thrown away and the card she hadn't, which made for a busy funeral for her.

"You're not surprised," Timmie accused Barb.

Her attention on the car ahead of her, Barb chose not to take offense. "Ellen's as human as the next girl," she said easily. "Just 'cause she's divorced doesn't mean she's a nun."

"It's just like your fireman's helmet," Cindy said.

"Her what?" Mattie asked.

Cindy leaned forward again. "Timmie has a brand-new Los Angeles Fire Department helmet in her closet. It fell on my head last night when I went to get my coat. Has her name stenciled on it and everything. Ask her about it."

Cindy had damn near worn it back out the front door when she'd gone home, too. But when she'd finally been alone, Timmie had sat for a long time just holding that helmet in her hands like a dried corsage.

"It was my going-away present," she defended herself.

"From who?" Barb asked with a knowing grin.

The helmet was still new enough for Timmie to blush. "All the guys," she protested. "Amazing how close you can get after sharing a couple of earthquakes and a riot or two."

"But especially one guy," Cindy chortled.

Timmie tried hard not to smile. "Fireman Dan," she finally admitted wistfully as she thought again of the fun they'd had with that helmet. "Finest turn-out gear in the city."

All three of them laughed. "So what happened?" Mattie asked.

Timmie shruggeded. "He went back to his ex-wife."

"And you moved out of phase three," Cindy prompted. "Tell them about the phases."

Timmie sigh. She should have just coldcocked Cindy with that damn helmet and been done with it. "The four phases of divorce," she said for the whole group. "It's kind of like the stages of grief, except instead of denial, anger, bargaining, and acceptance, what you go through is denial, anger, sluthood, and recovery. I am now in recovery."

"And Ellen is still in sluthood," Cindy finished for them all, and then offered a big grin. "Which sounds a lot more fun than recovery to me any day of the week. Especially if you're in love."

"I am not going to give her the dignity of labeling what they were doing as love," Timmie said. "Not in a coroner's truck."

"I did it in a meat locker once," Cindy mused. "But that wasn't love, either. Not like this time."

Timmie knew that Cindy wanted somebody to ask, "This time?" Nobody did.

"Ellen deserves better," she insisted anyway as they reached the top of the hill, where the town water tower could be seen past the Eternal Rest Crematorium.

"Shit, we all deserve better," Barb reminded her. "Doesn't mean we ever get it."

Taillights flickered like out-of-sync Christmas lights, and everybody slowed to a stop. Barb followed suit to the sound of unclicking seat belts.

"You don't think Tucker ignored Billy's death because he's been in Ellen's pants, do you?" Timmie asked as she stepped out onto the cracked asphalt.

Barb, Mattie, and Cindy were glaring at her when they joined her on the grass. "Let's bury him first," Mattie suggested. "Then we can dig him up and play with him some more."

"Can't," Timmie said, her attention briefly caught by a couple of Mayfield brothers who were shoving at each other over bumper proximities. "Can't test ashes."

"Then that takes care of that," Barb pronounced and led the way to the Eternal Rest Chapel, Mausoleum, and Gift Shop at the top of the small hill.

But it didn't take care of it. Just the mention of testing ashes made Timmie uncomfortable, as if she'd made a statement before understanding what it meant. She hated that.

"Mind a little company?" Timmie heard from behind her and turned to see Alex Raymond loping up from the end of the line. He was in a gray suit, his black cashmere coat open and flapping in the chilly breeze. The day was dank and dark and chilly, the sun missing in action behind a layer of slag-colored clouds. For some reason, it did nothing to dim his glow. He looked like a night-light, and everybody smiled at him.

"Of course not," Barb greeted him as every woman preened.

"I got caught at work, or I would have made the service at the chapel," he apologized a bit breathlessly as he slowed alongside Timmie.

"You didn't miss much," she assured him. "The minister tried to convince us that Billy was a good man, and Billy's family got into a fistfight and almost spilled him all over the carpet."

Alex grimaced. "Sounds like the best part. I couldn't leave till I said good-bye to Mrs. Salgado, though."

"That cute little old lady up on two west?" Cindy asked, laying a hand on his arm.

He nodded. "Yeah. Died in her sleep this morning. I really hated to lose her."

"She used to tell the neatest stories about growing up in Italy," Barb said. "I liked her."

She got general nods from the other women.

"At least she died in peace," Mattie offered. "Mrs. Winterborn's back in the unit."

"Again?" Cindy demanded.

"Again," Timmie assured them all. "Why they just don't put a bullet through that poor woman's brain and end her misery, I don't know."

"You were going to talk to Dr. Raymond today," Cindy told her.

"You were?" Alex echoed, his interest keen.

They'd reached the door to the chapel where the flow of people had clogged up waiting to get in. Turning to yell at Cindy, Timmie caught sight of Tucker Van Adder standing back on Valhalla Drive, smoking with one of the local uniformed cops.

"You don't suppose he's here on official business, do you?" she asked, knowing full well what she was doing.

All heads immediately turned. Several emitted noises of disgust.

"Don't be ridiculous," Mattie told her. "Like you said, it's too late."

"Besides," Barb added with a dignified sniff. "Even if he were looking for work, he's standing next to the most worthless cop in three states."

"He's not all that worthless, Barb," Alex protested without noticeable heat. "He came to my office to take my full statement after the incident, and he seemed . . . competent."

"Who is he?" Timmie demanded.

Barb snorted unkindly. "Oh, come on. You mean to tell me you haven't met the lovely Mr. Dr. Barbara Adkins?"

Timmie took a look at the skinny, acne-scarred man holding on to his leather equipment belt as if holding his pants up and hooted, which turned more than one head in the crowd.

"Oh, Barb, say you're joking."

"Only when I said 'I do,'" she assured her with another sniff. "And let me be the one to tell you that the only police work Victor's interested in is strip-searching that trashy little dispatcher he ran off with."

"What a guy."

"Oh, yeah." Barb made it a point to smile and wave at the police officer, who didn't seem quite so sanguine about it. "He doesn't understand why I don't want my kids visiting with that tramp there, who calls my baby girl a mongoloid, the bitch. 'Get used to it,' he says. '*She* loves me.' She loves his eight-inch dick."

"He has an eight-inch dick?" Cindy demanded, squinting in his direction as if she could actually see it.

"You don't want to go down that road," Barb warned her.

"You coming in?" one of the mortuary guys asked, since they were the last ones standing outside. "We're about to start the final prayers."

"Which better begin with 'Pass the marshmallows, it's gonna be a hot one tonight,'" Mattie offered as she tugged her church dress more smoothly over her backside.

Timmie was about to pass through the faux-granite walls when Alex stopped dead in his tracks to her left.

"If they aren't here to investigate something," he said, his attention back toward the street, "what's *he* doing here?"

That effectively stopped forward progression all over again. This time, even the mortuary guy took a look.

"It's just the reporter," Timmie said, seeing him picking his way along the line of trucks, notebook in hand.

"Reporter?" Mattie asked. "What reporter?"

"Daniel Murphy," Alex said with a bemused expression. "The man from the horse show."

"He probably ran out of people to save," Barb suggested. "Which means he has to do his job. Isn't this his job?"

"A funeral?" Alex retorted with no little disbelief.

"He reports for the *Puckett Independent*," Barb reminded him. "The *Independent* doesn't exactly cover trade embargoes. This is probably the most exciting thing he could find to do."

"Daniel Murphy cover just a funeral?" Alex demanded with a laugh. "I don't think so. That man has two Pulitzers."

This time Timmie's attention was caught. "He's *that* Daniel Murphy?"

Actually, she should have figured it out when she'd seen him before. There was something familiar about him, something about the way he walked and talked and looked that reminded her of the hardcore guys who used to cover L.A. Sexy as hell with his just-shaggy salt-and-pepper hair and hound-dog eyes, but tired and battered and faded at the edges. Clad in his army's uniform of shapeless old tweed jacket and jeans that were as worn as a battle banner nobody saluted anymore. As burned out as the cops he'd covered.

So there was a multiple Pulitzer winner in a town the size of Puckett. Alex was right. Timmie wondered what it meant. And why he'd come to this particular funeral.

"He's headed this way," Cindy said, patting at her stiff crest of hair. "What do you think we should do?"

"Anybody here have something to hide?" Timmie asked.

Every hand went up. Even the mortuary guy's. By the time the reporter reached the steps to the Eternal Rest Chapel, there was no one left to greet him.

* * *

Debriefing probably would have been a lot more fun if the waitress who was serving them at the Rebel Yell Bar and Grill hadn't also been Billy's first cousin on his mother's side. Other than that, it was a typical hospital party, with Travis Tritt on the jukebox and steins of beer on a constant slide down the Formica bar to where the hospital crew had assembled in the Jeb Stuart party room.

"I . . . hate funerals," Cindy moaned, her face almost in the salsa. She'd had three beers, and her hair was already flat.

"I hate Richard Simmons," Mattie retorted.

"I hate family court," Timmie chimed in.

Everybody cheered and lifted glasses. The SSS had made a strong showing at the bar, along with other hospital staff who had smelled a celebration and showed up before their shift. Even Alex had come along for one drink, although truth be told, his scrubbed-cheek appearance did put a bit of a damper on the celebration.

"What would your father say?" Cindy asked, veering her attention toward Timmie like a Yugo skidding on ice.

"About what, family court?" Timmie asked. "He hated it, too."

"No . . ." She waved, her gesture exaggerated. "Death."

"Ah." Timmie considered it. Lifted her glass, which held only 7-Up with a twist. Cleared her throat. "He would say . . ."

"Yes?" four people urged.

"Fuck it. The guy's dead. Let's drink."

She got an even greater cheer. She also got half a glass of beer over her head from the mourning cousin.

Timmie sputtered and wiped. The cousin cursed. "You wouldn't'a thought it was funny if it was your cousin that was dead. 'Specially if it shouldn't'a never happened."

"Hard to avoid in the long run," Timmie philosophized, accepting a bar towel from the outraged bartender, who was trying to pull the cousin away.

"He was only forty-four!" the cousin screeched, her heels skidding in beer as the bartender yanked her back.

Timmie paused for a moment as she blotted foam from her only decent dress. "Yeah," she said. "He *was* only forty-four."

"He woulda been okay if he'd gone in like I told him three weeks ago," the cousin insisted. "He'd'a got saved."

Timmie blinked. "Three weeks?" she asked. "He was only sick for four or five days."

"He was sick for a month!" the girl yelled, pulling away from her restraint and bearing down on them again. Everybody grabbed their beer glasses in self-defense. "Pukin' and gettin' numb and itchin' and feelin' bad. But that bitch of a wife of his told him he was makin' it up so's he didn't have to pay no child support. What the fuck did she know? He was sick!"

Only Timmie was really listening. "But nothing showed up on the tests."

The cousin snorted. "Like you really give a shit."

"Get outa here, Crystal," the bartender demanded. "Cool off."

Crystal got out.

A month, Timmie couldn't help but think. Sick a month. Like the flu. With numbness and itching.

That niggling thought about testing ashes resurrected itself right there in the middle of the bar. God, if only she weren't so distracted and tired, she knew damn well she'd be able to make sense of it.

"Don't even go there," Mattie warned.

Timmie swung her own attention wide. "I'm not goin' anywhere."

"Uh-huh. You in town one month and you got dead flowers in you locker and beer in you hair. Girlfriend, I think you askin' for trouble."

"Dead flowers?" Alex immediately asked. "What dead flowers?"

"It's nothing," Timmie assured him with a warning glare at Mattie, who was sitting right next to Cindy as Cindy regaled one of the unit nurses with tales of Johnny's funeral in Chicago.

"The line of cop cars went on for miles," she insisted. "*Miles.* He was a good cop."

"He was a cop?" Timmie echoed instinctively.

"Yeah," Barb said. "Didn't you know?"

Timmie shook her head. "No . . . I sure wish they hadn't dry-roasted him."

"Cindy's husband?"

"Billy."

Barb smacked her on the head. "Knock it off."

"Fine," Timmie snapped. "Ignore the obvious. We missed something, Van Adder was incompetent, and now we're not going to ever know what killed a damn near healthy man."

"He was an asshole."

Timmie glared. "Asshole is not a recognized cause of death."

"Is this what being a forensic nurse means?" somebody asked.

"Yeah," Mattie responded. "Forensic is Greek for 'pain in the ass.'"

"Forensic is Greek for 'no shit, *that's* what he died of?'" Timmie told them all. "And in a town like Puckett, I think every nurse could stand a little training. God knows the coroner hasn't had any."

"Training isn't the problem," Barb assured her. "It's the pain-in-the-ass part. Pains in the ass get threatened, ya know."

Timmie waved her off as if she were a fly. "It wasn't a big threat. It was a little threat. Flowers and a lovely note in my locker. Big deal."

"Forensics?" Alex asked. "How can you be involved in forensics?"

Three separate people at the table groaned.

"It's a new nursing specialty," Timmie explained, ignoring them. "In *other* jurisdictions, forensic nurses work as death investigators, rape investigators, or police-hospital liaison. Collecting evidence, intervening in abuse situations, stuff like that. That's what I did at L.A. County–USC."

Alex nodded, suitably impressed.

"It also makes her annoyingly persistent," Barb assured him. "As in, 'won't let a dead horse drop'?"

"Is that a proverb?" somebody asked.

"No. Big animal with four legs."

Timmie scowled at them all. "You were sure singing a different song when I taught you that trick with the fabric softener and the lighter."

"You learned that in forensics?" somebody demanded. "I thought you were just twisted."

"She *is* twisted," Barb said. "It's why she does forensics."

"So, how'd you end up working back at Memorial?" Alex asked.

Timmie slugged back some soda and turned to Alex, who was smiling. "An offer I couldn't refuse. After a divorce and a downsizing, I ended up in a city that couldn't afford me. So instead of trying to eke out a living there, I decided to come home and eke one out here." She shrugged uncomfortably. "Besides, my dad needed me home."

"He's not who you were going to call me about, is he?" Alex asked with such real sadness he made Timmie squirm.

"I'll call you about it tomorrow," she lied badly, certain he could see the ambivalence. "It's not urgent."

Thankfully, Cindy was hip deep in reminiscing about her post-Johnny depression and didn't pick up on it.

"Dr. Adkins?" a male voice interrupted.

Timmie looked up to see a rumpled, damp young man standing at the doorway alongside Jeb Stuart's dour photo and almost crawled under the table. Something was all too familiar about that stance. That manner. That rectangle of paper in his hand.

"What?" Barb asked.

The young man laughed and bounced over to her. "Wow, he was right. He said you'd be easy to find."

Barb was glowering now. "What?" she demanded again.

Timmie's reflexes were good, but she wasn't in time. Before she could bat the paper away the young man had handed it over. "You've been served, ma'am. Have a nice day."

He barely made it out the door alive.

Timmie had never seen Barb in full fury before. It was fast, it was devastating, it was noisy as hell. Timmie had lived through four good-sized quakes. They had nothing on this.

"I think we'd better—" Timmie had meant to say find cover. She was too late again.

Barb lurched from her chair like an Atlas rocket. "Son of a bitch!" she shrieked, her voice soaring so impressively that

Timmie expected her next words to be "fee fi fo fum." "That smarmy, insufferable, shit-faced sack of shit!"

Let Grimm put *that* in a fairy tale.

Even Travis Tritt shut up for this one. Cindy startled so badly that two people had to hold her in her chair. The pool players in the main room dove under the table as if expecting a tornado to take out the front window.

"That was what he was doing there today!" Barb howled.

Timmie swore glass trembled and weak men fled.

"What is it?" Alex asked, hand instinctively up to help.

"A subpoena! That tiny, worthless little putz is suing me for support. *Me!* The one who's raising his three children while he's muff-diving in his gun and handcuffs. Support!" Barb screeched, rattling glassware all over again. "I'll show him fucking support! Shit, I'll show him that trick with the fabric softener!"

"But I thought you said he was a *big* putz," Cindy objected blearily.

"He's a *dead* fuckin' putz!" Barb screamed.

"This calls for a forensic specialist," somebody offered.

"This calls for a lawyer," Timmie retorted evenly.

Barb swung on her, eyes wild. Nodded briskly. Smoothing her skirt, she stalked from the room with immense dignity, the subpoena by now nothing more than a tiny, misshapen lump in her fist.

"Well," Mattie spoke up brightly, gaze surreptitiously following her friend. "Anybody got a funny story?"

"Ellen looked just like that when Billy yelled at her," Cindy said, nodding. "Just like that."

Everybody stared at her, then turned almost as one to look after Barb. Thought of quiet, passive Ellen.

"Oh, be serious!" somebody objected.

Cindy lifted her head. "She did. He hurt her so much she—"

"He dead, girl," Mattie interrupted. "Enough."

"And Van Adder let him go," Timmie said to herself.

Mattie swung on her like an avenging angel. "Stop! Just stop."

Timmie glared right back. Secrets, she thought. The damn

town was full of secrets, and they were supposed to keep more. Everybody was afraid. Even Mattie. Even, when it came down to it, Timmie.

"It's a bad habit," she defended herself, even though she knew that Mattie wasn't fooled. "It's what I'm used to doing."

"Uh, Miz Leary?"

All heads turned toward the door.

"Oh, shit," somebody warned. "It's a cop."

Timmie's heart skipped a couple of times. "Yes?"

Another fresh-faced puppy. Nervous. "Uh . . . well . . ." His posture rigid, he delivered his report like a history paper. "I was told by your baby-sitter I'd find you here? It's your father. He's wandering around town in his underwear."

Timmie's first instinct was to flush hard, the old shame hot and familiar. So she laughed instead. Leave it to Joe to break up her life. It meant she really was home, she guessed. She turned on Mattie, determined to ride this out as a joke. "How'd you manage that?"

Mattie scowled. "Oh, yeah, I tol' that boy to come in here if you got rowdy and tell on you daddy."

It didn't keep her from following Timmie to her feet. In fact, everyone did. Timmie didn't want them to. Not when she knew what was going to happen. It seemed she didn't have a choice. The party streamed right out the door after her, and she was left with one less secret of her own.

"WHERE IS HE?" TIMMIE ASKED, HAND OVER HER FOREHEAD TO keep the sleet out of her eyes as they hurried up Elm Street. Alex had offered to ferry them all in his car, but the quickest route had been to weave through driveways up the hill to where her father had last been seen.

In his underwear. Out in the freezing weather. Timmie was going to kill somebody.

"They're trying to get him inside the church, ma'am," the cop was saying as he ran with one hand holding his holster in place. "We thought it was safer. He seems to be tryin' to incite people against the IRS."

"No," Timmie said, wishing one of the old-timers had filled the kid in. "He was trying to enlist you for the IRA. There's a difference."

"I wouldn't know, ma'am. All I know is that when Miss Charlton demanded he go home and put clothes on, he yelled somethin' at her about women needing to be struck regularly."

"Like gongs, yes," Timmie answered. "It's Noël Coward."

"Who is, ma'am?"

Timmie sighed. "Never mind."

They topped the rise at Elm Street and turned right up the sidewalk toward the church. It was just after two, too early even for hospital-induced rush hour. A few cars scattered water over the streets, and the lights were already on in the dingy gray. Timmie saw a few pedestrians catch sight of the phalanx from the bar and stop dead. No surprise. Several carried to-go cups. One or two had forgotten to get rid of pool cues. And Timmie was taking them to her father as if they were the villagers after Frankenstein's monster.

"Then he started singing bawdy songs," Officer Braxton informed her. "He really has a good voice." The boy sounded surprised.

Timmie almost laughed at that one. The kid was so stern faced as they tramped up the glistening, darkening streets of town like a pack of lemmings in search of a cliff.

"He spent some time singing intro for the Clancy Brothers in the sixties," she explained. "Got a lot of his music from Greenwich Village."

"Uh-huh." Which meant that he'd never heard of the Clancy Brothers or Greenwich Village. Hell, he'd probably never heard of the sixties.

Well, if there was one thing she could depend on from her father, it was diversion. Far be it from Joe Leary to simply age gracefully. Or, for that matter, quietly.

Considering that she could hear him from two blocks away, she doubted she could even hope for manageably.

" 'Too-rah-loo-rah-loo-rah-loo, they're lookin' f'r monkeys out in the zoo . . .' "

Uh-oh. Timmie ran a little faster and hoped that nobody'd bothered to get the local priest involved. Her father was in full and glorious voice, and the song was one of his favorites, "Sergeant McGrath." Not the best choice for church.

They were heading uphill, of course. St. Mary's of the River commanded the highest point of the small town that had been built straight up the hills on the banks of the Missouri. San Francisco to scale. The steeple could be seen for miles, stabbing its well ordered way through the ragged sky, the crown of a pretty little redbrick church that looked for all the world untroubled and serene. Except for the music issuing from inside, which was not in any way ecclesiastical.

"'. . . and if it was me, I had a face like you I'd join the British arm-y-y-y-y . . . !'"

Timmie was panting like a dog and freezing from the beer that hadn't dried yet on her hair before the sleet had hit it.

Damn that old man. Seventy-five years old, and he'd probably run all the way up. He had a heart like a fifteen-year-old. Timmie had chest pains, but she wasn't sure whether it was from the run or the fact that she was trying so hard not to laugh.

"'Too-rah-loo-rah-loo-rah-loo . . .'"

"Oh, Daddy, don't . . ." Timmie gasped, reaching the steps of the tall brick Gothic church and sliding right into the wrought-iron rail. She broke a heel and limped the rest of the way, trying to get inside the door before her father got to his favorite line.

"'They're lookin' f'r monkeys down in the zoo . . .'"

"We tried to hold him down," the police officer protested.

"Wrong thing," Timmie assured him, getting to the door.

"'But if it was me, I had a face like you-u-u . . . I-I-I-I-I'd . . .'"

"Daddy, no!"

"'FUCK the British army!!'"

She was wrong. The priest was here; standing right behind her father. The look on his face would have been damn near comical if he hadn't had a semi-naked septuagenarian singing obscene songs in his vestibule. That did it. Timmie burst out laughing and her father, delighted, laughed back. The priest was not noticeably amused.

"You want us to get hold of him?" the cop asked.

She shook her head. "No. I'll handle it."

Not one person in the church could have lasted three minutes against her father if they really got him riled. There were several more raincoated police standing by the priest, along with an outraged-looking dowager and, of all people, that damn reporter.

"What are *you* doing here?" Timmie demanded as the rest of the SSS and Alex pounded through the door behind her until the tiny vestibule was thick with humidity and the black-and-white-marbled floor puddled from too many dripping bodies.

Dripping from his own battered London Fog, Mr. Murphy shot Timmie an enigmatic smile and showed her his notebook. "You were the one who said your father was a character."

"'River-r-r-u-n-n . . .'" began the sonorous voice in near-Gielgudian tones.

"Oh, God, that's it." Timmie groaned. "He gets started on *Finnegan's Wake*, we'll be here till Easter. Daddy?"

He didn't even notice her as he recited on, effectively mesmerizing everyone in the vestibule. He was dripping wet, his white hair wild, his great arms thrown so wide he almost shut out the light, his voice majestic enough to fill a cathedral. This would be what Brian Boru would have looked like had he lived so long, Timmie thought. Cuchulain, Niall of the Nine Hostages. Maybe, she thought, it was why they had all died young, those huge Irish heroes, so they wouldn't have to betray in their eyes the longing for their once-legendary magic.

"Da, it's Timmie. Come on, sweetie, it's time to go home."

"'. . . to bend of day brings us commodious vicus of recirculation . . .'"

She reached way up to him, laid her hand against his thin white stubble. Smiled her best smile. "Yo, Finnegan. Wake's over."

He saw her finally, and his features crumpled straight into distress. "Kathleen," he whispered, his own great hands up to her face. "Oh, Kathleen, I'm sorry. I didn't mean it."

Timmie stopped smiling. "Da, it's me. Timmie."

"It was just me and some of the boys, ya know. Celebrating the series. Wasn't it a hell of a series? We won, girl. Surely that deserves a celebration."

Timmie pulled her hands back. Jammed them in her pockets. Fought like hell to maintain her poise. "It does, Joe. It does. Now, come on home."

He was crying now, big, sloppy tears and shaking shoulders. "Say you forgive me, Kathleen."

Timmie smelled the old incense, the beeswax the altar society still used on the wood, the damp of wool, and fought uncommon claustrophobia.

"I forgive you, Joe. Now let them close down for the night."

There was utter silence in the church. Timmie couldn't look. She couldn't take her attention from her father or she'd lose him. She couldn't stand to see the pity in all those eyes.

"Do you want a ride home?" the young cop asked behind her.

"No," Alex spoke up for the first time. "He needs to go to the hospital. He's too old to be out in this stuff."

"He can't," Timmie said, her focus still on her father. "It'll confuse him. And Medicare won't cover it."

"Yes it will," Alex assured her. "I'll see to it."

Timmie turned to see that Alex was smiling at her, and there was no pity in those lovely brown eyes. She could have kissed him on the spot. "Thanks," she said.

"After a couple of days at Memorial, we can figure out what else to do."

"Thank you."

And so she ended up walking her massive father out the doors of the church like a stunned bear, and spent the next two hours getting him settled in the hospital, where they tied him down and snowed him all over again so he wouldn't sing to the other patients or hit the staff. And then she went home to confront her baby-sitter for letting him get loose in the first place.

"You didn't tell me he could be that fast!" the baby-sitter protested. A strapping forty-year-old woman who claimed experience in children and adults, she'd come highly recommended and even more highly paid for. And she'd let that old man out on her first night.

"I've told you before," Timmie snarled, her temper worsening. "He could talk you into robbing the rectory for him. You *never* believe him unless he says he has to pee. Are we clear on that now?"

"Well, don't blame me," she objected, puffing her full chest out like a pigeon with a crow in sight. "I did my best."

Which meant Timmie was running out of relief baby-sitters, and it was a long way to go till the ninth inning.

The entire time Timmie had been confronting the baby-sitter, Meghan had been bouncing on the balls of her feet as if she'd saved her grandfather instead of letting him get loose.

"Well, what do you have to say, young lady?" Timmie demanded, swinging around on her. "Didn't you even notice your grandda walk out the door?"

"I was busy, Mom," Meghan apologized, eyes glinting oddly, her hands wrapped tightly around each other. "I was so busy."

Timmie definitely didn't like the look of this. "Doing what?"

"I had to answer the phone," the little girl all but sang.

Timmie's stomach dropped. She wasn't a nurse because she liked bedpans. She was a whiz at diagnosing symptoms. And she diagnosed Meghan's with no problem at all. God, no, not this.

"Who was on the phone, Meghan?" she asked, knowing.

Meghan beamed and spread her hands. "Daddy."

Timmie thought she was going to throw up. "Who?"

Meghan began to dance around. "Daddy. My daddy. I told you he'd find us, and he did. He said he'd figured we'd try and come here, and he was awfully upset with you for taking me away like that. Didn't I tell you, Mom? He misses me so much. He's coming to see us."

Timmie sat down so fast she unlodged a pile of health flyers and sent them cascading to the floor. Meghan kept pirouetting around the room like a sprite on high air. As for Mrs. Filpin, she was busy stuffing her knitting into her bag and mumbling about ungrateful clients.

Jason. Oh, Jesus, Timmie had known it. He'd finally come off that last high and decided to look for them, and now it was going to start up all over again. The lawsuits, the harassment, the control, just to prove he still could. And Timmie just didn't have the money or the patience to deal with him this time.

"Did he say when he was coming?" she asked, trying very hard not to scream.

"No," Meghan sang, still twirling. "He has some business to finish. He's so busy, but he's coming *right* here when he's finished. And *he's* going to buy me a pony!"

He was waiting, just like always. Playing Timmie along, stretching her out, lurking just below the water like the shark in *Jaws* until she let down her guard.

"I just can't do it," she muttered to herself, unable to move. Unable to think past the overwhelming urge to run to work and drown herself in some good, mindless trauma.

She was going to need a lawyer. She was going to need a nursing home. Hell, she was going to need a new baby-sitter.

Screw it, she decided, getting back to her feet. She'd think about it all tomorrow. She and Scarlett, soul mates to the end, the only difference being that Scarlett looked better in curtains and Timmie knew what to do with a parking lot full of injured soldiers. But both of them up to their elbows in manure, and neither of them knowing how to admit defeat.

Tomorrow. After she waded around in an accident or two at work, just to settle her nerves.

"Meghan?"

Meghan came to a sliding halt a couple of feet away, her hair still flying, her expression once again caught between warring emotions—this time, exhilaration and guilt. Timmie held out her arms.

"Come here, punkin. I need a hug."

"But you're mad at me."

Forget the exhilaration. The kid radiated a hundred percent apprehension from those big blue eyes. Afraid, even as high as she was, that she'd be left. If she were bad, if she were noisy, if she was too demanding. If she chose one parent over another. Her father had done it. Wouldn't her mother? Most days it wasn't noticeable. On a day when her grandfather had slipped his bonds and her father had called, it was glaringly obvious. And nothing Timmie could do would convince her otherwise.

"Yeah, I was a little mad," she admitted. "But mostly with Mrs. Filpin. She was the adult. She should have watched Grandda."

"What about Daddy?" Such a small voice.

Timmie grinned. "How could he watch Grandda?" she asked. "He's in California."

Meghan almost smiled.

"Do I love you?" Timmie asked, a game as old as her child.

"Yes."

"No matter what?"

A hesitation this time, which spoke volumes about how little a small girl trusted her father, no matter how excited his call had made her. "Uh-huh."

Timmie smiled right through the terrible comprehension. "Well, then, let's hug on it."

Meghan rushed at Timmie as if afraid the offer would be withdrawn, and Timmie hugged Meghan before she had the chance to back out, a tiny flood wall against the frustrations of Timmie's life.

"I love you," the little girl whispered.

"Me, too." Timmie picked her up and swung her into her arms. "Come on, munchkin. Let's go read *Charlotte's Web* and feed Renfield some flies."

"I don't think Mrs. Filpin likes Renfield, Mom," Meghan whispered in conspiratorial tones.

Timmie had to laugh. "Well, that settles it then. She's history."

She'd made it up only two steps before the phone rang. Setting Meghan down with a pat on the bottom, Timmie turned for the dining room. She picked up the phone on the fourth ring.

"Hello?"

"Don't you listen?"

Timmie stopped cold. The voice was a whisper, low and raspy. Creepy. "Just a second," she said, and turned to her daughter. "Head on upstairs, honey. This'll only take a second."

When she was sure she heard Meghan's footsteps enter her own room, Timmie returned her attention to the call. "You wouldn't be the thoughtful person who left flowers in my locker, would you?" she asked in deceptively sweet tones.

"Has it occurred to you yet," the voice responded, "that you can't afford to lose your job? Or worse?"

Never one for a slow temper, Timmie fought against absolute meltdown. "You threatening me?"

"Warning you. Leave it be."

She was sure her caller was set to hang up. Until she laughed, that is. "Listen, asshole. You want to intimidate me, you're going to have to do a better job. I've had better threats from fourteen-year-old girls."

"It's a warning," the voice repeated. "Pay attention."

"Get fucked."

By the time Timmie got upstairs, Renfield was asleep and Meghan was on chapter two. Even so, Timmie settled beside her on the window seat and read along, trying very hard to disappear into a world where the most important thing that happened was the perfect spinning of a web.

She was not going to be threatened. On the other hand, would she accept a warning? Nuzzling her daughter's peach-soft cheek and listening to her play the part of the pig with a decided Irish accent, Timmie wasn't so sure.

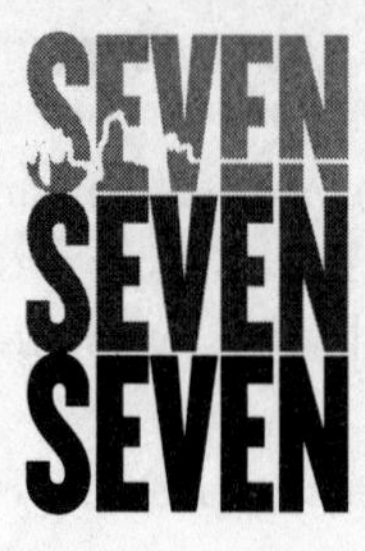

"NOW, YOU SAY YOU JUST TOOK OVER RESPONSIBILITY FOR YOUR father's care," the Restcrest caseworker said to Timmie the next morning.

Timmie squirmed in the faux-leather office chair she'd been shown to and looked around at the soft Impressionist prints and lush potted palms that decorated the office. Typical of a hospital in the nineties, the good stuff was reserved for paying customers. The better the hoped-for reimbursement, the classier the decor. This was about the best Timmie had seen in the entire Memorial campus, and it made her nervous.

"Yes," she said, doodling on the notepad the caseworker had provided her with for pertinent info. "I moved home about a month ago."

"And so far he's been in three different nursing homes."

"Yes."

The caseworker nodded, scribbled a little on her own notepad. MRS. EVERLY, said the nameplate that matched the prim, conservatively gray woman behind the comfortable oak desk. No first name. No jewelry, no personal mementos strewn about the office. Polite, professional, all business in a caregiving setting.

Timmie wanted to go home. She wanted to go to work. She wanted to watch Meg ride that little horse down the road. Instead, she was forced by Medicare restrictions to lay her life bare to this woman who only wanted to give her a chance to fork over whatever was left of her money so her father would have a safe place to live.

"And you've been relying on Medicare," Mrs. Everly said.

"Yes."

Timmie jotted a few words on her own pad. Her note wasn't about level-two nursing care or Medicare co-pays, though. She was doing what she always did whenever things got too uncomfortable. She was splitting her attention in as many different directions as she could. *If not flu*, she wrote, *what cause of death?*

"Do you know what kind of testing your father has had?"

*Jason Parker*, she wrote next, then scratched it out with furious strokes. No, that was definitely another road she didn't want to go down today. Stick to the fun stuff, even if she wasn't going to do anything with it. Which she wasn't. She just preferred to work on the puzzle of Billy Mayfield rather than the tragedy of Joe Leary.

"Mrs. Leary-Parker?" Mrs. Everly gently persisted. "Has your father been tested?"

Timmie looked up. "No," she admitted. "He really hasn't. He was already in the second home by the time I got back. So far I haven't had much of a chance to do more than catch up."

"Facility."

"Pardon?"

"We prefer to use the term 'facility.' "

Timmie smiled. "Of course. God forbid we should admit that our parents are as mad as March hares or more dependent than six-foot-four three-year-olds."

It was Mrs. Everly's turn to squirm a little. "We don't like to think of our clients that way," she protested.

That actually made Timmie laugh. "That's okay. I don't like to think of my dad as a client."

And far be it from Timmie to admit to this tightly wrapped little woman with her comfortable catchwords and plastic sympathy that Joseph Aloysius Michael Leary had been as mad as a March hare and as dependent as a three-year-old his entire adult life.

"Your father has been . . . asked to leave these other facilities."

"Thrown out," Timmie amended, her attention back on her list.

Liver failure?

No

Electrolyte imbalance?

Possible

Slow poison?

"Aw, shit."

"Pardon?" Mrs. Every asked.

Timmie glanced up. Smiled to cover the sudden lurch her stomach had just taken. She'd done it now. Admitted what she'd suspected all along. "Nothing. I'm sorry. What did you say?"

"I was asking why your father was asked to leave."

Timmie sighed. "It's in his records, Mrs. Everly. Besides, I thought you were only concentrating on the financial obligations today. We know he has need."

Sepsis?

No

Kidney disease?

No

It couldn't have been poison. Billy was a jerk, but there wasn't any reason to kill him.

Billy had been sick a month. Long enough to build up enough poison to knock over a rhino, given in small enough doses so his symptoms wouldn't be suspicious.

Cardiac failure?

No

Ebola virus?

Nice try

It *couldn't* be poison.

What Timmie couldn't understand was why, after all that damn forensic training she'd taken, poison hadn't been the first thing she'd thought of.

But if she'd thought of poison first, she would have had to consider the logical correlations. If Billy had been poisoned, then who was the most likely suspect?

"We think your father would certainly benefit from Restcrest," Mrs. Everly was saying. "We would begin by thoroughly testing him so that we could maximize his potential. Then, at Restcrest, he would have available to him the most progressive program for Alzheimer's patients in the state, which would include the latest in physical, occupational, and recreational therapy. We're even experimenting with aroma and music therapy at the moment."

Nausea
Numbness
Itching
Cardiovascular collapse

Generic symptoms to fit any disease . . . and, of course, most poisons.

"Dr. Raymond has also worked to include Restcrest in several pharmaceutical studies to avail our clients of the latest possible drug interventions. Our staff is highly trained and committed, and our unit has been newly redesigned with the latest innovations for patient safety and stimulation. But all that, of course, is expensive. We do our best to acquire grant and research money to cover some of the costs, but intensive care of any kind is . . . well, uh, costly. You understand that, don't you?"

"Quite well."

Thallium
Arsenic
Sodium fluoride

Don't do this. You have enough problems as it is. You weren't responsible for Billy Mayfield's death, and that's all that matters. Heck, you've even been warned off the playing field.

But poison . . .

"Was it a financial problem?"

Still preoccupied with the thought of Billy and murder, Timmie belatedly looked up. "Pardon?"

"Your father. Was he asked to leave the homes for financial reasons?"

"No. It was a behavioral problem. My father has decided not to go gentle into that good night, and at six foot five, he can make a lot of noise about it."

Mrs. Everly blinked. "What good night?"

Timmie sighed. Didn't anybody in this town study literature anymore? "It's a poem," she said. "By Dylan Thomas? About death. You know, 'rage, rage against the dying of the light'?"

Mrs. Everly thought for a moment. Nodded. "Ah. I see."

No, Timmie bet she didn't. "Let's get down to the bottom line here, Mrs. Everly. You might be able to find a bed for my father if we can cough up the cash. Is that right?"

Mrs. Everly went dangerously red. "We have the premier facility in the state here, Mrs. Leary-Parker—"

"And you could take really good care of my father. I know that. I just need to know if I can afford it, and I don't think I can. So I need straight answers."

There was an uncomfortable pause during which Timmie could see Mrs. Everly trying hard to find another way to sidestep. It must be hell to have to face a person with no use for euphemisms.

"A deposit of five thousand dollars," she finally admitted as if the words had been squeezed out of her. "One hundred ten dollars a day with the understanding that barring extraordinary situations, Restcrest is capable of providing permanent care for your father no matter his health. And understanding also that as one of the reasons we can provide such progressive care is the research we do, you agree to participate, and that after your father . . . passes, his remains be donated to the Price University Medical Center for the sole purpose of Alzheimer's research. You wouldn't have to worry about his being used for, say, med school."

"You only want his brain." Timmie nodded. "I understand perfectly well."

*Conrad T. Jones*, she wrote and smiled.

What a good idea. Conrad was a nearby medical examiner with a passion for pharmacology. He was also at least as suspicious as Timmie and far, far more knowledgeable about poison. Maybe Timmie would call him when she got out of this hothouse. Have lunch. Talk dead people. It'd sure as hell be more fun than this.

"Is there anything else I can explain?" Mrs. Everly asked, laying down her pen.

Timmie finally looked up. Smiled. "Yes. Where I can get the money. I don't have it."

"You don't have anyone else to help you?" the woman asked.

Timmie found herself going very still. When she smiled, she knew it looked forced. "I doubt it."

"In that case," Mrs. Everly said, closing Joe's file, "maybe one of the other social workers can help you find placement for your father at another fine facility."

"Just don't call Golden Grove," Timmie suggested, getting to her feet. "I don't think filthy and abusive is what I'm after, either."

And with little more ado, she was shuffled off the good furniture and sent back to the cheap seats.

"Poison," Conrad T. Jones sang over the phone line with unbridled delight half an hour later. "Favorite murder weapon of the passive-aggressive. Neat, sneaky, tough to spot. What do you think you have?"

Timmie leaned a bit outside the lounge door to make sure no one could overhear. "You tell me. Gastrointestinal symptoms for a month. Transient numbness in the extremities, rash, no real test anomalies. He came in complaining of the flu and went out plastic-wrapped."

"Symptoms for a month, huh? How about liver failure? Hair loss?"

"No real cirrhosis, even for a man fond of the bottle. He did look kinda yellow as I remember it, though. I guess I should have been surprised his enzymes weren't higher. As for anything else, I don't know. History didn't include it, nobody thought to ask."

He considered the problem a moment and then snorted. "Arsenic goes to the top of the class. A perennial favorite, arsenic. Romantic yet effective, creating just the right touch of suffering to make it all worthwhile. A favorite also of medical examiners and historians everywhere, because you can still catch it in the hair and nails forever afterward."

Which was probably what had made Timmie itch in the first place.

"Not if the official in question okayed cremation, you can't."

"Ah. So the call is merely academic."

Timmie sighed. "I guess so. I just wanted to know I was right."

"You're right. I'd stake my considerable reputation on it. So, *bella donna*, when are you coming back to town to visit?"

*Bella donna* being Conrad's favorite feminine form of address, his little forensic pharmacologist's inside joke, since belladonna was also one of the deadliest and most popular historical poisons.

"I have come back," Timmie admitted without noticeable enthusiasm. "I'm living in Puckett now."

She'd first met Conrad three years earlier when she was doing her initial death-investigation training at St. Louis University. A forensic pathologist with a minor in pharmacology and an obsession for all things Italian, Conrad had taught the course on poisoning and overdoses. He'd been fifty-five and randy as a goat, and Timmie had found herself adopted on the spot. She loved Conrad to death. It didn't mean she'd let herself be left alone with him for ten minutes. Not only did he look like Truman Capote on a bad-hair day, he considered the tongue an integral part of any kiss.

"Puckett?" he echoed with growing disbelief. "You're within spitting distance and you haven't called yet?"

"I am calling."

"Puckett . . . Puckett. *Madre mia,* Timothy Ann, don't tell me the official you're talking about is none other than the infamous Tucker Van Adder."

"How'd you know?"

"I think I just used the word infamous, didn't I? Good God. Over a hundred counties in Missouri and you have to pick the one with the worst coroner in the country. Come to St. Charles. Have lunch. I'll tell you all the details." He laughed. "And then I'll talk you into helping change it."

"No thank you, sweetheart. I have a full enough plate at this picnic as it is. I'll call you."

Hanging up, Timmie checked her watch. Ten minutes left in her lunch break. It was too late to use them to call another bank. The first three she'd contacted to inquire about a second mortgage on the house had been polite but very cautious. Not that Timmie blamed them. Not only had they never seen the inside of the house, they hadn't scanned Timmie's credit report. Once they did, they wouldn't hesitate. They'd just laugh themselves silly.

If she really needed to, she had a last option before throwing her father to Golden Grove. Like the craven coward she was, though, she preferred putting off the inevitable as long as she earthly could. So she sat back instead, propped her feet on the couch, and closed her eyes to think forensics.

Poison. Billy Mayfield had probably been poisoned.

Fine. Now what?

She couldn't prove it. Not without tissue. Besides, nobody wanted to know about it. Heck, nobody wanted to know about *anything* in this town. And to top it off, if she pursued this, not only would she seriously displease her friends, but a certain caller would be back on the line, her boss would fire her, and the coroner would probably have her run out of town on a rail.

If this had happened in L.A., her choice would have been easy. In L.A., she'd still had a certain sense of her accomplishments. She'd been crystal clear about her mission. She'd been Wonder Woman. Trauma Queen. The Forensics Fairy.

But she was in Puckett now, where nobody believed in fairies except the little girl and old man who looked to her for support. And she couldn't think of a single area of her life that would be improved by her walking out onto the work lane and announcing that somebody somewhere had poisoned Billy Mayfield for reasons unknown, and that since the coroner was too busy bumping boots with the deceased's ex-wife to do anything about it, she, Timothy Ann Leary-Parker, would prove it.

Tomorrow, Timmie decided, sinking farther into what was left of the cushions. She'd make her decision tomorrow, when she felt better. When she knew what she was going to do about Joe. When she knew what Jason was going to do about her. When she knew better how to make her boss like her enough to let her stay here for the next hundred years, which was what it was going to take to pay for that old man and that little girl, who both needed so much.

In the meantime, though, Timmie seriously needed to patch up a few bodies and yell at a couple of drunks.

"Timmie? You okay, girl?"

Timmie grinned at Mattie without opening her eyes. "I'm bored. You guys promised me action. I haven't even seen a tractor crash."

"Every case can't be forensics, girl."

Timmie sighed. "Only in a perfect life, Mattie. Now, what can I do for you?"

"Besides take over for me so I can eat?"

"Where's Cindy?"

"Been pulled to Restcrest. They got need, we don't, and Ellen lost the toss to go, although why those two like it up there is beyond me."

"She'll pass a happier shift."

"Amen and hallelujah. Now, if you want to get that lazy-ass white butt of yours off the couch, I got that new plastics guy, Dr. Babbaloo, or whatever—"

"Balanbarian."

"Yeah. Babbaloo. He stitchin' up a Tupperware lady did a header down somebody's porch steps. But be careful. You go in there, she'll try and sell you lettuce crispers. And next door to her, I'm waitin' for the Ancef to come up to mix for Vern. He the one got his hand bit by his wife's boyfriend last night."

"What else?"

"Uh . . . well . . . "

Considering the fact that Timmie had not in three weeks ever heard Mattie resort to the sound "uh," that got her to open her eyes. It was to find, of all people, Victor Adkins standing in full uniform in the doorway behind Mattie.

Timmie's first thought was that he'd found out. Somebody at the switchboard had plugged into her call with Conrad and tipped off the cops that Timmie suspected foul play in the death of one Billy Mayfield.

Then Timmie realized that the chances of anybody official caring about how Billy Mayfield died were on a par with insurance companies going back to nonprofit status. Unless an untapped oil well that could benefit the town was found under Billy's house, Timmie doubted it was going to change.

"Well, if it ain't the five-oh," she said to Mattie as if he weren't there. "What does he want?"

Mattie's eyebrows lifted dramatically. "Don't look at me, girlfriend. I'm just the jungle guide."

Timmie grinned and got herself off the couch. "I don't suppose Barb's coming in, is she?" she asked sotto voce. "I mean, so I could get my trauma time in. It's like flying, ya know. If I don't clock so many hours, I lose my magic cape."

Mattie chuckled, a lovely rumble deep in her considerable chest. "He stupid, girlfriend. Not dumb."

Timmie bent to retrieve her stethoscope off the table.

"Mattie, you take all the fun out of coming to work." Then she went to meet Barb's ex-husband, who was trying to screw Barb out of her own child support.

"What can I do for you, Officer?"

"Do you have a minute?" he asked. "I'd like to talk to you."

"If you want to follow me around. I'm on the clock."

"Your drugs are up, Mattie!" somebody called.

"You mean Timmie's drugs are up!" Mattie yelled back. "I'm eatin'."

Even so, she followed just a few paces behind as Timmie headed past. Timmie thought best on her feet. Therefore, she forced the policeman to follow her down the hall to the medicine cabinet, while everyone on the hall watched.

"What can I do for you?" she asked, rescuing her antibiotics from the vacuum tube and picking a 50cc bag of D5/W off the shelf to go with it.

Close up, Victor didn't look as bad as he had at the funeral the day before. He had pretty dark eyes with sinfully long lashes, and a cocky smile that probably worked a treat on female suspects. It didn't do a lot for a woman who had dated her share of cops. Especially a nurse who despised musk colognes and assholes who didn't stop screwing their wives just because they'd divorced them.

"You're Timmie Leary?"

Timmie worked by rote, popping the sterile seal on the antibiotic vial into the trash and swabbing the top with alcohol, all the while keeping her eyes on the officer. "I sure am. What can I do for you?"

He took hold of his belt as if it were his official tool of office, or he just wanted to be near his gun. "Well, I was here on an MVA and thought I'd stop by and talk to you. It's about the threat you got the other day?"

Syringe plunged deep into the vial to start aspirating, Timmie stopped what she was doing. Right behind Victor, Mattie was making a great show of updating the flow board. Timmie didn't even give her the satisfaction of a look.

"What threat, Officer?"

"Dead flowers, the way I heard it," he said. "And some kind of note."

"How'd you know about that?"

He pulled himself up a little taller. The "need-to-know-basis" stance some guys loved so well. "That doesn't matter. Do you know what it was for, Ms. Leary?"

Timmie went back to work. "We just assumed that it was the

local Klan warning me off saving any more colored folk, was all," she lied, making sure she didn't look at Mattie, who, come to think of it, still didn't know what was really in the note. "I threw it away."

Victor nodded, shifted his weight so that his belt creaked and several dangling items rattled against his butt. "Can you tell me what it said?"

"It just told me to stop. In cut-out magazine letters."

"And you're sure it was about the shooting?"

Timmie blinked. "Well, since I paid off that loan shark last month I don't think he'd see any need to go after more of my thumbs. And I haven't threatened anybody lately."

His expression darkened portentously. "Not even the coroner?"

She sighed. "Oh, that's right. I keep forgetting I'm not in Los Angeles anymore. I can't have PMS here without the paper printing my water weight." Jabbing the needle into the port, she injected the drugs into the IV bag. "I didn't exactly threaten him, Officer Adkins. I just voiced displeasure with the way he was doing his job. He's a public servant and I'm the public. It's my right. Besides, he doesn't strike me as the scissors-and-magazine type."

"You think this is funny?"

Mattie raised her hand behind him. "I do."

"Nobody asked you," he said without turning, which made Timmie think that if Mattie had been a man, he would have closed that sentence with "boy."

Ah, bringing out the charm now. Timmie decided it was time to put an end to this dance. "I swear to you," she said, her weight on one hip and the mixed bag in hand, "I haven't done anything more nefarious to warrant a note like that than save a couple of hospital administrators."

"Shoot," Mattie said equably. "I shoulda sent you a threatening note myself."

Timmie grinned at Mattie, which Victor didn't enjoy, either.

"You don't think maybe you might have said or seen something?" he asked. "Something you might not have told the police?"

That actually got Timmie to stop. "The police haven't asked.

Not since it happened. But now that you are, the only thing I can tell you is the man's description, which hasn't changed from what I told the cop on the scene."

"Nothing else?"

It was obvious Victor had read his interrogation handbook. The words were right. The tone, however, needed a lot of work. The last Timmie had heard, disdain was not the suggested tone of voice for inviting confidences.

"Nothing I didn't tell the officer who took my statement that day." She deliberately smiled. "But I'm sure you've read that already."

He gave her his best assessing look, the kind that said, "I know you're hiding something, and I'll find it out."

"Somebody'll probably get in touch with you about it." When you're old and gray and senile, Timmie interpreted. "If you remember anything else, or have any more problems like that note, please get in touch with me. I might be able to help."

"Tell you what I do need," she said, wondering why she was sticking her neck out. "A good lawyer. My ex-husband is coming back to jerk me around a little more, and I don't feel like playing his games. Got anybody in mind?"

Mattie froze in place. Work stopped all along the lane. As for the good Officer Adkins, he flashed her a look that made Timmie think there was something that bore watching behind all that "good ole boy" shit. "Wouldn't be my place to advise you on matters like that, ma'am." He jangled his belt one more time, which made Timmie think of a witch doctor shaking rattles to ward off evil, and headed for the door. "Let me know if you hear anything."

She gave him her best killer smile. "You bet."

The minute Victor cleared the door, applause broke out. Everybody, evidently, had heard. Timmie bowed, an eye instinctively cocked to catch Ellen's reaction where she was charting by the desk. Ellen just smiled without looking up from what she was doing.

"You got brass balls, girl," Mattie said on an awed whoosh of breath. "Big brass balls."

"I'm from California," Timmie said. "People expect me to be a little outrageous."

Mattie hooted like a truck in the passing lane. "That ain't outrageous, girlfriend. That's suicidal. That boy got you license number."

"Ah, he can't take a joke, the hell with him. Mattie—"

"You better not be gonna ask what I think you are," Mattie accused.

Timmie flipped the IV bag a couple more times, like a percussion instrument keeping rhythm. "If you were me, wouldn't *you* like to know how Officer Adkins found out about my little problem? Don't you want to know why he was *really* here, since I can't believe he's terribly concerned for my safety?"

"Not after you dissed him to his face, he isn't."

"I didn't dis him till he got here."

Mattie lifted a finger in exception. "I thought you was gonna steer clear of those waters."

Timmie took a final look at the back of Victor Adkins. Then she looked at Mattie.

"They know who it is," she said anyway, just to Mattie. "And they don't want anybody else to know. What is it they're afraid I found out, Mattie?"

Mattie drew herself up to her full height and put every inch of Baptist-raised, iron-hand-ruling grandma in her eyes. And said not a word.

Finally Timmie sighed, deflating like a party balloon. "Okay," she said, and realized she meant it. "You're right. No matter what's going on right now—and I'm still not convinced nothing's going on—it's not the time to fight city hall. I need to save all my energy to fight off my ex-husband again."

Mattie frowned. "You weren't kidding about that? I thought you left him at home."

"I did. He found me. And far be it from Jason Parker to ever miss a chance to screw up my life. But that's not something I feel like dealing with today, either. Let's go do us some trauma."

Mattie led the way. "I'm on break, girlfriend. That means I get to shoot 'em, you get to sew 'em."

"Stellar idea. Just as soon as I drug your patient." They made it halfway down the hall before Timmie gave in to temptation. "Mattie?"

"Yeah."

Timmie spoke very quietly, an eye still on Ellen, who was now laughing about something with Ron. "What if Billy Mayfield was poisoned?"

That brought Mattie to a dead stop. "See?" she demanded, stabbing a finger at Timmie. "There you go again. No wonder you always gettin' notes. And what does that have to do with anything anyway?"

Timmie didn't back down. "What if he was?"

Mattie never blinked. "Serve him right."

The shift ended up being busier than they'd anticipated.

Croup season had kicked in, which made the hall sound like feeding time at the seal pools, and one of the local fast-food restaurants had evidently gotten a bad shipment of guacamole, which made it sound like a frat house at 3 A.M. The only person dissatisfied was Timmie, who was now suffering serious trauma withdrawal. A gunshot. A car accident. Anything. Heck, Timmie would have settled for a river-barge injury. But she was stuck with abdominal pains and kids with runny noses. By the time she got the chance to take a couple of minutes, it was ten o'clock, and she had an abstinence headache.

"I'm gonna run up and see my dad," she announced as she dropped her last chart in the bin for recycling and dry-swallowed a couple of aspirin.

The minute she announced it, two people started to sing and one quoted "The Lake Isle of Innisfree" all over again. It was a good thing Timmie liked the damn poem, or she'd be the next one going postal in Puckett.

"Just in time," Ellen announced from where she was triaging. "Cindy's coming back from Restcrest."

"Shift's not over," somebody said.

"I'm afraid her patient is. I stopped up to see her about an hour ago, because, well, she just doesn't do well with grieving families and Mr. Abbot was already at end stage."

"Why didn't he get turfed down here?" Timmie asked. "I thought the policy was that anybody looking real sick at Restcrest traveled the ER road to heaven."

Ellen, who didn't have the skin to blush, did. Guiltily. "Because the family has been sitting by his bedside chanting 'law-yer, law-yer' if anybody so much as balances a hand on Mr. Peterson's chest."

"What a good family."

Mattie grinned. "Get our Gold Star of Excellence award this week."

"At least that means there's a bed available," Ellen told Timmie in all sincerity. "Honey, I bet Alex could get your dad in."

But does Alex want to pay for it? Timmie almost asked. Instead, she smiled at Ellen's perfect sincerity and said she'd see. Then she hit the switch to open the back doors before anything else could stop her.

She wasn't counting on the interruption waiting on the other side of the doors. Leaning against the back wall, hands in jean pockets, as if just waiting for her to show up.

That reporter.

"Ya know," Timmie greeted him, "there were people I worked with on the same damn shift at L.A. County I didn't see as much as I see you."

He pushed himself away from the wall. "L.A. County emergency department is bigger than Puckett."

"More fun, too," Timmie admitted without thinking.

The reporter's smile was much too knowing. Timmie wanted to tell him to shut up. Especially since that smile looked so damn sexy, even on that raggedy, beat-up face. She was too tired for sexy. Much too intelligent for raggedy and beat-up.

"What are you doing here?" she asked.

"Looking for you, actually. Can I talk to you for a minute?"

He had the damnedest eyes. Deep-set and pale green, like sun catchers in a dirty window, crowded with crow's feet and topped by thick eyebrows that were going to go a dramatic white in a few years.

Timmie flat-out shook her head. "Nope. I have filial duties to perform, and not much time to do them in."

He grinned like a bandit. "Your father? Great. I'll tag along."

The son of a bitch even had dimples. It just figured. Timmie did her best to smile and walk by. "No, you won't."

The reporter kept pace with her, walking backward. "I hear you were threatened."

Only disgust got her to stop. "Evidently everybody's heard about it. Amazing, since I don't remember telling anybody. At least anybody with a badge or a notebook."

He didn't seem particularly repentant. "Did it look like this?" he asked, dipping into a saggy tweed pocket and pulling something out.

Timmie found herself staring. It was her card. The one that had come with her flowers. Same paper, same letters, same threat.

STOP NOW BEFORE YOU GET HURT

"Where'd you get that?" she demanded, making an abortive grab for it.

He stuffed it back in his pocket. "In my mailbox at work. Wanna talk?"

Timmie thought about all the questions she had, and just what would happen if she shared them with a Pulitzer Prize–winning reporter with sharp green eyes. She shook her head. "Nope. I want to ignore it, just like this whole town seems to do. Got a problem with that?"

"On any other day, no. But it seems that I've been dumped into the middle of the same stew pot as you, and it has something to do with the suspicious deaths around here."

"Deaths?" Timmie demanded before she got the chance to think. "There are more?"

She knew she was caught when he raised an honestly surprised eyebrow at her. "There's been one?"

"WHAT ARE YOU TALKING ABOUT?" TIMMIE DEMANDED.

"What are *you* talking about?" the reporter echoed, looking as smug as snot.

Timmie stood there like a stunned ox, suddenly not sure what to do. Behind her, the hydraulic doors closed, shutting her friends off from her. The back hall was empty at this hour of the night, the only denizen the housekeeper at the far end polishing floors. Which meant it was going to have to be up to Timmie to get out of this all by herself.

Boy, this kind of thing had never happened to Scarlett when she'd put things off. She'd just had to eat turnips.

"You got a threat," Timmie scoffed. "Big deal. You'd think a world-class reporter like you'd be used to it by now."

"The threat doesn't bother me," he retorted, sounding, oddly enough, angry. "It *interests* me. Besides, once I found out you'd gotten one, too, I had to come apologize. I think I got you into this."

"What do you mean?"

His grin was sheepish enough for a Rockwell painting. "That's what I wanted to talk to you about. I was given your name—"

"*My* name? What for?"

"I got a call the night of the shooting. Mysterious, hushed voice begging me to do something about the deaths here."

"Not a threat?"

Murphy squinted at her. "You getting calls, too?"

Timmie shook her head decisively. She was going to have to learn to keep her mouth shut. "Nah, I just figured . . . "

She could tell he didn't buy it. He didn't push it, though.

"No threats. Somebody asking for help."

"And they gave you my name?"

"Go figure."

"And we both got notes."

"Well, after I might have mentioned your name a couple of times when asking questions. Yeah."

Timmie rubbed the heel of her hand against her sternum, behind which settled most of her more intense emotions. She sure wished she had a baseball bat in her hands. "So, what are you going to do?"

"That's what I wanted to talk to you about."

Timmie screwed up the courage to take another good look at the reporter, who was now standing foursquare, hands on hips, his jacket splayed out behind, foot tapping in staccato bursts. Antsy. Unsettled. As out of place in Puckett as she was.

She could talk to him. Tell him what she'd found without him laughing over the idea that a nurse could have a certification in forensics. She could share war stories and stoke up on them like an exile pulling out old family movies.

She could give him the stuff about Billy and let him run with it.

Or not.

He didn't know Ellen. He wouldn't care why she was doing the horizontal hoedown with the coroner. It wouldn't matter to him that the fallout would contaminate Timmie as much as anybody.

So she shoved her hands in her bulging lab coat pockets and headed off again. "Thank you, no. Now, I really have to go."

"How is your father?" the reporter asked, keeping an easy pace.

"Fine," she answered just like she did to everyone. "Just fine."

"Good. That means he'll be happy to see me."

That brought Timmie back to a dead halt no more than five feet from the elevators. "No. You leave him alone."

"He's a legend."

"He's a sick, lost, childlike old man who can still remember on the odd day that he has immense pride. I won't have him humiliated."

"That's not what I was thinking of doing. I wanted to write about the effect he's had on people around here. The stories they all like to tell." He grinned again, and Timmie had to give him points for looking sincere. "I think it's worth a line or two when I get gas station attendants and pool sharks quoting Yeats and Blake. Don't *you* think that's pretty incredible?"

Timmie glared at him for a moment, unconsciously rubbing. The last thing she was sure she needed was Daniel Murphy scavenging around in her life for insight. So she turned on her heel and walked. "Public elevators are around the corner."

He walked right alongside. "I don't suppose you want to tell me which death you were talking about."

Reaching the staff elevator, she punched the button. "I wasn't. I was talking about the fact that the coroner's incompetent, but you can't quote me on that or I'll lose my job, and then you'll get to keep that wonderful old man who quotes Yeats at *your* house, because I won't be able to afford him."

"But if the coroner's blatantly ignoring the rise in the death rate around here, you could get him out of office."

Suddenly Timmie forgot where she'd been going. In fact, she damn near forgot to breathe.

Murphy leaned toward her, and his eyes widened. "I'm talking about the fact that the death rate has gone up in Puckett since Price U. bought in," he said. "Aren't you?"

The door slid open. Timmie was so busy staring at Daniel Murphy that she completely missed it. "Don't do this to me," she begged.

He all but whistled. "You didn't know, did you? Timmie, I think you and I have been having two completely different conversations here."

Timmie turned to the wall and ignored him. She ignored the silence that built behind her.

"Oh, my God," he suddenly said, truly stunned. "You *do* think William Mayfield was murdered, don't you?"

Timmie decided she'd damn well better be having a heart attack, or that squeezing in her chest was an omen of disaster.

"Timmie, hi, where are you going?"

It took Timmie a full five seconds to realize that Cindy had appeared around the corner from Restcrest and was even now faltering to a halt beside to them. She looked wilted and tired, which meant she'd had a hard time with Mr. Peterson. Timmie knew she should be ashamed, but all she could see was a means of escape.

"Up to see my dad," Timmie said. "You remember Mr. Murphy?"

Cindy nodded, her hair bobbing low over her forehead. "There's a bed available in Restcrest," she said in what Timmie thought of as "Johnny tones." "You know I lost my little old man."

Timmie nodded. "I'm glad he got to stay up with his family," she said, her hand on Cindy's arm. "You know we just would have tortured him."

Cindy closed her eyes and sighed. "I know. He was just so nice. Both Alex and Ellen stopped by to help, but they didn't need to. I had it in hand."

Timmie must have reacted, because when Cindy opened her eyes again, she looked hurt. "I am good at some things," she said, defending herself.

"I know, Cindy," Timmie apologized. "I know . . . You know, Mr. Murphy's doing that series of articles on Restcrest. You could probably help him if you were to talk to him about what happened tonight. After all, it's as much a part of the story as anything else." Okay, so she was underhanded. She was desperate. And Cindy had never minded talking about herself before. "Maybe now, while you're thinking about it."

Cindy actually shook her head. "Maybe some other time. I need to go talk to Ellen."

Timmie was stunned. Usually nothing short-circuited Cindy's

libido. But there was no mistaking her distraction. She really must have felt this one. It had been so long since Timmie had reacted to anything on that level, she almost couldn't imagine it.

"That'd work better for me, too," Murphy agreed, hardly deceived by Timmie's ploy. "Maybe in a day or two?"

Cindy smiled. "Thank you, yes."

Which meant that when Timmie finally did get on the elevator, Murphy got right on with her.

The door closed and Timmie punched buttons. "I'm still not talking to you," she said.

"Why not?" Murphy asked. "I don't think I need to remind you that you've already been threatened. Maybe I can help."

"And maybe you can get me more involved."

"You *are* involved. You'd just have answers."

Timmie turned on him hard, suddenly very afraid. She'd been working on the assumption that what she was facing was a limited problem. One suspicious death. Maybe an unexplained shooting. Murphy wanted to take it to a whole new level of play. "You know, Mr. Murphy, at this point in my life, my impulse control isn't what it once was. And my impulse right now is to use my knee to render you completely immobile so I can enjoy the rest of this ride in peace. You might want to think about that before asking another question."

He didn't even blink, and Timmie realized just what kind of power plant hummed behind those laser-green eyes. "You were sure singing a different song the last time I saw you. What happened?"

Timmie actually laughed. "What happened is that my father wandered out into the streets in his shorts to remind me of my priorities. Muckraking is for loners."

"Like me?"

"I'm not talking to you."

He nodded, eyes pensive as he scratched his chin. "Probably be the best for both of us, I guess. The last thing I need at this point in my life is to get involved in a messy investigation."

"It's not exactly one of the twelve steps," Timmie retorted.

That got Murphy's attention. "My reputation precedes me."

"Nah. I'd recognize a reformed drunk at a hundred paces."

He laughed. "Not reformed at all. Warned off. Is that why you won't talk to me?"

She heard the door open onto the fifth floor and gave him the benefit of one more glance. "No. I won't talk to you because I have nothing to say. Now, let me go see my father in peace."

And much to Timmie's eternal surprise, Murphy just held the door for her. "Give him my best."

Timmie, of course, believed that once Murphy left her alone, the rest of the trip would be easier. She should have known better.

"Do you realize what you've been doing to this man?" the nurse taking care of her father demanded.

A reformer. Timmie could spot those faster than old drunks. Those nurses who knew better than anyone else and saw it as their mission to impose the benefit of their wisdom on the unworthy, like circuit riders scattering Bibles to the savages. Tight, controlled, disapproving do-gooders with less humor than flexibility. This one had her zealot's eyes set squarely on Timmie and the grocery list of Joe's medications she'd brought.

"I've been trying to keep him safe," Timmie assured the woman, doing her damnedest to hold on to her temper.

She hadn't even made it into the room, where the lights had been turned low and Joe could be heard humming—"Carrickfergus," Timmie thought, which meant he was lonely. And Timmie, who might actually be able to help, was stuck out in the hallway like a fly in a bug light.

"You've been torturing him," the nurse accused, her posture aggressive. "I won't have it. He's a human being, not a side of beef."

Timmie sighed. "Fine. Good. Thank you. I beg forgiveness. Now, I'm going to go in and see him."

"I've just gotten him calmed down."

Timmie smiled. "Calm him down again."

She walked into the sterile, silent room while the nurse bristled back in the lighted hallway. "We've taken him off everything," she informed Timmie in arch tones. "Just so you know when you take him home."

"Home?" Timmie echoed, turning back to see the nurse silhouetted with hands on hips like Patton surveying the Nazis.

Home. Just the word was enough to drop a rock in her chest. She'd gotten a full night's sleep last night for the first time in a month. She'd had time to play with Meghan without having to keep an ear open for problems. She'd been able to pretend everything would be all right.

"Day after tomorrow. You didn't expect us to warehouse him for you, did you?"

Timmie fought hard for a calming breath. It would have been easier to take if she hadn't thought that very thing about relatives of some of the old people she'd housed. All those families she'd judged so blithely when her father had been a thousand miles away.

"And a nursing home?" she asked.

"He's on waiting lists."

Fuck. Shit. Timmie couldn't breathe all of a sudden, just with the thought of going back into that old house.

And then, to make it all worse, she turned back to her father, who lay open-eyed and still on the bed, the wailing notes of the lament drifting off him like old smoke in the dark.

"Daddy?"

Slowly he focused those old blue eyes on her. "Timmie?"

Timmie did her level best to smile for him when all she wanted to do was scream. "Hi, sweetie. How are you?"

His eyes teared over and he reached for her hand. "Take me home, Timmie. Please. I want to go home."

As if that would make it all better.

As if anything would.

It took another week for Timmie to have at least one wish granted. She got her trauma. Before she could get that far, of course, she had to spend the week settling her father back home without benefit of the major psychotropics that had been keeping him under control. She hired and fired three more baby-sitters and finally sent Meghan to stay down the block for a few days, just to keep the little girl safe from her grandfather's furies.

Timmie wasn't safe anywhere. She collected a bouquet of bruises, a cracked finger, and a loosened tooth from the evenings when baseball didn't help, and a wagonload of frustration at the restrictions that kept her father out of a safe place.

The good news, she supposed, was that being that preoccupied effectively squashed any wayward urges to change the system. She didn't have the energy to so much as give a damn that Ellen might have gotten away with murder. She didn't say bad things about Van Adder or call Murphy about suspicious death rates. It was all she could do to handle the trauma at home, much less dig up more at work.

Murphy did call, but only to ask again for a chance to talk to Joe. Nursing her sore finger and a crashing headache, Timmie almost agreed. But she knew that until she got Joe really settled somewhere, a talk about his life would only make matters worse. As it was, Joe swung from delightful, rambling lectures on the precious gifts of history, literature, and baseball to harrowing rages that ate up the nights, when the darkness stole his sense of certainty.

He wanted to run away. He just couldn't remember how to get there, or why it was Timmie would keep him from doing it. Timmie, his baby. Timmie, who had always sneaked off with him for day games at the stadium and night toots on the town. Timmie, who smiled at his singing and cheered at his heroes.

By the time Friday came, Timmie was at the end of her rope. Her friends had helped, her daughter had invented an imaginary playmate who had two parents and no grandfather, and Timmie had learned her own limitations. She was a trauma nurse. She acted quickly and thought on her feet. But she had no business struggling for inches with a man who would never get better, because she simply didn't have the patience for it.

She'd always said she'd use her last resort as a last resort. The last resort came when she walked back into the house from shopping to find her father pointing a pistol at her

"Joe, knock it off," she said, by now at least comfortable with the fact that his memory of Joe was more solid than his memory of Daddy.

He straightened, stained and rumpled and frightened, the gun shaking so badly in his hand he'd probably hit the ceiling before he hit Timmie.

Where'd he get the damn thing? she wondered as she set the grocery bag down on top of a pile of old curtains. It immediately tipped over, spilling tomatoes and cantaloupe and lettuce like vegetarian boccie balls. Timmie didn't bother to notice.

"Joe, put the gun down. You don't need it."

"I . . . you know how tough this neighborhood is?" he demanded, swinging the gun around in punctuation. "I need protection."

"Tell it to the cop who's behind you," she suggested, sidling closer. Sweating. Wondering what had happened to the latest baby-sitter. Had there been shots fired? Were the police even now on the way here?

Her father smiled suddenly, like a choirboy caught cadging a smoke behind the rectory. "Oh, Timmie, my girl, you lie like an amateur."

"You need to put the gun down, Da. It's going to hurt somebody."

"Yeah," he admitted, studying the thing as if it were an insect. "Me. If I'm lucky."

New shakes. Terrifying images of her father blowing his brains all over her grandmother's cabbage rose wallpaper.

"But not today," Timmie insisted. "Today's the seventh game of the series. Milwaukee, Dad, remember? You can't tell me you're going to miss finding out if the Cards can pull it out."

Flickers of disquiet marred his face like ripples on a lake. Uncertainty, embarrassment, fear. He chuckled, but it was the chuckle of someone terrified that they'd forgotten something important and didn't know what.

"Daddy, come on," Timmie pleaded, praying she knew where the videotape was, chancing a few steps closer through a minefield of fruit and vegetables. "Game's going to start any minute. You don't want to miss Ozzie's backflip."

The gun wavered, lowered. Timmie heard the sirens at the same instant she made that last leap and took the gun from her father's hand.

"We have to hurry," he insisted, turning without a qualm for the back room.

Timmie stood there and shook and knew that it was time to grovel.

"Timmie? Is that you?"

Timmie sat in the stiff old brown wingback in the living room, the phone in one hand, her best Louisville slugger in the other. She'd already knocked the Nerf ball clean off its line with it. Now she was just using it for balance.

"I need some help," she admitted, closing her eyes. If she opened them, she'd just see the van Gogh print she'd cut off a calendar and framed for her wall. One of the later ones, all energy and hot, weird color, laid down in the scatological brushwork of madness. Like she needed the reminder.

There was silence on the other end of the line. Jack Buck was talking from the back room again, where Mrs. Falcon had been found crouched beneath the bed two hours earlier. It was where she'd hidden to call the police when Timmie's dad had escaped. It was where she'd tendered her resignation when Timmie had followed the telephone cord to unearth her.

"Please," Timmie added now, as if it would help. "Just this once."

Another pause that almost made her hope.

"I don't think so."

Timmie fought hard not to cry. "I can't do this alone. The only home that can control him is too expensive, and it doesn't take Medicare. I need a loan, but the banks won't help. Please."

"It wasn't worth a free house after all, was it?"

Timmie closed her eyes. Fought the bile at the back of her throat. Rubbed hard at her chest. "Please."

"Just like that? What makes you think after all this time I care what happens to him?"

"How about your granddaughter, Mom? Do you care what happens to her?"

Timmie heard the click and didn't believe it. Not until the phone beeped and the recorded operator came on to suggest that if Timmie intended to make a call she could hang up and try again. She hung up. She didn't think she could try again.

"Timmie Leary, it's your lucky day!" Ellen greeted her when she walked into the lounge.

"You couldn't tell by how it's gone so far," Timmie assured her, setting down her nursing bag and dropping into the chair.

Ellen's homely flat face immediately folded into planes of concern. "Your dad?" she asked gently.

Even as exhausted as she felt, Timmie found a smile for Ellen. "Yeah, I'm afraid so. We just didn't have a good day today." Nothing like an understatement to clear your palate.

Ellen was a good nurse. She smelled the euphemism and sat down, hand on Timmie's knee. "Oh, honey, I'm sorry. What can I do?"

Put him out of his misery, Timmie thought immediately, and regretted it even faster. God, she must be tired if she was even admitting to that kind of temptation.

"Figure someplace better than the back of a hall closet to hide a handgun," she said, then regretted that, too. Ellen looked appalled. "It's okay," Timmie soothed her friend. "He's fine."

"You haven't heard from anyplace?"

Timmie grimaced. "Golden Grove. The flagship in the GeriSys fleet of old folks' warehouses."

Ellen gaped. "Oh, Timmie, you can't. GeriSys is awful. Three different states are investigating them for neglect and fraud."

"I know I can't. But it may get to the point where I can't not. Megs isn't safe in that house with him anymore."

Rolling her neck to loosen it a fraction, Timmie began pulling out her supplies for the shift. It occurred to her that she should have been grilling Ellen, figuring a way to get evidence from her to prove she'd killed her husband. In fact, she'd thought it pretty much every day for the last week.

And then done nothing.

"I still think you should have gotten in at Restcrest," Ellen was saying. "It would be such a wonderful place for him."

"So would Ireland," Timmie said. "I can't afford that, either."

Ellen frowned. "I mean it, honey. You know Dr. Raymond would take good care of him. He'd be so happy there."

What should she say? Timmie wondered. I'll try? "I'll try," she said. "Now, did you have a present for me?"

Ellen brightened. "How does a bus accident sound?"

Timmie looked up. "You're not just saying that to make me feel better."

"It hit two motorcycles."

"Donor cycles?" That got her to her feet. "Really?"

Ellen's smile was beatific. "We're saving them just for you, honey."

At that moment, Timmie decided that she didn't care if Ellen killed off every ex-husband in the hospital. She'd personally nominate her for lifesaver of the year.

Draping her stethoscope around her neck, Timmie stuffed her pockets with the tools of her trade and strapped on her watch. She was just turning for the hall when the door opened again.

"Timmie, there you are."

Timmie looked up and blinked, fast. Alex. No, she thought. Not now. Not when she'd been promised trauma to escape to.

"What can I do for you, Alex?" she asked, wrapping a hand around each end of her stethoscope, as if balancing herself with it. Next to her, Ellen just stood there, everything she'd said still telegraphed in her expression.

"I only have a second," he said, "but I wondered if I could have a word."

Timmie made it a point not to look at Ellen. "Sure thing. What's up?"

"Your dad," he said baldly, and Timmie noticed for the first time that he stood as stiffly as a man delivering unwanted news. "I heard what happened today," he said. "I'm really sorry, Tim."

The room seemed to close in on her. Timmie didn't question how he knew. She just didn't know what he wanted her to say about it. Or what she could do about it. "Thank you, Alex," she said because she had to. "Everything's okay, though."

Alex actually looked away for a second before speaking. "That bed he needs. I want to give it to him."

Timmie just stopped breathing. She saw Ellen's eyes go wide and couldn't bear it. "Thank you," she said, her voice unforgivably small with shame. "I really appreciate it. But I can't. I talked to one of your people . . . "

He was already nodding. "I know. I talked to her, too. But why did I come home if I can't help old friends? And Joe is an old friend. It'll probably take a couple of days, but somebody will call you. We can work out particulars later."

Timmie couldn't think. She saw Alex's gaze stray to the new bruising along her jaw where her dad had clipped her the night before and fought a new wave of embarrassment. "But . . . "

He pulled himself straight and smiled. "But nothing. I'll see you in a couple of days."

And without another word, he walked out. Timmie stood stock-still, stunned to tears, her hands still clenched tightly against her chest. Numb and shaking and trying to believe that the fairy godfather of old people had really just tapped her head with his magic wand.

"Well, for God's sake," was all she could manage on a gulped half sob that infuriated her even more.

Ellen wasn't nearly so shy about things. She gave Timmie the hug of a lifetime. "Timmie, that's wonderful!"

Safe. He'd be safe now. He'd be waited on by people he could charm, people who knew how to be patient with him. And Timmie would be able to have her daughter and her peace back again.

Jesus, she thought, fighting hard against the urge to hyperventilate herself straight into a coma. She just wasn't made for a day like today. One more emotional high *or* low, and she was going to just cash it in.

"Well, then," Ellen said as she held open the door. "Shouldn't we go out and play?"

The ER reverberated with pandemonium. It had been a full hall to begin with. Word of the accident sent the staff into a frenzy. Nurses scurried back and forth, trundling loaded carts from room to room. A couple of techs were tossing IV bags and procedure trays through open doors. The radio chattered and the computer stuttered. Timmie stood for a second at the foot of the hallway and breathed in the activity like an ocean wind. Her heart rate picked up. Her headache eased, and she smiled.

Traumawoman stepped out of the phone booth.

The bus accident was only the beginning. As if rewarding Timmie for her patience, Puckett went on a rampage. Accidents, overdoses, heart attacks. One woman even gave birth in the backseat of a Geo Metro, and a ten-year-old came in wearing the three-inch pumps he'd Super-Glued to his feet. For the first time since she'd signed on, Timmie sang as she worked.

"Girl, you are havin' way too much fun tonight," Mattie accused as she delivered the chart for Timmie's latest patient, a three-hundred-pound man complaining of chest pains who was even now being maneuvered onto the cart by the tech.

Timmie flashed her friend a big grin. "Way too much."

"Oh, no . . . ooooh, no!"

Both Timmie and Mattie spun around at the same time, but Mattie was closer. Which meant she ended up on the floor under the patient when he went down in cardiac arrest. Timmie burst out laughing. Mattie growled and the tech tugged.

"Call a code!" Timmie yelled, gasping for breath, and added her shoulder to the job of getting the guy off Mattie. "How many times I gotta tell you, girl? You the nurse, you get to be on top."

"You really are having fun," Ellen all but accused when she skidded in to help.

Busy inserting an airway, Timmie didn't bother to deny it.

"Everybody needs to know they're good at something, Ellen. And I'm very good at this."

They conducted the code on their knees, looking for all the world like worshipers at a hirsute altar. Timmie kept singing Irish rebel music, and Ellen patted the patient's mottled hands. Neither the code, the musical interlude, nor the comfort did him any good. But Dr. Chang had caught the patient at the end of her shift, and hated to give up what she'd started.

Then Ron hit the door at warp speed. "Township 105 is on the way with a crispy critter," he announced shrilly. "Will *somebody* get out here and talk to them?"

Everybody but Chang jumped to their feet. "Code is called at 11:01 P.M.," Timmie announced, peeling off her gloves.

When Chang didn't move, Timmie leaned down. "Principles of triage," she said quietly. "This guy isn't going anywhere but the express train to God. We need to get to the burn victim we can save. And if the ambulance is already en route, the guy's too bad to treat on scene. Let's go talk to them."

When Timmie held out her hand, Chang, a petite, wide-eyed pile driver of a doctor, shook her head. Even so, she took hold and pulled herself up.

"You asked for this," Ron accused as Timmie sprinted by.

"No," Timmie admitted with a silly grin. "I begged for this."

"I'll take the radio," Chang told Ron as she picked up the headset. "Dr. Adkins is due in for her shift. Let her do the patient . . . Township 105, this is Memorial, go ahead."

Timmie ran for another space suit. She collected morphine from the drug locker and fluids from the supply cart, singing all the while. She got sterile sheets and cut-down trays and intubation kits and wondered why she'd started the day in such a bad mood.

"He's a total crisper," Ron announced from the doorway. "House fire, completely involved. This guy didn't know a thing."

Finally, thankfully, Barb strolled in to start her shift, her coat still thrown over her shoulder.

"What's coming in?" she asked, leaning in the door.

Timmie traded Barb's coat for a laryngoscope. "Crispy critter. House fire. And you're up to bat."

Barb nodded. Sucked in a huge breath, the laryngoscope drooping in her hand like unwanted flowers. "Don't suppose a helicopter's handy to just turf this puppy east?"

"Not for another forty minutes."

"Well, then, let's be ready to do gasses and a carboxyhemoglobin. How are you on these things, Timmie?"

"I hate 'em. You?"

"Yep. Me, too." Then she snapped the laryngoscope into place and headed for the crash cart.

The patient was every bit as bad as they'd feared. Charred and hairless and rasping for breath, an indistinguishable hunk of protoplasm that reeked of charred meat, his clothes singed tatters of blue and white that hung off like sloughed skin. The team chose up tasks, Mattie doing assessment, Ellen at the cart, and Timmie working on starting IVs, which would be the only way they could medicate the patient if he decided to live past that evening. Trying her damnedest to find an inch of uninvolved skin, Timmie didn't think he stood much of a chance.

"His airway's as black as a chimney sweep's face," Barb pronounced as she suctioned for a better look. "He's been sucking bad shit."

"He was drinking," the paramedic offered as he helped hook the patient up to monitor and oxymeter. "We damn near killed ourselves on the beer cans in there."

"Let's get an ETOH, too," Barb suggested. "Was he smoking?"

"Nah. Fire jockeys found cans of kerosene in the garage he was evidently using to clean machinery with. They think it was spontaneous combustion."

Half-listening as she dug for an already collapsed vein, Timmie suddenly stopped. "Spontaneous combustion?" she asked.

"Yeah. There was plenty of stuff. Rags and shit. Once it went up, it went up quick."

"You said kerosene?"

Bent over the other side of the cart where she was trying to get breath sounds, Mattie shot Timmie a warning stare. "What is it you tryin' to say?"

Timmie looked at her. Looked at the paramedics and shook her head.

"His $O_2$ Sat's only fifty-six percent," Barb announced, oblivious. "I don't think this camper's gonna make the final singalong. Get X ray in here for his chest films. You got a CVP line for me?"

"His pressure's dropping," Ellen added, her voice tightening. "It's eighty over forty."

"Timmie, you got a line? Dial up the fluids. Hyperventilate him on a hundred percent. Let's start with some sodium bicarb and a Dopamine drip, huh? And somebody call the helicopter back and tell them to hit the afterburners."

Timmie was so busy with the sudden pop of a vein at the edge of her needle that she barely took note when a burly, red-headed cop walked in the room.

"You sure you should be taking care of him?" he suddenly asked.

Everybody else looked up before Timmie.

"Why not?" Barb asked, her pocket *Merck Manual* open in her hand like a hymnal at a Sunday service. "You want him to die?"

"No. I don't. That's why I don't want you taking care of him."

That even got Timmie's attention. "Why?"

"Don't you recognize him, Dr. Adkins?" He pointed at the patient's face, but it was already hidden beneath ET tape and saline packs. "That's your ex-husband, Victor, you're taking care of."

MURPHY REALLY SHOULDN'T HAVE BEEN HERE. HE PROBABLY wouldn't have if he hadn't been so frustrated. It was the one thing he hadn't counted on when he'd gone into hiding. That the kind of normal, everyday life he'd been so intent on recording for posterity, now that he wasn't going after real news anymore, was so damn boring.

So here he was sifting through the ashes of a house fire, just because the guy involved had given him a hard time.

If this had been a movie, the sky would have been overcast. The leaves would have already been off the trees so that the limbs looked skeletal and threatening to match the destruction they surrounded, and the air would have been as heavy as the smell of smoke. There would have been yellow police tape stretched across trees and neighbors clustered together on the grass talking in hushed tones.

But the sky was gem-quality blue, the yards empty, and the trees still flaming with a dozen colors that flickered in a brisk breeze, which made the lumpy, soggy remains of Victor Adkins's house look almost surreal in their midst. A rotten tooth in the midst of a carefully tended, rigidly blue-collar mouth.

The remains were real enough. Murphy could smell them, the unmistakable roux of ash and smoke and melted plastic. A cheap, small, prefab house that had once had Colonial blue siding and white shutters, and now wasn't much more than toxic waste. It had lasted, from all accounts, a full twenty minutes from the first sighting of flames. A good ten minutes past the moment a neighbor had braved the heat and smoke to drag an unconscious Victor out the family room window from the eviscerated couch Murphy could now see through the maw that had once been a window.

It was a mess. Murphy stood there with his hands in his pockets staring at the evidence of mortality and couldn't think of a damn thing to say but that. A mess.

Well, thank God, he thought with black humor. And here I thought I'd lost my talent.

That was when he saw her. Straight through the gaping holes that lined up through the walls like rifle sights into the backyard. There was a picnic table back there, regulation cedar with benches, the kind a family bought for barbecues and kids. She was sitting on the table with her feet on a bench, wearing a pair of lurid pink scrubs and a black leather jacket, her elbows on her knees, her chin in her hands, considering the house as if it were a painting in the art museum. And she was laughing.

Murphy found himself wanting to smile and didn't.

It took him a good few minutes to pick his way through the debris in the yard to get to her.

"You know, there were people who worked with you in that ER at L.A. County I didn't see as much as I see you," he greeted her.

She didn't bother to look away from whatever had her attention. "Shut up."

He reached the table and followed her line of sight, but he didn't see anything other than the flip side of what he'd been studying in the front yard. A little more trash on the back lawn than the front, a good view into the kitchen that had once been decorated in gingham and eagles, a gutted roof and exposed garage. Tumbled bachelor furniture and tattered, black-singed walls.

Murphy returned his consideration to his surprise companion. "What's wrong with this picture?" he asked.

For some reason, that made her laugh again. "Exactly."

Which was when Murphy realized she wasn't laughing because something was funny.

Murphy waited, but that was all he got. He did notice, however, those four earrings she wore, like dime-store constellations, right up the curve of her ear. Four simple, multicolored stones in an arc. All he could think of was how they fit her. And how long her neck was. He liked long necks even more than tight little bottoms on the kind of self-reliant women who'd have the gall to teach a renowned reporter manners. Which Murphy knew didn't bear thinking about, since he only thought about those things in the abstract these days anyway. So he sat down alongside her on the table and watched the house, too.

"When does the show start?" he asked.

She didn't look over. "He didn't make it, you know."

"I know."

"Died at two-thirty this morning. Not of the burns, though. Those were kind of an afterthought. He'd sucked in enough hot gases and smoke to drop a rhino."

"Assuming a rhino would have the bad luck to get caught in a house fire."

"Van Adder's dying to call it an accident. The arson guys are waiting till they clear their paperwork to agree." She watched a while longer, weighing something. "You find anything out this week?"

"Not a thing. I took your advice and went back to interviewing PTA presidents. Was I wrong?"

A sigh, heartfelt. "Ah, hell, who knows? He came to see me."

"Victor?"

She nodded, one ringless hand rubbing the back of her bare neck. "Wanted to know if I'd *seen* something . . . heard something at the horse show. The one thing he didn't want to know was what the shooter looked like. Don't you find that interesting?"

"Is that why you're here?" he asked. "Trying to make sense of this?"

"Nope. Trying to decide what to do about it."

"Do? What do you mean?"

For a second she didn't move. Then she sighed and straightened. "Do you still like what you do?"

This was beginning to give Murphy a headache. "Not really."

She didn't seem to expect more. "That's what I figured."

"How about you?"

That actually made her smile, and the smile was real. "Love it. Shit, I scarf it up like peanut butter and chocolate. Dive in face first and paddle around like an idiot. I swear to God, I can almost come just with the sound of a fire engine." She kept staring at the house, as if it were a threat to her. "I've been trying to think of what else I could do that would make me this happy, and I just can't."

"But that might happen?"

Again, she decided not to answer him. Not exactly. "You can have that appointment with my father if you want," she said. "I'm going to be taking him to Restcrest, where he'll be safe. Where he will, God willing and the fates be with us, be happy. After almost two years of actively beating my head against the wall, I finally have some semblance of stability for myself, my daughter, and my father. I felt so damn good last night."

"And?"

"And then Victor Adkins comes in my door in end-stage life impairment. So, tell me what you see in that house."

Murphy looked. "The house."

"Yep."

"Secondhand furniture. Lots of fireman damage. No reason to be surprised that Victor didn't get out of that alive."

"The curtain rods," she said without pointing. "Tell me how they look to you."

Murphy felt that first flutter of disquiet. Old warning bells that should have gone off the minute he'd stepped into this yard. "The curtain rods?" he echoed, finally turning to look.

He found them right where they should have been, above three of the windows, one with shreds of an awful brown-plaid curtain dangling from it. As for the rods, there was nothing noteworthy about them. They were singed and sooty, but basically intact. "They look fine. Why?"

"See what I mean?"

"No."

She waved a hand in the direction of the rods. "A little lesson I learned at death investigator's camp. Fires go up."

"I learned that one in Boy Scouts."

She nodded, not particularly insulted. "And since a fire goes straight up across the ceiling and then works its way back down the wall with a usual temperature variance of almost a thousand degrees between top and bottom, it follows that a curtain rod would get hot before the curtains that hang down from it, right?"

Murphy kept looking. He even pulled out a cigarette to help him think. "Okay."

She nodded. "And if the rod heated up before the curtains caught fire, the weight of the curtains would have pulled the rod down so that as it heated up to the point of being malleable, it would bow in the center. Especially those curtains. I checked. Victor had heavy curtains everywhere to keep out light so he could sleep during the day."

Murphy stopped halfway through his first drag of smoke, now sure he felt bad. "All the rods are perfectly straight."

"Which means that there were no curtains left to pull them down by the time they heated up."

"The curtains burned first," Murphy finished, "because an accelerant was used across the floor."

"You should go into forensics, Murphy. You're a natural."

"The arson guys said it was badly stored kerosene."

"They used the words 'spontaneous combustion,'" she said. "Problem is, hydrocarbons are completely incapable of spontaneous combustion. Absolutely, positively. Common mistake to make, evidently. Not such a common mistake, however, is ignoring the smell of kerosene in the front hallway when it supposedly combusted in the garage. Can I have a cigarette?"

"You smoke?"

"Only when I'm not going to be home. My dad can smell it on me at twenty feet and it makes him nuts."

Murphy pulled out his pack and shook one out for her. Oddly enough, she looked like a furtive high schooler when she lit it. It made Murphy think of the first time he'd moved away from home and the bottle of bourbon he'd gone through in two days just because he could.

"So, what are you going to do?" he asked her.

"I don't know. What are you gonna do?"

Finally, Murphy laughed. "We do seem to be the only two gunslingers left in Dodge."

She took a second to inhale her cigarette, eyes closed, entire body wrapped around it as if making it a high-contact sport. Murphy watched her and wished for the first time in a very long time that he had the energy left to court that kind of disaster. But he was much too old and she still loved the sound of sirens.

"You and I seem to be holding up both ends of this problem," she said, straightening, with a half-finished cigarette between her first two fingers. "Somebody calls you about some murders that I'm supposed to know something about, and we get threatened. We see the shooting that Victor comes asking us about, and then Victor gets ashed. I just want you to know right now that if anything happens to me, I'm signing responsibility for my father and my six-year-old over to you."

"She's six?"

"And she has an imaginary playmate and a pet chameleon. Do you like tea parties?"

"I get the message."

"Still . . ." She sighed again.

Murphy ground out his cigarette butt on the table and field-stripped it. "It is a question," he admitted. "And questions make me curious."

"Curious is a good word."

"And you must have it worse than I do. You're trained to act."

"There is that."

"And you still *like* to act."

She just grinned, which made Murphy taste ashes in his mouth.

They sat for a while longer, and Murphy wondered why he was doing this. Why he was going to get involved. He didn't want the story. He didn't want Sherilee to find out what he was digging into and expect him to investigate everything that made her mad. He didn't want the hassle and pressure, just to find out once again that nobody really wanted to know about what he'd unearthed.

Because they wouldn't. Nobody did, really. Bad news upset people and good news bored them. Scandals just demanded attention, and nobody had any left after a hard day in the rat race and a harder night on the riverboats.

But the only thing Murphy hated more than exerting himself was leaving a question unanswered. Like why a policeman asking the wrong questions about an attempted murder nobody else had questioned had now been murdered himself. And why the only person who had picked up on it was an out-of-town nurse.

"You really went to death investigator's camp?"

She dropped her chin back into her hands. "I am a certified forensic nurse, trained in the investigation and prevention of all manner of violence against persons. Right now, that seems to translate into nothing more than a license to lose sleep, friends, and gainful employ."

"Handy if you need to investigate a murder, though."

"Bite your tongue."

"If you were going to investigate a murder, what would you do?"

She finished the cigarette and flipped it into the wreckage of the house with practiced fingers. "Annoy the coroner some more. Talk to some friends in arson, then check back with the police and fire puppies here. Make a general nuisance of myself."

"Fire puppies?"

This time her smile was a little easier. "Technical term. Arson squads with more energy than experience who end up getting wagged by the ass."

"Uh-huh." Murphy looked at her a minute. An adrenaline junkie. A young, hungry adrenaline junkie with an unbusted cherry of a sense of honor and blue eyes the size of dinner plates. She could damn well be more exhausting than Sherilee, given the chance.

But then, Sherilee didn't have any old ghosts in her smile. Timmie Leary did. Old ghosts and a refreshingly honest hint of rage. And Murphy could only hope that that combination would make all the difference.

"I'll tell you what," he finally offered, already regretting the impulse. "What if we come at it from different sides? You check into the fire, and I'll look into the big picture."

"The big picture."

"What an attempted shooting might have had to do with a mysterious phone call might have to do with Memorial Med Center."

"Ah."

"If you can get me Victor Adkins's social security number, I can also get you background information. You also might want to just listen around the hospital for a clue as to why we got contacted and why somebody tried to shoot up a fund-raiser."

She nodded absently. "Any ideas?"

"Alex Raymond," he said without hesitation.

She turned on him then, genuinely stunned. "Alex? Good God, why?"

Murphy considered another cigarette and decided against it. "Because he's perfect. Perfect people make me itch."

She laughed again, and it sounded a little lighter. "I hate to ruin your day, but Alex probably is perfect. I haven't even seen him get into a fight since he was twelve."

"He spent a few years away from home."

"So did Christ. Didn't make him a gang-banger. You want a motive for the shooting, my money's on cost-cutting and HMOs. One opinion I got was that certain white citizens of Puckett objected to a certain black administrator firing friends."

She made Murphy want to laugh again. They were sitting behind a burned-out house planning to make their lives unnecessarily complicated, and she was making him look forward to it. Damn her.

"All right, then," he conceded. "The hospital death rate. If you'll casually look into the specifics, I'll look into Price University. Good enough?"

She straightened and raked both hands through her hair, which just made it stand up. Then she took another considered look at the house. "The first thing I have to do," she said, "is challenge the accepted perception of what is or is not arson."

At the house just east of Victor's a curtain lifted in what was probably the kitchen, and then fell back into place again. Which meant that if the neighbor was active as well as nosy, Murphy and his accomplice had about five more minutes of quiet before a cruiser showed up to evict them from their perch.

"There is one more thing," Murphy said. "How do you think Billy Mayfield's involved?"

Timmie's face immediately clouded over. "Oh, God. Billy."

"You do think he was murdered, don't you?"

No answer. No eye contact.

"He have something to do with the hospital?"

For the first time since Murphy had spotted her, Timmie Leary-Parker turned to take a considered look at him. Murphy noticed how sunken her eyes had gotten. How she seemed to be a little puffy and discolored in places. She also had a splint on her little finger. She'd been a lot busier this week than he had, that was for sure.

"You know," she said, oddly enough brightening. "I didn't even think of that. I don't have a clue what he did. But it would make sense. You know, if he knew Victor, which he probably did. Their wives worked together. Maybe he worked there at some time. Maybe he was a patient."

"He was. You killed him."

"*I* didn't kill him," she retorted, stiff with outrage. "Somebody else did."

"You gonna tell me about it?"

After his last meeting with her, Murphy expected an argument. What he got was a chagrined smile.

"Yeah, I guess I am."

"And then you can get his social security number, too."

She told him about it. Murphy probably could have easily lived the rest of his life without learning about the interesting connection between Billy Mayfield and the Puckett County coroner. He probably would have lived a happier, albeit more boring, life if he hadn't heard the word "poison."

But once she said it, she couldn't take it back. And Murphy knew that if nothing else, he at least had to salve his curiosity. And so, with that in mind, he sent Timmie Leary-Parker back out into the world of hospitals to check on the results of Victor Adkins's autopsy, and he headed for the phone.

"Price University?" Pete Mitchell asked the next day over lunch. "You think Price University is doing something nefarious?"

Murphy took a second to sample his chili before answering. God, it had been a hundred years since he'd eaten at Crown Candy. A lifetime ago when he'd worked for the *St. Louis Post-Dispatch*. He'd been fired from that job, too, of course. Not for being a drunk or a drug addict. Nobody much cared as long as he got his stories in. Cops had driven him home from cop bars and crime scenes, and editors had shrugged off complaints. Like a star athlete with a penchant for punching girlfriends, Murphy had been immune as long as he'd produced. And he'd produced one of his Pulitzers for the paper. It wasn't until he'd been caught with his pants down by a TV crew that they'd finally shown him the door. That had been about eight years ago.

Pete Mitchell had worked under him then, the junior woodchuck assigned to keep him out of major trouble. Now balding and paunched and content, Pete edited the business section. And instead of inviting Murphy to Missouri Bar and Grill, where the print news guys really hung out, he'd suggested Crown Candy, one of the few standing buildings in the wasteland that had become north St. Louis, where TV camera trucks vied with police cruisers for parking, and the town's politics were discussed over chili and ice cream instead of scotch and cigar smoke.

So Murphy sucked down four-alarm beans under a high

stamped-tin roof and ticked off the aging, balding, uniformed faces he still recognized around the room, all the while fighting that old feeling of a visit from Christmas past.

"There's just some action going on out in Puckett, and Price seems to be involved," Murphy finally hedged.

Pete laughed so loud that half the room turned. "You're lyin' like a dog. But that's okay, because I still owe you for the Growth and Commerce Association story."

"And Price?"

Pete went back to his sandwich. "Nothing. Not a whisper of distress. The university is in the top ten, which is crowding the other med schools in town, and the hospital seems solid. Too many beds, but working hard to stay a contender."

Murphy ate some more chili. He might have had lots of problems, but his stomach had never been one. It obviously still wasn't. "And Memorial?"

Pete paused, belched, and waited, as if expecting applause. "A master stroke." Waving his sandwich at Murphy like a soggy wand, Pete grinned. "Every hospital in town has been layin' odds on where the next big population shift is gonna happen. Barnes went into St. Charles, St. John's into Washington, and Price bet on Puckett. The word on the big Monopoly board is still out on who's going to win, but I'm betting on Price. Not only the population, but the population with expendable cash. Price is also giving every sign that they believe it hard, too."

"How?"

"Feasibility studies. Busy real estate lawyers. Spending the money to bring in a hotshot like Paul Landry and then stuffing him out in Memorial instead of the university hospital itself."

Murphy forgot his chili. "Landry, huh? Johnnie Cochran clone with a degree in corporatespeak?"

"The very same."

The man standing right next to Alex Raymond when the shots had been fired. The one Timmie had said made white folks nervous.

"He's hot, huh?"

"Specializes in hospital turnarounds. He just came off a big job in Dayton, where they wanted to give him the keys to the city and an armed escort out of town. Within another four months, I guarantee you'll see a solid business where a charitable hospital once stood."

"Definitely a man of the nineties."

"My own considered opinion is that Price set him up out there to lay the way for the big shift in Price services. I figure that in another ten years the only thing left of Price in the city is gonna be clinics for the med students to practice on. The real money-making services are going to be out in beautiful, bucolic Puckett."

"Like Restcrest."

Pete nodded happily. "Perfect example. I mean, they set that place up as the Temple of Aging. Did everything but cement Mother Teresa into the cornerstone. It is, my son, the way of the future, and Price is preparing itself to own the market."

Murphy was so out of practice that it took him a good few minutes to recognize his reaction. Itchy. Restless, like somebody was pumping electricity through him, right below his skin.

Instinct.

For a second he forgot the hum of conversation in the echoing room. He lost the clink of china and the almost constant whine of sirens beyond the green screen door. He was thinking of big business. Big money. Big power. Big risk.

Money and power and sex. Murphy's trinity of motivation.

The kind of motivation that could lead to murder.

He damn near smiled. "And Alex Raymond?" he asked.

Pete picked a stray shred of lettuce off his white shirtfront. "Mother Teresa's twin brother," he said. "I don't know what you want to hear, but the guy is beloved. He and his partner are really making advances in Alzheimer's research. The partner's a geek of the first order, but like a good Frankenstein, he stays in the lab. Alex Raymond pats hands and fights governments for medical breakthroughs."

Murphy did look at Pete then, and it was to see a familiar edge in the editor's eyes. A faint reflection of old reporter's lusts, which both of them had long since used up and washed away.

A perfect man in a perfect hospital doing good works. Nothing a reporter distrusted more.

"You'll keep an eye out for me?" Murphy asked.

"For like considerations."

This time Murphy gave Pete the kind of smile that would once have sent half the people in that room running for cover. "I do have a small one. Save it up for when you need it."

Pete's leaned forward. "Yes?"

"Paul Landry. Have you heard his 'poor marine wounded in a foreign war' story?"

"The beginning of his long and illustrious career as a savior of hospitals, from what I hear."

Murphy nodded as he finished the last of his chili and let his spoon clatter into the bowl. "You might want to check to be sure, but my guess is that he missed a paragraph in his military history. He put himself in Chu Lai about three years after the marines had gone."

Pete damn near held his breath. "You're sure?"

"That's what I heard him say. My guess is that he hasn't been any closer to Vietnam than the *Time-Life* series."

Pete wasn't glowing anymore. He was laughing. "You want some help on the rest of the story?" he asked. "Like old times?"

Murphy was touched. There hadn't been any old times. By the time Pete had signed on, Murphy's ship had been sinking fast. All Pete had been able to do was hold his coat and the door.

"Thanks, Pete," he acknowledged. "I'll let you know. Right now, though, I have somebody helping me. And, unless I'm mistaken, she is already, even as we speak, doing undercover work right inside the hospital itself."

TIMMIE WASN'T AT THE HOSPITAL. SHE WAS AT ANOTHER FUNERAL. Victor Adkins was being laid to rest in the same cemetery as Billy Mayfield, and the sense of déjà vu was just a little too intense.

The good news was that at least Timmie didn't feel nearly as bad about it. Not that she was thrilled to be burying Victor. Victor didn't deserve to die any more than Billy had, no matter what the SSS had to say about it. But at least this time Timmie didn't have to wade through a morass of ambivalence on the way to the services.

There was no question about the cause of death. Victor had died from smoke inhalation and thermal injuries to the bronchial tree. Hot smoke and gases, just like Timmie had told Murphy out in Victor's backyard the day before. Definitely not a survivable diagnosis. ETOH level of 350 mg/dL, which meant that Victor had drunk himself into a coma and slept right through the working smoke alarm, the flames, and the searing heat that had, in effect, melted his lungs and airway. Which also meant that the murderer had at least had the decency to anesthetize him before burning him to death.

Also no question. Victor had been murdered. Timmie was sure

the fire had been set, which meant that Victor had probably been deliberately . . . what, drunked? Tanked up? Intoxicated with intent? In any case, premeditated to death.

If Timmie could have gotten the fire puppies to pay more attention to her, she might at least have gotten them to send someone to Victor's neighborhood to ask about recent Greeks bearing beer. But her second contact with them had been as productive as her first. Fire puppies did not appreciate being told their jobs by as-yet-unknown nurses.

She'd also spent a solid twenty seconds considering a phone call to Van Adder, who had demanded primary jurisdiction as coroner on Victor's case. But if the fire puppies had trouble talking to a nurse, Timmie could well imagine Van Adder's attitude.

At least this time she wasn't out there staring into the sun all by herself. Murphy listened. Murphy believed. Murphy would at least help her solve the puzzle, which was enough right there to propel her out the door this morning with a smile on her face.

Murphy also had the potential of being a real predicament for her on an entirely different level. Murphy was sexy, and Murphy was sharp, and Murphy was walking the end of the same road she was on, which made him a heck of a conversational partner in a town without many. And while Timmie was into stage four of divorce, she wasn't all that far from three, which meant that her hormones still tended to rampage like juveniles.

But Timmie knew better than most that hormones weren't enough for anything but a stockpile of batteries or a pile of regrets. Murphy might hold down a job. He might even smile on occasion so that she could see that cute dimple of his, but he still walked with that brittle "I haven't been out long" air Timmie knew much too well and hated far too much. She knew a dead-end street when she saw one, and Murphy was the poster child for dead-end streets, no matter what Timmie wanted.

But that was a problem for another day. Today, her job was to watch and see if anything of interest happened at the funeral.

And to that end, the other difference. Today Timmie was the one driving Cindy, Ellen, and Mattie in her battered old Peugeot as they followed the procession up toward the Eternal Rest Chapel.

"You sure we shouldn't just bury this thing along with Victor?" Cindy demanded from the backseat as the car coughed into a gear change.

"I'll have you know that old Cyrano here got Meghan and me all the way from L.A. to Baltimore in four days to see Cal Ripken break Lou Gehrig's record at Camden Yards," Timmie said proudly as she patted the car's cracked and faded dashboard, which carried not only a statue of the Virgin Mary, but St. Christopher, St. Patrick, and St. Jude, who as patron saint of the impossible was Timmie's most important talisman against automobile decrepitude.

"Cyrano?" Ellen asked.

Timmie grinned. "Ugly but faithful. A heroic car with many good, unnoticed qualities."

"You really drove all the way cross-country just to see some skinny white boy play baseball?" Mattie asked.

Timmie smiled at the memory of hot dogs and fireworks and a lone man trotting all the way around a stadium to say thank you. It had almost restored her faith in the game. In the memories she'd hoarded since childhood of perfect summer days and her father bent way over her so she could smell Old Spice and Lucky Strikes as he taught her to keep score.

"Some things are worth a little extra effort," she said.

"Not baseball," Mattie assured her. "But you might think of putting a little time in on the air filter on this thing."

"I've been busy," Timmie said.

"I drove cross-country once," Cindy offered. "I decided to go surfing and just took off. Had a great weekend in San Diego with a bisexual biker named Jose."

"Did you get your father taken care of?" Ellen asked Timmie.

Timmie just nodded and kept her attention on the cop car in front of her. They'd had a good turnout for Victor. Police had shown up from twenty or so municipalities and the highway patrol to form the procession that snaked through the often-repaired cemetery lanes, and the last thing Timmie needed to do was ram old Cyrano's nose into the ass end of a cop car.

"Alex Raymond really got him into Restcrest?" Cindy asked, leaning forward between the seats.

"This morning."

Timmie had badgered her father to get dressed. She'd lied to him about where they were going. She'd strong-armed him from the car and then walked away from him when he'd pleaded with her to tell him why she was abandoning him to strangers.

He was going to be happy there, the staff had kept assuring her. He was going to be busy and active. They kept patting her hand when they said it the same way she'd patted her father's when she'd promised he could come home again if he'd just stay at Restcrest for now. He'd sobbed as she'd left. Even though she'd done it before, even though she knew this time was really for the best, Timmie had cried all the way home.

But that wasn't something she was going to think about right now, either.

"I think he likes you," Ellen offered.

Timmie looked away from the procession for a split second to check Ellen's passive face in the mirror. "Who?"

"Alex Raymond. Why else would he go out of his way for your father like that?"

Timmie's laugh was abrupt. "Because he's a nice guy?"

"Of course he's a nice guy. But there's a waiting list for every one of those beds."

"And just what would he see in her he doesn't see in me?" Cindy demanded, damn near sitting on the stick shift. "I can tie a cherry stem with my tongue."

"And my girl here can quote Tennyson and Shakespeare," Mattie said, arms across chest where she was shoehorned into the other front seat. "Whatchyou got to top that?"

Cindy's smile was rapacious. "The *Kama Sutra*."

" 'The pleasure is momentary,' " Timmie quoted instinctively, " 'the position ridiculous, and the expense damnable.' "

"Tennyson or Shakespeare?" Ellen asked with a grin.

"Lord Chesterton."

"He never dated *me*," Cindy assured them all.

"He the only one," Mattie retorted.

"You really want the truth, I think it was my contribution got your father in," Cindy offered with another big, secretive smile. "I laid it all out for you, ya know."

"I'm sure you did, Cindy," Timmie agreed.

"You've been known to lay it all out for ice cream and a bad movie," Mattie retorted.

"Not this time," Cindy assured her with a pat to her arm. "This time it's love."

"Uh-huh."

The procession was slowing to a final stop. Taillights flickered like before, doors opened. Men in uniforms spilled from sedans and lifted hats to heads with gloved hands. It was time to watch the crowd and see if anything shook free.

"It reminds me . . ." Cindy said inevitably.

"We're not going to the chapel again, are we?" Ellen said in a faint voice.

"No," Timmie assured her, pulling to a careful stop behind a Puckett cop car and yanking on the brake. "Up by the green tent."

Just another little irony in life. Billy had ended up ashes, and Victor, who was already ashes, was going to take up ground space with a bronze casket. Go figure.

Billy. Timmie had to ask about Billy, how he might have known Victor. A lot of the same people had showed up at his funeral, but Timmie wasn't sure whether that was because there was a connection or just because this was a small town.

Up by the limo, Timmie saw Barb bending to adjust the coat on her youngest daughter. Barb looked no different than usual, cool, composed, deceptively relaxed. No one who saw her take that fragile little girl into her huge arms and gently guide her other children toward the grave site would have recognized her two nights earlier when the red-headed detective had identified the disaster on their table as Victor.

She'd laughed. Loud. High. Hard. With astonished tears in her eyes, although no one could have said whether she'd been astonished at Victor's appearance or her own reaction. Dr. Chang had taken over from that point and they'd at least managed to get Victor as far as a burn unit in St. Louis before he died.

"I hope this isn't going to become a regularly scheduled event," Timmie announced as they all collected purses and prepared to decamp. "I like cemeteries about as much as I like working the ortho ward in winter."

" 'Specially *this* cemetery," Ellen agreed heartily.

"There has to be one more," Cindy allowed as she tugged her micro Lycra skirt a millimeter lower over pencil-thin thighs. "Everything comes in threes, ya know. Maybe we should start drawing names from a hat."

"This isn't a game," Ellen retorted as hotly as Ellen knew how.

Halfway out of the car, Timmie turned to see Ellen sitting as stiffly as a hurt child. Cindy must have seen it, too. Her own expression wilted and she laid a hand on Ellen's knee. "I'm sorry," she apologized. "You're right. It's not a game at all."

Ellen, being Ellen, patted back. "It's okay, Cindy," she said gently. "I know you didn't mean it that way. You've been such a good a friend these last few days."

"My Johnny wasn't perfect, either," Cindy said, her voice soft and almost as hurt as Ellen's. "You want the honest truth, he hit me sometimes. It didn't mean I didn't miss him. It didn't mean that I didn't want to die right along with him."

"I know," Ellen soothed, wrapping her arms around the other woman. "I know."

Timmie shot Mattie a look over the top of the car. Mattie just rolled her eyes. Amazing, Timmie decided. Ellen comforting Cindy. But then, maybe that was what Ellen needed right now.

"Excuse me, Ms. Leary?"

Timmie had just bent over to release the driver's seat so Ellen could get out. She straightened instead at the sound of the familiar voice.

"Yes?" She turned before she'd gotten her balance, and almost lost it again.

The redheaded detective. Standing in the middle of the cemetery drive as if he'd been waiting for her.

"Yes?" she asked again, forgetting Ellen completely.

People passed the two of them like a stream sweeping past rocks, but the detective didn't budge. He was medium height, but wide. Solid. Unsmiling, as if he weren't given to it, not as if it had been taken away. Kuppenheimer suit and Lenscrafters steel-rimmed glasses, regulation-cut mustache and suspicious brown eyes.

"I'd like to talk to you," he said.

Timmie actually laughed. "Now?"

"Yes, ma'am."

"Timmie?" Ellen asked, still caught.

Chagrined, Timmie spun around and released the seat. "My name is Leary-Parker."

He didn't answer. He didn't move. Neither, once they managed to get out of the car, did Cindy, Mattie, or Ellen. The rest of the procession, however, was picking its way around tombstones and tree roots to get to the green tent.

Finally Timmie waved her friends on. "Go ahead. I'll be there in a minute."

"You sure?" Mattie asked in her most intimidating mode.

Timmie grinned. "Yeah."

"All right," she conceded. "Just remind that man who he has to come see, he ever gets hisself shot." And then she turned and led everybody else off.

Timmie turned back to the cop. He didn't seem amused by Mattie's threat. On the other hand, he didn't seem upset by it, either.

"And you are?" Timmie prodded him.

"Detective Sergeant Bernard Micklind. You a friend of Victor's, were you?"

"A friend of his wife. Why? Was I headed to the wrong side of the aisle?"

For just a second, Sergeant Detective Micklind let his gaze drift up the hill to where the ranks were forming up for the service. Then he was right back with Timmie.

"You've been asking questions. Talking to the medical examiner up in St. Louis and the arson investigator here."

"Yes, I have."

He seemed surprised by her honesty. "Why?"

"Several reasons. I knew the St. Louis ME had done Victor's post, and I wanted to make sure Victor's death wasn't preventable in our ER. And, as I tried to explain to your arson investigator, I think that fire was set. I thought he should know."

Actually, he'd laughed. Kind of the way Van Adder had when Timmie had mentioned the words "forensic nurse." Don't teach a grandmother to suck eggs, the fire puppy had told her, and then hung up. Interesting that a cop now showed interest.

"But you said you're a friend of his wife," the officer said, not relaxing his posture a millimeter.

Timmie did her best to keep her patience. "Even assholes don't deserve to end up charbroiled."

A common theme lately, she thought blackly.

"He was a good cop," Micklind retorted finally, with some emotion.

Up on the hill the preacher opened his book and asked the gathering to pray along. Timmie considered the taut line of officers who had come in their off hours in uniform when it hadn't been necessary. She thought of Micklind's instinctive defense.

"I'm sorry," she said, relenting. "You're probably right. Just 'cause he was a lousy husband doesn't mean he was a bad cop. It also isn't reason enough for me to overlook a possible murder. I thought something was wrong, so I told somebody. I wasn't aware that was an indictable offense."

"Not indictable. Just . . . complicating. We're investigating the fire, Ms. Leary. We'd prefer you didn't interfere."

Timmie would have felt relieved if this guy didn't still seem so evasive. There was a message here, and she wasn't getting it just yet. "So you do think it was arson?"

"The file isn't closed."

"Uh-huh. Well, that's good. I'm glad. I don't suppose you want to tell me if you have a suspect."

He didn't. It didn't matter. Timmie saw it by the way his attention drifted back uphill as surely as if he'd pointed a finger square at Barb's back. "We're looking into that."

Timmie's jaw dropped. "Are you nuts? Barb couldn't have done anything like that! You saw how she reacted when she found out that was Victor. My God, she was there when he came in!"

"She wasn't when the fire started."

Timmie opened her mouth to argue. She couldn't. He was right. Barb had walked in right after the call had come through.

But Barb couldn't have committed murder. Especially not that murder. Because if Barb had, Timmie would have to go back to suspecting Ellen, too, and Timmie simply couldn't stand that. Not Ellen, with her quiet comforts and gentle words. Not either of them.

"No," Timmie said with a definite shake of her head. "It's something to do with the shooting he was investigating. I'm sure of it."

Micklind gave her a stone-faced cop glare. "Shooting? What shooting?"

"At the horse show."

"Don't be ridiculous. He wasn't investigating any shooting. Vic was a patrol sergeant, not a detective."

"Of course he . . ." It took that long for it to sink in.

Micklind was standing there staring at her as if she'd told him Victor had set the fire himself. Blank, solid, noncomprehension. Micklind was telling the truth. He didn't have a clue that Victor had been making the rounds.

Suddenly everything shifted again. Timmie had just assumed that Victor had come in an official capacity, there to fill out forms until the problem went away or was forgotten. But he'd been serious. He'd also been working outside the loop.

Which meant what? Which meant she should *do* what?

"Victor *was* asking questions," Timmie insisted deliberately. "He talked to Daniel Murphy and me. He even showed Mr. Murphy some pictures. Doesn't that even interest you, when you know the fire that killed him was probably set?"

Micklind just stood there as if this weren't the biggest surprise of the day. Behind Timmie the crowd responded to a prayer in hushed tones. A breeze cut through the leaves in the mature trees that survived in the older part of the cemetery. Nearby, a maintenance worker was swinging one of those big tractor-mowers in around tombstones as if it were a timed obstacle course.

And Timmie stood there thinking she should ask something. Well, hell, she thought. She was trained to question victims, survivors, perpetrators. She wasn't trained to grill cops. Especially cops who might be involved somehow. What the hell was she supposed to do?

"Why do you think Victor was investigating the shooting on his own?" she asked.

Micklind froze completely. Wrong question first time out. Oh, what the hell. She might as well go for it.

"Are *you* investigating the shooting at the horse show?"

Wrong again. Now he was glaring.

"Is *anybody* investigating the shooting?"

"It's an ongoing investigation," he recited dutifully.

Timmie laughed. "Don't insult my intelligence, Detective. Just tell me why nobody wants to know any more. Is it because you're pretty sure it was a one-time deal and you don't want to hurt the person involved for making a stupid decision in a moment of stress, or is it something else?"

Now he sighed. "It's nothing, Ms. Leary. This might be a lot for an overeducated bedpan handler from L.A. to understand, but we take care of our own here. And we're taking care of it."

"If you were," she retorted, cheeks hot, "don't you think Victor would have left it alone?"

Another SSS wrap party at the Rebel Yell. Another several rounds of drinks, fueled by Cindy's close encounter with another cop funeral and Ellen's with the Eternal Rest cemetery. Alex showed up again for one drink and spent the time asking Timmie what she thought of Restcrest. Barb arrived for the first toast. Calm, collected, pretty in her testifying duds, as she called the sharp red suit she said made her look like a brewery wagon. Timmie drank and laughed and recited the best of her father's lines and wished she were home with a pencil, ruler, and sheet of paper so she could graph out what little information she had.

Micklind had clammed up like a pregnant teen. And by the time Timmie had made it up the hill to watch the rest of the service, the service had been heading back down the hill.

She did ask Alex if he'd heard anything more about the shooting investigation, only to be met by bland indifference. She asked the general crowd what they'd heard from Van Adder, only to be booed. She sipped her soda and watched people having a wonderful time and decided that she shouldn't have listened to Murphy after all. If she hadn't, maybe she could enjoy her first afternoon out without having to worry about anything more than what she was going to fix Meghan for dinner. As it was, she spent it watching everyone for ulterior motives and deciding that she was the worst detective since Clouseau because she didn't see a one.

"I didn't come home with you to play another game o' Clue," Mattie griped as the two of them closed Cyrano into the detached garage at the side of Timmie's house an hour later.

"They think Barb killed Victor," Timmie argued, her keys jangling in her hand as she turned back toward the front walk. "Don't you think that's reason enough to ask questions?"

It was getting on toward three. Meghan was due home from school, and traffic had picked up on Timmie's block. The sun was losing out to a thin layer of clouds, and the wind seemed to whip around at ankle level. Timmie shivered with the as-yet-unaccustomed chill.

"Why bother me with it?" Mattie demanded.

"Because I trust you. Because you watch everything and keep your mouth shut. Because you're not sleeping with Van Adder."

Mattie did everything but spit on her fingers. "Don't even go there, girlfriend. I got nightmares enough as it is."

Timmie laughed, her attention on separating her door key as they walked. "I'm telling you, Mattie. There have been two murders and one attempted murder that nobody's talking about, and I just don't think it's all a silly coincidence."

"Why not?" Mattie demanded, yanking off her gold lamé church hat as if this were a statement itself. "People get murdered all the time where I grew up. Shoot, girl, you wouldn't'a had a job in Los Angeles if people didn't get capped on a regular basis. Why you got a problem with this?"

"Because they suspect Barb. Now, if they're right, let me know and I'll shut up. But if they're not, and there isn't any connection between Billy and Victor that could explain what I'm finding, then Barb goes to the head of the suspect pool." Timmie stopped, agitated all over again. "And right behind her in line might just be Ellen, and do you really want to see her have to face that Micklind guy?"

Mattie stood stock-still in front of her, eyes narrow, stance aggressive, chins quivering with frustration as she made up her mind. "The only time I know Billy met Victor was when Victor arrested him for breaking a restraining order. Memory serves, Victor broke a few things hisself. Now, you happy?"

"They didn't work together?"

"God, no."

"Billy didn't work at the hospital?"

"Billy didn't work noplace. Not regular. He gambled to get his support payments. Made Ellen crazy."

Timmie lifted a finger in exception. "Don't say that."

Mattie scowled. "You way too serious, girl."

Timmie snorted and turned for the house. "So was whoever turned Victor into a minute steak."

She had thought she would enjoy walking back into her house. Her empty house. Her silent, undemanding house that might still be a mess on a scale with a carnival teardown, but at least wouldn't pop out surprises like old men waving pistols.

Somehow it didn't work. Timmie had just put her foot on the first step to the porch when it hit. Smack, right in the face, sucking out her breath like a force field. The depression. The realization that it all waited in that house, no matter what she wanted. Even though her father wasn't going to be waiting for her. *Because* he wasn't going to be waiting for her. Mattie walked right up the steps, but Timmie faltered to a halt out there in the cold sunshine trying to think how she could put it off.

Piles and stacks and mountains of trash. The smell of mold and memories. The dim recesses of responsibility. And Timmie, in her knee-jerk reaction, wanted out. Away. Free. Even though she knew she couldn't.

"Girl, you all right?"

"Oh, I'm fine, Mattie." Still she didn't move. "I mean, what could be wrong? I have my little girl, a job, an intriguing puzzle to solve that actually involves forensics, and my father neatly tucked away out of sight where I don't have to see what a waste product he's become."

Only Mattie could laugh and get away with it. "Shit, girl," she retorted, leaning her bulk against the porch support. "You gonna spend all day whinin', forget this party."

Timmie managed a grin. Then she shrugged, a completely ineffectual gesture. "I didn't want to do that to that old man."

"He too much for you," Mattie said. "Get over it. You got enough to worry about without beatin' youself up 'bout that."

Her view taken up with the pretty brick and white-wood house, Timmie sighed. "I thought I'd feel better, that's all."

"Not till the day you die," Mattie assured her blithely.

And made her laugh. Timmie heard the car pull up behind her, but didn't pay any attention as she re-slung her purse and headed up the steps. "Okay, then," she said, opening the screen door. "You notice anything different at the hospital?"

Right beside her, Mattie laughed. "Besides a new administration, all those goddamn HMOs to memorize, and a new computer keeps goin' down when we need it? Something else?"

"Something that would make somebody think that our death rate has suddenly gone up."

"Sure it has," Mattie said, waving her hat at the question as if it were an annoying insect. "We seein' more people, too. What's you point?"

"Ms. Leary-Parker?"

A car door slammed. Obviously a connection with the voice.

"Yeah?" Timmie didn't bother to turn from where she was opening the front door.

"Timothy Ann Leary-Parker?"

This time she turned.

So did Mattie. "Oh, no." She groaned. "Not again."

Timmie made it around just in time to recognize the young man who was loping up her steps.

"No!" she protested, hands up in instinctive defense. She probably even cringed back in horror. He never flinched. Never stopped smiling. He just slid a rectangle of folded paper in between her upraised fingers and wished her a good day.

And Timmie was left standing on her porch with a summons in her hand.

"Uh-oh," was all Mattie said.

Timmie stared at the paper with the great seal of Missouri on it. She started to laugh.

"What are you gonna do?" Mattie asked.

Timmie knew perfectly well how terrifying her expression was. She was just glad Meghan wasn't here to see it.

"I think I know," she said, stuffing the paper away like an overdrawn notice, "just who the third husband should be."

And then, because it was the only thing she could do, she showed Mattie into the house and began asking her more questions about Billy Mayfield.

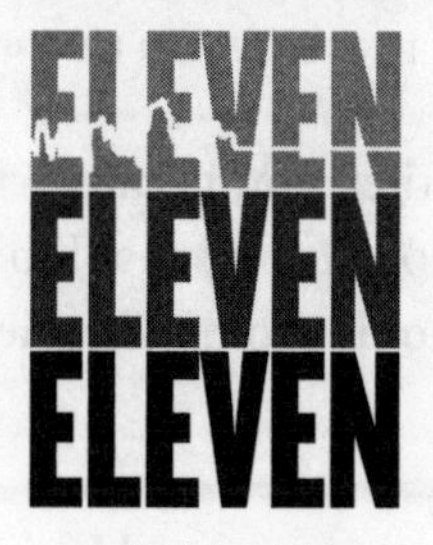

# ELEVEN

MATTIE DIDN'T KNOW ANYTHING ELSE ABOUT BILLY MAYFIELD. As was fairly common with swing shift hospital personnel, Mattie saw Ellen at work and at hospital functions and at the Rebel Yell after a tough shift. If family was called for at something, Ellen brought her kids. It was nothing anyone commented on. Victor hadn't made any more get-togethers than Billy had. After all, even spouses who understood the stress weren't necessarily enthusiatic about sitting through the war stories and whining.

All Mattie could really say for sure about Billy was that he'd been a drinker, a wife beater, and a general argument for birth control—unfortunately also not that unusual for the spouse of a caregiver like a nurse. Victor, on the other hand, had been a workaholic cop with an eye to skirts and a belief that nobody could get the job done as well as he. Not reason enough, Mattie agreed, to serve him up on a spit.

As for the hospital, Mattie hadn't noticed unexplained deaths any more than Timmie had, hadn't picked up any outrage over the grapevine other than the usual "administration sucks" variety, and couldn't come up with any suspects the police might like more than Barb.

Which was as far as they got, because right about then Meghan came slamming in the door from school to remind Timmie that on this, her first full day home from exile, her mother had promised her dinner and a movie.

Timmie got back to business after Meghan went to bed. Armed with hot tea, cold lead, and unlined paper, she decided to wade through the players and incidents in this mess and find out how they were connected.

Two murders, an attempted murder, and at least a dozen people, all needing to be positioned on the paper according to their relationships. Alex, Landry, Billy, Victor. The entire SSS. Van Adder and Mary Jane Arlington and even Murphy. Timmie and her dad and Micklind the red-headed detective. All having had some contact with at least one of the intended victims, and a possible motive to kill. Timmie figured that if she could find just one person who might connect to all the incidents, she might well not have to pull out the second chart, which would be the one about who would benefit the most from what had happened.

After forty-five minutes of work, Timmie stopped to consider what she'd come up with. A spider's web. A spider's web on acid. Good lord, she thought, considering the crisscrossing lines. The only person not potentially involved was her father, and that was only because she hadn't let him near scissors in a month.

But she'd been right. There was a figurative center. A single name from which all the other lines radiated. One person who was connected to everyone else.

Her.

Wonderful. She'd just solved both murders and the shooting. She'd done them all. Now if she could just figure out why.

It was probably as good a time as any for the phone to ring. Unfortunately, when Timmie reached over to the wall recession where the black rotary phone sat like a telecommunications Buddha, she knocked a mountain of newspapers over and almost ended up buried in baseball stats from 1965. Timmie and the phone and the papers all ended up on the floor, which raised a cloud of dust that smelled like newsprint and mothballs.

"What?" she snapped, rubbing her hip.

"You must be psychic. You're already in a bad mood, and you haven't even heard what I have for you."

Giving up the idea of trying to get back to the table, Timmie just dragged the phone right into her lap on the floor and reclined against newsprint. "That's not the way to encourage a continued conversation, Murphy," she assured him. "Especially since I've just found out that I'm the murderer."

Anyone else in town would have blustered. Ellen would have protested. Murphy didn't miss a beat. It was why Timmie liked talking to him. "Good. If it wasn't you, it was looking to get complicated, and I'm still not sure I want to expend that much energy."

"My thoughts exactly. You ready to take my exclusive confession?"

"Sure. Why'd you do it? Enquiring minds are certain to want to know."

She grinned. "Greed?"

"Neither of them had a dime that wasn't going to their wives."

"Revenge?"

"They didn't screw you. . . . Did they?"

"Watch it, newsboy."

His laugh was as dry as statistics. "And you realized you killed them when?"

"When I made a chart to show how everyone is connected to the murderer, and lo and behold, I was the only one who connected to everybody."

"If you want to escape the razor-sharp minds around here, I'd burn that thing. They'd probably hang you with it."

Timmie found herself grinning again. Damn it, she liked Murphy. Ellen thought he was too cynical. Mattie thought he was trouble. Barb thought he wasn't serious about staying sober. Timmie thought they were all right. But she liked him anyway. Listening to him, she could almost smell the smog.

"What did you find?" she asked.

"Billy Mayfield didn't work for the hospital."

"I know."

"He wasn't even ever sick enough to need admission there."

"Not even detox?"

"As my old friends on the circuit are so fond of saying, a person has to want treatment to get it. Billy evidently didn't want. He did, on several occasions, send his wife to the ER to be treated, however, which did not put him in good stead with her compatriots."

"The SSS had a wanted poster made up."

"The what?"

Timmie laughed. "Suckered Sisters Sorority. The honored society of duped women and family court frequenters."

"I don't suppose you have any male members."

"As a matter of fact, we do."

"Good. Fill me out an application. I have three clusters to my commendation."

Strike three, as it were. "Did you ever think you should just be a spectator, Murphy?" Timmie demanded. She resettled against the pile of news and felt something jab her in the small of the back.

"Some people just take longer than others to learn those important lessons in life, Leary. Now, back to Billy."

"It wasn't Ellen."

"I didn't say it was. But just for the sake of hypothesis, why couldn't it be her?"

"Because poison is sneaky. It's calculated. It's cold. If there are three adjectives no one in his right mind would use about Ellen, those are the ones."

"Even if the guy who was offed was still practicing conjugal batting practice without a license?"

"Even then. He's connected with the other murders somehow. But it's not through Ellen. I won't let it be through Ellen."

"He was a loser with a petty record and a gambling habit who couldn't hold down a job long enough to get a W-2. Which pretty much makes him a worthless waste of protoplasm."

Timmie fought the instinctive urge to defend. She closed her eyes so she couldn't see the musty piles of history in the room and answered him. "Careful with those some-all fallacies, Murphy. Maybe he saved a baby when he was young. Maybe he had dreams nobody else saw. Maybe he coulda been a contendah."

"Yeah. Right. Wanna hear about Victor now?"

Timmie reached around behind her and pulled out whatever had been jabbing her. A tin whistle, old and battered and rusty. Of course. "Snap military man," she answered, twirling the instrument through her fingers like a coin. "By-the-book cop, friend to all, especially those big-eyed blonds with mall hair and Lycra wardrobes down at the Rebel Yell."

"Up to his eyeballs in debt. Seems he liked those trucks with the oversized tires."

"And women."

"And powerboats."

"And women."

"Adds up."

"Did you know he was the only one asking questions about the shooting the other day?"

That got her a very satisfying pause that awarded her the ace. "Really."

Timmie smiled, just for herself. "The impression I get from the regular constabulary is that they're content that the perpetrator will go and sin no more. One of those 'a small town is like a family' things, ya know?"

Murphy considered that for a moment. "You're the one originally from the small town. What do you think?"

"I think I surprised the hell out of them when I told them Victor was still looking. Their suspect of choice for Victor's premeditated barbecue is Barbara."

"And you don't agree."

"No more than I agree that Ellen killed Billy."

"Dr. Atkins has just as much reason. I read about the court order for support. I know what she's making and what it's taking to raise her kids. One of them has Down syndrome and a heart defect, did you know?"

"Yep. But Barb worked her way through med school as a bouncer. You tell me. Would any bouncer you know be timid enough to drink a guy stupid and then set a fire?"

Another pause. A consideration. "You think she'd just club him like a baby seal?"

"I think she'd beat him till his eyes bled. If Barb wanted Victor to pay, she'd make him pay. She wouldn't make sure he missed the main event. Besides, if you keep looking, you'll find that that baby with Down syndrome was covered under Victor's health insurance. Which I'll bet isn't going to transfer now."

"All right, then, what?"

Timmie sighed, knowing just where she was heading. "We need to look at the hospital."

"I have been. Nothing stands out except that it's well run, it's planning to get bigger, and it's probably going to move its center of operations out to your neck of the woods, which is why Mr. Landry is there now."

Timmie looked at her chart. At her mess that had delusions of being a chart.

"Landry, who would lose a lot if something went wrong."

"He's a suit," Murphy protested. "Suits don't get personally involved. Besides, can you imagine anybody in Victor's neighborhood passing up the chance to tell everybody they knew that a black man had been at the scene of the crime a short time before the flames were spotted?"

"He could have sent somebody else."

"A stranger. I'll bet Victor didn't have many strangers at his house, either. Would anybody rat on Dr. Perfect, though?"

Timmie huffed impatiently. "You really are hung up on Alex as a suspect, aren't you?"

"I told you. He's too good to be true."

"Fine. Be that way. You look up Alex, and I'll check the death info at the hospital."

"And you'll reach Loch Lomond before me?"

"Play it any way you like. Just keep me informed."

"Okay. I'm going to see your father Tuesday."

Timmie opened her mouth to say something, only to shut it again. Let Murphy find out for himself. "That's nice."

"What?" Murphy demanded. "No warning? No 'Don't hurt that defenseless old man?' "

This time Timmie did laugh. "My father is many things, Murphy. Defenseless is not one of them. Did you know he was a Golden Gloves finalist?"

"Figures."

"Just remember that he telegraphs his roundhouse and you'll do fine."

"No other advice?"

"Don't make fun of the Cardinals or Ireland or you'll be picking your teeth off the floor."

Murphy snorted. "Baseball. It has to be baseball."

"You got a problem with baseball, Murphy?"

"You're not going to give me this 'metaphor for America' crap, are you?" he demanded. "I mean, for Christ's sake. It's a ball. It's a bat. It's boring."

"What'd your father take *you* to?" she retorted. "Ballet?"

"Opera."

Timmie snorted just as hard. "Oh, yeah, there's something on a par with hibernation. I've seen one opera. Woman dying of tuberculosis singing loud enough to wake hogs in Hawaii. Please, give me some credit. If that woman were dying of kidney stones or childbirth, then maybe all that noise'd make sense."

"You're a heathen, Leary."

"And you're a snob, Murphy. Try and sell my father the concept of opera. I dare you."

"Right after I prove Alex Raymond is behind those two murders."

"Can I put money on this? I could use the cash."

"And you think it's . . . "

Timmie sneaked another look at her chart. "I'll let you know."

Right after she figured out who'd benefit the most.

The first thing she did was find out who benefited the least. The next day, when she should have been calling trash-hauling places, she walked over to the hospital on the pretense of checking schedules. Then, when Angie McFadden left at exactly 11:45 for lunch, like she did every day of her supervisorial life, Timmie sneaked into her office and booted up her computer.

It took Timmie a full five minutes to pull down the hospital Morbidity and Mortality records, and another minute to print them out, all the while keeping a weather eye out for interruptions.

She needn't have worried. She had no more than hit the Print button when she heard a code called in trauma room one. Since the day-shift nurses tended to be the most placable, least aggressive of the staff, it was a sure bet they'd all be bunched up trying to figure out Dopamine doses for the foreseeable future.

So Timmie scanned numbers, names, and dates as they appeared on the serrated paper that unfolded from the machine and blessed the technology gods for the ability to collate information as it was gathered. Only a year's worth of names. Any more than that she'd have to pull from the county registrar's office. But what she found in Angie's computer was probably enough.

The numbers for the hospital were going up, most notably in the last four months. The good news was that none of them looked particularly confusing. A cancer here, a heart failure there. An auto accident with a three-for-one special. The ages tended to skew high, but that was to be expected. After all, it kind of went with the territory. You counts your birthdays, you takes your chances.

The important thing was that Timmie couldn't spot any discrepancies in the Restcrest dismissals. The numbers weren't in the least disproportionate to the rest of the hospital, maybe even a little lower. It meant that Murphy was going to be frustrated in his crusade against Alex. Those deaths were on somebody else's head, just as Timmie had known all along.

Timmie did notice that she was seeing "emergency department" on the dismissal unit line more frequently, but she didn't think that meant anything. Patients who died in the ER never saw more of the hospital than the morgue. They wouldn't have had any contact with the rest of the hospital, where the problems were alleged to have happened. And if the care was that shaky in the ER, Timmie would have picked up on it.

She did notice one other thing. The coroner didn't seem at all interested in the cases that should have been his. In the state of Missouri a coroner had jurisdiction on any patient who died within twenty-four hours of admission to a hospital, any patient who died after an invasive procedure, and any patient who'd been in law enforcement. And yet Timmie couldn't seem to find a "hold for coroner" anywhere.

But that was just the first pass. She'd take more time with it later, when she couldn't be caught. She was also going to make that appointment to have lunch in St. Charles with Conrad. Maybe he'd find that lack of coroner involvement more telling than she did. In the meantime, she let the printer do the work for her. And, while she was waiting, since there wasn't anything else going on . . .

It was probably illegal. It was certainly going to be boring. It could get Timmie tossed on her scrub-clad butt faster than slapping a rich drunk. It didn't matter. Armed with the password Angie had so thoughtfully taped to her corkboard, where she wouldn't forget it, Timmie checked the supervisor's E-mail.

Most of it involved territorial disputes. Housekeeping wasn't keeping Angie's trash empty enough. Central supply had misplaced another set of plastic instruments. Outpatient kept trying to use her rooms when they were full. Predictable, uninteresting.

Not so the notice from Paul Landry.

> Due to certain negative attention paid to the medical center in recent weeks, it has been deemed inadvisable to promote our newest policies to the public. No changes will be made in the timetable, which so far has been effective, but to prevent further problems and possible costly misunderstandings about what might seem like negative results, please refrain from discussing the matter with anyone until further notice. Any questions are to be directed to Mary Jane Arlington, my office.

"Well, well."

What policies, Timmie wondered? What results? Could she actually be this lucky to find something incriminating pointing right in the direction of an increased death rate from a bad policy? Could that undue publicity just mean Murphy snooping around, or could it be a corporate reference to the shooting?

The only changes Timmie had heard about so far had been the focus on increasing trauma response and the integration of Restcrest into the hospital system. And why would that cause problems? Just to be sure, though, she printed out the page with the memo on it to add to the M and M list.

Timmie also tried her best to work her way back into Angie's menu to see if she had a file of policy changes, but nothing showed up. She was so engrossed in her hunt that she almost missed the page that would have sent her straight to the bread lines.

". . . to the ER stat. Angie McFadden to the ER stat."

Timmie started to attention as if Angie had walked through the door herself. She had to get out of her office. The chain of command was inviolate in Angie's small world. Whatever they needed, they'd get from her here. And the only thing worse to her than ignoring the chain of command would be invading her privacy.

Timmie had just enough time to shove the printout under her jacket and flip off the computer midfunction. Then she slipped down the back hall as Angie lumbered up the front.

"We just got that CVP monitor," the supervisor was protesting to one of the day docs, who was hot on her heels. "Nobody knows how to use it."

"I do!" the doctor was yelling. "Now break it out!"

Timmie took a peek in trauma room one to find about six people in the process of scrambling out of the way of an arc of bright red blood that had pretty much soaked a portable X-ray unit. Two or three people were evidently trying to corral a pumping artery while everyone else played code team.

"Anybody ever see the movie *Giant*?" somebody was asking as they ducked again, like kids running through a sprinkler. "Don't you feel like James Dean when the well comes in?"

"Better cap this well fast," another voice suggested laconically, "or James isn't gonna have anything left to celebrate."

"Can't celebrate much without kidneys anyway," somebody else said.

A loose dialysis shunt, Timmie guessed. The permanent line must have accidentally been pulled free from the artery during the code. Standing beyond the bottom end of the cart, all Timmie could see besides scurrying staff were shriveled, yellow legs. Horny nails. Calloused, bunioned feet, one still dangling a fuzzy pink mule. They were coding an old lady with no kidneys. Made perfect sense.

"Do you think they'd like some help?" a soft baritone asked behind her.

Timmie almost dropped her papers in surprise. Alex had sneaked up on her. Well, not sneaked. He'd probably walked like a regular person, but when a body is holding illicitly obtained information that could endanger her employment, any arrival is a surprise.

"I don't know that it's going to make any difference," Timmie said with a quick smile.

Alex smiled back. "You working today?"

"Nope. Checking the schedule. Then I'll probably make a run up to see Dad."

His smile grew. "Did you bring the mementos?"

One of the first requests the staff had made. Representative items from Joe's past to put in a glass case at the door of his room so he'd always know which one was his. So he'd recognize his place, his past, maybe connect it to his present. Easily asked, terrible to fulfill.

"Uh . . . some of them," she hedged. "He's hidden anything important, since he's so sure somebody's stealing from him. I just found the house's papers in a shoe box in the garage last week."

"It's a very common thing," he assured her in a gentle voice, a hand to her arm. "And I know it's difficult. But it is important, Timmie. Especially pictures, all right? Sometimes those are the most important."

Photos. Yeah. There were no photos in her father's house, hidden or not. She'd have to go far afield for those. She really wished a signed baseball and an Irish flag were enough.

"How's he doing?" she asked.

"He's a strong man. It'll take him a little longer to settle in, I think."

Timmie's answering smile was wry. "You're a master at euphemism, Alex, but I know just what Dad's like."

He gave her a sheepish grin. "Force of habit. You're right, Timmie. Your dad's a challenge. But, oh, when he's lucid, it's all worth it. He's a great man, honey. I'm thrilled we can help."

Timmie wished with all her heart that she could tell Alex how he'd saved her life. "Thank you," was all she could manage.

He laughed. "If you really want to say thanks, have dinner with me."

"What the hell did that mean?" somebody in the trauma room screeched.

Timmie almost turned to answer that she didn't know. Then she realized that they were talking about the code. Not Alex, who had just asked her out.

*Her.*

Jesus, suddenly she felt twelve again. Traumawoman, the forensics fairy. All shot to dust by a question from one guy with drop-dead eyes and a history of being a gentleman.

"Uh . . ."

Alex shrugged, as if he were feeling just as uncomfortable. "It's bad timing, I know. But we haven't gotten a chance to catch up. And I'd really love to talk to somebody about something other than DRGs and Medicare funding. Please?"

"Hey, hey, where are you going?" another voice demanded, farther away.

Dinner, Timmie wanted to say. No matter what Murphy thought, because she was hiding the proof of Alex's innocence under her coat. Besides, Murphy had never spent his summers watching Alex Raymond from afar. A girl could learn a lot about a guy from afar.

"Sure," she said. "Give me a call, okay?"

His smile was everything a little girl might have imagined.

"Stop! Stop, damn it!"

This time the voice came from not ten feet down the hall. Timmie turned to find that one of the day nurses was headed her way, hot on the heels of a scruffy-looking teen who was barreling toward her like a loose horse. Only this horse was carrying a wrapped instrument tray under his arm like a tight end, and the nurse, an even scrawnier guy with a four-pack-a-day endurance challenge, couldn't keep up.

"Stop him!" the nurse bellowed, just too late.

The kid slammed the tray into Timmie's stomach like a cow catcher and then tried to run right up her chest. Timmie instinctively dropped what she was holding to grab him. The kid kicked. Timmie bit and bit hard.

She only got jacket. He screamed anyway, and the kid, Timmie, and Alex cartwheeled over into a skidding heap on the newly polished floor.

"She bit me!" the kid howled in Timmie's ear. Timmie couldn't breathe. Alex had an elbow in her back and his face in her neck.

"She bit me!"

"Shut up," the nurse demanded, hauling him free of the mess. "Or I'll bite you again, you little prick."

Timmie couldn't seem to move. She was flat on her back with a diaphragm that had been surprised into nonperformance and a hundred-and-eighty-pound physician on her hip.

"Timmie?"

The nurse, a guy named Eddie with buckteeth and more gold chains than Cindy, bent over her, his laughter more of a gasp. The kid bent alongside him, rubbing his well-padded arm.

"Timmie?" Alex echoed, readjusting his position so that he was over her somehow. "Honey, you all right?"

Timmie couldn't speak. She couldn't much think. So she nodded, and finally, with a lurch, her diaphragm rewarded her with a gasping breath. "Yeah."

"Here," Eddie said, handing something down to her. "You dropped these."

Her files. Her secret, hidden, dangerous files. That did it for lounging on the floor. Timmie made it as far as her butt, where she sat next to Alex, who was trying to right his suit.

"What's going on?" somebody demanded behind her. Somebody who sounded suspiciously like Angie.

Hand still out with the sheaf of papers toward Timmie, Eddie looked up. "Stupid little SHPOS here tried to steal an instrument tray."

Timmie gurgled, gasped, grabbed the papers before Angie could see them. Repositioned her sweatshirt just enough to hide them.

"Why?" Angie demanded.

"Great roach clips," Timmie allowed with a grin.

For the first time, the teen grinned along with her.

Alex frowned. "Shpos?" he asked.

"Subhuman piece of shit," Timmie told him, arm tight to her side as if protecting sore ribs.

The kid lost his grin. "Hey!"

"You all right, Ms. Leary-Parker?" Angie asked in the kind of voice that let everyone know how long-suffering she was.

"Fine."

Angie squeaked as she turned on her heel. Eddie grinned like a yenta, and the kid muttered about abuse. Alex climbed to his feet and held out a hand to pull Timmie up. She took it, still wondering why the hell Alex Raymond would possibly ask her to dinner.

Two miles away Daniel Murphy was smiling, too. But for an entirely different reason. He'd spent the morning out in Victor's neighborhood finding out that nobody, after all, had paid much attention to who had been at Victor's house before the fire. TVs had been tuned to *Oprah* and *Barney*, and dinner was on the stove. It wasn't until the next-door neighbor heard the smoke alarm while barbecuing that anybody thought to look that way.

Dejected, Murphy had sat himself down at the Stone Age computer back at the paper and waded his way through the life and times of Alex Raymond. He'd searched NEXIS/LEXIS, and he'd tapped into one of the credit bureau lines he'd borrowed from once or twice. He read how Alex Raymond was a golden boy of golden parents in a golden little town in the Midwest. He read how the golden boy got scholarships and had ambition and compassion in equal amounts. Eagle Scout and senior class president of Puckett High. Top of his class in premed, top third in med school. Gifted, smiling, committed to the welfare of old people everywhere.

There was even a piece in there about his mother, the brewery heiress who had fallen tragically ill in her early fifties and succumbed shortly thereafter to Alzheimer's disease.

It was enough to turn a reporter's stomach.

And then Murphy's day brightened. The golden boy had a tarnish.

Three years ago, in Boston, where he'd so diligently schooled and trained, he'd helped set up another Alzheimer's prototype unit. An experimental site coadministered by his now-famous partner, the nerd researcher Dr. Peter Davies. Pictures were included of two smiling, white-coat-clad physicians who looked like Jekyll and Hyde in person. Raymond the bright light, Davies the dark loner.

Only the two of them evidently hadn't gotten it right that time. The unit folded, and they declared bankruptcy, leaving behind some seriously displeased creditors and more than one cranky customer. They had given the press the usual, "a great idea that needs better funding" line, and then split town.

And four years before that, they'd done the same in Philadelphia. The pictures looked younger, brasher, more hopeful. The results were dismally the same.

And now, they were the toast of Puckett with the same song and dance.

Murphy smiled. It wouldn't hurt to get in touch with somebody involved in the other Alzheimer's units. See what might have happened, what tastes were left in what mouths. It might not even be a bad idea to venture deep into the bowels of Price University labs and see just what the dark, intense Dr. Davies looked like now that he was working on a possible third strike.

It might even be a good idea to ask Leary out to dinner. Just to ask what she'd found out. And then he'd tell her what he'd found out. For the first time that day, Murphy laughed.

# TWELVE

"WHAT DIFFERENCE DOES THAT MAKE?" TIMMIE DEMANDED when given the news two days later.

"What do you mean, what difference?" Murphy retorted, now close to seriously enjoying himself as he walked down the hall alongside her. "Money and power and status. Tough stuff to give up, Leary."

"Alex isn't giving anything up. He's trying again."

"With somebody else's money."

That stopped Leary dead in her tracks and spun her around. "I imagine you've already figured out why a guy trying his best *not* to go bankrupt would be killing off his paying customers?"

"That's what this visit is all about."

The two of them stood face-to-face about halfway along the connecting tunnel between the hospital and Restcrest, where Murphy was due for an appointment with not only the good doctor himself, but Mary Jane Arlington and Joseph Leary, their newest resident. Or client, as Mary Jane had put it.

Murphy hated the word "client." The minute the public relations queen had used it, Murphy knew he wanted to find dirt under Restcrest's rugs. He just hadn't realized he'd have so much trouble getting Leary to help him.

"I won't be party to a witch-hunt," she insisted.

Murphy started walking again. "I'm not hunting anything. I'm doing an in-depth piece on the wonders of Restcrest and the Neurological Research Group. I'm tying that in to the character piece I'm doing on your father."

Leary followed along, her heavy shoes thunking on the tile. "Which is the only reason I'm coming along."

Ten feet from the open fire doors into Restcrest, she stopped again. Stood there, hands on hips and fire in her eyes. She was wearing jeans today, old, worn ones, with an oversized pea green sweater and what looked like heavy brown work boots. She also sported a black-banded Mickey Mouse watch with the dial against the inside of her wrist and those tiny four earrings in each ear. Other than that, she was unadorned. A straightforward force of nature.

"I just think we need to look into the main hospital more," she protested, sneaking a look past the doors as if somebody might hear her. They probably could. Her urgent voice echoed down the hall like a soft wind. "I still haven't had a chance to look at the death stats, but I didn't see anything at all that indicted Restcrest."

"You've had two days," he reminded her, just to see her get mad.

She did. "You're right, I have. I also had a six-year-old with the flu and a backed-up toilet. I'm afraid in situations like that, murder just has to take its turn. Its turn will be right after work tonight, after I finish making my daughter's Halloween costume, and probably after dinner tomorrow night."

"Dinner?"

Suddenly Leary was the one looking like a six-year-old. "Yes. Dinner. You know that word."

"You can't read a printout while you're eating?"

She ducked her head, shoved her hands in her pockets, and headed off again toward Restcrest so fast that Murphy almost missed her answer. "Not when you have a date."

"A date?" he demanded, knowing damn well he was reading her

reaction right and following hot on her heels to prove it. "Tell me you're not going out with the golden boy. Tell me, if you are, that you're just doing it to grill him for me."

Leary stopped. She glared. She spun back along her original course like a comet snagged by a vagrant sun. "I'm going out with him to talk about family and memories and the outside world."

"And murder," Murphy insisted, watching her neck mottle.

"Don't be ridiculous."

Murphy found himself grabbing her arm. As if it would make a difference. As if she weren't a big girl and knew just what she was getting into, or he wasn't the last person to offer advice to anybody on the planet.

She turned on him like a mad cat. And, suddenly, smiled.

Not at him. And not with any warmth.

"Ms. Arlington," she said with almost-clenched teeth to a spot over his left shoulder. "Nice to see you."

Murphy spun to see the perfect Junior League poster child clacking their way in her Bruno Magli shoes, her pageboy bouncing with her step, her trim figure wrapped in something gray and Ann Taylor. The public relations queen looked confused.

"Are you helping Mr. Murphy?" she asked Timmie, clutching her soft leather daybook to her chest like a baby.

Murphy quickly let go of Timmie and watched her smile grow the way a prizefighter's did before the first bell. "Only with my dad. I don't have to be at work for another couple of hours, and Mr. Murphy asked if I might sit in. I'm going up to visit Dad while you all do . . . whatever it is Mr. Murphy plans on doing."

Ms. Arlington nodded, her hair bobbing just once. "I see. Well, thank you. That's . . . um, generous of you."

"No it isn't," Timmie assured her as she turned on down the hall toward the patient wings. "I'm here to make sure nobody bothers my father."

Ms. Arlington didn't know quite how to react. Murphy did it for her. "Helluva nurse, I hear," he said, taking hold of Ms. Arlington's arm and walking her the other way. "But don't ever pull a gun on her. She'll drop you like a rock."

* * *

Murphy was going numb. There was just so much PR babble he could ingest in one sitting without wanting to make Stooge noises. And Mary Jane Arlington was fonder of PR babble than Ross Perot was of pie charts. For the last hour she'd guided him on a micromanaged tour of the wonders of Restcrest as if he were a first-time visitor to a space station, all the while dispensing Alzheimer's statistics like Pez.

"We've begun to find early Alzheimer's indicators in people as young as twenty," she was saying as she walked. "Which makes you wonder how many more people out there are gestating the disease like time bombs ticking away in their brains."

She also made Murphy want to count backward from a hundred and recite the state capitals, just to make sure he still could.

The unit, Murphy had to admit, was impressive. Set up in a daisy pattern, it contained a complete twenty-patient unit in each petal with support services tucked into the core area. The sections were open and airy, with walking paths laid out around the perimeter of the central activity area for the people who needed to roam, and other paths snaking through a well-tended garden outside within very secure high walls. Semiprivate bedrooms circled the outside along with frequent and well-identified bathrooms.

Mary Jane led Murphy to the center of the high-ceilinged recreation area, where couches and beanbag chairs were gathered into islands of intimacy and tables displayed the clutter of constant activities. The atmosphere was quiet and soft, the staff well-evident and patient. Even the old people seemed happy. They certainly looked clean and well cared for.

"Right now we're only equipped to handle a hundred inpatients and selected outpatients," she said. "But Dr. Raymond is expanding outpatient services and research. Our ultimate goal, of course, is to one day make any Alzheimer's unit obsolete."

Toward the center, two or three people sat around picnic-type tables, beyond which gleamed a tidy, state-of-the-art kitchen. At its edge, a pencil-thin old guy in brown cardigan and lime green golf pants carefully plucked an apple from an open shelf.

"Mr. Veniman there is using our cafeteria-style dining area," Mary Jane announced like a narrator in a theme park. "As you can see, all our refrigerators and cabinets are either open or glass-fronted. Often, if a client sees food, he'll remember that he's hungry. Isn't that right, Mr. Veniman?"

Startled by the sound of his name, the old guy looked up and smiled. Nodded vaguely and then went back to studying the food he held. Ms. Arlington barely took a breath before plunging on.

"You see, as Alzheimer's progresses, the connection of certain needs to certain tasks becomes lost. A patient may recognize hunger and not remember what to do about it. If he can't see the food, often he forgets the need. We try to keep everything necessary as open and immediate as possible. We break tasks down into easily manageable functions, with reminders to help."

They did a lot of reminding here. Every wall bore big corkboards with announcements in huge letters.

IT IS TUESDAY, OCTOBER 29: SQUARE DANCING TONIGHT, PARDNER!
THE WEATHER OUTSIDE IS: CLOUDY AND COLD, TEMPERATURE 30 DEGREES.
TWO DAYS UNTIL BERT BRINKERHOFF'S BIRTHDAY.

There were smily faces and frowny faces everywhere, bright paintings, yarn sculptures, photos of the neighborhood. Kind of like the dark antithesis of a preschool room.

"This is one of my favorite advances in Alzheimer's care," Ms. Arlington continued as they approached the patient rooms, her hand sweeping out in a gesture familiar to anyone who watched game shows. "Our memory cases. We put them at each patient's room to help him easily identify it. To cement his own identity."

Murphy had to admit that he was impressed by the brightly lit Plexiglas cases. Built into the wall by each room, they displayed mementos from the patient's life. Old photos, uniforms, bric-a-brac, children's artwork. The guy who'd gotten the apple headed toward one now, hand out a little as if reaching for it, his eyes on a big wedding picture from the fories and the set of crescent wrenches that lay in the light. Passing by, he stroked the Plexiglas, as if his connection were frail enough to need physical contact to maintain it.

It was like ancestor worship, Murphy thought, itching with discomfort. Little shrines built to forgotten memories and worshiped every time a person walked by. A mental mezuzah tacked to the door to reestablish reality.

Murphy had spent most of his life deliberately severing that kind of connection. He wondered, when he saw the old guy smile at the sight of himself in younger clothes, what he'd have left for a shrine of his own. Whether he'd be able to recognize himself from just two Pulitzers.

Screw that, he decided with an almost superstitious shake of the head. The important thing here was that the place looked . . . legit, damn it. Upscale, well run, well planned, well intentioned. Murphy had investigated more than one nursing home in his career. He'd spent an unforgettable week from hell in one place outside Detroit that offered cockroaches in the soup and mice in the mattresses. Whatever he would end up saying about Alex Raymond, it wouldn't be that he extracted profit from patient misery. The patients here were not miserable. The equipment was first rate, from diagnostic tools like CT and PET scanners to rehab equipment. All space-age stuff, all for these frail, smiling people and the frail people who would follow them.

Not at all what he'd expected from this trip. Not, truthfully, what he'd wanted. He'd started this story as a relief from boredom. But the more he learned, the more he suspected there was a worm hidden somewhere in this perfect apple. He just couldn't find it, damn it, and that made him have to work harder.

Which he didn't want to do, either.

"Everybody seems pretty mobile here," he said, deliberately walking on. "What happens to them when they aren't?"

"Unit five," Mary Jane answered gaily, somehow clacking along on carpeted flooring. "It's a full nursing wing for any of our clients who are ill or have progressed on to the third stage, which is the final physical decline of the illness. Care here is never discontinued because of physical problems. Right now we're lucky, though. We have very few patients needing advanced care."

"Lucky?"

Mary Jane's smile could have been used to teach condescension to acting students. "Nobody likes to see suffering, Mr. Murphy. By the time our clients have reached stage three, they've lost most of what has made them the people they are. It's not easy for anybody. Especially Dr. Raymond. He suffers every time he has to graduate a client. We seem to be preventing that better, don't you see?"

He didn't, but then, he didn't work here day in and day out.

"It's expensive, though, isn't it?"

Her smile brightened, as if she could stun him into forgetting he'd asked such an impolite question. "We have the very latest in care here, Mr. Murphy, the most advanced research. And Dr. Raymond does his very best to offset every cost he can. Fund-raisers, research grants, that kind of thing." She took a quick look around, then leaned closer, in confidence mode. "He'd probably be angry with me if I told you, but a good example is Mr. Leary. Dr. Raymond is picking up much of the cost of his care himself. That should definitely tell you something right there."

Murphy would like to think so. Of course, Murphy naturally hoped it was because Raymond wanted something in return. "Is that why he went bankrupt before?" he asked.

For a second, old Mary Jane's features froze entirely. Murphy spent a moment wishing he had a cigarette. It would have been a good time to light it to give her a chance to recover, him time to assess. Besides, it would get the smell of Giorgio out of his nose.

"Excuse me for being rude," Mary Jane said with the kind of controlled vehemence that betrayed real outrage. Personal outrage, the first Murphy had seen from the plastic woman. "But I don't find that line of questioning pertinent. Or productive. I imagine you'd have to get those answers from Dr. Raymond."

"You bet we went bankrupt," the golden boy answered twenty minutes later. "What, specifically, did you want to know about what Pete and I are so fond of calling 'our youthful excesses'?"

"You'll pardon my saying so," Murphy said, settling back into the comfortable leather chair across from Raymond's simple teak desk, "but I'm a little surprised that you didn't have any more trouble setting up a unit for the third time."

And damn if Raymond didn't laugh. "Who says I didn't? Don't get me wrong, Mr. Murphy. I grew up in Puckett. I love it here. But is Puckett, Missouri, the first place that comes to mind when you think 'premier medical facility'? The people here gave me a chance. I'm trying to pay them back."

"What makes you think you won't have the same problems here you had before?"

Raymond leaned back himself. Tented his hands as if building an antenna to search for the perfect answer. Dressed today in blue shirtsleeves, Looney Tunes tie, and nicely tailored gray slacks, with his white lab coat slung over the chair behind him like a casually assumed mantle of office, Raymond looked supremely unconcerned with his image. Murphy wished the guy at least seemed more nervous. That he needed to display himself more, with diplomas on the walls or community service awards strewn around. Hell, even a picture or two with Raymond's arm around a semifamous person.

But the golden boy had decorated his office in high-quality Monet prints, and left it untidy with books and magazines stuffed into simple shelving units along with the obligatory anatomy models and a couple of reproduction Chinese horses.

Raymond didn't even have pictures of the legendary mother to elicit sympathy. He had paperweights made out of geodes and a dollar goldfish swimming around in a kid's bowl. And Alex Raymond smiled as if he really did enjoy watching that stupid fish swim around on his desk.

"I don't think I'll make the same mistakes as before, because I have Paul Landry looking out for me this time. Peter and I are committed to what we do. It doesn't mean we're not fiscal idiots. Paul, on the other hand, is a genius, and I'm more than happy to leave the financial end up to him. Between him and Mary Jane, they've freed Pete and me up from everything but patient care and research."

Murphy didn't even bother to take notes. He just sat there wondering if this guy could really be serious. Hell, he wondered if this guy could be real. It certainly seemed that Mary Jane had a real investment in the guy. From what Murphy had seen so far, Landry would probably be stupid not to be involved as well. But there wasn't any way Murphy was going to buy into the myth that Alex Raymond was completely oblivious to everything but holding hands and separating genes.

"Which brings us to Joe Leary," he said, regrouping.

Dr. Raymond beamed like a kid talking about a favorite big brother. "Which does, indeed, bring us to Joe Leary. What would you like to know?"

"Why you're paying for his care, for one thing."

The perfect face fell a little. Surprise, disappointment, caution. "I imagine Mary Jane told you. I'd really rather not let that get around, if you don't mind. It's a personal matter."

"Personal how?"

And now, as if choreographed, that smile. The smile Murphy had seen from damn near everybody in town with the notable exception of Timmie Leary when Joe Leary was introduced. "Joe is . . . special. He's a true original who won't come this way again, and I already miss him."

"That's it?"

The smile grew, shifted. "Why don't we go see him now? After you spend some time with him, I think you'll understand."

"Like most of our residents in the inpatient area of Restcrest," Raymond said as they walked, "Joe is in what we term the second stage of Alzheimer's. Affected enough that he can't safely remain in a home environment, but still mostly able to care for himself. The first stage, when he was beginning to forget, is the toughest stage for the patient, I think; the second stage, when he begins to lose touch with his world, is toughest for his family. He only remembers Timmie occasionally now, which must be terrible for her. The two of them were inseparable when she was a little girl." For a second, Raymond remembered, smiled, and nodded. "It's something you just don't forget. That great, huge man with his booming laugh walking down the sidewalk in the summer holding hands with that tiny girl and singing and reciting poetry to her."

"He still seems to remember the poetry, anyway."

"Magnificently. I wish he'd taught me English lit instead of Mrs. Beal. I might have actually passed the class."

"He taught?"

"For a while. He did lots of things for a while. He entertained us all for the sheer love of it, though. Bars, town square, church suppers. He always said there wasn't enough music in the air. If nobody else was going to provide it, he would. He did."

He still was, evidently. Murphy heard the distinctive voice even before they'd opened the doors.

" '. . . Oh, how may I call this a lightning? O, my love! My wife!' "

Raymond grinned like a kid. "Romeo," he crowed, pushing open the door as if expecting to see Julia Roberts on the other side.

The only thing on the other side was more old people. More staff. More glass-fronted storage and brightly lettered memory boards. And Joe Leary standing foursquare in the center of the beige carpet, his frame bent, his massive hand cupping the face of his daughter, who was sitting at a table littered with coffee cups and orange rinds. Even from where he stood Murphy could see the glitter in her eyes.

" 'Death, that hath sucked the honey of thy breath,' " Joe Leary whispered so that every person in the room could hear, " 'hath had no power yet upon thy beauty. Thou art not conquered . . .' "

"Act five, scene three," Raymond told Murphy in awed tones. "Romeo's about to die for her."

Nobody moved. Nobody breathed. Murphy watched them, watched Raymond quiet to attention just like the rest. He turned and took in the show himself.

Joe Leary mesmerized. His great voice was hushed, his eyes grief stricken, his movements small. Murphy could damn near see a crushed, callow seventeen-year-old standing in the place of the rumpled, white-haired old titan.

Evidently, so could everybody else. They remained in suspended animation as the words built like a soft, sad storm in the artificially bright room.

" 'Come, bitter conduct, come, unsavory guide! Thou desperate pilot, now at once . . . now at once . . .' "

Nobody noticed the hesitation but Murphy. It seemed a natural pause in the play if you didn't know it by heart. But the old man's eyes flickered, his hand trembled.

"Now, at once . . ."

Murphy wanted to jump in to save him. He didn't have to. Joe Leary's trembling grew until Murphy thought the people in the room would surely see. His gaze sharpened on the face of his daughter. She didn't move. Murphy could barely see her mouth work the lines the old man had temporarily misplaced, the whispered words so soft the audience could barely tell. The perfect prompter, she kept the focus on him.

And then, as if she'd hit a light switch, Romeo returned.

" 'Now at once run on the dashing rocks thy seasick weary bark!'" he cried. "'Here's to my love! O true apothecary! Thy drugs are quick.'" Lifting an imaginary vial to his lips, he drank, and all eyes went with him. "'Thus with a kiss . . . I die.' "

They all burst into applause.

"He do this all the time?" Murphy asked as he joined in.

"All the time," Raymond assured him. "He's the best thing that's happened to this place since music therapy."

Everybody clustered around the old man, all with that same damn smile. Old people wept and staff laughed and Joe stood there, the power draining away from his features like a flashlight with a failing battery, the tremble reappearing.

He began to look around, as if trying to remember something, and then one of the staff asked him to refresh her about the rest of the story. Joe settled, turned to her, smiled.

"The story is as old as time," he said, reaching to take her small hand, and everyone listened.

Murphy knew then why Timmie didn't want to indict Restcrest for anything. What he didn't understand was why, as everybody else crowded around in rapt attention to catch some of Joe Leary's infectious enthusiasm, the one person who walked away, movements as tight and contained as fury, was his daughter.

It was two more days until Halloween and Timmie hadn't finished sewing the damned costume yet. Why couldn't Meghan want to be Pocahontas like every other kid on the block? Why couldn't she even want to be a pumpkin, like last year? That costume was still around somewhere, a masterpiece of orange-and-green felt, and Meghan certainly hadn't grown out of it yet.

No, Meghan had to be Scheherazade, just like in one of Grandda's stories, and that meant she had to have yards of netting and those stupid bloused pants. It meant that all that damn material was draped over Timmie's dining room table like a taunt as Timmie skimmed pages of death notices.

She should be finishing the costume, or Meghan was going to be trick-or-treating with straight pins in her crotch. She should be getting ready for work so she could afford to extend her father's run at the Restcrest Playhouse. Instead, she read about dead people.

Normal dead people. Old people, young people, all reduced to a single line of print. Name, age, date of birth, date of death, unit, cause of death, disposition.

William Anthony Marshall, 47, 1/15/50,
2/25/96, CCU, Acute MI, Breyer's Mortuary

She had to find some direction other than Restcrest for Murphy to point his finger. Somebody other than Alex Raymond to be responsible.

Minerva G. Wilding, 71, 6/23/25, 6/30/97,
Oncology, CA, Liver, Breyer's Mortuary

Some of the names she recognized. Some of those spare statistics could still ignite melancholy or delight or frustration, like surprising scent from long-pressed flowers. Some just made her sad.

William R. Porter, 8, 11/1/88, 8/15/97, ER,
MVA, Head Trauma, hold for coroner

Well, so there *had* been cases Van Adder had investigated. Timmie could swear his numbers were awfully low, though. Especially when she considered the fact that the hospital mortality rate was an average of thirty a month, increasing to almost forty in the last few months. What were the odds that in over 360 people, not one was a suspected suicide or homicide?

Maria Salgado, 76, 10/1/22, 10/22/97, ER,
Cardiac Arrest, Van Adder Mortuary

Timmie looked again, all the way through, just at the disposition line. She checked every time she found the word "coroner," and what it was for. Two gunshot wounds and a stabbing. An overdose. Little William who had died in the car accident, and another motorcycle accident. Two other overdoses that went to Breyer's and a head injury that was taken back up to St. Louis to bury.

Van Adder wasn't doing his job. Not a huge surprise, after meeting the man. But it would take that lunch with Conrad to get the whole skinny on that.

Timmie flipped the pages back to the last few months, running her finger down the lines just to see if anything stood out. Anything she should have noticed as unusual.

"Don't you have to go to work?" Meghan asked, skipping over from where she'd been finishing her homework.

"Yes," Timmie assured her daughter, her eyes still on the page. "I do. You probably could have figured that out when Heather came to baby-sit."

A name. Something about a name that niggled at her.

Wilhelm Reinholt Cleveland, 76, 7/1/21,
10/20/96, ER, Cardiac Arrest,
Breyer's Mortuary

What should she be noticing here? What made her uneasy?

"Heather's boring," Meghan complained, leaning against Timmie's arm.

That was Meghanese for "I need some hugs here." Meghan was not the type of kid to demand emotional outbursts. She expected them as her right. Far be it from Meghan to admit that all the upheaval in the last few months—not to mention the last few days—would make her need them a little more.

Leaving a pen in the fold of the printout, Timmie turned to put her arms around her daughter and squeezed hard.

"At least she likes Renfield," she bargained.

"I can't go over to Mattie's again?"

"Sorry, hon. You're going to spend the night there tomorrow so Mommie can go out."

"*Again.*" Meghan sighed like the orphan kid in a melodrama. "You're *always* gone now."

Timmie gave Meghan another squeeze. "Don't give me grief, kid," she teased. "This will be the first time I've put on panty hose for anything but a funeral since your dance recital last year. Mommies need to play, too, you know."

"But Daddy will be mad," Meghan insisted. "Especially if he comes here and finds me gone."

*Daddy*. Timmie did her best not to flinch. She'd forgotten. Well, probably not forgotten. Done another Scarlett. She had to find that lawyer and head off that "miscellaneous action" Jason had filed to harass her about not being able to get in touch with him. She had to start looking for him around every corner so she'd be ready when he walked up to her door to delight his daughter and harass his ex-wife. Damn, it was always something.

"We'll leave Daddy a note," Timmie promised.

Meghan leaned her little head against Timmie's chest just as she'd done since she'd been a baby, so that Timmie could smell Johnson's shampoo and fresh air. "I want to go to Mattie's tonight," she said.

"I know."

"I like them. Mr. Mattie lets me help him barbecue."

Timmie stroked silky brown hair and smiled. "Not mister. Reverend. And his name isn't Mattie. It's Wilson. Reverend Wilson."

"He thinks it's funny when I call him Mr. Mattie. He says it's okay. What's vengeance, Mom?"

Timmie pulled back. "What?"

Meghan screwed up her face. "I thought he said penguins. I thought he said penguins were the Lord's, and I thought that was silly, so I asked. He said it was vengeance, but that wasn't for little girls."

"When did this happen?"

"The night before you took Grandda away, I think. Cindy was there, and, oh, Barbara. I remember Barbara because she took us all out into the street to play corkball after dark. *After dark*, Mom, isn't that cool? Do you know we even went for a walk and saw a shooting star? *You* never showed me a shooting star before."

"We never lived anyplace we could see them, my little city mouse."

Another wrinkle of the nose so that she did, indeed, look the part. "I'm not a mouse, Mom. But if I was, I don't think I like being a city mouse anymore. I *like* shooting stars. What's vengeance, and why can't little girls have it?"

Timmie gave up the stats for good. Just keeping pace with this kid was dizzying. "Were, honey. If I were. And vengeance kind of means getting even. Like if Crystal Miller pulls your hair, you pull hers back. Which you can't do—"

"Because it's not for little girls. But why would the Lord pull Crystal's hair?"

Timmie laughed. "I think what the reverend meant was that if the Lord doesn't pull Crystal's hair, then neither should you."

That didn't seem to work either. "Well, if she's being mean, *somebody* has to. And why would the Lord pull Ellen's hair?"

"Ellen's hair?"

"They were talking about Ellen. And . . . uh, how she's alone. And how Cindy's glad. Is that nice, Mom?"

Timmie interrupted this little intelligence with a small swat on the butt and stood up. "You're much too nosy, little girl. Enough. I had a hard day at the sewing machine. I don't need an ethics class, too. Come up and help me dress for work."

Meghan's grin was a hundred percent imp. "Why, just so I can be bored?"

"By me?"

That got a giggle. "No, silly. By Heather. Couldn't Cindy come over? I'd rather have Cindy."

Now, that Timmie hadn't expected. She'd thought Meghan wouldn't have had time for a woman not much more mature than she was. "Really?" she asked, with a tickle for good measure. "How come?"

It took a few shrieks and wriggles for Meghan to answer. "Because it's fun scaring her with Renfield."

Ah. Some sense at last.

Timmie just picked Meghan up and carried her so she could keep her close as long as possible.

"Did you know she was locked in a herbi . . . herbi . . . snake house once?" Meghan asked, legs wrapped around Timmie's stomach. "All night, all by herself, and she had to hold very, very still so the snakes wouldn't smell her. Snakes can't smell very well, you know. Especially in the dark. When the lights went on, there were snakes curled up all around her."

"My, my."

"Yes, and her daddy had to leave when she was a little girl, too. She said it made her very sad, but he was an explorer, so she knew he was finding new places she could visit someday."

"Uh-huh."

"Do we have to go back, Mom?"

It took Timmie a while to catch that one. "Back where, baby?"

"California."

They'd reached the top of the stairs, where the books lived. Piles of them, masses, mountains. Literature, philosophy, history, tomes in English and French and Latin. A few in Gaelic, but her father had come to Irish late and had lost interest quickly.

Timmie still considered this place haunted and holy, the sum of words and ideas that had tumbled so easily from her father's brain all those years. The real Joe Leary when the other one went away, just like the explorer in Cindy's story

But tonight Timmie didn't look. She didn't stroke old leather or visit well-known titles. She focused instead on her daughter.

"I thought you didn't like it here."

Meghan didn't quite face her. Meghan hated to admit she was wrong. "I can't have a horse in California," she whispered.

Timmie probably should have told her that she couldn't have a horse here, either. But she knew what her little girl meant. Meghan had already begun to be seduced by those quiet, dark nights and corkball games. By walking home from school and having a pony down the block she could feed apples to on her way by. And Timmie had no right taking those things away from her.

Even for the sound of sirens.

She sighed. "So you've decided to be a country mouse?"

Meghan nodded, head still tucked into Timmie's neck. "Only if my daddy could find me."

Timmie held on tighter. She fought all the old anxieties. "Your daddy knows where to find us," she assured her little girl. "As long as we're where he expects us to be, he'll find us."

*Where he expects us to be.*

Where he expects us to be. Why did that suddenly make her want to turn around and go back down to her statistics . . .

Timmie froze midthought.

Oh, God. Oh, no. She was wrong. She had to be wrong. That couldn't have been what she'd seen.

Timmie almost dropped Meghan down the stairs. She squeezed her hard, then set her on her feet. "Hang on a second, hon. I have to check something."

"Mom!"

But Timmie was already back down the stairs. Grabbing a highlighter out of the pen forest she'd been collecting in an old popcorn tin, Timmie bent back over the printout. She highlighted the names that were familiar to her. Lila Travers, Milton Preston, maybe Clara Schultz. Patients she'd personally dismissed from her ER. Added to the ER statistics as their own, as if they had come from the outside with only moments to live so they just brushed along the fringes of the hospital.

Except they hadn't come from the outside. That was what suddenly stood out to her. She had worked on the assumption that the numbers were okay because she was checking familiar ratios to see if they were wrong. ER, OR, ICU, Med/Surg. The ER numbers had been higher, but that didn't reflect on the hospital proper. The ER stood separate, individual, like an island in a larger sea. And Timmie would have seen a change in the ER. She would have heard, would have sensed or smelled.

But she'd been wrong. Not about the ER. About the ratio. It wasn't right. The ER numbers weren't honest. Timmie hadn't taken into account the patients they'd been seeing from Restcrest. The policy had changed no more than six months ago so that any Restcrest patient with a resuscitation order would be immediately transported to the ER if they needed treatment.

And if they died, they were dismissed as ER patients.

No, no, no, she wanted to say with her whole heart. It can't be that. I'll find it isn't that when I look closer.

She had to get back to that computer. She had to double-check which patients had come in from Restcrest. Because if her suspicions were true, it wasn't the ER's numbers that were going up, it was Restcrest's. And intentionally or not, the hospital's new policy was camouflaging that.

They were hiding the fact that there were more people dying in Restcrest than anybody knew.

ANOTHER GEEK, MURPHY THOUGHT WITH NO LITTLE FRUSTRAtion. Another undernourished, overeducated freak of nature who seemed unable to communicate with anything but a microscope and, evidently, Alex Raymond.

No wonder these guys got into so much trouble.

Lanky and dark, Peter Davies was good-looking in an absent-minded professor kind of way, with unkempt hair he kept dragging out of his eyes as he talked, deep-set hazel eyes, and a sheepish grin that probably delighted the ladies. If they wanted to put up with that six-week-old lab coat, that is, or the constant chatter about gene therapy and amyloidal plaques.

Davies's realm was much more impressive than his hygiene, anyway. Definitely high tech, gleaming white, with acres of test tubes, herds of centrifuges, walls of gleaming stainless-steel refrigerators. Light microscopes and electron microscopes and enough DNA testing equipment to staff the FBI. There was great work going on here, as reflected in the serious young faces of the research assistants and the static of excitement that permeated their conversation. Science was their god, and they were its priests facing down demon Alzheimer.

"I've already shown you the PET scan pictures," Davies said, shoving his hair out of his eyes with one hand and waving a color-enhanced photo of a shriveling brain with the other as they walked away from the populated area of the lab. "So you see the progressive destruction of the cortical areas, yes?"

His eyes still full of desiccated brain, Murphy nodded. Here he took notes. He was hearing about hippocampuses and neurofibrillary tangles and serum amyloid P. Words so familiar to Davies that he didn't stop to explain them to the reporter. The reporter, frustrated, tired, and disappointed by finding just what people had said he would, desperately wanted a cigarette. Instead, he got a stool at the far end of the lab, which made him think Davies had probably forgotten where his office was.

"It is the amyloidal plaques we're interested in," Davies said, pacing. "They're sort of like neurological junk piles that build up in certain areas of the brain, yes? Our focus is to keep them from forming and interfering with the neurotransmitters that link neural synapses and form thought. You understand?"

No.

"Sure."

A quick nod and he was off again. "To do that, we have concentrated on the part played by a substance known as apolipoprotein E, or Apo E, which seems to collect the plaques like a . . . well, a lint catcher."

Murphy jotted the words *protein lint catcher* and left it at that. He didn't give a damn about proteins he couldn't pronounce. He just wanted to know what they had to do with Restcrest.

"And how does your unique arrangement with Restcrest help you do this?" he asked.

Davies blinked a moment in response to the change of conversational direction. "Research money, of course. Alex is a whiz at that kind of thing. And we do excellent work because of our relationship with Restcrest. Restcrest gives us access to raw material other research labs are begging for."

"Raw material?"

Davies blinked again. "You do know that right now the only way to definitely diagnose Alzheimer's is through autopsy, yes?"

"You can't just mock up the problem on a computer simulation, you mean."

"Exactly. We need affected tissue to study it, and Restcrest provides that. It also enables us to correlate a patient's symptomology and family history with the postmortem microscopic changes on a scale not easily matched. A rare opportunity."

"I imagine."

Davies bounced, then leaned close. "Most people don't appreciate how important that is," he insisted, his eyebrows telegraphing his intensity like furry semaphores. "Without a facility like Restcrest, we would have to rely on donations. We wouldn't have complete access to the patients to study them while they're alive, not to mention the next generation of potential patients before they're symptomatic. As a matter of fact, because of the good image Restcrest has, we're starting to see donations of nonsymptomatic brains with familial histories. Young brains, Mr. Murphy. We don't get many of those, you see?"

Calling Mel Brooks. Your Frankenstein is waiting. It was all Murphy could do to keep a straight face.

*Nursing home supplies raw research material*, he scribbled, knowing that he'd never use it. Not like that. It was too scary. Too confusing. The truth was that the geek doctor was probably as sincere as hell. He performed a service, and inflammatory stories would only scare possible donors away from a good cause.

Unless, of course, the doctor's good luck had something to do with Murphy's mysterious phone call.

"Have you been getting more donations lately?" he asked.

Davies paused a second to sign off on some result a staff member presented. "More?" he asked, his attention on the clipboard. "Yes, I suppose we have gotten more. It happens like that sometimes, though. This week, in fact, we've already had three. Two from the unit and one from the coroner."

Murphy looked up from his notes. "Coroner?"

"Yes. The healthy donation."

Did Murphy remind the guy that if a brain had been healthy it wouldn't have been in his refrigerator? "Murder victim?"

Davies looked up. "No, no. An accident. It was just released today, in fact. Not perfect, of course. Heat damage. But usable."

Did Murphy hope for recognition or misapprehension?

"Name of Adkins?" he asked.

Davies started a little, then blinked. "Of course, you work for the local paper. You'd know about him, yes?"

"Yes," Murphy said, knowing damn well he shouldn't have felt that flush of triumph simply because he'd just heard an interesting coincidence and he hadn't believed in coincidence since the day a brand-new twenty-dollar bill had shown up on his dresser not two hours after he'd caught his father playing sink the Bismarck with his cousin Mary. "I knew about him."

Not enough, obviously.

"You want to tell me why you're investigating Alex Raymond?" Sherilee demanded an hour later when Murphy dragged himself back into the newspaper.

Punching his blinking answering machine, Murphy feigned innocence. "You were the one who told me to do the dry-good series on the Neurological Research Group. I'm doing."

Sherilee aimed a computer printout at him like a signed confession. "And personal finances are, like, important to the spreading of the unit's good name how, Murphy?"

"I don't go through *your* desk, Sherilee," he said agreeably. "Don't you think it's bad manners to go through mine?"

"Not when you're not telling me what's going on," she retorted. "You work for me, Murphy, remember?"

Murphy held up a hand as he waited for his messages. It was better than laughing at Sherilee when she was serious. The only words he'd heard more in his life than "You work for me, Murphy, remember?" were "Closing time."

"Something came up I'm investigating."

Three messages. *Beep.*

"Not about Alex Raymond."

*Beep*. "I'd say you owe me," the deep, laughing voice announced on his recorder, "but I've been saying that for years. Call me back. I've dug into your boy, and I'm afraid I came up empty. But I might have some other tidbits you'll like."

Marty Gerst. City-desk editor of *The Philadelphia Inquirer*, which would have covered one of Alex Raymond's failed units.

"Murphy?" Sherilee insisted, up on her toes now. "You aren't going after Alex Raymond."

*Beep*. "Just thought I'd let you know," Pete Mitchell offered in tight tones that betrayed his excitement. "Your boy kept more to himself than just his service record. Call me."

Hmmmm. This town was like an old knit sweater. Pull one loose strand and the whole thing began to unravel.

*Beep*. "You haven't listened—" Murphy hit the button at light speed. He'd been threatened enough over the years to recognize another of the breed. Definitely not the voice he'd heard before. Probably the one Leary didn't want to talk about.

"Murphy?" Sherilee asked, on alert.

Murphy turned to her, leaned his hip against his desk. Dealt with Sherilee like every other editor he'd worked with before.

"You were right, Sherilee," he said. "Something is going on at the hospital. I'm just looking for some answers."

"Just tell me and every city official who's called today that you're not climbing up Alex Raymond's butt just for the fun of it."

Murphy lifted a wry eyebrow. "Alex Raymond is too fragile to protect himself?"

"No . . ." She huffed, shifted from foot to foot. Reddened. "Not exactly."

"Oh?"

"You're not from around here," she insisted, suddenly frustrated. "You just don't know what kind of person Alex is."

"So tell me."

"No way. Tell me what you think first."

He grinned. "I don't think anything. I'm just looking. Although I will admit that I'm having a little trouble with this shining-knight routine. I mean, do you really expect me to believe that this guy would keep coming back like George Foreman just because his mother died of Alzheimer's?"

"She didn't die of it," Sherilee said. "She killed herself. Like, hung herself in their garage, and Alex walked in on her when he came home from school. You don't think that's a good enough reason for him to be, like, a little obsessed?"

Yes, he did. He didn't want to, but he did think that would be plenty of reason. Damn it.

"Give me my reports," Murphy said, snatching them out of her hands.

"So?" Sherilee asked. "What are you going to do?"

"Find out why the coroner released a murder victim and then see if you might be right about Paul Landry."

Sherilee brightened like a kid hearing a snow day announced. "Really?"

Murphy couldn't help it. He knew he could get hauled up on any number of harassment charges, but she was so damned enthusiastic. He tweaked her nose. "Really."

He waited till she'd left to replay the threat.

Actually, Timmie got to Van Adder first, for the simple reason that when she stopped in the ER on the way up to see her father, Van Adder was ensconced in the lounge with Angie.

She probably should never have gone near him. She was in a bad enough mood as it was. Her fingers were sore from trying to finish that damn costume, she hadn't had any luck in matching the Restcrest deaths to the ER without access to a computer, and the nurse on her dad's unit had called again about his memory case items. So Timmie had been forced to root through mountains of trash in the hopes of unearthing the treasures her father had buried.

At four, when she should have been primping for the date she'd dreamed of since her seventh birthday, Timmie stalked into the hospital carrying a grocery bag under one arm and a rolled-up poster under the other. Three separate people asked her why she was scowling. She was scowling because she'd had to dig through history she'd done a lot to forget, and now she was going to have to present her findings to her dad like tarnished medals commemorating his accomplishments in a long-forgotten war.

That was why she was scowling.

Then she spotted Tucker Van Adder slouched in the lounge with his oversized butt on the sprung couch and his feet on a wheelchair, laughing with Angie like he owned the place, and she decided she shouldn't be the only one in a bad mood.

"Barb tells me you released Victor's case as an accident," she said, blocking the doorway.

Angie started like a philandering wife.

Van Adder just frowned. "I thought you didn't want to think your friend killed him."

"She didn't," Timmie assured him. "But somebody did."

Van Adder lay the newspaper in his lap. "Somebody didn't. Victor had too much to drink and didn't move in time to save himself. That's what I think, and the police couldn't convince me otherwise."

"You're absolutely right," Timmie said with a gentle smile anybody who'd worked a hall with her would have recognized. "He *was* too drunk to notice. But it's what he was supposed to notice that's the problem. That fire wasn't an accident."

"How many arson cases have you investigated, Ms. Leary?" he asked.

Timmie straightened, fully aware that there were witnesses. It didn't seem to matter. Incompetence demanded comment.

"How many have *you* investigated, Mr. Van Adder?"

Setting aside his paper and coffee, Van Adder climbed to his feet. "If you weren't Joe's daughter," he threatened, "I'd just take you over my knee. You have a couple of courses in nursing school, and you think you can teach me my business. Well, little girl, I've been doing this for almost thirty years. I don't need a *forensic nurse* to tell me how."

"Maybe you do."

It was Angie's turn to react. "You'd better watch yourself," she warned, on her feet as well. "You're on probation here."

Van Adder waved her off as unnecessary. "Really?" he asked Timmie with an offensive smile. "You're going to teach us all how to do our jobs, huh? You're going to show me how it's done? What the hell can a forensic nurse do, anyway?"

It was Timmie's turn to smile. "She can run for coroner," she said, and then walked out.

Bad nurse. Bad, bad nurse.

Timmie spent the entire walk to Restcrest berating herself as a pigheaded fool. She'd probably just cost herself her job. Any hope of a job. But she couldn't let that smarmy son of a bitch dismiss not only her but his own responsibilities as if they were insignificant.

Little girl, was it? He was going to put her over his knee, was he? She hadn't had any choice after that. She'd had to finish him off, just to see the look on his face. The only problem was that she'd also effectively sabotaged any hope she'd had for a future in this town.

Worse. She'd probably talked herself into running for an office she didn't want, just to prove a point.

Bad, *bad* nurse.

"Oh, good, you brought them."

Timmie looked up, startled. She hadn't even realized she'd made it all the way to her dad's unit. But there she was, faced with the inevitable proof that it was THURSDAY, and that the weather was COOL AND DAMP. Timmie guessed they weren't allowed to use the much more appropriate SHITTY. If the weather didn't clear up by tomorrow, Halloween was going to be a bust. But that wasn't her problem right now. Her problem was smiling at her with all the dedication of a true believer.

Timmie held out the bag. "All here."

The nurse, a bright young thing with enough energy to exhaust Timmie, peeked into the bag as if she were looking for Halloween candy. "Oh, I really love this part of the job. It's like *This Is Your Life*."

Timmie almost laughed. That wasn't Joe's life at all. It was Joe's life the way Timmie wanted to remember it, which bore no resemblance to the truth. The truth she'd left back with all the piles of tax returns and half-finished crossword puzzles.

"It's the best I could do for now," she said instead as the nurse lifted out a 1982 World Championship pennant. Also in the bag were the 1964 and 1967 pennants, a baseball from the forties signed by the Gashouse Gang, a poetry textbook, a leather bomber jacket from the Eighth Air Force, a small, amateur painting of a little white house in a field, and a battered tin whistle. The poster was from when he'd opened for the Clancy Brothers at The Bells from Hell, a club he'd played in the Village, the tin whistle visible in his immense hands as he smiled over Tommy Clancy's shoulder.

"This is wonderful," the nurse said, her eyes alight as she lifted the painting. "Is this his house in Ireland?"

Timmie looked at the clumsy rendering with sheep standing as large as cows in the background. "It's his grandmother's home. Dad's never been there."

"Really?" the nurse asked, really surprised. "I could have sworn he grew up there."

Timmie smiled. "So could he."

"How about photos?" she asked. "Those are very important. Especially the rest of his family, your mother and sisters."

"I'm working on it. For now, though, it'll only be me."

The nurse blinked, trying hard to understand. This kind of nurse would, Timmie thought. A lovely woman, truly delighted to be here with her little old people, happy to reacquaint them with their treasures every time she passed by. This was the kind of nurse who saw her career not as a convenience, but a calling.

It was to Alex Raymond's credit that he could still command a staff like that, which was one of the reasons Timmie knew Murphy was wrong.

"Your dad's in his room, if you want to see him."

Timmie knew the nurse would probably be very understanding if Timmie said no, she didn't want to see him, especially after spending all day wading around in the detritus of his life.

It wouldn't make Timmie understand any better. Or feel any

better about herself. After all, one of these days she was going to have to grow up and deal with it all. So she went on in to where he was sitting on the edge of his bed, hands on knees, patiently watching the wall.

The room was lovely, sunny and pastel and comfortable, with her father's easy chair along one wall and the sunflower quilt his grandmother had made him neatly folded on his bed. The staff had even figured a way to tuck a bookshelf in the corner so he could be with some of his beloved books. Not that he could read them anymore. He remembered their friendship, though. He stroked them like cherished children every time he went near.

"Hi, Daddy."

Slowly he looked over, his eyes clouded and vague. Fogged, ruined mirrors that could no longer reflect. Timmie fought the same damn old clutch of grief she'd struggled with for as long as she could remember.

"What do you want?" he asked, frowning.

Timmie sat down. The nurse, walking in behind her on crepe-shod feet, put a hand on her shoulder. "Don't expect it to get better yet just because he's here," she said quietly.

Timmie wanted to hit her. She wanted to hit something.

"I just wanted to say hello, Joe," she said instead, understanding more than the nurse thought.

He tilted his head in that odd, wry greeting he'd learned from his own father. "Then, hello."

As she sat there in that quiet room beside her silent father, Timmie tried to convince herself that there might well be some danger in Restcrest. People might be dying here who had no business doing it, people whose only illness was confusion. Her father could be in real danger.

Timmie studied the sharp relief of his cheekbones, the broken ridge of his hawk nose, the deep well of his eyes. She thought about the brilliance of his words, the terror of that gun.

Tentatively, the way she did to Meghan while she slept, Timmie lifted a hand and stroked her father's hair. It was cleaned and shiny from the staff's attention, brushed into a thick, noble cap that looked nothing like it had when he'd been tied to his chair at home. She stroked his hair and hummed a few verses of "Only the Rivers Run Free."

If she left him here, he could die.

If she took him home, he would certainly die.

Knowing that he would never need to understand her decision, Timmie kissed him and walked out into the hall that seemed suddenly much too bright for her eyes.

By eleven that night, the weather had cleared. The moon skirted fitfully among the ragged clouds, and a crisp breeze teased the trees. There was soft music drifting from the car stereo and the subtle scent of Aramis in the air.

"Surely you'll let me see you to the door."

Timmie looked over to where Alex's head gleamed faintly in the passing streetlights and smiled. She'd been preparing for this moment since she'd met Alex at Café Renee three hours earlier. Actually, she'd been dreading it. She'd intended to avoid the moment when Alex walked into her house by meeting him at the restaurant. But that had been before Cyrano had decided to have an uncommon hissy fit. Timmie had ended up walking over, and knew better than to think Alex would let her walk home. So she moved to plan B.

"This is Puckett, Alex," she assured him. "Nobody's going to mug me on my sidewalk. Besides, you've been yawning for the last hour. Get home and get some sleep."

Alex slowed his silver-gray Lexus to a perfect stop at the cross street before turning onto Timmie's block. "I'm really embarrassed about that, Timmie. I don't want you to think I haven't had a good time. I really enjoyed myself this evening."

Timmie smiled. "So did I."

Alex was a gentleman. He was dear and polite and sincere. Timmie was sure that it was the fact that she'd been distracted by everything on the planet that had made him seem so . . .

Nope. A woman who had just had a twenty-year-old fantasy fulfilled did not court words like "boring."

Alex was tired. Timmie was frustrated. She had had the evening scripted for almost a hundred years. Somehow it had never included endless paeans to her father, intensive instruction on everything to do with Alzheimer's, and a blow-by-blow description of the struggle to attain a new PET scanner for the unit.

Next time they would talk about world events, places each had traveled, the effect of any national policy that didn't have a direct impact on health care. Next time they'd laugh like kids over silly jokes and the foibles of lesser humans.

"I haven't had much sleep the last few nights," he apologized for the third time. "I just can't figure out why Barnaby graduated."

"Graduated." The favorite among the vast and varied euphemisms for dying Alex was so fond of using. It still amazed Timmie that Alex couldn't actually say the word "died." His patients graduated or passed or expired or went on. They never just died. Which was what they did. Another one two nights earlier.

She should ask now. She should demand an explanation.

"It's almost enough to make a new customer nervous," she said. "It does seem we've been seeing a lot of your . . . residents in the ER lately."

She couldn't say clients. She just couldn't.

His expression stayed tight. "It happens like that sometimes. You know that. But it's been a really tough autumn for me."

She was going to ask more when they turned into her drive, and Alex abruptly smiled. "I've always loved this old house," he said, leaning forward a little to catch sight of the old Victorian with its soft red brick washed in porch light. "It's such a dignified old lady. Our house was brand new when I was a kid. No ghosts at all."

Timmie almost said that there weren't any ghosts in this house, either, but she couldn't quite believe it. "Yeah," she said instead, "our house in St. Louis was pretty boring, too."

"You never did tell me," he said, pulling the car to a stop. "How's your mom? Last I heard she was working up at Barnes Hospital."

"She still is. Assistant director of nursing. She's fine."

"And Rose and Margaret?"

The girls who, if Alex had ever thought to look their way, would have been much more of an age to attract him. "Fine."

Timmie heard the snap in her voice and almost apologized. But if Alex heard it, he didn't interpret it. He only nodded and smiled, a handsome man wearing his regulation-gray tailored suit and blue-and-red-patterned tie, in his perfectly nice car. Putting the car in Park, he yanked on the brake, and turned to her. "I'm glad you're back, Timmie."

Timmie smiled back at him. "Me, too, Alex. Thanks for dinner."

Murphy would be waiting to hear that she'd finagled a confession out of Alex. He'd want something more than Alex's admission that his own first marriage had failed because of his commitment to his work and that he was troubled by people . . . graduating in his unit. Timmie couldn't pry any deeper, and not because she'd dreamed of Alex since she'd been seven.

"I'll probably see you at Restcrest tomorrow," she said, fiddling with the tiny bells that dangled from her earrings.

His smile grew. "You're a good daughter."

Timmie damn near laughed. Just the testimonial she wanted in a darkened driveway from the man of her dreams.

"He's quite a dad," she said, as she always did, and unhanded the bells to grab her purse. Definitely time to go.

"He's a lion of the hills."

That almost did it. Timmie nodded and struggled to get the door open. "He is that. Good night, Alex."

She made it all the way up to her front porch before it dawned on her that she hadn't even waited to be kissed. Or that Alex hadn't pressed the point. Definitely out of stage three of divorce, then, she decided, pulling out her house key.

Trying hard not to giggle, Timmie turned to wave good-bye. After she put that key in, Alex would go home and she'd be faced with that house again. With all the crap that she kept hidden behind that door. Well, hell, she might as well get it over with.

Except that the door was already open.

Timmie realized it when she went to slide in the key. The door creaked with the pressure of her hand. It swung in a little, and for the first time Timmie saw that she was standing in a pool of shattered glass. Somebody had broken out the door window.

She froze for a second, staring. The door kept swinging and she got a good look at her living room. "Aw, hell."

She should have expected this. A lovely night out with a man, and she came home to find her house broken into.

Her first reaction was that somebody was going to be mighty disappointed. Her second was that only one person had ever broken into her house before, and that that person had started calling again.

He'd warned her. He'd served her with a notice. She'd ignored it, as she'd tried to before.

"Jason Michael Parker," she snarled, "if this is your work, I'll fry you like a hush puppy!"

Furious and frustrated and frightened, Timmie shoved the door all the way open and stormed inside.

"Timmie, don't go in there!"

Timmie hadn't even realized that Alex had gotten out of the car. But there he was, loping up the porch steps. Timmie didn't have any choice. Whirling to face him, she threw her arms wide to block his way in.

"Alex, no!"

But Alex didn't hear her. Before Timmie could get the door shut, Alex was pushing her out of the way. "Get in my car," he demanded. "I've called 911 . . . Oh, my God," he gasped, stumbling to a sick halt. "You've been vandalized!"

And Timmie, more ashamed than she'd been since her father had thrown up on her at the father-daughter dance, had to stand there next to Alex as he took in the sight of the living room she'd been rooting through for two days and admit the truth. "No one's touched anything, Alex. This is the way it looks."

He hit his head on the Nerf ball as she ushered him in.

* * *

The police came five minutes later to dust the door and peer at the broken glass and gape at the sight of Dr. Alex Raymond calmly seated on a pile of *Life* magazines in the middle of the floor. Waiting until Timmie had made sure Meghan was still safe at Mattie's, they reluctantly asked Timmie if anything was missing, and agreed too quickly when she said no.

When they left, Timmie ushered a still-protesting Alex out right after them. And then, only bothering to board up her front door and take off the stiletto heels she'd pulled out for her famous date, Timmie spent close to an hour with the bat in her hand trying to knock that Nerf ball back off its line.

She was forty minutes into her therapy, her red dress hiked to her thighs and her stockings torn, when she saw the blinking light on her answering machine.

Nope. She didn't want to check it. After all, it was probably Jason calling to see if she'd checked his handiwork.

Nothing had been taken. Nothing moved. To Timmie's mind, that meant Jason. After all, if somebody'd broken in to rob her, they would have at least tried. She did have a few valuables tucked in her freezer. If it had been another one of those amateur threats, the perps wouldn't have settled for the front door.

No, it was Jason, which meant he was getting started again. He wouldn't hurt her. Jason considered violent men weaklings. His torture *du jour* was the subpoena, his chosen calling card the simple hit-and-run attack.

And he wanted to stay in touch with Meghan. Timmie had to get the hell to a lawyer and stop him.

When she had finished working off her rage.

Smack! A three-bagger at least, with Willie McGee trundling along the bases ahead of her.

After a while she ran out of energy. Barb called at one, and Ellen shortly thereafter, evidently having been contacted by the Mattie express. Then, finally, Cindy, who didn't understand when Timmie declined her offer to come over and sit.

"But I'm still at work," Cindy objected. "I can be right over there. I mean, my God, Timmie, you're there all alone. What if something else happens tonight?"

Timmie wasn't sure whether Cindy meant that she could help or that she didn't want to miss it. Either way, Timmie's answer was the same.

"Cindy, I lived in North Hollywood and worked in Central L.A. for almost ten years. I don't think the homeys here are quite so tough. So if everybody will stop calling, I'm going to bed."

She wasn't making Cindy happy. "I'm trying to be a good friend."

Timmie sighed, chagrined. "You are a good friend."

"I'll go right home. Call me if you need me."

"I promise." She'd made the same promise to Ellen and Barb. Maybe three promises like that was critical mass. By the time she shut off the phone Timmie had had it with just about everybody in this town. She was going to shut off the lights and go to bed and the hell with all of them.

She was halfway across the living room when she heard the creak.

The porch. The first board after the steps. It always creaked when people tried to walk too carefully on it. She knew. She'd tried to sneak past that board herself too many nights.

Her heart shouldn't thump like that. She shouldn't suddenly want to call Cindy.

It was nothing. Nobody. All those careful friends had succeeded in making her afraid, which was stupid. She'd survived more than a stupid B&E artist in a one-horse town.

*Creak. Scrape.*

How could silence be so loud? It seemed to roar in her ears, with only the hum of the refrigerator in the kitchen to encroach on it. It was so quiet Timmie could almost hear herself sweat.

She should call for help. She didn't want to be laughed at again.

There was somebody at her front door.

Somebody who knocked.

It wasn't much of a knock. More like another series of soft scrapes. Syncopated and slow. For some reason, Timmie thought of every old urban legend, from the Hook to the hung guy with his shoes scraping the top of the lovers' car, all making slow, syncopated noises in the dead of night.

"Who's there?" she called out, feeling like an idiot.

All she had to do was check out the window. Make sure there was somebody on her porch. Call the police.

She took a step. She took another. She heard a muffled sound like a man's voice on the other side of her door. It was the Hook. She just knew it. Or worse. It was Jason, finally deciding to escalate the issue into insanity.

"What do you want?" she called more loudly, feeling really stupid now.

Timmie pulled back the curtain to check out front. She could see the porch, glossy gray flooring, clean white rails and wicker furniture. Empty sidewalk bordered by twin yellow columns of chrysanthemums. Some kind of large, lumpy shadow at her door.

"Move back so I can see you!" she yelled.

She got an answer. She just couldn't make it out. So she picked up the baseball bat and opened the front door.

And screamed.

The shadow hadn't been leaning over at her door. It had been leaning *on* her door. The minute she opened it, the weight forced it wide open. Timmie jumped back. A body landed on her floor with a smack and lay sprawled at her feet.

"Oh, for God's sake," she snapped in disbelief. "Murphy!"

That was when she realized that he hadn't fallen because he was been drunk. He'd fallen because he was bleeding like a stuck pig.

# FOURTEEN

"JESUS, MURPHY, WHAT HAPPENED?"

There was blood on his face, all down the front of his shirt, caked in his hair. There were bruises and scrapes on his knuckles, a couple of good rips in what was probably his only sports coat, and a funny catch to his breathing Timmie recognized all too well. Either Murphy had run afoul of the only grizzly in the state of Missouri, or he'd had the crap beaten out of him.

Timmie didn't even notice her nylon snag on the hardwood floor as she dropped to her knees next to him. "Murphy?"

"Nnngh."

At least he was getting his eyes open. Timmie tossed aside her bat to check his pulse. A little fast, but not thready. Not slow and bounding, which would have signaled a head injury. She lifted both eyelids to make sure his pupils were round and reactive to light. They were. Timmie also saw a spark of cognizance flickering in that deceptive green. He was in there, he just hadn't decided whether or not he wanted to make an appearance.

"Oh, Murphy!" she called as if he were a kid she wanted to come out and play. Unbuttoning his shirt and pulling his tie loose, she did a quick assessment with knowing hands to find a couple of lumps behind one ear, an impressive cut at his hairline, and more than one tender area over his left ribs and right kidney. "Come on. You got all the way to my house. Now tell me what happened."

He blew out a breath and flinched. So did Timmie. She could have stoked a Bunsen burner on that breath.

She sat back, disgusted with them both. With him for having evidently jumped off the wagon right into a bar fight and herself for feeling disappointed.

"Tell me what happened or I roll you right back out the door," she demanded, ready to get back up.

He didn't open his eyes again. "You're going to tell me . . . I had a drink."

"I don't think it'll come as a surprise to you."

He nodded his head fractionally and winced again. "Couldn't seem to . . . get here without a little painkiller."

"So you got beaten up *before* you got drunk?"

That at least got one eye open. "I'm not drunk, Leary. Trust me . . . I know the difference."

"And you got beaten up how?"

The eye closed. He spent a moment bracing his ribs with his hand. "Nice dress, Leary. Was the big date tonight?"

It was all Timmie could do to keep from hitting him. "You're asking for another bruise, Murphy. What happened?"

"I got jumped . . . Oh, Jesus, I forgot how much that hurts."

"You got jumped?" she demanded. "In *Puckett*?"

"By somebody with jackboots."

Jackboots. Oh, boy. Timmie let her own breath out and rested back on her heels. The only jackboots she'd seen in this town had been worn by the cops. "Where? When?"

"Ten . . . I think. My place. Three of them, maybe four. It all kind of blurred after that first boot."

"And so you came here instead of calling 911 because you didn't want to run into the same cops who jumped you?"

He managed a twitch of a smile. "You did live in L.A., didn't you?"

Even considering the evening she'd had, she had to grin. "You need to get checked over, Murphy."

"Thought you were a forensic nurse."

"That doesn't make me an X-ray machine. Let me call the paramedics. I'm not licensed to handle this. Especially if you've ended up with a pneumothorax or a bad kidney."

"And if I refuse?"

"I don't have any release-from-responsibility forms around here."

He bent a jean-clad leg to evidently ease the discomfort in his stomach and grunted with the effort. "I need some . . . stitching, Leary. Some ice. Not a new kidney."

She grimaced. "Familiar with the symptoms, are you?"

He grimaced right back. "Occupational hazard. I can breathe fine, my neck's not even sore, and I already peed on my own."

"No blood?"

He grinned. "No blood."

It finally dawned on Timmie that cold air was swirling in the still-open door. Jumping to her feet, she closed it, locked it, and returned to shove aside the pile of magazines to get to the Chippendale secretary in which her grandmother had stored the linen napkins. Perfect for stanching blood.

"Have you been . . . uh, tested lately?" she asked.

He grinned like a teenager. "During my latest unfortunate incarceration. I may be a headcase, but I'm a careful headcase."

She went back to getting her hands bloody. "And when you were dancing with these guys, did they deliver any message?"

"Your basic 'Be on the noon train outta town.' "

She nodded. "So you're upsetting people again."

"In my line of work, we prefer to say I'm getting close to the truth."

"Uh-huh." Pushing a stiff mass of hair back off his forehead, she assessed the two-inch cut that looked like it had been made with a blunt object. Maybe a nightstick or a flashlight. "You know the drill?"

He was still smiling, as if this were all faintly amusing. "Daniel

Patrick Murphy. Timmie Leary's living room floor. Thursday, October thirtieth."

Oriented to person, place, time. He really did have the routine down. Timmie pressed a napkin against the cut and got a muffled oath for her trouble.

"I'll call Barb," Timmie said. "I can trust her."

"No. Just you."

Timmie sighed, furious with herself. With him. With whoever had done this. Murphy really did look like hell. And he'd brought it right to her door, as if she could make it better. What the hell was she, Caregivers "R" Us? With her own muffled oath, Timmie swiped an old olive-green throw pillow from the couch and slipped it beneath his head. "I don't have my own suture kit, Murphy. Besides, Barb can at least get you some Darvon."

Damn him if he didn't chuckle with his eyes still closed.

"No good. I was hooked on that, too."

Timmie wanted to laugh, damn him. "Anything you *weren't* hooked on?"

He considered. "Not that I can remember."

"A full life lived, huh? I'll just go throw out all the cough syrup and aftershave so you don't end up crawling across the floor in the dead of night."

"Won't happen," he said, then offered another crooked grin. "Not this time, anyway."

Timmie had been about to get to her feet. That one stopped her cold. Well, wasn't that just the story of her life? The man she'd dreamed about was a disappointment, and the one she was attracted to was a dead-end proposition. *Not this time*. It pretty much closed the conversation.

"Well, then," she said, wiping her hands as she finished her climb. "I guess I should probably at least get the name of your next of kin, so I know who to contact if you croak on my floor."

He seemed to think about that, too. "My wife, I guess."

Another double take. Her third in only five minutes. It was definitely not her night. "I thought you said you had three strikes against you."

He grinned again, which was making her testy. "I do. I just haven't worked up the energy to walk away from the plate . . . Oh, God, I must feel bad. I'm doing baseball analogies."

This time Timmie did laugh as she walked over to the phone. "So, what's the opera equivalent? The fat lady's sung but the curtain puller's asleep?"

He laughed back and groaned. Served him right. Timmie was just about to lift the receiver when the thing rang. For a second, all she could do was stare at it.

"I think it's for you," Murphy suggested in that hurt-rib-careful voice he was using.

"Uh-uh," she disagreed, shaking her head. "The way my luck's been going tonight, it's probably Jason wanting to gloat about breaking in."

The phone kept ringing, shrill and threatening in the early-morning quiet.

"Breaking in? What are you talking about?"

"The board over the door," she said. "You weren't the first one to make a surprise appearance tonight."

Timmie looked over to see Murphy open his eyes, assess the hastily attached boards on the graying door. "Leary . . ."

But she couldn't wait anymore. She just picked up the phone. "What?"

"You didn't listen."

Oh, shit. It wasn't Jason at all.

"I think I'm getting my phone threat," she informed Murphy dourly, then turned to her caller. "Okay," she said, infuriated by the fact that her heart rate had just doubled. "I give up. Who is this?" She also hit the Record button on her answering machine, because half-whispered threats in the dead of night pissed her off.

"Your voice of reason. You should have listened."

"Listened to what?" she demanded. "You think I'm going to pay attention to somebody who cuts his threats out of a *Cosmo*?"

"Take a look at Mr. Murphy. You think that's a joke? How about your front door?"

Her front door. Wonderful. Better and better. She had the creeps harder than she'd ever had them in L.A. Well, at least that meant that Jason wasn't harassing her. Yet. He'd probably show up right after she got the glass replaced. And she didn't even want to think right now about what the hell they'd done to her house if she hadn't noticed anything out of place.

"Okay, I'll bite," she drawled. "Who are you and what are we supposed to stop doing?"

"We're just people with the welfare of this town in mind. You and Mr. Murphy obviously aren't."

Timmie probably shouldn't have, but she laughed. "Great. I'm being threatened by the Puckett Chamber of Commerce. I would have thought you guys were too busy printing up complimentary calendars to bother with breaking and entering."

"You're not taking this seriously enough."

"You still haven't told me what we've done."

"You know what you've done. Do you think Dr. Raymond would still see you if he knew you were trying to ruin him?"

Timmie actually found herself spluttering. Stunned, furious, frightened all over again.

Alex.

No, no, no. It couldn't be Alex.

She tried to form a coherent answer, at least a noise of real outrage, but the caller had already hung up.

"Leary?" Murphy asked from behind her.

"Well, that tears it," she snapped, slamming the receiver down so hard the phone jumped in its little alcove. "I'm on the next stage out of town. Los Angeles was way more fun than this."

"Leary? Who was it?"

That finally got her to turn around, only to find that Murphy wasn't where she'd left him. He was, in fact, tottering toward her, his free hand leaving bloody smudges on the dingy brown couch, his arm tight around his ribs, his face the color of her front door.

"You idiot!" she snapped, truly mad. "Lie down somewhere before you fall again and knock all this crap over and I just have to clean it up right after I clean you!"

His grin was probably about sixty watts shy of what he was trying to project. "It is an . . . interesting room."

"Shut up." She stalked over and grabbed him by the armpit.

"Ouch."

Timmie at least got him on the couch—after she'd swept it clean of the insurance forms her grandmother had seemed to collect on a par with Christmas cookie recipes.

"Hey, Leary?" Murphy asked as she stuffed another pillow under his head.

"What?"

"Tell me that's not a tattoo on your thigh."

Timmie instinctively looked down to make sure her dress hadn't hiked up. It hadn't. But it did tend to float out a bit.

"Great view from the floor," Murphy allowed, eyes half open. "Good thing I'm an honorable man. Is it a tattoo?"

"What's it to you?" she demanded, hand instinctively covering the spot even over her dress.

Murphy groaned. "It's a rose, isn't it, Leary? I love rose tattoos. They're sexy as hell, especially there. I don't suppose you'd want to have my babies, would you?"

There he went again. How could he be this offensive and this funny at the same time? How could he make her feel so itchy with just that damn smile? Timmie grabbed a particularly vile puce afghan and plopped it over him as if she were burying not only him, but every wayward thought in her head. "I'd rather skin myself alive with a nail file than have another relationship with an unreformed drunk, Murphy."

He smiled. He smiled! "Okay, then, how about some meaningless sex?"

For just that second before her better sense kicked in, Timmie actually considered it. Thankfully, her better sense was stronger than her libido, and she remembered just what a disaster it had been when she'd followed the meaningless-sex dictates of stage three of divorce. "I only have sex after I jog, Murphy. If you can get off that couch and run six miles right now, it's a deal."

She got another groan. "You're heartless, Leary."

"No, I'm not," she said, feeling a little better. "If I were heartless, I'd tell Barb what you just said before I let her stitch you up."

And with that, finally, she went to call her friend.

"This probably isn't a good idea," Murphy managed almost an hour later.

"Shut up," both Timmie and Barb answered in unison.

"But you shouldn't be involved," Murphy insisted as the sleep-tousled giantess pulled his shirt off to check him.

He was colorful, that was for sure. The bruises were brick red and purpling, even with the Baggie-loads of ice Timmie had already supplied. Clad in bright orange sweats, Barb examined him with gentle efficiency. Murphy winced and cursed under his breath as they moved him, but he behaved. Having already seen the worst when she'd cleaned him, Timmie kept her mouth shut and her mind on the newest problems they had.

Alex.

It wasn't going to be Alex. She wouldn't let it be, no matter what.

But if not Alex, then who? If she was right about the death rate going up in Restcrest, why wouldn't he have noticed? And why the hell couldn't she just have focused on cleaning the house and teaching trauma nurse certification courses instead of always getting into trouble?

"So, you're telling me that the long and short of this evening is that you got beaten up because you're sure Vic was murdered, and it has something to do with that little dustup at the horse show," Barb said, squinting into Murphy's retina through an ophthalmoscope. "Which might lead back to Restcrest, if not—and I don't believe it for a minute—Alex."

"Shouldn't you be more surprised?" Murphy asked.

Barb just kept working. "The last time I was surprised was when my children told me that they'd walked in on Daddy handcuffing his girlfriend to the bed. If Vic had to die, I'm glad it wasn't from stupidity."

Standing beyond Murphy, Timmie could see the glitter in

Barb's eyes that belied her brisk words. She offered the only consolation she could. "He was trying to be a good cop."

Barb nodded, spared Timmie a quick glance that betrayed too much, and picked up her percussion hammer and Murphy's elbow. "Then what do we do about it?" she asked.

"We do nothing," he answered, his attention on the gig-twitch of his arms in response to her deft taps. "It might just be time to take this to the state police."

"State police wear jackboots, too," Timmie quietly offered.

Murphy glared at her.

She shrugged. "In a little while. Can't we just kind of make sure we've got the right field of wheat before we bring in the harvesting equipment?" Now both of them were staring at her. She scowled. "All right, so there are some drawbacks to being raised in a literary household. I think in analogies. What I mean is that Restcrest is a wonderful place. I don't want it leveled in a panzer attack for the truth."

"It may end up leveled anyway," Murphy told her. "Even if it isn't Raymond, an investigation of any kind could cost the facility its license."

Timmie was already shaking her head. "That won't happen," she insisted. "Alex Raymond is the heart of Restcrest. As long as he isn't the culprit—which he isn't—Restcrest will be fine."

Barb leaned over to look Murphy full in the face. "Mr. Murphy," she said, gesturing to Timmie. "I'd like to introduce you to Cleopatra."

Murphy grinned. "Queen of denial, huh?"

"I am not," Timmie insisted out of habit. "I'm serious."

Besides, she thought without bothering to tell them, I'm Scarlett. No denial necessary when you can just put things off till tomorrow.

"You really think somebody's killing gomers?" Barb asked as she tapped knees and Achilles tendons. "Why?"

"Could it just be negligence?" Murphy asked.

Both women shook their heads. "That'd make Alex the culprit," Timmie told him. "Alex may be many things. He isn't negligent."

Murphy rolled his eyes again. Barb, on the other hand, looked pensive. "Then who? And why?"

"Could be a number of things," Murphy assured her. "Could be cost cutting. For some reason right now, Restcrest doesn't have very many patients in its most expensive division. Then there's the researcher, Davies. He's happy as a clam that he has lots of fresh brains to play with. Or you could have one of those mercy killers on the loose."

Timmie shook her head. "That usually doesn't involve a police cover-up."

"Even if the hospital involved is the town's biggest industry?" Murphy asked. "Awful lot of good publicity generated in that facility, not only for the hospital, but for the town and the county. It's top on the local job hit parade right now."

"Well, that would definitely explain the chamber-of-commerce angle," Timmie admitted.

"You're sure it's Restcrest?" Barb asked.

"It's sure Alex they mentioned on the phone," Timmie said.

"It's not Alex," Barb said simply. "Think of somebody else. Lie down, Mr. Murphy. I'm going to make you beautiful again."

Murphy laid down and in quick order had sterile towels draped over head and bare chest, and his forehead painted a bright Betadine orange. Settling herself on the coffee table like a ripe pumpkin waiting for a good carve, Barb set to work.

"Okay," she said, drawing up the lidocaine. "If there is something going on, what about that Mary Jane Arlington? I wouldn't put anything past her."

Just south of the sterile towels Barb had draped, Murphy's eyes followed the movements of the syringe. "How about if we wait to discuss this?" he asked in astonishingly faint tones. "I'm not sure I want you to be wielding sharp instruments close to my face if you get upset."

Barb snorted unkindly. "Oh, don't be a baby. I've sewn up screaming kids, fighting drunks, and hallucinating psychos. I even sewed up a hysterical poodle once."

Timmie grinned. "Didn't even leave a scar."

Murphy just sighed in resignation and closed his eyes. His fists were still suspiciously tight, however, as Barb first numbed, then sutured the laceration with stitches as delicate as any master seamstress.

"Mary Jane," Barb reiterated. "You see the serious Hinckley eyes she puts on Alex? I think she'd take out the town council with a machete if she thought it'd help. When was your last tetanus?"

Murphy didn't even hesitate. "Last year. Mary Jane, huh?"

Barb nodded. "Rabbit in the stew pot, you know what I mean?"

"What about Paul Landry?" Timmie asked. "Mattie doesn't like him at all."

"Who knows?" Barb asked, snipping a pair of hairlike threads. "He's sure a big-time player in a nasty league."

"Would people be upset that he's involved with GerySys?" Murphy asked, bringing the proceedings to a screeching halt.

"What?" Timmie demanded before Barb could.

"You know about GerySys?" he asked, opening his eyes.

"You are talking about the worst nursing home chain since the invention of the bedsore," Barb informed him. "Parent of the notorious Gulag Golden Grove. That GerySys? Why?"

"Because Paul Landry is negotiating with them to cosponsor Restcrest. I found out today from a contact at the *Post*."

Murphy almost ended up with a pierced eyebrow. "Alex would never let him do that," Barb informed him tightly.

"Alex has no say," Murphy said. "It was part of the deal. Landry's in charge. And Landry's talking GerySys into helping defray a much more expensive unit than anybody at Price had anticipated."

"Oh, God." It was a chorus now. Distress, disgust. Disbelief.

"This'll kill Alex for sure," Timmie said.

"So they—Landry or Mary Jane or whoever—killed Victor because he found out people were dying at the home," Murphy said. "And maybe it had something to do with this new deal with Golden Grove—"

"Or maybe they're keeping it quiet so GerySys won't be scared off," Timmie said.

"And somehow they have Van Adder involved so the deaths go virtually unnoticed."

"If they killed Vic," Barb said, "why not just kill Murphy, too?"

Murphy was once again eyeing the instruments. "Because I got the impression that this was stage one. If somebody had threatened Victor, would he have listened?"

Barb laughed, a booming intrusion in the echoing room. "Not Victor. It would have been an insult to the memory of Jack Webb."

"But it does mean they're serious," Timmie admitted.

Murphy allowed himself a minimal nod beneath the towel. "Hard to believe, but I think you're right. We need to make sure your kids are safe."

Timmie shared looks with Barb, her stomach knotting. She could tell that Barb's was doing the same. Decision time. Unfortunately, Timmie couldn't go back on the one she'd already made.

Barb clinched it by bending back to work. "We can take care of our kids," she said. "And I'm not about to insult the memory of Jack Webb, either. The question is, what do we do now?"

"Well," Timmie said, grabbing the scissors and snipping threads to speed things up, "I have an appointment to meet with the St. Charles ME to talk about it. And I have a Morbidity and Mortality printout I'd like you to—" She got that far, and froze.

*The printout.*

The very same printout she'd sneaked out of the ER like a counterfeit diamond and perused like secret missile plans. Oh, damn. Dropping the scissors at the edge of the tray, she spun on her heels for the stairs. "Excuse me."

Upstairs nothing seemed changed. The same mountain range of books commanded the hallway, now in disarray from where Timmie had burrowed for items for that damn memory case. Her room was still awash in fabric samples and purloined wallpaper books and outdated missalettes. Timmie did a quick check to see if she could spot a strange hand at it, but she couldn't tell because she'd tossed the room too many times herself looking for her dad's things.

In the end, it didn't matter. There between the old sleigh bed and the wall where she'd left it with all her busy work was her cloth nursing bag. And inside that was the list.

Timmie chuckled with embarrassment. As if this would made a big difference. Unless three separate computer systems crashed, the printout was like an extra roll of prints. Yanking the sheaf of papers from her bag, Timmie carried them back downstairs where Barb was telling Murphy what a lucky boy he was.

"I think I found something on the M and M printout," she said, reclaiming the scissors. "I need you to look, too, Barb."

"There's one other thing you have to do," Barb told her in a tone of voice that portended trouble, her attention still on the tiny needle and thread in her large hands.

Timmie held still. Murphy opened his eyes. Barb smiled, and it wasn't pretty.

Timmie blanched. "Not . . . "

Barb nodded, enjoying herself much too much. "You know damn well that if there's something hinky going on at Restcrest the staff knows about it, and at least one person over there's pissed as hell. You *know* it, Timmie. And there's only one way to find out who it is."

"No."

"Oh, yes. You're going to have to go undercover."

"*You* go undercover," Timmie demanded of the big woman, now truly distressed. "I'd rather play coroner truck with Van Adder."

Barb was laughing now. "Sorry, girl. I'd stick out like a sore thumb. But they're always needing nurses over there. And you are, even with all those fancy initials behind your name, a nurse. The next time Restcrest calls for help, you're going to have to go on gomer patrol."

"We could ask Ellen to do it."

"She's sleeping with Van Adder."

Timmie's grimace was purely reactionary. "Well, then, Cindy. She *likes* it up there."

Barb lifted an eyebrow. "You'd trust Cindy with delicate information? You *are* desperate."

Timmie shut her eyes. "Oh, man. The things I do for the truth."

"Now," Barb said, dropping the instruments on the sterile towel and ripping off her gloves. "Let me look at that list."

She looked while Timmie cleaned Murphy's face, dressed his cut, and handed back his shirt and ice packs. She hummed and whistled and paged back and forth as if she were going through a company ledger. And then, when Timmie had all but run out of patience, Barb sat back on the wingback she'd commandeered, crossed her leg over her other knee, and nodded.

"You're right. This is weird."

Timmie looked up from the trash bag she'd been filling. "You do recognize them, then?"

Barb blinked. "Recognize who?"

Timmie's heart sank. "The patients from Restcrest who were dismissed out of the ER. Because of that new policy of transferring all seriously ill Restcrest patients to the ER, the Restcrest mortality numbers are skewed. On the printout, it looks like they're declining. They're really going up."

"Oh, that," Barb retorted. "Sure. I figured that out." She opened the pages again and pointed to several lines. "The thing that bothers me is that they almost all died of cardiac arrest."

Timmie dropped what she was doing. "What?"

Now it was Murphy's turn to look confused. He'd just tottered to his feet and was tucking his blood-encrusted shirt back in. "I guess I don't have this right. I thought cardiac arrest was something you died of."

"Of course it is," Barb snapped. "It's what *everybody* dies of, if you want to get technical about it. Your heart stops beating, you die. But something else causes the heart to stop beating, and that's what should go on these lines. You understand?"

Timmie imagined that Murphy nodded. She didn't see, though. She was already bent over the printout, furious at her own oversight. "Oh, my God," she whispered, seeing the evidence for herself. "You're right."

Barb kept skimming with a blunt finger. "See? There's Mr.

Cleveland, and Mrs. Salgado?" She stabbed at one line in particular and smiled an oddly whimsical smile. "And here's Mr. Stein, you remember him? He always dropped by with cookies."

Timmie shook her head, still too stunned. "I missed it."

Line after line, Barb pointed out the obvious, tucked in among the myocardial infarctions, the cardiovascular accidents, the sudden infant death syndromes, the multiple traumas from MVA.

Cardiac arrest
Cardiac arrest
Cardiac arrest

At least fifteen of them. And they'd never been caught by the hospital, the coroner, or the physician who was the heart and soul of the most advanced Alzheimer's unit in the country.

"They're all Restcrest's?" Timmie asked.

Barb nodded. "I recognize enough of them."

Now even Murphy was looking. "Weren't you suspicious that you had so many people coming in from the same place?"

"Why should we be?" Barb retorted. "They were old. You expect old people to die, ya know?"

That was when Timmie felt the worst. The most ridiculously, pompously, self-delusional worst. "Which is why it's so easy to murder them," she admitted, wanting suddenly to cry. "It's one of the first lessons I learned in forensics. The easiest people to murder are the elderly, because nobody's really surprised when they die."

"Especially people with Alzheimer's," Barb agreed.

Murder. They *had* been murdered. Maybe not all of them. Probably not all of them. They were, after all, all over the age of sixty, some well into their nineties and frail and high risk.

But enough. Enough that Timmie the death investigator, the Forensics Fairy, should at least have asked. Instead, she'd just wrapped them up and rolled them out and only questioned their disposition when the coroner had been an asshole.

And now, the only way to make amends was to spend at least ten hours up to her hips in meandering, muttering, miscast phantoms from a thinking person's nightmare. She was going to have to do time at Restcrest. And then she was going to have to face her father and then admit that she was putting him in danger by even asking the questions she needed to ask. She was going to have to face every demon that had sent her screaming from this town. It was enough to make her want to vomit.

And to think that the only reason she'd gotten into this in the first place was because she'd decided it would be better than dealing with Jason.

Jason.

Hell, she hadn't decided what to do about him, either.

Well, Scarlett, she thought, so close to tears she had to leave the room, tomorrow's just come, and you're not ready.

# FIFTEEN

MURPHY HAD SURVIVED OTHER MORNINGS AFTER. THIS ONE was pretty typical except for the fact that he didn't have alcohol mucking it up. He was sore in a thousand places, dizzy if he turned too fast, and moving on a par with an arthritic octogenarian. It didn't make a bit of difference to his stomach, which was as much a tyrant as ever. So when he awoke right on cue at dawn, he only managed to stay in bed another couple of hours before venturing out into Leary's kitchen.

Besides, even the kitchen was better than that back bedroom he'd slept in with its stale smells and sad mementos. Murphy couldn't imagine having to live in this house with all its discarded history. He couldn't imagine Timmie Leary moving through it as if it all didn't exist. But then Timmie Leary was a series of contradictions that intrigued an old newsman almost as much as that red-and-green tattoo on her right thigh.

The outside of her thigh, just at panty line, where nobody but a beaten-up drunk lying on the floor could have seen it.

Damn tattoo. Murphy hadn't been actively libidinous in years. It wasn't worth the effort. But he'd dreamed of that tattoo at least twice during the night, even knowing perfectly well it wouldn't do him any good. Timmie Leary didn't want to come within spitting distance of him, and in his more cognizant moments, Murphy couldn't agree more.

If only he hadn't seen the tattoo.

"That's disgusting," he heard behind him.

Murphy probably turned too fast, but then guilt will do that. He grabbed the edge of the old gas stove for balance when the room spun and he saw two or three Learys standing in the doorway in jeans, Marvin the Martian sweatshirt, and bare feet.

His first instinct was that she'd overheard his more objectionable thoughts. Not quite. Her focus was on the eggs that were spitting in her frying pan on the stove.

"Like some?" he asked with wry amusement.

Timmie's smile was not pretty. "I hope you'll be sufficiently warned if I just tell you that not even coffee helps me at this hour of the morning."

He didn't even bother to smile. Just turned back to the stove, picked up the RABID NURSE coffee mug he'd been drinking his own coffee from, and flipped his eggs.

"Make yourself at home," she said and padded in.

From the looks of her, Timmie hadn't slept any more than Murphy had. Her eyes were sunken again, and her hands trembled. And he was positive she didn't want him to notice. So he didn't.

"I left a dollar on the refrigerator," he said. "Sorry to be so presumptive, but I'm always up long before this."

Timmie groaned. "A day person."

Murphy shook his head, sipping coffee and nudging eggs. "Not by choice. I get up to run every morning. Penance for my sins."

"Which are undoubtedly numerous. Too bad you couldn't jog last night, huh, Murphy?"

He caught the very dry humor in her voice and turned around, properly chagrined. "Considering what mayhem you had the chance to wreak after that . . . unfortunate slip of the tongue, I'd like to say what a lady you are for not considering it."

She poured herself some coffee and took a good slug of it. "I've been propositioned by more than one concussion victim in my time," she said with a tired smile.

"Which I hope means you won't be bringing me up on charges."

She allowed a brief flicker of attraction to spark those huge blue eyes, then purposefully locked it away again. "It means that if you don't ever mention the rose, I won't mention the meaningless sex."

Murphy sighed. "Used to be, I'd at least get the meaningless sex before I couldn't talk about it."

"Times are tough all round these days."

He gave up and went back to his eggs, which were crisping around the edges from inattention. Timmie reached into a cabinet and pulled out a chipped Melmac plate for his eggs and a bottle of generic acetaminophen for his headache.

"Thanks."

"You're welcome. You dizzy or seeing double?"

Murphy dished up his eggs and shut off the gas. "Not much. How do I look to the trained eye?"

She squinted hard. "Like a train wreck trying to pass itself off as performance art. Good thing Halloween's today. You'll fit right in. But the scars will be minimal."

"You guys do good work."

Timmie eased her jeaned bottom down in one of the three mismatched Naugahyde chairs that surrounded the metal table. "Of course we do. We're the wave of Memorial's future."

"I thought that was Restcrest," Murphy said, gingerly sitting himself down across from her.

Timmie's laugh sounded awfully fatalistic. "Not after we get through with it."

Murphy heard every nuance in that statement and forgot the eggs he'd been anticipating since dawn. "Can I ask a question?"

"As long as it isn't about sex."

"Aren't you worried?"

Timmie raised eyebrows at him. "Worried about what?" she retorted, suddenly cautious. "Crime on the streets? The rising cost of medical care? The chance of contracting the ebola virus?"

"How this whole escapade is going to affect your father. I know what he means to you, Leary. You're putting him in a pretty vulnerable spot."

Murphy could see her jaw working as if she were chewing up her words before she spat them out. He saw how tight her eyes were and wondered at every little secret he didn't know.

"What brought this up?" she asked.

"His room. Sleep isn't very productive the first night after a crack on the head, and I didn't have anything to smoke. So I got to spend a lot of time looking at memorabilia." He retreated to his eggs as he spoke, the residue from those long, dark hours a little too fresh. "Raymond may be an android, but he's right. Your dad is something special, even only working on three cylinders. Raymond told me how he used to watch your dad lead you down the street singing to you when you were a little girl. Tough to get an image like that out of a person's head. Tougher to imagine that that guy could end up as bait."

She sucked in a breath that hissed in the quiet kitchen like a flaring match. "How do we know he isn't in danger already unless we find the murderer?" she asked carefully.

"Then why leave your father there at all?"

Murphy couldn't imagine her going any more rigid without just shattering. "The benefits outweigh the risks."

"You're sure about that."

Her laugh was dark. "I'm not sure about anything, Murphy. But if you'd like to take him home with you, the whole thing will be settled for the foreseeable future. But don't forget that he likes to roam around the streets in his underwear scaring church organists, and that when he gets frightened he swings."

Murphy went back to his eggs, cutting them into bites small enough to satisfy an anorexic. Timmie drank the very last dram of coffee in her cup. The sun, making it past the next-door neighbor's, splashed sun-catcher colors on a dingy wall. Murphy tried hard to focus on food rather than the easy sensuality that had so quickly vanished from Leary's movements the minute her father had been brought up. He missed it. He also wondered at it.

"I know it's an imposition," he said, "but would you mind driving me back home? I want to start making background calls."

That made her laugh as she dropped her cup on the table with a thunk. "Not unless you're better with a metric wrench than I am. My car died last night, and I'm going to have to spend the morning trying to find out why. You might as well use my phone."

He tried smiling again. "You're holding me against my will?"

"Of course not. I'm laying odds you won't make it down my front steps without ending up on your nose. I also don't think you really want to be seen at work looking like Rocky Raccoon."

His smile grew into near-genuine proportions. "You know far too much about male egos, Leary."

Her eyes still looked sore and tired. "More than you'll ever know, Murphy."

"All right, then," he said. "Let's work together. If you or Dr. Adkins can gig the hospital computer for more information on those patients and I can get more background on the business angle, we can maybe find out exactly what the death rate might have to do with the bid by GerySys. Working together we can get answers in half the time."

She was already shaking her head as she climbed to her feet. "Not today. I have a car to fix, a costume to sew, and after that, I don't care if Alex Raymond is the Green River Killer, it's Halloween. I am spending the evening with my daughter. Tomorrow's soon enough."

"Okay, then," he said, a lot slower following to his feet, his plate only partially emptied. "I'll start. When you get the phone bill, forward it to the paper. Sherilee'll be happy to pay for a scoop like this. She's been smelling exposé since I hit town."

That brought Timmie to a dead stop, her cup caught between her hands and her gaze off somewhere out the window. Murphy didn't have to ask why.

"Leary?"

Timmie turned to face him, and Murphy wondered if she knew how frightened she looked.

"You can still back out of this. It could protect your dad."

Out in the living room, the doorbell chimed. Neither of them turned to it. Timmie Leary stood there in the doorway to her kitchen as if caught in warring winds, her hands wrapped tightly around that old brown coffee mug, her posture taut.

"I'll tell you something, Murphy," she said, her voice way too soft. "This may sound ugly, but I'm getting real tired of always having to balance what's right against what's good for my father. Just once I'd like to act without having to worry about how it will affect him."

Murphy heard the anger, saw the sorrow, and couldn't think of a thing to say, except the obvious. "I didn't think you'd been back that long."

The door chimed again, more insistently this time. Timmie seemed to come back to life. She smiled with the kind of bleakness Murphy knew too well. "Don't kid yourself," she said. "You know that lovely picture Alex likes so much of Dad and me walking hand in hand when I was a little girl?"

Murphy nodded, the perfect straight man.

"I was the one leading him, Murphy."

And then she walked out to answer the door, and Murphy was left behind wondering why he was so surprised.

It was Cindy. Of course it was, Timmie thought, pulling the door wide to let her in.

"I don't know what to do," Cindy was saying before the door was even open. "That asshole's dropped me. *Dropped* me. After what I've given him. Timmie, what do I do?"

Timmie saw the tears that streaked Cindy's mottled face, the bedraggled state of her hair, and thought, Oh, what the hell. It was easier than talking to Murphy about her dad.

"Come on, Cindy," she said, turning her blithely back in the direction of the front yard. "Let's go work on my car."

"I don't want to work on your car!" Cindy wailed, distress lifting her voice like a curtain in high wind, then dropping it into misery. "I just want to feel better."

Any other morning Timmie might have been surly. But Cindy

hurt. Timmie could hear it in every syllable. So Timmie smiled and put an arm around her shoulders and guided her away from Murphy, who didn't need to hear this. "I know, hon. But the sunshine will help. And I can teach you to be self-sufficient enough not to need another asshole again as long as you live."

"You do that," Cindy said, sniffing, "and I'm your slave forever."

It seemed to work. Not only did Cindy not notice Murphy in Timmie's house, but within twenty minutes they'd discovered Cyrano's problem and been joined by Ellen, who bore with her the name of a lawyer who was just dying to get her teeth into a delinquent husband.

"I was cleaning out some things this morning," she said by way of explanation. "And I came across this. I guess I just never had the guts to use her when I still could . . . Cindy, are you okay?"

Which gave Timmie the perfect chance to skip on up to the house to use the phone. The good news was that the lawyer was interested. The bad news was that, of course, she would cost money. Timmie bit the bullet and hired her when she said that since Timmie had filed her need to move with the California court, Jason's latest paper chase was nothing short of imbecilic and could be taken care of in short order. Timmie hung up feeling better than she had all night.

"Did you know that Mary Jane Arlington was head nurse at that Boston nursing home your golden boy ran?" Murphy immediately asked, puffing away on a cigarette he must have found under her father's bed as he made quick shorthand notes on a pad of paper he was balancing against his leg. "Her name was Mary Jane Freize then, but it's her. My old editor's sending pictures."

Timmie glared at him. "It's Halloween," she reminded him. "Tell me tomorrow."

So even with Murphy on her phone and her friends in the driveway, Timmie spent the rest of the day without having to deal with anything more than Cyrano's distributor, the cranky bobbin on her sewing machine, and the fact that Ellen and Cindy didn't seem happy unless they could play endless games of "my love life has been more screwed up than yours."

As for Murphy, he was deemed a little too frightening to be answering any doors, so he got dropped off the minute Cyrano was in service and Timmie's friends were out the door. He lost any grace points he'd earned by smiling at Timmie's ugly little car and saying, "Oh, look. I have a Cabriolet, too." His Cabriolet, of course, wasn't a 1983 Peugeot. It wasn't even rusted.

And that evening, with the clouds scudding in appropriately creepy fashion across an old yellow moon and jack-o'-lanterns lit into leers, Timmie took a very excited Scheherazade out to trick or treat in a costume that billowed and sparkled when she whirled. Since sundown signaled a temperature drop, Scheherazade had to deal with a coat over her lovely outfit, but at least she didn't have to worry about being ambushed by wayward straight pins.

After Meghan's pillowcase sack of candy had been inspected and half-consumed and all the other porch lights on the street flipped off to signal the close to the evening, Timmie ended her long day awake and watching Megs sleep in her veil and lipstick. It was enough for her, even though Megs let Renfield be the one to wake Timmie the next morning from her place curled up in the armchair in the corner of the room. It had to be. The first thing Timmie had to do that Saturday morning was go see her mother.

"I suppose you think this is an improvement."

Timmie bent over to kiss her mother's taut cheek. "Hi, Mom. Good to see you, too."

Her mother, a prim, petite, precise woman of sixty-five, couldn't drag her eyes from her daughter's hair or mismatched clothing or jangling earrings. Not that Timmie was disconcerted. She'd spent most of her childhood bearing up to similar scrutiny.

Kathleen Leary saw the world as a place that never met her standards. All it took to remain in her good graces was to allow her to attempt your conversion. Timmie had not been in her good graces for a very long time. It didn't increase Timmie's self-respect to know that she'd spent an hour choosing the outfit most likely to elicit maternal outrage. It didn't keep the smile off her face when she saw her mother's reaction to the short brown skirt, oversized

Insane Clown Posse T-shirt, and Doc Martens Timmie wore, either.

"I have the pictures you wanted," Kathleen said, closing the door behind Timmie and following her into the beige-and-peach living room Timmie had always thought of as her mother's ode to conformity. "You're more than welcome to them. Where's Meghan?"

Timmie's attention was already drawn toward the spotless white kitchen, where she could hear the distinct sounds of snuffling. Oh, hell. It was going to be worse than she'd thought.

"Meg is on an overnight," she lied rather than explain why her very opinionated daughter did not want to see the grandmother who'd never quite managed a kind word to her.

As for the grandmother, she pursed her features in a quick moue of displeasure. "Oh. Well, you'd think she could take a little time out to see me. After all, you two have been back over a month and haven't been up once."

"That's okay," Timmie answered, heading unerringly toward the center of her mother's life. "I figure Rose gives you enough attention for the two of us. Hello, Rose."

Her older sister by twelve years, Rose had been intended to be the last of the Leary children. Rose had never gotten over the fact that she wasn't. She was sitting at the teak kitchen table with a cup of tea and a box of Kleenex, a puffy, unattractive woman with lank brown hair and basset hound eyes.

"I'm . . . sorry, Timmie," she said, sniffling. "I shouldn't be intruding. I just needed to talk to Mom for a while. It's Bob. I just don't know what to do with him anymore."

Bob being her husband of fifteen years who was nasty, shallow, mean, and philandering. But without whose unending ill treatment Rose would not be able to play her favorite role of long-suffering martyr.

"I just want to feel better," she said with a much-too-familiar sigh.

Timmie found herself fighting off the urge to laugh. Poor Cindy. No wonder she got snapped at so much.

"I know," Timmie said and remembered all over again why

she'd started tagging along after her father in the first place. "I won't be long. I just needed to get some pictures for the nursing home and talk to Mom about a little financial help."

Kathleen Leary stiffened as if Timmie had cursed or thrown a baseball in the kitchen. "I think we've had that discussion. After forty-five years of supporting that man, I don't think I should be expected to flush any more money down that toilet."

"It's not a toilet," Timmie protested. "It's the only place he's safe. It's not nearly as much as I thought, and I'm not asking for him. I'm not asking for me. I'm asking for Meg so she isn't afraid to live at home."

Wrapped around her hot tea and misery, Rose laughed. "Like she should have it so much better than we did?"

"You were never afraid," Timmie retorted, falling much too easily into old arguments.

"I was terrified," Rose insisted. "He was a drunk, Timmie. He never had a job, and we never knew what he was going to do from one minute to the next. Don't you remember?"

Timmie's smile was as cold as her sister's eyes. "At least he was interesting, Rose."

"Girls!" her mother snapped. Ever the guardian of propriety, she never allowed a harsh word in her house she herself didn't speak. "Enough. We'll talk about this later, Timmie. After I get Rose settled."

Kathleen, ever capable, ever doing, did. She refilled the teapot and set out cookies and patted Rose with a longtime nurse's absentminded efficiency. And Timmie, standing aside, had to wait to do her pleading.

"Besides," Kathleen said as she poured a cup of tea Timmie didn't want, "from what I've heard at work, Price is overplaying Restcrest. I don't think it's going to be what you think it is." She smiled with the relish of being able to dispense bad news. "I have it on good authority that they're courting GerySys." Then she laughed, and Timmie wondered just how her mother would have defined herself without her father's wild excesses. "It'd just serve that son of a bitch right."

* * *

It took Timmie forty minutes to drive from her mother's uninspiring town house in Brentwood to the restaurant in St. Charles where she was to meet Conrad. The day was another beauty, a perfect, crisp, St. Louis autumn, with sharp blue skies and trembling trees spread out beyond the highways like tumbled, variegated comforters that had been laced by frost. Timmie cranked up the car stereo until the windows rattled, and still she couldn't get the sound of her mother's voice out of her head.

"I'm sure it makes you feel better to be the martyr, Timothy Ann," she'd said with that tight cant to her mouth that conveyed both displeasure and distance. "But don't forget that we've been the ones dealing with him."

"I couldn't—"

"You could. You decided to run. While your father got more and more difficult you married the first man who asked you and ran as far and fast as you could. The only reason you came home was that you'd run out of money. If it weren't for your grandmother's house, you wouldn't have anyplace to go."

Yes, Mother. Thank you, Mother. Timmie bit the acid back in her throat and downshifted into third to swing into the passing lane on Highway 70. She could see the sweep of the Missouri River Bridge ahead, and accelerated. Conrad would wash the bad taste away. He'd make her laugh. He'd make her forget that she wanted to belt her own mother for laughing because Joe could end up in a place like Golden Grove without any means of escape.

Her mother had finally lent her the money. But the price had almost been too high.

She'd also dispensed information Timmie didn't want. The other hospitals in town were nervous about Restcrest. Always a cutthroat business in St. Louis, the medical community had decided to focus on Alzheimer's care about half a beat after Alex Raymond had set up shop, and now they all wanted in. More important, they wanted Alex Raymond out.

The competition couldn't have something to do with the deaths at Restcrest, could it? Timmie deliberately shook her head

Nope. That would make it too complicated, and she had complicated enough for the rest of her life.

Timmie swept up over the bridge, the river stretching somnolent and silver out beneath her and St. Charles tucked behind the bluffs beyond. St. Charles had been the first Missouri state capital. Its downtown area by the river still boasted cobbled streets and rows of period brick buildings that now housed antique shops and restaurants. Quiet and shady and as slow-moving as the river, it was a lovely place to visit on an autumn morning. Especially if Conrad was waiting for you in the street.

Timmie parked the car, grabbed purse and bag, and ran to greet him, already smiling at the new white Panama hat he had affected with his white Armani suit.

"Timothy Ann, *mi amore!*" he sang like an opera singer. "You look like . . . *madre mia*, you look like a terrorist!" He laughed, crowed, swung her around in a hug that could have crushed ribs, and deposited her back on the street again. "And you've brought me something to nibble on, haven't you?"

They sat together on the glassed-in balcony of an open-brick-and-hanging-plant kind of restaurant that overlooked Main Street and enjoyed lunch and final diagnoses and gossip. Within ten minutes Timmie had forgotten the acrimony she'd carried across the river. After ten more, she'd lost herself in Conrad's bubbling laugh and rapier-sharp intelligence.

"Conspiracy?" He hooted, turning heads all across the high-walled tea room. "Tucker Van Adder? *Bella donna*, you watch too much television. Tucker Van Adder doesn't have the brain power to conspire against his breakfast, much less the community. He's vain and stupid and locked into the politics of that town like a tick on a whippet's ass. If there is an evil plot afoot, the best they could do is keep it from him, so he doesn't screw it up."

"You don't think he'd need to be in on this?"

"I think they know they can count on his laziness. Now, exactly what do you think is going on?"

Timmie leaned forward so the people at every other table didn't hear, and she told him. While he listened, eyes focused entirely on

Timmie, Conrad sipped tea and juggled cutlery and hummed faintly familiar arias. And then he laughed.

"But this is wonderful!" he insisted, slamming the spoons down with a clash.

Timmie blinked. "Wonderful."

"Of course! If we can prove it, we can ride Van Adder out on a rail."

"If we prove it, I'll be tied to the tracks right in front of him, Conrad. Nobody wants to know."

"Bah! They'll live. You're sure about this problem, now?"

So she pulled out the printout and showed it to him. And he tapped and hummed and read, and finally nodded.

"Your friend the doctor is right, *carissima*. There's something here that bears looking into. What can I do?"

"Make sure Van Adder doesn't close the file on any Restcrest patient who gets turfed to God. Demand postmortems."

He nodded. "Absolutely. Well, I do have friends, you know. We'll try. Even better, I'll talk you into taking his place."

Timmie grimaced. "Better yet, talk yourself into it."

"Absolutely not!" he was shouting again, his method of gentle emphasis. "I want you as coroner! That way," he said with a grin, "I can consult, and we could work together frequently."

Timmie leaned close, laughing. "*Caro*, the last man who propositioned me like that ended up needing stitches." She didn't bother to say that he'd needed the stitches before propositioning her.

It didn't make any difference. Conrad laughed. "It's why I love you so much. You don't take any crap off anybody. But most of all, you don't take it off me!"

"What should I look for, Conrad?" she asked, deadly serious.

His expression didn't change a bit. His words, however, were quiet and professional. "The agent that's being used?" he asked. "If I were to do this to harmless old people, I would do it with digitoxin. One of the paralytics, maybe, succinylcholine. Or just zap them with too much of any of their prescribed medication. It probably wouldn't take much, and nobody would notice."

Timmie's scowl was heartfelt. "Thanks. You've really narrowed it down."

"I'd also find out why these people in particular died. What do they have in common?"

"They were all Restcrest patients . . . I think. I'm asking Barb Adkins to do some checking on the computer for me to make sure."

Conrad lifted a finger in exception, and Timmie noticed the perfectly manicured nail. "Even if all the victims were Restcrest patients, not all Restcrest patients were victims. Why these?"

Timmie nodded. "Maybe the families can tell me. I'll talk to them. I'm also doing a couple of shifts at Restcrest."

Conrad grimaced for her and patted her arm, knowing perfectly well what that meant. "*Bellissima*, you come see me. I'll comfort you. In the meantime, why don't I just trundle this little gem of a list off to my friends in the FBI and see if they have something familiar in their famous computer?"

"Ooooh," Timmie answered, her eyes lighting for the first time. "A pattern? You'd do that for me?"

"I'd slay neurosurgeons for you, *mi amore*. Now, eat your pasta. The garlic will protect you from doctors." And he laughed, as if everything they had discussed were light and silly.

Timmie couldn't remain quite so sanguine. "Don't be too noisy about it, Conrad. I don't know who's all involved. I know it's enough people to spare at least three of them to beat up a reporter who's helping me, and some of them might have been cops."

Conrad nodded vigorously and attacked his soup, his attention still on the printout. "Well then, we'll be as quiet as church mice until we find something. And then I'll personally call some very trustworthy people and have them sweep in like the Valkyrie and clean up that town. How's that sound?"

"Distressingly operatic."

Conrad dropped his spoon. "You *must* love opera, *bella donna*. Don't break my heart."

Timmie found she could laugh again. "Conrad, I'd rather sit through a four-day hemorrhoidectomy marathon."

First Conrad grimaced, hand to chest. Then, in typical fashion, he threw back his head, laughed, and finished his soup.

By the time Timmie began to wend her way back home, she was humming. She had an ally. Not that Murphy wasn't an ally, but Conrad was a known quantity. He was an official with enough pull in the state to take care of matters once they were brought to his attention. He'd given her hope that she could get out of this fairly unscathed. All she had to do was survive a shift over at Restcrest, a furtive dig through the lives of patient families, and her regular shifts down in ER with Angie, one of which she was due for in less than three hours.

That three hours gave her enough time to take the scenic route home. Instead of whizzing out the very uninspiring Highway 70 with all the other harried commuters and over-the-road truckers, she turned off onto Highway 94 and drove the north bank of the Missouri River.

It was worth it. The sun was high and the clouds moving fast. The fields still held their green and rolled away toward a horizon of trees that sparkled with their last clinging leaves. Farm buildings gleamed where they sat tucked into the folds of land, and around some corners, the Missouri appeared, glistening and grand and silent.

Once away from the heavier suburbs, the road twisted and climbed and dropped like a rural roller coaster, the only sounds filtering past Timmie's rock and roll birdsong and church bells. Altogether a lovely reward for the trip. Timmie cranked up the radio, this time to accompany the choreography of the road, and reacquainted herself with the joys of a stick shift.

She wasn't really paying attention to other traffic unless it was somebody she had to pass on the two-lane road, or a car she didn't want to demolish coming the other way. So when the black Bonneville showed up in her rearview mirror, she noted it and downshifted to set up for the next corner. The Bonneville moved closer. Timmie saw a sign for the Herman wineries and thought about taking Meghan on a Katy Trail bike ride and stopping over

She heard Willie Nelson on the radio and turned it up even louder, the perfect companion for a back road. She'd just noticed that she had a long clear ribbon of road ahead when something smacked into her car.

"Son of a . . ."

Cyrano lurched, shuddered, swerved. Timmie tightened her hold on the wheel and lifted her foot off the pedals just long enough to see what had happened.

The Bonneville had hit her, right in the ass. Timmie thought of stopping. Getting out and yelling at the jerk. She thought of slowing and just letting him pass if he was so bent on it.

He wasn't. She realized that in the split second before the Bonneville rammed her again. Harder. Smack against the right rear fender so she'd swerve right off the road down toward the river.

Her adrenals kicked in like afterburners. "Shit!"

It took a little maneuvering, but she regained control and accelerated. Timmie tried hard to see into the car, but its windows were tinted. A guy, she figured, because most women didn't handle cars like that. Which was probably why this guy thought he could just take her out in the middle of the afternoon on a country road. He probably figured he had a nurse in an old French car, what could it take? One or two good hits, she'd be over the edge.

And then what?

Which was when it hit her that he very possibly wanted her dead. He certainly wanted her disabled. He'd backed the Bonneville away a bit. For another try, Timmie realized suddenly when she heard the growl of a couple hundred horses revving up. The son of a bitch really was trying to run her off the road.

It made her smile. The guy had picked the wrong road and the wrong girl. If this had been a straightaway, she wouldn't have stood a chance. That car had at least a hundred horses on her. It was newer, and it was sure as hell heavier. But this stretch of Highway 94 was nothing but curves and hills, which made the driving just as important as the horsepower. And if there was one thing Timmie knew after besting just about every canyon road and interstate in Los Angeles County, it was how to drive.

"You want me, asshole," she said, sucking in a breath and spitting on her stick-shift hand, "you come get me."

With an apology to Cyrano's old engine, Timmie slammed him into second and took off. Cyrano screamed like an outraged woman. The road ahead bent on itself like a frying snake. Howling with the kind of sheer, stupid glee she hadn't felt in months, Timmie took it like a rocket. Swooping over the hills, she tracked across both lanes as she set up the apex of each corner to make its cleanest turn, one hand on the wheel, one on the stick shift, her right foot rocking constantly between brake and gas as she double-clutched into each turn and then eased up to let her gas foot have the fun along another stretch of clear road.

She kept her focus on the road ahead rather than the road behind. Unless this guy was road-race trained, he wouldn't keep up with her. But she didn't want to run down some unsuspecting grandma just trying to get to her daughter's. And the way the hills folded up against one another, it was tough to judge too far, especially doing seventy.

The Bonneville fought valiantly against gravity. Its wheels screamed. Timmie thought she could see the brakes smoke on more than one turn. She heard more than one squeal of protest from overdriven tires. Which meant, she figured, that the guy driving wasn't the cop who'd gone after Murphy. Cops drove better than that. A cop would at least have made it a tight contest.

Timmie spent a millisecond too long assessing her pursuer, missed her line around a tight turn by inches and almost ended up on two wheels, saving herself with a little heel-toe action as she double-clutched down into a tight S turn that had a twenty-mile-an-hour warning sign on it. Timmie took it at fifty.

She was doing eighty when she passed the YOU ARE LEAVING ST. CHARLES COUNTY sign. The road leveled out for a bit and Timmie downshifted for better acceleration. She was going to lose ground here, and she knew it.

So did the Bonneville. Timmie could hear that engine winding out. She saw the next curve coming, hoped it would be soon enough, knew that if this guy smacked her at this speed she wouldn't come to earth till she hit the far bank of the river.

He was inching up. Timmie found herself leaning forward, as if she could get a few more mph just by gravity. The curve was close, closer, beckoning like a mirage in a terrifying desert. Timmie's heart was knocking against her chest like every poor, overworked piston in her engine. But she was going to make it. She could get to the next set of curves and keep going, because there was a town nearby. People. Witnesses this guy didn't want. She reached for the stick shift and stomped her foot on the clutch, and knew the guy behind her had lost.

Timmie had forgotten one important thing. She hadn't driven in Missouri in over ten years. In that time, she'd never had to deal with ice on the road. It was one o'clock in the afternoon on a sunny day. The temperature still hovered at freezing, though, and the hills to the north kept the sun off the road. Timmie didn't even see the patch of black ice she hit. She just suddenly found herself airborne, with a panoramic view of the Missouri River out her windshield, and knew she was screwed.

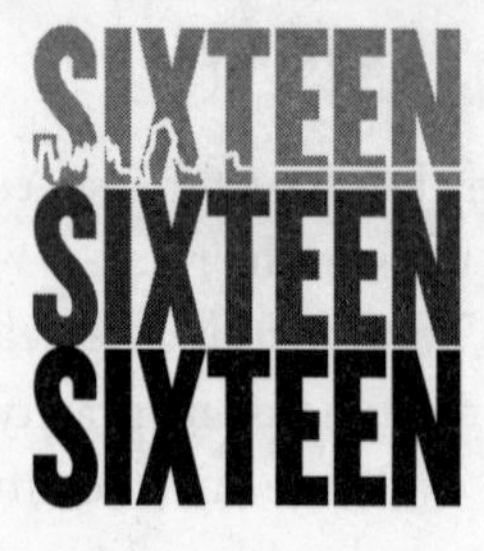

THANK GOD FOR SEAT BELTS. IT WAS ABOUT THE ONLY COHERENT thought Timmie had for about fifteen minutes as she stared blankly out her front window into the bushes that had ended up catching her. She would have been pavement pizza if she hadn't been strapped in. As it was, she was hanging from the shoulder strap like a parachutist who hit a tree. Her head hurt, her chest hurt, and her hands, still wrapped around the wheel as if holding her in the car, felt as if they'd shattered on impact.

Amazing. She could still see the river, not more than twenty yards off. Rolling, rolling . . . no, that was the Mississippi. Besides, it wasn't rolling at all. She'd sailed right to the edge of some farmer's pond. Oh, well. Maybe that was the farmer himself she heard trying to get into her car.

He wasn't going to have any luck. The door was locked. Another legacy of life in the fast lane. Timmie locked her car doors if she was going to sit in her driveway to think.

Now the person was tapping, scraping around the car as if trying to find a better way to get in. Timmie sighed. She guessed she was going to have to move. She tried to reach around for the seatbelt release and couldn't. Something was in her way. Besides, her shoulder hurt when she stretched.

"Just a . . . minute," she called out, which made her head hurt.

He didn't wait. He punched out her rear window. Timmie couldn't see him. She couldn't get her head around. But she heard the distinctive pop and crunch and tinkle of glass tumbling onto her backseat. She felt sick. She smelled gas and remembered how to feel afraid.

"I need a little help getting out," she ventured, trying again to reach her seat belt. Failing.

"Where the fuck is it?" he said, a baritone with a south St. Louis accent.

Not the farmer, then. Timmie finally remembered the reason she'd been sailing over farm silos and fought a new rush of fear. The smell of gas was even stronger, and the man who'd broken into her car wasn't there to get her out.

"If you get me unlatched I'm sure I can help you look," she tried.

Timmie could hear him rifling through the backseat, and then the front. She actually caught sight of a head of hair. Dark. Thick. Oily. No face to go with it, though. Kind of like talking to a badly groomed Cousin Itt.

"You took it with you this morning. That's what they said."

"Who said?" she asked. "And if you knew I had it this long, why the hell didn't you just break into my car when it was sitting on the street? You didn't have to chase me through two counties."

"Shut up."

"And I expect you to pay for that window," she said. "Not to mention the rest of my car. Asshole. You ran me off the road."

He laughed. "You misjudged the turn."

"I did not. I hit ice."

Timmie did give a passing thought to how ridiculous the conversation was. Better than screaming for mercy, she guessed.

"What'd you do with it?" he demanded, shaking her by the

shoulder this time. Like that would help. All it did was dislodge a few more brain cells so they probably scattered over her seat like broken glass.

"Find it yourself."

She didn't have a clue what he was talking about.

"Hey!" an old voice yelled nearby. "You all right there?"

Timmie could hear the guy moving toward the back of the car. "Call 911!" he yelled. "A drunk ran off the road!"

That was what cleared Timmie's head. "Drunk?" she demanded. "I'm not drunk. I am not drunk!" she yelled for whoever was outside, as if that would make a difference.

"Do yourself a favor," the guy said almost in her ear. "Ditch that piece of paper. And forget I was ever here."

She would have if she hadn't caught sight of his hand scrabbling through the nursing bag she'd left on the passenger seat. If she hadn't seen the gold-and-cat's-eye ring on its pinkie. Its bent pinkie. Its square, pale, scraped pinkie. Timmie took one look out of the corner of her eye and knew she could identify that fifth digit anywhere. She didn't say anything to the guy, though. She didn't even say anything to the farmer when he finally returned leading a parade of fire engines and police cars. She waited until she was in her own ER, strapped to a backboard like a bagged deer and blinking in the overhead lights.

"The printout!" she gasped, coming to her senses.

Of course. The carefully guarded, top-secret, all-revealing Morbidity and Mortality printout they'd been tossing back and forth for the last week or so like a hockey puck in overtime. It was the only thing Timmie had been carrying in that nursing bag except an extra pair of nylons, and if that guy had run her off the road just for used panty hose, she had more problems than she'd thought.

"Pardon?" Dr. Chang asked as she bent over her upside down, her face as round as a moon. The Halloween moon, except this one was frowning and kind and much, much younger. And the goblins chasing Timmie weren't pretend.

Timmie began to shake. "Nothing. Isn't Barb on?"

"You don't like me?"

"I love you, Chang. Really. I just need to ask Barb something."

"She busy. And you need c-spine films."

"My c spines are fine. I need to get up."

"No. No, you stay. We get films. Behave."

Great. A third-year resident from Beijing sounding just like her mother.

Other people came in. A couple of day-shift people and the portable X-ray tech and one of the other day docs. A couple of local cops in jackboots who tried not to laugh when Timmie told them a guy in a Bonneville and a pinkie ring had tried to run her off Highway 94. Timmie lay on the board getting stiffer by the minute and trying her damnedest to pretend she wasn't affected by what had just happened.

Maybe the guy who'd done this had just been stupid. Or maybe he hadn't cared whether she'd lived or died. Or maybe she would have been dead no matter what if that farmer hadn't shown up.

Definitely not things to consider when tied down so a person couldn't walk off the news. Which meant Timmie lay there shaking hard from adrenaline and a delayed terror she refused to admit, and focused everything she had on eavesdropping on the hallway. Which really didn't make her feel much better, either.

"Well, it's not really such a surprise," somebody said upon being informed of the identity of their newest patient. "She drives anything like she walks, she should be crippled."

"I should have known," Ellen all but wailed when she arrived for work to hear the news. Timmie wondered if Ellen thought she walked too fast, too.

And then, at least to amuse Timmie, Cindy's reaction.

"She's luckier than I was when it happened to me," she informed the person who'd told her, even as Ellen walked into Timmie's room in high-comfort mode.

"Are you all right?" Ellen demanded, patting the first available arm she could find.

"Although, of course, if it hadn't been for the accident," Cindy was going on, "I never would have met Fireman Dan."

Fireman Dan?

"Timmie?" Ellen said, patting harder. "Who did this? Is Meghan okay?"

"Ah, Fireman Dan," Cindy was saying outside the door. "Finest turnout gear in the city . . . "

Timmie's first reaction was to yell. That was her life Cindy had absconded with out there. Aw, what the hell. She laughed instead, which just made Ellen frown.

"I'm fine," Timmie said. "Meghan's fine. She wasn't there."

"You have to be more careful," Ellen insisted, still upset.

Cindy called greetings from the door on her way by. Ellen headed off to be Restcrest's relief, and Timmie was left behind with the boring ceiling, the boring light fixtures, and the boring wait for negative films. And, of course, the boring fact that she was getting more frightened by the minute now that the real danger was over. Good trauma nurse that she was.

"Timmie! My God, Timmie, is that you?"

Timmie still couldn't move her head. There was surgical tape stretched across her forehead and chin to stabilize her to the c-collar and board. She could tell that voice, though, and wondered what the hell he was doing down here.

"You didn't have another graduation ceremony, did you?" she asked, swiveling her eyes as far as she could to catch the golden head just inside the door, conferring with the black one.

"What?"

She sighed, teeth chattering. "Nothing, Alex. I'm fine, really. Convince Chang, will you?"

Alex floated into her vision like a balloon in the Macy's Thanksgiving Day parade. "The ambulance crew said your car was totaled. He said something about alcohol. Honey, what happened?"

"There was no alcohol, Alex," she said simply. "You know that. I hit a patch of black ice on 94 and did a Bullitt over some guy's cow pasture. That's all."

Alex's smile was fond and worried. "It's enough, honey. You look like you lost a prizefight. Although I hear you have a heck of a tattoo."

Timmie blushed, scowled, and grumbled, "I know some EMTs who should be running for their lives this very second."

"Are you really okay?" he asked, all joking aside as he lay a hand on her shoulder.

"I'm sore," she said to the ceiling. "Do you have any idea how hard these damn backboards are? My butt's asleep, and I'm gonna be picking adhesive off my chin for a week."

He grinned. "You don't sound too injured to me."

"Yeah, well. That's what I've been trying to tell them."

"I'm glad you're okay." His smile was radiant. "When I heard from Ellen, I ran right down. If you need anything . . . I mean, I have to head out of town for a couple of days, but if there's anything, I mean, anything I can do."

*Tell me why people are dying in your unit. Tell me if you told someone to do this to me.*

"Thank you, Alex. I'm fine."

"My car. You can use the Lexus while I'm gone."

Timmie's laugh was a surprised bark. "Why? You need that crash-tested, too?"

"I'm serious."

"Okay. Thank you. If you really want to help, though, tell Chang to get me off this damn board before I walk it down the hall."

Alex, knowing better, just patted, and Timmie was left to wonder.

Timmie ended up with X rays of everything but her ankles, four staples in her head, and an excuse from work that afternoon, which Angie accepted with predictable bad humor.

"But that's all right," she said with an alligator smile. "I have the perfect place for you to recuperate. Since you're supposed to work tomorrow, why don't you just do your ten over in Restcrest? They're short, and we're not, and you shouldn't be running around anyway, isn't that right?"

Timmie didn't have to lie about wanting to go to Restcrest after all. She did everything but call Angie a Republican. Ellen saved her job by appearing just then to take her home.

Barb caught up with the two of them as they reached the driveway. She was wearing virtually the same expression as Alex, although Timmie had to admit that it didn't look quite as attractive on Barb.

"You idiot!" the big woman snapped.

Alex had also said "I worried about you" better. The problem with that was that Barb was the one who was going to make Timmie cry. So Timmie bluffed her way through it.

"You shoulda been there, Barb," she teased. "I could see all the way to my house. I swear that poor farmer thought we were doing a remake of *Smokey and the Bandit*."

Barb just planted herself in Timmie's way, tears sparkling in her soft gray eyes. "You . . . total . . . idiot!"

No, Barb. Laugh. Don't make it real. Timmie swallowed hard against the fear Barb's concern was going to let loose again.

"I'm fine," she insisted, holding her arms out as if to prove it. "Really."

Barb glared harder, the tears brighter. "Don't . . . *ever* do that to me again," she said. "When I heard what happened—"

Timmie didn't know how else to shut her up. It looked silly as hell, but Timmie didn't know what else to do but put her arms around her friend. Which she did, barely. On her toes.

"I'm not in the mood for more funerals," was all Barb could manage.

It took a few moments, but when Barb straightened, she was dry eyed and in control. She held her hand out to Ellen. "Give me the bag. I'll take her home."

"But . . . "

Barb didn't say another word. Ellen just handed it over. "Thank you, Barb," she said. "I really did want to get back over to the unit. Little Mrs. Worthmueller isn't doing very well right now."

Timmie thanked her for taking the time, and Barb held her tongue until Ellen had made it inside the door. Then Barb, carrying the plastic personal effects bag that held Timmie's bloodied and scissored clothes like a dead mouse, turned a scrub clothes and Doc Martens–clad Timmie back toward the parking lot

"So what happened?" she demanded.

Sucking in a steadying breath, Timmie told her.

"Why?" Barb asked. "It makes no sense. All that stuff's in the computer already."

Her attention more on negotiating a suddenly high curb with very sore hips, Timmie shrugged. "To give them a chance to change something on the records they didn't want anybody else to know?"

Barb shook her head. "Then they would have done it by now. I spent the morning looking everything up, and it isn't any different. There were fifteen patients from Restcrest turfed to the ER to die, another six who died in the unit because the family wouldn't allow them moved, and four more who died of cardiac arrest before the policy change. Of those, only six died of something else definable."

Timmie slowed almost to a near stop right in the middle of the traffic lane. "You really think they were killed."

"I looked through at least seven charts. Every one of those deaths was a surprise. Sudden respiratory arrest. Sudden cardiac crash. Amazing how surprised a nurse can sound with just the words 'patient had been stable until arrest.'"

Timmie had almost made it past that first jolt of fear. This stopped her dead in her tracks. Last chance to escape the inevitable, and Barb had closed the door. There were people dying, and other people covering up the fact. Not a huge surprise in a hospital. It happened. Nobody liked to admit mistakes, especially when mistakes tended to cost lives and millions in litigation. But this . . .

This.

Timmie sighed, closed her eyes. "Fuck."

Barb looked way down at Timmie the way a mother does when her child first realizes that the world isn't a place Santa Claus would live in after all. "Let's get you home," she suggested. "We can finish the editorial portion of this program then."

Timmie started walking again, but the questions began to circle relentlessly. If that guy hadn't wanted the list, what had he wanted? If there were deaths being covered up, just who was committing them? And who was covering them up?

Timmie stood there shivering while Barb unlocked the Volvo's door, and all she could think of was that she wanted to sleep. For hours. Days. Weeks. Amazing how predictable the body was. When in danger, run. Or hide. Or both. Down at the end of the lane, one of the security wagons was trolling for problems. Timmie didn't pay a lot of attention.

"I'm going to have to talk to those nurses up there tomorrow," she said, thinking specifically of one very dedicated nurse. "They'll know . . ."

Something. She'd been about to say it. She lost the word somewhere in the millisecond of time it took to see the security guard waving hello to Barb as he trundled past. The guard with the thick black hair and potbelly.

The guard with the cat's-eye-and-gold ring on his left pinkie.

Well, no wonder, Timmie thought as she stood there gaping like a Kansas farmer in Manhattan. She'd been right. It hadn't been a cop. It had been somebody who played one on his job. A security guard. From the hospital.

"O-o-o-h, shit," she muttered, struggling not to make eye contact or run. Probably a good thing. The look the guard shot her on the way by left no doubt that he was here to make sure she didn't recognize him.

"Oh shit what?" Barb asked, throwing the bag with Timmie's clothes in the car and holding the door open for Timmie to follow.

Wondering how it could be that nobody else seemed to be able to see her shake, Timmie tried to grin. "I'll tell you later at the house."

"Think," Barb demanded an hour later as they sat sprawled in Timmie's living room with sodas and ice packs. "You have something somebody in that hospital wants pretty badly."

"Nothing!" Timmie insisted again. "Not if they haven't changed the M and M sheets."

"He didn't hurt you in any way."

"No. I think he just wasn't good enough at his job to lift my bag earlier." She hoped he just wasn't good enough. "He probably saw that running-a-car-off-a-road stunt in a Sylvester Stallone movie somewhere."

"Seems pretty stupid."

"So did he."

Barb finished her soda like a shot and grimaced. "So, what do we do now?"

Timmie pushed herself off her chair and tried not to groan. She was not a very good victim, especially when she ached. She was a worse target, though. "I need to catch Conrad before he disappears with that list. Maybe he's spotted something I missed."

But Conrad had already disappeared. All Timmie had to talk to was his answering machine, which pleaded for her to make him a happy man with a message and then wished everyone a musical "*Ciao, bambini.*"

Timmie left her message. Standing there doing it, she saw that her answering machine was blinking and instinctively hit the Replay button. There was a message to call her insurance company and the leftover one from Murphy, who had wanted to warn her about new phone threats. Then there was one other.

"What games are you playing now, Timmie?" an aggrieved male voice demanded, making Timmie flush so hard her head spun again. "You telling the courts I gave Meghan drugs? Got her drunk? I've had a little trouble and you get righteous and vindictive. Well, I have my rights. I'm here, I'm going to see my daughter, and then I'll show everyone just what pain you've caused me. Think about it, Timmie."

Timmie just stood there as the machine beeped, clicked, and went silent.

"Obviously the ex," Barb suggested dryly. "He does have the West Coast concession on rationalization, doesn't he?"

Well, at least it washed out the fear for a while. Timmie was so angry she could hardly speak. "The pain I've caused *him*?" she demanded, not realizing how much she sounded like Barb had with the court order in her hand. "The games *I've* played? He's got almost three million stashed away somewhere and I haven't seen a penny's child support since he walked out the door, and he's dragged me through court for thirteen months just to do it, and *I'm* playing games with *him*? How *dare* he!"

She was trembling now. Barb, her own rage buried along with her ex, leaned back and smiled. "He's a man. That's how dare he. Because, like most men, he's never grown up. And you want to know why? I've thought about this a lot lately, you know."

Not in the mood to be anybody's straight man, Timmie just glared.

Barb grinned. "Because we never wean them off the breast, that's why."

The doorbell didn't even ring. The door just flew open and hurried footsteps echoed in the hallway. Timmie had been expecting Meghan. But unless Megs had graduated to size thirteen large overnight, this wasn't Megs. It wasn't. Like the perfect punctuation to a senseless conversation, there stood Murphy.

Timmie couldn't help it. She laughed. She laughed so hard her ribs hurt where the seat belt had bruised them, and she had to sit down. "I never thought of it that way, Barb. You're right."

"About what?" Murphy demanded, panting.

"That you never grew up," Barb said over her shoulder.

"If I'd grown up, I wouldn't have been a reporter," Murphy assured her, then turned to Timmie. "You okay?"

Timmie smiled more than she'd intended. "I look worse than you. I got staples."

He faltered to a halt right at the edge of the section of floor where he'd spent the other night sprawled. "I got more."

"You win. What are you doing here?"

He grimaced and leaned over, hands on knees, panting a little. "You kidding? There's a police scanner at the paper. The minute Sherilee heard who was involved, she made it a point to call me personally. She still smells an exposé. Is this exposé material, or did you just fall asleep at the wheel?"

Amazing how many words he could fit between panting breaths. Timmie motioned him to the couch. "You sure you jog?"

That made him glare. "You know how much fun it is to run with busted ribs?"

"What about that fancy-ass Cabriolet you have?"

Barb finally lost her temper. "Just sit down, for God's sake. You're both idiots."

So Murphy sat down, and Timmie gave him the Cliff Notes version of her amazing feat of aerodynamics. She also filled both of them in on what her mother had said about Restcrest and Conrad had said about the deaths. Which led her inevitably back to her aborted ride home.

"But who's doing it?" Timmie asked. "Who told that guy to get . . . whatever it is he was after?"

"What about old Mary Jane Arlington?" Murphy offered. "Remember how I tried to tell you she'd worked with the golden boy before? She has, in fact, been promoted from floor nurse to supervisor to vice president since the first unit failed."

Barb sat right down.

Timmie blinked. "She's worked in all three of the units?"

Murphy's smile was on a par with a shark's. "It pays to have drunk the best editors in the country under the table. I found out that Mary Jane has managed to parlay a nursing degree and a night school bachelor's in generic science to a hundred-thousand-dollar-plus-a-year job as senior vice president of the Alzheimer's Research Unit and Restcrest Nursing Home. Pretty heady stuff, don't you think?"

Barb whistled. "Pretty big stakes to forfeit just because one nurse and a reporter don't like the way she does business."

Murphy leaned forward, elbows on knees. "Bigger when you consider that she'd rather poke her eyes out with a stick than disappoint Dr. Perfect. She's been known to toss patients out and scythe through staff like the reaper if they weren't properly respectful."

Timmie was feeling sicker by the minute. "Imagine what she might do if she thought a third unit might have problems due to patient cost."

"Or a bad reputation." Barb wagged a finger at both of them. "What'd I tell you? Rabbit stew all the way."

"I'll find out when I'm there," Timmie said.

"Carefully," Murphy warned. "We're both limping already, and we don't even know what the hell it is we know."

"Don't worry. I had that impressed on me this afternoon. Barb, can you get next-of-kin addresses from those victims?"

"Sure."

Timmie nodded, leaned her head back, and closed her eyes. "Then it's time we visit a few of them to see what they have to say about those sudden deaths."

"I'll do it," Murphy said.

Timmie shook her head. "I don't trust you alone. You don't know what to ask."

"Thanks for the vote of confidence, Leary," he said. "Ought to really help me on my road back."

Timmie snorted without opening her eyes. "You're not on the road back, Murphy. You're just on the road."

Murphy laughed. Barb climbed back to her feet. "On that note," she said, "Timmie, you need a nap. I need to get back to work, and Mr. Murphy needs a ride back to wherever he ran from."

"We need to send our kids to camp somewhere, Barb," Timmie said, still not opening her eyes. "Until this blows over."

Barb stalled at the edge of the room, a looming shadow of condensed energy. "I can take care of my kids," she said.

Timmie opened her eyes and focused hard on her friend with every truth that afternoon had left her evident in her expression. "It was pretty scary today, Barb. I don't think we want our kids to know scary like that. And if we're not giving up, then whoever we're after is going to get more serious."

Murphy nodded. "Either back out now or take them out of the equation. Your kids make you vulnerable."

It was tough for an ex-bouncer to admit she couldn't protect her own children. Barb fought the inevitable in silence, her stance at once aggressive and frustrated. Finally she sighed. "They've been through enough. Let me talk to the Rev. If nothing else, he's the biggest black man in the county. I don't think even the cops'd screw with him."

"Who's the Rev?" Murphy asked.

"Walter Wilson," Timmie said. "His wife, Mattie, works with us."

"And you trust him?"

Timmie laughed along with Barb. "The day we stop trusting Walter, we might as well just give up."

"Now then, Mr. Murphy," Barb said. "It's time to go."

Murphy got to his feet with a grin. "Caller ID on the phone, too, Leary. Before our friend phones again."

Behind them the door slammed open again, and finally, it was Meghan. Timmie wrapped her daughter in a hug and the other two showed themselves out the door.

While Cindy entertained Meghan with her shrieking response to Renfield the next night, Timmie spent a lifetime in the Restcrest advanced care unit. She gave medications and she gave tube feedings and she cleaned and rolled and cleaned and rolled again. She feasted her eyes on the empty husks that had once been active, individual persons, and listened to the dissonant music of the gomer chorus, endless ululating wails, repeated words, questions, all carried in high, fractious voices.

"Nurse! Nu-u-u-urse!"

"What'd he do? What'd he do? What he d-o-o-o-o-o-o-o?"

"Help me, please, oh, please, oh, please help me, they're taking me, help . . ."

All conspiring to freeze her brain into immobility and her sense of humor to stone.

It wasn't just an exile into the wilderness far away from trauma. It was an exercise in prognostication. An unerring view into her father's future. This was where Timmie would spend her afternoons watching her father disintegrate into vegetable matter, until he lay sprawled out on the bed like the Scarecrow after the monkeys had gotten through with him, scattered and brainless.

And alive.

Repeating over and over again, " 'I will arise and go now, I will arise . . .' " until Timmie would want to throttle Yeats himself for finding Innisfree in the first place. Until she was tempted to stuff a blanket in her father's mouth just to get him to stop. Until she was crushed by the impulse to simply put him to sleep, like an old dog who'd gone blind.

Which made her wonder just what good she was doing tracking down the people who were doing that very thing. Putting these poor, empty shells out of their misery and saving their families the money that should have gone to their children's education and instead went to care for their parents.

Timmie doubted sincerely that this was what Barb had had in mind when she'd suggested the trip. She'd probably wanted Timmie to find empty vials of tubocurarine among the linens, or notations on charts about tripling Digoxin doses. Timmie found neither of these. She found a well-run unit that spared nothing for its patients. She found a place where the administrator came to stroke old faces, and where the patients might not be better, but at least they were clean.

She did get to meet the reclusive Dr. Davies, which was a trip to Mars in itself. She spotted him wandering into the room of one of the newer patients, a fractious little lady named Alice who had lots of money, a heart like a jackhammer, and a truly foul mouth. Since Timmie also knew that Alice had no in-state family, she tried to toss Davies's rumpled butt out of the unit until one of the other nurses introduced him. Davies pushed his wirerims up his nose, muttered something about late stage-two deterioration, and walked on into the room without even saying hello.

And then, weirdest of all, at seven o'clock on a Sunday evening, Mary Jane Arlington herself came blowing in. Clad in razor-pressed chinos and a pink silk blouse, she looked a bit frazzled when she came upon Timmie standing by the nurse server.

"Well . . . you're . . . helping?" she asked, blinking.

Timmie smiled. "You guys need more staff. I got pulled from the ER."

"Your father . . . uh, he's not . . . "

"Here? No. He's on his regular unit."

"Well, that's good. That's . . ." Mary Jane squinted, peered closer. "What happened to you?"

Probably the last question Timmie thought Mary Jane would be asking this evening. "I was run off the road yesterday. Why?"

Mary Jane actually blanched. "Run off the road?" she asked. "Intentionally?"

Timmie didn't know how to react. "Looked that way to me."

It seemed to take Mary Jane a few moments to process that kind of information. Timmie saw a range of reactions, from confusion to disbelief to revulsion, chase across those perfect blond features. Which meant one thing. Mary Jane was more surprised by the incident than Timmie had been.

"I didn't know," she all but stammered. "I took a holiday, you know?"

No, Timmie didn't. Timmie wasn't sure she was following any of this. Mary Jane was standing flat-footed in front of her, one hand rhythmically clicking a pen, the other rubbing against her thigh as if wiping a damp palm. Definitely upset. Definitely surprised.

"You have to understand," she said, clicking faster, "that some people might not understand . . . they . . . might feel . . . threatened . . ."

Timmie wasn't sure what Mary Jane wanted her to say. She opened her mouth to at least agree when the administrator simply turned away. And then, ten feet down the hall, turned back, looking more frantic than ever. "Just remember this," she said. "Alex is your friend. He's the best hope these people have, no matter what." She paused, seemed to gather purpose. "No matter what."

And that was it. Timmie was left behind with the most unholy feeling that not only did Mary Jane know nothing about whatever that guy had been after in her car, but that she did think she knew who did. And that she thought Alex Raymond was somehow involved.

If not responsible.

"You're not helping at all," Murphy accused her when she told him about it the next morning.

Timmie shoved a cup of coffee at him and poured her own, not yet prepared to trust her own reactions. She'd managed only a few hours sleep the night before, and dreamed all night of being chased down the hall by every one of those poor old gomers she'd cared for the night before, stalking her, arms out, tubes dangling, all crying out in their individual gomer voices.

"Nurse, nurse, nurse . . ."

"Help me, please, oh help me, please, somebody . . ."

And interspersed in there somehow, Mary Jane. "He's their only hope."

It didn't take a shrink to figure that one out. It didn't help Timmie get any rest, either.

"I thought you said the golden boy couldn't be behind this," Murphy said, leaning against the kitchen doorway as he drank his coffee.

"He can't."

"But if he is—"

"It's too early for that, Murphy," she threatened. "Why don't we just go see families?"

"You want to separate these or see 'em together?" he asked, keeping a careful distance.

Timmie slammed down the rest of her coffee, hoping for a miracle of coherence, and sighed. "Together. I'm not in a careful interrogation kind of mood."

He lifted an eyebrow. "Does that mean you'd like me to drive?"

"Since Bobby's Garage is still picking soybeans out of my transmission, and I don't want to drive a Lexus, yes."

Murphy didn't say anything. He just walked into the kitchen and came back with the bottle of acetaminophen. "Here."

Timmie tried not to laugh. "Shut up."

She took the medicine. Then she grabbed the list of surviving family members Barb had handed off the night before like the plans for a nuclear sub and walked out the door.

There were ten names on the list. Timmie decided on the places to go and Murphy asked the questions. Nonthreatening general information on care given, benefits derived, family's reaction to the patient's disease, deterioration, and death.

They stuck to that plan of attack at the first three homes and learned nothing. The children and spouses of Mr. DiSalvo, Mrs. Frieberger, and Mrs. Rogers, respectively, were saddened by the deaths, but not surprised. Relieved, a few admitted, considering what their loved ones had gone through. Getting on with life, eternally grateful to Restcrest, Dr. Raymond, and Memorial Medical Center for everything they'd done for the person in question. Not one mentioned Joe Leary because Timmie had introduced herself as Annie Parker, which kept the interviews properly focused. Not one had offered any surprises, either.

Limping up the steps to the fourth door, Timmie asked Murphy to let her try her hand at the questions. She was feeling a bit more alert, and with it, a bit more patient.

Their target here was Mr. Charlie Cleveland, son of Wilhelm "Butch" Cleveland, seventy-eight, who had died of cardiac arrest the morning Billy Mayfield had come in. Mr. Cleveland lived in a nice neighborhood of two-story brick bungalows with mature trees and carefully pruned hedges. Lots of effort, little imagination. Butch had lived with him and his wife, Betty, until admission to Restcrest two years before his death.

As she waited for Mr. Cleveland to answer the bell, Timmie wondered what the poor man would think when he opened the door to catch a pair of bruised, battered creatures waiting to ask him about his father.

It was nothing to what Timmie thought when the man finally opened the door on the second ring. But Murphy said it first.

"Oh, my God."

Mr. Cleveland just stood there, morning paper still clasped in his hand, a finger tucked into the page he'd been reading. He was wearing half reading glasses on a chain around his neck and a carefully pressed cotton shirt and slacks. A handsome man with dignified wings of gray hair and a ruddy complexion.

His complexion this morning was pale, though, his eyes wide. Stricken was the word that came to mind. Timmie knew how he felt.

"Mr. Cleveland," she greeted the man who had tried to shoot Alex Raymond at the horse show. "Can we talk to you?"

# SEVENTEEN

MURPHY EXPECTED JUST ABOUT ANY REACTION BUT THE ONE they got.

"Well, it's about time," Mr. Cleveland said. Then he laughed and shook his head. "Listen to me. I'm about to be taken in on attempted manslaughter charges, and I'm saying it's about time. Well, it is. I've been sitting in this living room for two weeks waiting for that doorbell to ring."

He looked nice. *Nice*. Now there was a word Murphy hadn't thought to use in connection with that guy with the gun. Standing here in his own doorway, though, Mr. Cleveland looked as if he belonged right here, reading his morning paper in his boring, predictable living room, not in a police lineup. But Murphy had done enough of these interviews to know just how many people in police lineups looked just the same.

"We're not the police," Murphy assured him. "We're from the paper. My name is Daniel Murphy, and this is—"

"Annie Parker," Leary interjected, just like the other three times. And damn if she didn't look more like Annie Parker than Timmie Leary, her short hair curled and her usual tights and long sweaters traded in for tailored blouse, vest, and slacks. "We wanted to ask you about Restcrest, if you don't mind."

They couldn't seem to surprise the guy. "Of course you do," he said. Carefully folding his paper out of the way, he pushed open the door.

As Murphy stepped in, he catalogued the house. Not much more imagination inside than outside. Solid pastel furniture, beige rugs and curtains, walls decorated in stiff family portraits and framed pastoral prints. The smell of Pine Sol, old coffee, and pipe tobacco. All well cared for, all showing wear and tear, as if the budget had been stretched to the limit a long time ago.

Mr. Cleveland led them both to the light-blue floral couch and reclaimed his easy chair across from the television.

"You want to know why I tried to shoot Dr. Raymond."

Murphy saw Leary actually flinch at the statement. He didn't know whether to feel sorry for her or satisfied. At least one of the questions had been answered.

"Excuse me for asking," Leary said, leaning forward. "But haven't the police been here already?"

"Nope. Not a soul. Except for the Adkins boy, of course, but he didn't come on official business. Heard Father had been in and was thinking about having to do the same for his mother. Wanted my opinions." Mr. Cleveland smiled. "I tried to tell him what I'd done, but he just wasn't interested. Typical of the boy. Always has had a one-track mind. He does so love being a policeman. Makes a lot of noise when he moves."

Present tense. Probably not the time to fill him in.

"Nobody else, though," Leary said, nudging him back on track.

A quick, decisive shake of the head. "And you'd certainly think they would have figured it out by now. It's not like I'm a complete stranger. Father played bridge with Chief Bridges's father every Tuesday for twenty years."

Which neatly explained the "keep-it-in-the-family" angle. Obviously the chief had figured that if Mr. Cleveland wasn't going to say anything, neither was the police chief, who probably knew perfectly well what had become of Mr. Cleveland's father.

"Have you talked to anybody about it?" Murphy asked.

"Just my minister. Told him how stupid I felt after it happened. Never tried anything like that before. Don't know what came over me then."

Leary gently forced the issue. "Your father . . . "

Cleveland's features clouded over. He seemed to deflate a little, as if the truth would take the stuffing out of him. "Was very sick," he said quietly. "For a very long time."

Leary's voice got as soft as his. "I know," she said. "My father's in Restcrest."

Cleveland exchanged a quick smile of empathy with her that betrayed what the two of them shared. What Murphy knew nothing about. He wisely kept his mouth shut and let Leary take the lead.

"Then you know," Mr. Cleveland said.

Leary just nodded.

Cleveland sighed. "Father was an exceptional man. He fought in three wars, earned the Distinguished Service Medal and the devotion of the entire Marine Corps. He raised me on Plato and Aquinas and Rousseau. By the time he died, he was incoherent."

"You weren't surprised by his death," Leary said quietly, her posture folded forward. A picture of sincere interest, concern, understanding. She sat as still as a mirror, which amazed Murphy. He'd never seen her this subdued before.

Mr. Cleveland shook his head, slipped his glasses off so he could rub at them with his fingers, his attention completely focused on his precise movements. "I told them no," he protested in a very small voice.

Leary leaned forward just a little more. Murphy didn't dare break the fragile silence to prompt her. He didn't have to. "But first," she said even more quietly, her empathy a tangible thing, "you told them yes."

When Mr. Cleveland looked up at her, there were tears in his eyes. "How could I?" he demanded. "He was my father. I loved him. I really did."

Leary's smile was sadder than those tears. "I know."

Again, for just that second, the two of them shared that odd bond of guilty children. And Murphy, wondering what mementos they'd put in that old man's memory case, sat outside, watching.

"I think you want to tell us what happened," Leary said, a hand out to that pressed and creased knee. "Who made the offer, Mr. Cleveland?"

Mr. Cleveland kept looking at his glasses, a safe place to focus his anguish. "I don't know," he admitted. "It was a phone call. Early one morning. Just an anonymous voice in the dark giving me a way out. Father was so sick and I was so stretched financially. And I wasn't even paying as much as I would be now. He was one of the last of the old ones left."

The old ones? Murphy thought, itching. He held still and waited for Leary to ask the question.

"What did the person say?" she asked instead.

"Just . . . didn't it hurt to see my father that way? Wouldn't it be better if he were at rest."

"A man or a woman?"

For the first time since he'd started confessing, Mr. Cleveland looked up. "I don't know. Isn't that odd? I never even thought about it until later, after I'd tried to . . . you know. I just assumed it was him. I mean, he *is* Restcrest, do you see? I'm not so sure any-more. The voice on the phone whispered, and Dr. Raymond really did seem more upset than I did when father died."

"How did they make the offer?"

"They . . . they asked if I wouldn't want my father at peace. I said . . . I said yes."

"How did you let them know you'd changed your mind?"

"They called back. I was frantic by then, realizing what I'd said. What I'd told them to do. I told them to stop, just to forget it. I wouldn't tell anybody, but don't hurt my father . . . but they'd just called to say it was okay now. Father was . . . um, at peace. I guess I went a little crazy after that."

"Did they ask for money?" Leary asked, surprising Murphy all over again. He hadn't even thought of that.

"No," Mr. Cleveland said, his hold on those poor glasses warping the frames.

"Do you think anybody else might have had a call like yours?"

For the first time, the precise, quiet man smiled. "Oh, yes. I know they did. I ran into a couple of other families in town, and they obviously thought I was as relieved as they were that it was all over. You might want to ask them if they donated money."

"Did you?" she asked. "Donate?"

A flush. A tic. A tiny nod. "A thousand dollars."

He got another pat of understanding. "What other families, Mr. Cleveland?"

He told her. One of the couples had told Murphy and Leary not an hour ago how surprised they'd been by Mother's untimely demise. Murphy could see from the tight cast of Leary's mouth that she was disappointed. Murphy envied her those last vestiges of idealism and wondered how much longer they'd last.

"Have you heard from them again?" Leary asked, her hand still out on the middle-aged man's knee.

Mr. Cleveland shook his head, re-slung his glasses around his neck, as if putting himself back together again. "Are you going to the police?" he asked. "If you are, would you mind giving me the time to tell Betty? She doesn't know."

Leary spared Murphy a quick look. Murphy lifted his hands. Her call. She shook her head. "I don't think so, Mr. Cleveland. Would you be willing to help us investigate these deaths?"

"If you want."

Leary's smile this time was purely feminine, and Murphy was impressed. Mr. Cleveland beamed back like she'd offered him sex.

"Thank you," Leary said. "That would help a lot. You said something about your father being one of the last of the old ones. Can you tell me what you meant?"

Cleveland wagged a finger at her. "I bet you're paying through the nose to keep your father in that place, aren't you?"

Murphy saw a flush creep up Leary's neck. Even so, she smiled. "In a word, Mr. Cleveland."

He nodded, satisfied. "Father was a patient at Restcrest in the old days, before all this new rehabbing business happened. We had a lifetime contract locked in at a much lower rate. That new guy, Landry, tried to break the contract, but he couldn't. So they had to put Father right alongside the people who were paying fancy prices for all that high-tech care."

"Landry tried to break the contract," Murphy echoed quietly.

Mr. Cleveland laughed the way all people do who outsmart the big guys. "Did everything but threaten our pensions. Lucky for us, the lawyers from the original Restcrest were old socialists and sharp as tacks. Didn't stand for old folks being taken advantage of. We paid a flat fee of eighty-five dollars a day, no matter what, till Father died. Drove that Landry guy bats."

Murphy was itching again. "I'll just bet it did."

While Murphy was still taking that one in, Leary slung her purse over her shoulder and got to her feet. "Thank you again, Mr. Cleveland. We really do appreciate the help."

She held out her hand and Mr. Cleveland took it in both of his. "Thank *you*," he said, his soft face disheveled with relief.

Murphy was getting to his feet, too, when Leary blindsided him yet again.

"And thank you for the phone call," she said, hand still wrapped in Cleveland's. "It helped quite a bit."

Murphy made it to his feet just in time to catch the confusion on Mr. Cleveland's face. "Phone call?"

Now Leary looked tentative. "To warn us about what was happening at Restcrest?" she said. "I thought it might have been you."

Mr. Cleveland shook his gently graying head. "No. I didn't even know who you were. How could I?"

She beamed. "Of course. I'm sorry. I guess we might have another family who wasn't as relieved as they might have been. Thank you again. I hope we can visit under better circumstances."

"You give your father a hug tonight, young lady," he admonished, and Murphy saw those tears glitter briefly again.

Leary smiled, nodded, and fled.

* * *

"Landry," Leary mused, gingerly climbing back into Murphy's car fifteen minutes later with her bag of doughnuts. "That wouldn't be a huge surprise. Not if those people were costing him money."

"I don't see it," Murphy argued, slamming his own door shut and handing off a cup of coffee.

It was almost noon, and the streets around the Donut Hole were fairly crowded with traffic headed toward real food farther out toward the highway. The Hole sat in the middle zone, where used car dealerships and strip malls dominated. Almost developed, never quite successful, usually crime free, since the local constabulary didn't see fit to break the stereotype and opt for popcorn over doughnuts.

As for Leary, she was twitching like a gigged frog. Probably too much forced inactivity at the Cleveland house. Too many revelations she hadn't wanted to share with that sad, middle-aged man. Murphy watched her bounce around as she juggled coffee, doughnuts, and painkillers, and wondered if she knew how damn brittle she looked.

"What do you mean you don't see it?" Leary demanded as she threw back the acetaminophen and washed them down with a quick swig of coffee. "Landry's ruthless, he's hungry, he'll obviously do anything to make that unit fly. Why not off a couple old farts who are costing him money?"

Murphy popped the lid of his coffee and took a long slug that damn near seared his esophagus. "Not his game. He only murders on the books. Not in person."

Leary snorted. "You just want it to be Alex."

Murphy had to smile. "We do know he recognized the shooter, now, don't we?"

"No, we don't," she argued, her nose stuck in the doughnut bag in search of her cholesterol of choice. "He might not have seen his face before we broke it all up."

"Nice try. He knew him, he knew what it was about, and he won't admit it."

"Wrong. He's not that complicated."

"We could go ask him now."

"We could if we were in New York. He left for a conference this morning right after leaving the keys to his shiny new Lexus in my mailbox."

Murphy reached in the bag alongside her chin and grabbed the first doughnut he found, a cruller. "Bribery now. We'll nail him the minute he gets back."

Leary shook her head, still intent on her hunt. "We'll nail Landry as soon as I find out just how many of our early graduates were 'old-timers,'" she said, finally snagging a chocolate-covered longjohn and taking a big bite. "Then we have to decide just how to ask the rest of the relatives whether the offer was made, or if they just woke up one morning to find Grandma dead."

There was chocolate on her chin. For a minute Murphy couldn't take his eyes off it. A tattoo on her ass and chocolate on her chin. He was in lust all over again, and it was only noon. Even worse, he found himself beset by the most absurd urge to calm Leary down. Ease that stretched-thin look she was getting around the eyes. And that didn't just make him wary, it damn near made him afraid. He hadn't been compelled to do something that stupid for about twenty years now.

"If it's an exercise in cost cutting," he said instead, his focus never wavering from that daub of brown, "why bother to make an offer? Isn't that overkill?"

Leary took another bite. "Who knows? Maybe he gets off on the power. God knows he seems to at the hospital. Wouldn't you just love to know what Victor found out before he died? Although I don't think that's the way I would have handled Mr. Cleveland if I were him."

"It wasn't. Where'd you learn your interrogation techniques?"

She grinned and slid her coffee cup between her knees so she could fiddle with it. Murphy couldn't take his eyes off that, either. "Best homicide dick in L.A. Her name was Corinne Jackson, and perps dropped like flies for her honey-tongued little number."

"I bet. Tell me again you don't want to have sex."

Leary didn't miss a beat. "I don't want to have sex."

But she was grinning. At least she wouldn't be bringing him up on charges yet.

"Heavy necking," he offered, leaning back in his seat so he was actually, at least in his mind, farther away.

She finished off the doughnut with a very suggestive flourish. "No thanks."

Murphy closed his eyes, content that he'd at least gotten her to smile. "I guess this means that accident wasn't a life-altering experience."

"No," she said. "The divorce was."

He opened his eyes again and saw it. That crackle of attraction. The regret that she was going to let her head rule. Ah, well, definitely for the better. He just wished he didn't feel that that smile was a personal accomplishment.

As if just the thought of necking compelled community response, there was a brusque tapping on the window. Murphy leaned forward to see a red-headed guy in a detective suit bent over Leary's side of the car. He had coffee in his hand and white icing on his Jerry Garcia tie.

"I hope impure thoughts aren't an ordinance violation around here," Murphy said.

Leary laughed as she rolled down the window. "Nah. Detective Sergeant Micklind and I are old friends. Aren't we, Detective?"

The guy bent a little farther over to lean an elbow on the car door as he continued to sip his coffee. "Ms. Leary. How are you today?"

"Leary-Parker, Detective Sergeant," she countered brightly. "But I guess it's worthless to insist anymore."

The detective didn't so much as twitch. "Hear you did a gainer and a half over some farmer's silo."

"Yes, sir, I did. Thank you for asking after my health."

Murphy actually saw a tic of humor at the corner of the detective's mouth. "You look healthy, Ms. Leary. I was wondering if I might stop by to talk to you later today."

Leary grabbed another chocolate doughnut and took a big bite. "You heard my ex-husband is in town and decided to arrest me before he turns up dead?" she asked brightly. "Get all your paperwork out of the way before the rush?"

Another tic, minimally bigger. "You thinking of killing him, are you?"

"Ever since the day he sold all my furniture to pay off his girlfriend's boob job."

"I'll keep that in mind. What time would be good for you, Ms. Leary?"

"How's fifteen minutes after he shows up at my front door, Detective? Give me time to find my baseball bat and you time to respond."

"I think it would more of a challenge if you didn't tell me when you were going to kill your ex-husband, Ms. Leary," Micklind retorted easily. "I just need to know when to stop by today."

Leary bobbed her head briskly. "Well, if you're going to be a good sport about it, then how's two? We'll be finished by then, and you'll still have an hour or so with your thumbscrews before my daughter shows up from school."

"Finished, huh?" he asked, leaning farther over so he could give Murphy the once-over. "Something I should know about?"

Leary shot Murphy a glance of pure mischief. "Not unless assignations are against the law. We're having a hot affair, Detective. Got a problem with that?"

"Over doughnuts?"

She grinned like a kid. "I knew a cop would understand. See you later, sir." And then, with his tie still almost hanging over the door, she started rolling the window back up.

All Micklind had to do to delay her was lay a beefy hand over the top of the glass. "You, too, Mr. Murphy. I figured you wouldn't mind a little insight into that collection of bruises you have."

Murphy had to admit surprise. "Not at all."

Micklind nodded, lifted his hand, and recovered his tie.

"This town gets more interesting by the minute," Murphy mused.

Leary laughed. "And you thought you wouldn't like it here."

"I don't. The last thing I want right now is interesting."

She laughed again, which just told him that she understood him much too well.

* * *

They saw six more families. Not one other person even flinched when asked about whether they'd been approached to end a parent's life. A few got downright surly. Most showed the usual mix of grief, guilt, and relief that Murphy had come to expect. He got his fill after the first set. By the last, he was surlier than anybody except Leary, who was actively grinding her teeth. Which made up Murphy's mind about where they were headed next.

"Are you telling me I'm not good company?" she demanded, the manic humor phase of her mood long since dead and withered.

Murphy swung the car into her driveway and parked. "Enough is enough for one day, Leary. Even I can take only so much of this at once. I figure you're about to implode."

She was picking at the stitching on her purse until the whole thing threatened to come apart. "I'm nothing of the sort, Murphy. I'm just keyed up and sore."

"You've spent four hours wallowing around in what's going to happen to your father. Go play with your kid. Play baseball if you have to. Remind yourself there's something else."

"Is this part of your recovery?" she demanded. "Counseling the huddled masses?"

"I'm not going to do any investigation when I get back to the paper," he informed her. "I'm going to check over the article I wrote about your father. It's coming out tomorrow."

Even her restless fingers stopped. "Great. A brand-new round of 'Innisfree' and 'Foggy Dew.' I may shoot myself."

"I'll save you a copy for later when you feel more like reading it."

The inside of that car was getting mighty close. "I'm a big girl, Murphy. You don't have to protect me from that old man."

Over on the side of Leary's yard an oak tree was losing its leaves. Murphy watched them drop, one by one, onto the unraked lawn.

"I was a great drunk, Leary," he said. "Entertaining as hell, everybody's friend. Won two Pulitzers and broke in some of the finest newsmen in the business when I was so fried I couldn't remember to unzip before I took a piss." He sucked in a breath to deliver the judgment it had taken him four treatment centers to make. "I also drove my first two wives to nervous breakdowns. Which means, I guess, that I'm familiar with the territory."

There was a tiny pause. And then a sore laugh. "All the gin joints in all the world." She sighed. "Leave it alone, Murphy. Leave me alone."

"And sex is . . . "

She sighed again. "I'll let you know." And got out of the car.

And Murphy, who hadn't had to recheck an article since he'd been twenty, went home for a while to hide.

CONRAD HAD BEEN WAITING ON TIMMIE'S ANSWERING MACHINE when she got home. So had Cindy, the insurance company, and the lawyer, who had called to tell Timmie that Jason's latest salvo had been successfully blocked. After the day she'd had, Timmie decided that the only person she wanted to talk to was Conrad.

"*Bella donna*!" he crowed in her ear as she sat half sprawled on her couch with the phone cord stretched all the way from the dining room. "You found me at last."

"Quite a way of putting it," Timmie had to agree. Having tossed the good clothes she'd donned for the interviews the minute she'd hit the door, she now reclined in T-shirt and jeans. She ached like a sore tooth, her scalp itched, and she was tired and as crabby as hell after spending the day talking to those relatives. "Conrad, this is important. Where's the printout I gave you?"

"Right here, of course. I've been poring over it like the Dead Sea Scrolls, seeking truth and inspiration."

"Seek this. Somebody ran me off the road on the way home from our little visit to get hold of that list. Any ideas why?"

For the first time since Timmie had known him, Conrad was

struck dumb with surprise. "Are you all right?" he asked in a hushed tone Timmie almost didn't recognize.

Timmie damn near teared up. "I'm fine. I'm mad as hell and out for revenge, though. Wanna come along?"

"More than I want to see Domingo sing at La Scala. Tell me what you need."

That made her sigh and rub her face. "I don't know. I thought they were after the original M and M list because they meant to change the one in the computer, but the computer version is still identical. Evidently we're the only ones who've figured out how suspicious those cardiac arrests are."

"Then what?"

"Take another look through it. Is there anything else that speaks to you?"

She closed her eyes to the sound of rustling paper and thought about taking a hot bath before Micklind got there. She thought of the visit she should make out to her father that afternoon and the inevitable arrival of Cindy to remind her of just why she hadn't visited her sisters since she'd been back. She thought of her daughter, who would be walking home from school with a bodyguard.

Well, that was so much fun that she went back to considering the interviews. The not-so-surprised reactions of the relatives. The unspoken pleas to just let it all go. The ambivalence that still lay on the back of her tongue like old ashes, and the fact that if she didn't come up with something soon, she was going to have to endure another shift at Restcrest.

"There's nothing," Conrad finally said. "Only this last thing you copied along with the list."

"What last thing?"

"The notice about policy changes."

Timmie's eyes flew open. Her heart thudded with surprise. "Oh, my God."

Landry.

The gag order he'd sent Angie about that questionable policy change nobody would like. In all the hoopla over the M and M list,

Timmie had forgotten. Was it enough to inspire that bit of nonsense that had landed her in Farmer Johnson's pasture?

Who knew?

On the other hand, was Landry powerful enough to find out Timmie had gotten hold of that notice and then coerce a security officer at work into chasing her down for it?

Of course he was.

The question was, what was he so afraid of? And who knew about the policy he was protecting?

"I take it this means something," Conrad said.

"Oh, I think it does," Timmie assured him. "How fast can I get that from you?"

"Let me keep it for now, *cara*. I think maybe it's safer here."

Timmie took a deep breath to slow the spin of her thoughts, which skipped from Mary Jane, who hadn't known about Timmie's accident, to Alex, who was at the mercy of an administrator who thought nothing of using covert ops for problem solving, to Mr. Cleveland, who had assumed that a man had offered to grant his most terrible wish.

"Okay," she finally said. "Send me a copy so I remember specifics. Did you find out anything else?"

"Yes and no. I checked through my friends at the FBI for a pattern of hospital deaths elsewhere in the country that might match yours, and found quite a few. Hospitals just aren't safe places to be, *carissima*, you know?"

"And we're not even talking managed care."

Conrad's laugh was dark. "Ah, yes, well. That would take years to unravel. This is, blessedly, easier. About a dozen different series of suspicious patient deaths under investigation, some with suspects at large, some with suspected suspects, some with no inkling about who could be involved. Most, though, involve intensive care settings."

"Superman syndrome," Timmie agreed.

Not a terribly new phenomenon. Timmie had known a practitioner, a young guy at USC who had been caught pushing tubocurarine into an indigent patient's line so he could be the first one to the rescue when the patient had the inevitable respiratory arrest. Kind of like a fireman setting his own fires. The difference here was that these weren't the kind of patients anybody rushed to save.

"The open cases are pretty much all over the country," Conrad continued, obviously reading from notes. "Hospitals from Joliet to St. Petersburg to Boulder. I'll send you a copy of the list along with that note. Guard it carefully, and don't show it around, *bella*. Because he is a good man and wants to help, my friend even included the suspects' names, which are not for public consumption. The real news, though, is that your doctor has never worked in a hospital at a time that corresponds with any of these cases."

Timmie's breath whooshed out in relief. "He has no pattern."

"None that's ever shown up."

Timmie didn't thank him. That would be too much. "I need you to check another name, Conrad. Paul Landry. He's the new CEO here."

"The one with his name on this order somebody went to great lengths to try and get back."

"The same."

"What dates, *bellissima*?"

That caught Timmie up short. "Um, I don't . . . know."

"How long has he been at your little medical center there?"

An easier answer. "Four months. I know because he got here about two months before I got home, which would make it July."

Conrad hummed to himself as he riffled through papers. Out in the entryway the doorbell rang. Timmie held a hand over the phone and yelled for them to come in.

Conrad cleared his throat. "A problem, *cara*."

Timmie forgot the door. "What?"

"You think this man is responsible, maybe, for the cardiac arrests?"

"I was kind of hoping he was." More like desperately hoping, but that wasn't important. "Why?"

"Because the deaths started three months before he arrived, that's why."

Timmie was on her third cigarette, and she still hadn't settled down. "It's not fair," she complained.

Slouched in his own chair with his feet at right angles to

Timmie's on the coffee table, Murphy didn't even bother to open his eyes. "You'd consider it fair that Landry killed old people?"

"I consider it unfair that there aren't any answers at all."

"There are answers," Murphy allowed as he shortened his own cigarette. "You're just not ready for them."

"Shut up."

"The golden boy has been in town for the entire run of this show."

"So have Mary Jane Arlington, Tucker Van Adder, and the entire population of the town."

"He also knew about Charlie Cleveland."

"Same answer. This never happened before at a hospital Alex ran."

"Which means it never happened before at a hospital where Mary Jane worked or Davies researched. But then, the three of them had never been sitting on their third strike before, either."

That didn't make Timmie feel any better.

"There is one good thing," Murphy mused, eyes open and wry. "At least you know *you're* not doing it."

Timmie snorted and ground her cigarette out in the ashtray. "Evidently nobody's doing it. But everybody's killing themselves trying to cover it up."

She was going to have to go back in. Just the thought of it made her stomach curl. She was going to have to get those lovely nurses over in Restcrest to admit that old people had been dying under their very excellent care, and that they hadn't done a thing about it. And then she was going to have to try and get the truth from them about just who might be responsible.

The doorbell rang again, and Timmie lurched to her feet. "I don't suppose we can hope that Micklind has a smoking gun on him."

"Wouldn't that be a smoking syringe?"

Timmie opened the big front door to find Micklind scowling at the porch floor.

"Detective?"

He didn't look up. "You missing a lizard?"

Timmie opened the door to find Renfield considering her with a wide-eyed lack of interest from a position across Micklind's highly polished wing tips. "Sorry," she said, retrieving him. "He likes shiny things."

Micklind's eyebrows lifted. "Then he is yours?"

"My daughter's. She considers anything cute and furry a cliché. This is Renfield, eater of flies, who is supposed to live in her fish tank upstairs."

"Uh-huh."

Timmie draped Renfield over her shoulder and held the door open. "Come on in. We were just talking about you."

It took Micklind a moment to move, all the while casting a wary eye toward the chameleon that glared at him from beneath Timmie's left ear. "You're going to put him away, aren't you?"

It was Timmie's turn to admit surprise. "You don't like chameleons?"

Micklind's wrestler's neck darkened a little above that regulation Arrow shirt and half-yanked maroon tie. "Uh, no."

Timmie fought a smile. So Micklind was human. How nice. "I'll just be a minute, Detective."

By the time Timmie made it back downstairs, Micklind had usurped her place on the couch and was glaring at Murphy much the same way he had the lizard.

"I've obviously missed the small talk," Timmie ventured, sweeping a pile of papers from a third chair and pulling it over. It occurred to her that if she kept having to seat guests in the house, she wasn't going to have any floor space left. "To what do we owe this honor, Detective?"

Micklind didn't look appreciably easier now that Renfield was safely out of sight. Even ensconced on an ugly, droopy couch, he straightened himself up to interrogation posture and pulled out a regulation police notebook. "A couple of things," he said, considering it. "First, Vic Adkins."

Well, he had Timmie's attention. "He was murdered," she said.

"Yes, ma'am," Micklind admitted, looking back up with calm cop eyes. "He was. And his wife didn't do it."

Timmie recognized an apology when she heard it. She settled into her seat for the ride. "And?"

"And I wanted to talk to you about who it might be."

"Isn't it a little late?" Timmie asked. "From what I heard, nobody could convince Van Adder there was a problem. Case closed. And when a coroner's case is closed in Missouri, it stays closed."

Now she got that twitch of incipient smile. "Yes, ma'am. Unless it's a cop. Then we can do pretty much what we want. Now, you want to go over this all again?"

Timmie considered him for a minute. She thought about reaching for another cigarette, but she really hadn't wanted the last one. She only smoked the damn things as a last vestige of rebellion.

"One question," she said, also ignoring the urge to scratch her staples. "Why?"

Micklind spared a quick look Murphy's way. Murphy waved him off. "I'm off the clock till you tell me, hoss. I'm just as curious as you are."

It still took Micklind a few minutes to let go. When he did, it was facing that notebook, which he held in his hands like an archaeological find. "I hear you were at Charlie Cleveland's today."

"Word does get around," Murphy allowed.

"Victor visited him before he died, too," Timmie said. "Most amazing thing. Charlie kept trying to confess, only Victor wouldn't let him."

Micklind nodded equably. "Victor wasn't allowed to let him. Charlie's had his problems. The decision was made to just let him be."

"He needed to confess," Timmie said. "But that's not why you're here. You're here to tell us that Victor found out that Charlie wasn't so delusional about people offering to kill his father for him, aren't you?"

Finally Micklind raised his eyes, and Timmie discovered the detective lurking there. "Yes, ma'am, I am."

"How?" Murphy asked.

Micklind lifted the notebook Timmie had assumed was his. "Found this in the locker room the other day. It's Vic's. Seems he was carrying on his own investigation after all."

Timmie leaned forward. "And?"

Micklind shot Murphy a quelling look. "This is all off the record."

"Then why am I here?"

Micklind gave him a ghost of a smile. "So I can let you know the reason behind that little set-to you had the other night. Has to do with Restcrest, economic opportunities, and a mayor who's going to run for reelection on the strength of the town's rebirth."

Murphy looked poleaxed. "The *mayor* was behind that little escapade?"

"Not in any official sense. It was probably more like the misunderstanding between Henry the Second and Thomas à Beckett. A halfhearted complaint taken as an order."

Timmie almost laughed aloud. Go figure it'd be the detective who'd finally show some residue of a real education. Timmie wondered if he knew poetry, too. "General opportunities?" she asked. "Or specific?"

Micklind didn't bother to dissemble. "You should go see the mayor when this clears up. He has a great model in his office of the hotel and convention complex that's being planned. Lots of important decisions being made right now by potential investors. Decisions made on the assurance that Dr. Raymond and Restcrest will continue to be part of the town's picture."

Money and power. Another puzzle piece neatly slotted into place. Murphy smiled a reporter's smile.

"I'm afraid there's not much you can do about the . . . uh, messengers," Micklind continued. "But though nobody else will do it, I apologize for the . . . enthusiasm of the message."

Murphy nodded. "Apology accepted. Now, what about Restcrest?"

Micklind went back to meditating, until Timmie thought she'd scream. "Nothing about it," he said. "At least nothing official. We've all been warned as far off as possible. But . . ." He lifted the book, weighed it. "I figure you haven't been listening to the warnings anyway. And I'd like to know what the hell's going on."

"You won't help?" Timmie asked.

"I am helping. I'm giving you what Vic had and staying out of your hair, which is not what my directive is. Besides, if something's going on over at that hospital, no cop is going to get the truth like a nurse is."

Much to Timmie's chagrin, she had to admit his point. "And any further . . . warnings?"

"I'm afraid you're on your own. Just remember that no matter what's behind this, it's a real hornet's nest. You're swinging your stick at the most important opportunity to hit Puckett since the railroad. Which means that whatever's going on, nobody wants anybody else to know about it."

Timmie grimaced. "We've already picked up on that. What about Victor, though?"

Micklind gave a tight little shrug on a par with his smiles. "I'd appreciate a regular update on what you find. With your experience I'm confident you won't compromise a possible case."

Now Timmie was stunned. Good lord, the second person in this town who actually acknowledged that her training meant more than knowing alternate uses for the paper bag. "That you can count on," she said. "You want our theories?"

Micklind pulled out a second, almost identical notebook and flipped it open. "Yes, ma'am, I probably do."

For the first time, Timmie smiled. "Tell me, Detective. You're not from Puckett, or I would have recognized you. Where are you from?"

"Chicago." His grin was brief, bright, and telling. "I came here looking for some peace and quiet."

When Timmie and Murphy settled at the table to study Victor Adkins's notebook a little later, two things stood out. Victor had been more careful with his private deliberations than with his public interrogations, and Detective Sergeant Micklind had done more than just find that notebook. The notes Victor kept were neat, concise, and objective. Micklind's additional comments showed up sporadically in a hastier scrawl.

Unfortunately, Victor hadn't gathered a whole lot more than Timmie and Murphy. He'd talked to quite a few people under different guises, dug through Van Adder's records, and pored over the charter for the revamped Restcrest. He'd visited families and talked to both Cindy and Ellen about their time in Restcrest, and all he'd been able to garner had been disdain for Van Adder, respect for Alex Raymond, and frustration with the families.

It was on the very last page of notes that Timmie struck gold. A list of names, meticulously recorded in Victor's round, careful, grade school–level hand. Familiar names, listed with ages, times and dates of death, and one other item. Their original admission date to Restcrest.

"Well, I'll be damned," Timmie muttered when she saw Butch Cleveland's name almost all the way down and realized what it was she was looking at. "I think it's a list of the old-timers."

Pushing the notebook at Murphy, she jumped up for her knapsack purse, where she'd been carrying her own list of cardiac arrest victims. "You don't think we could be this lucky, could we?" she asked, yanking them out and adding them to the pile.

"Of course we can," Murphy assured her, his finger steadily tracking down the crinkled, lined page. "That's how reporting works. Just ask Geraldo Rivera."

Even so, when they matched up every name but one, Murphy was the one to let out the low whistle. "It's almost a dead match. Fifteen out of sixteen are on that cardiac arrest list."

Timmie grimaced. "Nice turn of phrase, Murphy. You should be a reporter . . ." Reaching out to the list, she pointed to the only name that didn't match up. "Bertha Worthmueller," she said, tapping the paper. "I know her. I took care of her the other night. Tiny little woman with a big nose. Looks like a mole."

Murphy scowled. "Don't ever take care of me, Leary. I don't think I could stand the affection."

But Timmie was already shaking her head. "No, that's not the point. She's the only surviving old-timer, and she hasn't been doing well. I remember Ellen saying it when she was taking care of her, and she was right. She's been weak and nauseated. They've had her on parenteral nutrition only for the last four days."

Murphy raised an eyebrow. "She's also ninety-three and has Alzheimer's."

Timmie glared at him. "What if she's already being poisoned?" she demanded. "Nobody'd notice. Like you said, she's old, she's sick, and she has Alzheimer's, just like all the others."

Murphy sat back and pulled a pack of cigarettes from his shirt pocket. Shaking one out, he didn't bother to light it, just stuck it in his mouth, as if the oral stimulation was all he needed in order to think. "And you think who, exactly, is poisoning her?"

Timmie glared at him. "Not Landry, okay? It still doesn't mean it can't be Mary Jane or Davies or anybody who works up in that unit."

"Or the golden boy."

"No."

"He'd have access. He'd have motive. He'd have the weapon."

"*No.*"

Murphy leaned back, crossed his arms, raised his eyebrows. The farther away he moved from her, the faster Timmie's heart worked. Timmie was amazed how quickly one could go from elation to distress. The thrill of the hunt had just become "Oh shit, the tiger's turned on me."

"Only one way to make sure," he said easily. "Watch her. Watch him. Make sure he never sees her alone."

"I can't."

"Which? Check the drugs? Control access? Take care of her?"

She got to her feet. "Do it alone," she said, walking. "And who else will help? Who can we trust up there?"

There was a tiny silence, and then Murphy's quiet question. "You don't trust the golden boy after all?"

Timmie still couldn't look at Murphy. "You don't understand." She was pacing now, using every inch of space in the room. Swinging at the Nerf ball as she walked past.

"Make me understand."

"What, in twenty-five words or less?"

She couldn't look at him. Hell, she couldn't even breathe. She'd known this was coming. She should have prepared. Set aside some of her store of guts to ride it through.

Behind her, Murphy rustled in his chair. "Are you saying you're falling in love with him?"

Well, at least that was worth a laugh. "You've been watching way too much *ER*, Murphy."

"Then what?"

Again, that terrible feeling of claustrophobia. The weight of inevitability she'd been running from all these years. Timmie walked over to the window, where she could see the tidy columns of yellow mums marching along her clean walk to the street. The last of the leaves were falling, leaving behind spectral trees against a cold sky. The lush, soft town of summer was being stripped of its guise and left with reality.

"I *need* Alex to be innocent," she said, not knowing how to say what she'd never before admitted. "If he isn't, there isn't anybody for my father."

Timmie didn't see Murphy, but she heard the hesitation in his voice. "There's you."

"You want coffee?" she asked, spinning around and heading straight for the kitchen. "I want coffee. Hell, I want a drink, but I don't drink. So coffee it is."

He followed her right to the edge of the kitchen, and just stood there.

"Leary?"

Timmie refused to look at him. She slammed through cabinets as if she were chasing cockroaches.

And Murphy waited.

Timmie pulled out coffee. She pulled out filters and she pulled out cups. Finally, though, she couldn't pull anything else out, and she couldn't manage to actually put everything together. So she stood there, her hands on the counter, staring at an empty coffee machine and thinking how much she hated what she had to do.

"You have kids, Murphy?" she asked.

"Yep." He sounded a tad confused.

Timmie nodded to herself. Sucked in a slow breath for courage, lifted her head, and stared out the window.

"I wonder if you know how much they hate you."

Silence. She hadn't expected anything else. So she faced him, and she told him.

"I have a feeling that you weren't just a great drunk, Murphy. You were a magnificent drunk. Larger than life, charismatic as hell. Brilliant and funny and beautiful. And when you got home, still a drunk. Still undependable and forgetful and unintentionally cruel. Still smelling like piss and vomit in the morning when your kids crept into bed to find a safe place. Still provoking massive, howling arguments that were more terrifying than storms, and walking back out to drink some more as if none of it mattered."

She wasn't going to cry. Not in front of Murphy. Not in front of anybody. She hadn't done it in years, and she wasn't going to do it now. But, God, faced with Murphy's tight, closed expression, all Timmie could think of was how her chest hurt. "Your kids would do anything," she said, her voice hushed, "*anything* to belong to you, because that's all kids want. But you've never noticed, and so eventually they'll give up and belong to something else."

She blinked fast. Swallowed. Finished.

"Alex only knew my father when he was brilliant and beautiful," she said. "So I know he'll fight for him, no matter what I say."

Murphy was so still Timmie wondered if she'd frozen him into immobility. Or insulted him to death.

But Murphy was made of stronger stuff. Most great drunks were.

"You really hate him?" he asked.

She couldn't help but smile. "Oh, yes. Every bit as much as I adore him. I was the lucky one in the family. I got to see him when he was beautiful, too. So I may be the queen of denial, but I'm also the grand empress of ambivalence."

Timmie didn't know what she expected after that. She didn't expect Murphy to really understand, no matter how smart he was. She certainly didn't expect him to forgive her. So she turned back to her coffee and braced herself for his reaction.

"I'm sorry, Leary," he said.

She closed her eyes. Son of a bitch. How dare he?

"Don't be sorry, Murphy," she said. "Just help me catch the son of a bitch who's doing this so I never have to talk about this shit again as long as I live."

# NINETEEN

TIMMIE MADE HER COFFEE. MURPHY MADE HIS OWN COPY OF THE list and went home. The house got very quiet. Too quiet, with just the hum of the refrigerator and the hall clock for company. Too still with nothing in motion but a second hand. Timmie hummed. She paced the kitchen and consigned a couple of piles of debris to the trash. She took a dozen swings at the Nerf ball and cleaned up the sewing box she'd left out and watched the clock until Meghan was due home, like a prisoner ticking off the days of her sentence.

At exactly 3:10, the door slammed and hard-soled footsteps clattered across the floor. Timmie and Meghan met in the middle like those freight trains in the infamous math problem. And Timmie did it looking much saner than she felt.

"Hiya, punkin, how goes it?"

"Look who I found outside!" Meghan crowed, swinging around in Timmie's arms like a carnival ride.

"Not Renfield again," Timmie begged. "I just put him back upstairs."

Meghan slid out of Timmie's reach. "You let Renfield out?"

Timmie tousled the dark head of hair and thought again how much she wanted her little girl to belong to her. "Funny, that's the very same question I was going to ask you. I don't think I'm the person he always talks into breaking him out of stir."

Meghan straightened with outrage. "I would *never* let Renfield out. He might get lost or run over or eaten by a cat!"

"I did it," Cindy announced from the hallway. "Disguised him as a tree frog and bribed the guards to look the other way."

Meghan giggled. Timmie wondered if Murphy knew how lucky he was that he'd missed this. "Hi, Cindy. How's it going?"

"You didn't answer my calls," she said, clacking across the hardwood in the new red-leather cowboy boots she sported with her studded denim dress. "I thought something was wrong."

"I just got home myself. Anybody for milk and cookies?"

Meghan pulled quite a face. "Really, Mom. That's so retro."

"Retro?" Timmie echoed. "Where the heck did you learn that?"

"Billy Peebucket."

Timmie turned her little troop for the kitchen. "That's Parbagget, young lady...ooh, Cindy, eau de Betadine. You working today?"

Cindy sniffed her armpits, which made Meghan giggle all over again. "Half a shift. I didn't know I carried it home."

"My mom has the best nose in the West," Meghan boasted.

"How was it?" Timmie asked because she didn't want to talk about boyfriends, which was what Cindy had come to talk about.

"Biker heaven. I think I'm in love."

"Which means, I guess, that you're over your loss."

Cindy's grin was fierce. "You don't want Meghan to hear what I think of that. There's some hot gossip at the hospital, by the way. Word's going around they're trying to hush up some patients getting intentionally stiffed." She snorted unkindly. "Like with the doctors we have they'd need any help."

Timmie opened the refrigerator and pulled out sodas instead of milk and apples instead of cookies. "Who says?" she asked, trying hard to be nonchalant.

"Ellen, I think. She heard it over in Restcrest. They're all on full alert over there. Seems to me, somebody should man the ICUs first. You ever worked with some of those Nazis up there? They'd drop you with a look."

"Why Restcrest?" Timmie asked as she passed out the snacks. "Have you seen anything up there to make you suspicious?"

"You want the truth?" she asked. "Mary Jane. She creeps me to the max, and she's always around when something happens."

"It's her job to be around when something happens."

"I don't know," she said with a shrug. "Ellen said to tell you, though, that she thinks your dad's safe. She doesn't think his unit's involved."

"I'm heading over to see him now. Might not be a bad idea to make sure. Want to go along to see Grandda, Megs?"

Meghan didn't exactly stop in her tracks. She did dip her head and clutch her apple with white-knuckled hands, though.

"I'll be happy to stay with her," Cindy offered.

Meghan said not a word. Timmie got the message, though. Meghan did not like Restcrest. Not for her grandda.

"That would be fine," Timmie allowed. "I'll pay you in pizzas. You call, I'll buy."

The offer was met with enthusiasm, and Timmie was caught between the dread of visiting Restcrest and staying home to hear about the boyfriend Cindy had decided to stop mourning.

"I should tell you who he is," she said, as if Timmie had asked, which made Timmie decide. Restcrest it was.

It could have been worse. By the time Timmie arrived, dinner was over and Joe was washed and clean and smiling from a beanbag chair in the main room. Timmie knew the chair kept him from wandering off, but she couldn't imagine trying to get him out of the thing.

"Hello, Da," she greeted him, crouched down on her haunches.

He blinked at her.

"He's been kind of quiet today," one of the nurses admitted. "We've been watching him for a fever or a urinary tract infection, but we haven't caught anything yet."

Timmie did her own laying on of hands and came away with

the feel of cool, papery skin. Her father blinked again and turned away. Timmie fought that stupid sense of abandonment that hit every time he failed to recognize her and climbed back to her feet.

"No recitations?" she asked. "No obscene army tunes?"

The nurse, another young soul named Tracy with tidy brown hair and small hands, actually patted Joe on the head. "Not even a limerick. He may just be a little tired. He's still trying to settle in."

"I understand."

Timmie found herself looking off toward the fifth wing, where Mrs. Worthmueller waited in silence for that last graduation party. She needed to check on her. Make sure nobody was shoving something lethal into her IVs. Even so, Timmie curled up on the floor next to her father for a requisite twenty minutes or so, all the while trading aimless chatter with other residents who wandered through.

It wasn't until she got ready to move that she realized she'd wrapped her arm around her father's leg, or that he'd rested a hand on her head. The customary position they'd assumed all those years ago when he'd ruled story hour at the Brentwood Library up in St. Louis.

Timmie could still call up the sensual memory of it: the scents of lemon wax and binding glue and paper; the hush of reverent voices and careful feet; the tactile joy of those first books her father had placed in her hands. It had been a magical place, set to the music of her father's voice and the laughter of the children he'd enchanted on Wednesday afternoons. And Timmie had spent every one curled up at his feet like a faithful pet waiting her turn.

Only it had never been her turn.

"Going already?" the nurse asked when Timmie lurched up.

Timmie started. Why had she told Murphy? What good had it done? Now he was confused and she was ashamed and her father was still her father. And she had some investigating to do.

"Uh, no," she said, straightening her clothes. "I thought I'd go check on a couple of folks I took care of the other night."

The nurse looked surprised, then relieved. "Oh, that's right. Mary Jane told me. You got pulled from ER, didn't you?"

"Yeah. I'm amazed, but I kinda got attached, ya know?"

The nurse patted the top of Joe's head again as if he were a Labrador, which made Timmie want to tell her to stop. "I know. I can't imagine doing anything else."

Timmie couldn't quite take her gaze off her father, whose eyes were closed to the touch of the nurse's hand. "I wish I had your talent."

She didn't mind the bald lie so much when Tracy smiled. Nurses like Tracy were needed. Nurses who walked that slow walk and didn't mind repeating an action a thousand times a day because the person they were working with forgot. Nurses who didn't have to carry the baggage of an imperfect life for the patients they liked. But Timmie wasn't that kind of nurse, so she smiled, checked her father a last time to find his eyes still closed, and headed off the hall.

The funny thing was that after all those nerves, Mrs. Worthmueller looked good. Sitting up in her bed, her Posey neat and clean across her chest, her hands picking at the sheets. Timmie noticed that her cheeks were pink and her vitals stable.

"Can I help you?"

Timmie turned to find the regular unit nurse smiling that "You'd better explain yourself fast" smile at her. Timmie gave her a professional recognition version to negate the picture she presented of a stranger in jeans and Cardinals T-shirt holding a patient chart. "Oh, hi, you must be Gladys."

Gladys, for God's sake, on a thirty-year-old. She even looked like a Gladys, a little tight, a little prim, as neat as hell, and as organized as an accountant. What she wasn't was amused by Timmie's intrusion.

"I am. And you are?"

"Timmie Leary. Joe's daughter from over on unit three. I work down in the ER and got pulled here last night when you were off. When I came in to see Dad I thought I'd make sure little Bertha was okay. She really had me worried."

Gladys's defenses flickered and died in the space of Timmie's speech. "She had us all worried. Isn't she a dear?"

Considering the fact that the only communication Timmie had shared with Bertha the night before had been a bellowed "Bertha?" or two, Timmie couldn't really consider her opinion valid. She smiled harder anyway. "A dear. She looks a lot better tonight. What was wrong, the flu? I have to tell you, this just isn't my gig. I felt like an alligator on ice up here."

Gladys patted Timmie as if she were one of the patients. "Oh, you'll get used to it. I'm sorry I was so defensive. It's just that we have to be very careful to protect our clients."

Timmie nodded enthusiastically. "I can't be more impressed with the care my dad gets over here."

That got a real smile from Gladys as she retrieved the chart Timmie had been perusing. "Well, you must have done something right," she said, turning toward the room. "She's so very much better today. We figure she just had a little upset. It seems all better now, though, DOESN'T IT, BERTHA?"

Timmie checked to see Bertha picking away, oblivious as ever to the sound of her name being brayed. "We've been getting a lot of your old folk lately, it seems," she said to Gladys.

Gladys clutched the chart to her chest like a Bible. "I know."

"It must be hard on you. You get so attached to them."

A nod, a wince of pain that seemed all too real. "Mary Jane keeps saying I'll understand some day. I don't think I will."

"Understand?"

"Why they're so afflicted. Why they have to suffer. Why we lose them . . ." Gladys actually gasped, tapped Timmie's arm again in odd commiseration. "Oh, I'm sorry. Here I am saying that, with your father here. You know, of course."

"It does worry me a little, Gladys," she said, leaning closer. "I mean, I know what kind of care you give up here, but people in the ER have been questioning . . . well, *all* the patients who've been . . . uh, graduating lately."

Gladys patted her again with a hand that trembled just a mite. "Nothing to worry about, I'm sure. You know how it happens. One of the dears fails, and the others tend to follow. They just want some rest, I think, from their suffering. You aren't worried about your father, are you? Why, he's as hale as a teenager."

Which meant that Gladys wasn't the one yearning to share her outrage. On the other hand, she might be one to watch.

"Thank you," Timmie said, sidling away. "I really appreciate the update. I told Mary Jane she needed more staff up here so you guys didn't keep getting amateurs filling in."

Gladys followed Timmie right to the door. "It would be nice," she agreed. "But I can't say a bad thing about the girls we get from the emergency department. Especially Ellen and the other girl. Our little people just love them."

Timmie nodded. "That sounds like Ellen."

Gladys waved Bertha's chart once like a salute and slid it back in its door slot. "You thank her for me when you see her."

"I will. And you take care of Bertha for me, okay?"

"Of course."

Timmie headed back to unit three to be greeted by the smell of popcorn. It was snack time, and the old folks were making for the kitchen like zombies trolling for fresh blood. All the way across the room, Timmie could see her father's nose twitch and then his head swivel unerringly toward the smell. She couldn't help but grin. He adored popcorn. All his favorite taverns had served it. She was going to have to get him a bowl. And maybe one for herself. Nothing sent a hospital staffer's saliva glands working faster than the smell of fresh popcorn.

Timmie had just turned to take her place in the migration when she heard the commotion behind her. A yell. A clatter. Even through two sets of doors, the clear notes of a distinctive voice screaming, "Oh, no, help! Call a code somebody!"

Oh, hell. That was right behind her, which meant unit five.

Which meant Bertha.

Timmie spun on her heel and crashed back through the doors into unit five in time to see Gladys desperately trying to punch three successive nines into the phone without any luck. Nursing home nurses were wonderful at patience and encouragement and calming. They didn't manage crises quite as well.

Grabbing the phone from Gladys, Timmie punched the numbers. "Code blue, Restcrest, unit five," she announced. "Room four."

"No!" Gladys shrilled, grabbing her arm. "Not Bertha. Alice!"

Timmie stared. "Alice?"

"Code blue, Restcrest," the announcer droned. "Unit five, room four."

Gladys spun for the patient, and Timmie ran for the crash cart. "Alice?" she demanded, incredulous. "Are you sure?"

Alice. No doubt about it. The skinny, cranky doyenne Dr. Davies had been so interested in the night before was in there thrashing on the bed like a landed fish, her eyes rolled, her tongue lolling, her skin mottling to quick purple. And Gladys, her nurse, stood there patting her head as if that would make all the difference.

Timmie checked for pulses, knowing already what she'd find.

"Gladys, does Alice have a gate pass?" Timmie demanded as she pulled out airways and leads.

"What?"

"A gate pass! A 'Do Not Resuscitate' order." As in, *Hi, my name is Peter, I'm going to be your guide through the Pearlies this afternoon . . .*

"No. Of course not."

Timmie sighed. The operator's announcement would bring the ER traveling code team. One look at the chaos in room two would send them in the right direction. In the meantime, Timmie guessed she should do something more productive than say, "*Alice*?"

"Here, Gladys," she instructed, passing over an ambu-bag. "You bag her, I'll compress. Come on, let's go."

Gladys had tears running down her face. "She wasn't even sick!"

Timmie dragged over a step stool to get better leverage. "Well, honey, she is now."

It was a cluster fuck, but then most codes coming over from Restcrest were. Luckily, Alice didn't know any difference, and the ER crew didn't mind in the least when they arrived to find Timmie balanced over Alice's skinny chest doing CPR. The code attempt made it back to the ER in ten minutes and then lasted another twenty before Barb called it. No matter what they did, Alice didn't respond. And Timmie was left to wonder just what the hell had made Alice a victim.

"We have to get an autopsy," she told Barb, who was signing off on the chart with a flourish.

Barb looked up without noticeable reaction and proceeded to strip off her gloves.

Already pulling useless lines, Mattie didn't manage the same. "What do you mean?" she demanded, her hands full of tubing. "This poor old thing's nothing but brain waste. Leave her alone."

Timmie looked at Mattie a moment, but she knew she didn't have time to make her understand. She turned back to Barb. "I mean it," was all she said. "Can you do a drug screen on the blood you got? Double-check the levels of her prescribed meds? And don't send her downstairs without letting me know. I'll try and force Van Adder into doing something."

"It's not a coroner's case," Barb reminded her calmly. "How you gonna pull it off?"

"Friends in high places. Just hold her. Please."

Over at the cart, one of the other nurses was hanging long strips of tape to the edge of the bed to begin wrapping the body.

Barb just shrugged. "Why not? I didn't like working in this county much, anyway."

"What are you *talking* about?" Mattie demanded. "Does this have something to do with why Walter's walking your girls home from school?"

Timmie didn't have time to answer, because Ellen was leaning in the door. "Mattie, those old ladies need you back in five."

Which was when Timmie heard it. Wafting on the breeze like a birdcall. Continuous, keening, impervious to soothing or shouting or sedating.

"Help! . . . Help! . . . Help!"

Timmie knew then why Mattie was so upset that they'd tried to save Alice. Timmie understood why she had tears in her eyes even as she turned for the door where Ellen waited.

"Help! . . . Help! . . . Help!"

Mrs. Clara Winterborn was back. Just as brain dead as before, just as brittle and empty and sere. Even older than when Timmie had been forced to save her the last time for another trip to the unit to be tortured and tormented and saved.

Timmie tried to pass the old woman's cubicle without looking in at the disaster that had once been a human, the two frail and fluttery jailers who held her here. She really did.

"Help! . . . Help! . . . Help!"

She didn't quite make it. Like the time she'd caught sight of her father naked in the bathroom, the first adult male she'd ever witnessed. Hairy and huge and alien. Timmie had been terrified, repulsed, appalled. She'd looked anyway, and kept on looking, because she just couldn't seem to stop. She looked now, just as repulsed. Just as terrified.

"Wish somebody'd do for this soul what they seem to be doin' upstairs," Mattie muttered on the way by. "No matter what Walter and his God say. It just ain't right."

"Mattie, you can't mean that," Ellen whispered. "Not you."

Shifting the Chux and catheter supplies in her arms, Mattie glared. "Me."

Mattie was right, Timmie thought. She should just go home. Leave them to tag Alice with her statistics and then wrap her like a pork roast and send her off to the freezer where someone would mourn, but not as much as if she'd lived.

Instead, Timmie turned and walked back upstairs.

When she reached Restcrest, it was to find even more of a commotion than when she'd left it an hour earlier. Not raucous, by any means. That would have upset the patients. The patients were upset anyway, because like children and horses, they could sense distress just from the way they were handled.

The cries were harsher, more strident, more frequent. From the level-two areas Timmie could hear the heightened babble of conversation and more than one argument. And on unit five, where she'd planned on talking to Gladys and collecting Alice's medications for analysis, she found not one nurse, but two, stiff-lipped, dry-eyed, and as tense as a terrorist cease-fire. The second nurse was one of the evening supervisors, which suited Timmie's purposes perfectly.

"I'm sorry," Timmie said, greeting Gladys. "She didn't make it."

Gladys closed her eyes. "I don't understand it," she insisted. "I just don't."

"Well, Miss Arlington's on her way in now to make us understand," the supervisor said dryly.

Miss Arlington. That meant Timmie didn't have much time.

"I need a favor," she said, holding up the evidence box she'd scooped up on her way out of the ER. "Alice's medications. I need to get them analyzed."

Gladys blanched. "Oh, I don't know . . ."

The supervisor, God bless her, held firm. "Well, I do. Take 'em before Mary Jane gets here. If something's going on, she's the last one who's going to want to know."

Timmie hesitated. "You're sure."

"I'm sure. Just make sure it's worth my job."

"I'll need you to sign and date the sealing tape," Timmie told her. "So we can protect the chain of evidence."

Gladys looked as if she were going to pass out. "Evidence."

The supervisor didn't say a word. She just reached out her hand until Gladys handed over the nurse-server key.

The supervisor helped Timmie clean out the medicine drawer and came away with handfuls of Dulcolax and Maalox dose packs, Ticlid, Digoxin, Tranzene, Nitropaste. Vials of Lasix and Compazine, and bottles of IV potassium chloride. Haldol and procainamide and half a dozen things Timmie recognized but couldn't immediately identify. Nothing Timmie wouldn't have expected, though.

Timmie and the supervisor both signed the red tape that Timmie stretched over the edge of the box, and Timmie thanked her. They were just finishing up when they both heard Gladys's surprised greeting. Ms. Arlington had wasted no time.

"I'm holding you responsible, Gladys," she was saying.

Timmie walked out of the room to see Gladys's mouth opened wide enough to show her uvula. "How could I . . . ?"

Which was about when Mary Jane caught sight of the coconspirators. "What are you doing here?"

"She helped code Alice," Gladys defended, now flushed and trembling. "And now she's—"

"Going back to see my father," Timmie allowed, the sealed evidence box safely tucked inside the jacket she'd balled up and held in her arms.

"I just can't believe that Alice is gone," Gladys said to no one in particular.

"Me, either," Timmie said. "I expected it to be Bertha Worthmueller."

Mary Jane's eyes snapped open so fast Timmie could see the tiny scars from her lifts. Her mouth opened, too, but she couldn't seem to manage anything. It was as if Alice's death was the final straw. It certainly seemed to be for Gladys, who was crying and glaring at the same time.

"It shouldn't have happened," she insisted, wringing her hands. "It never should have happened."

Timmie tried her best to assess each reaction. Gladys was distraught, the supervisor outraged, and Mary Jane . . . Timmie couldn't figure out what Mary Jane was, except cautious. Ah, hell. She might as well go for the gold.

"You really don't know who's doing this, do you?" she asked Gladys.

"No, we don't," Gladys said, her eyes lighting a little. "Do you?"

"Doing what?" Mary Jane asked just a little too late.

Timmie knew way back in her head that Mary Jane outranked her by at least ten levels of administration. She even remembered that Mary Jane might be a murderer with about as much conscience as Lucrezia Borgia. It didn't prevent her from reacting to that little piece of disingenuity with disdain.

"Come on, Ms. Arlington. At least twenty people have died on this unit. Fifteen of them have been the old-timers who've been costing this unit a ton of money. That's why I was worried about Bertha in there. She's the last one. What was it about Alice that made her a target?"

"There are no targets," Mary Jane insisted with less enthusiasm. "This is just an unfortunate . . . uh . . . "

"Murder," Timmie filled in for her. "And if it wasn't to save the unit money, what could it have been for?"

"That's why it shouldn't have been Alice," Gladys insisted. "She was going to leave the wing a grant. A fortune!"

Mary Jane snapped to attention. "Gladys!"

"I can't anymore, Miss Arlington. I just can't! Somebody needs to know. Alice isn't from here. Her family transferred her from Kentucky, and they were going to meet her here next weekend, after she got settled. They were so excited she was going to be safe and cared for. What we heard was that if they liked what they saw when they came to see her, they were going to donate a huge amount to the unit. Well, they won't once they find out she's been murdered!"

"She has not been murdered!" Mary Jane insisted.

"But somebody murdered those other people," Timmie retorted, her voice still very quiet. "And you all know it. Why didn't you say anything?"

It was Mary Jane's turn to glare, and she did it quite well. "Do you know what you're doing to Restcrest's reputation?"

Timmie wanted to scream. "I'm not the one doing it, Ms. Arlington. The murderer is. And the people covering it up."

Mary Jane damn near had a stroke. "Don't you threaten me, young lady."

"She told us not to say anything," Gladys insisted.

Mary Jane spun on her, but Gladys had had one too many deaths on her hands.

"But you knew what was going on, didn't you, Gladys?" Timmie asked. "How did you know?"

"They were dying for no reason at all," Gladys all but wailed. "I took such good care of them. Such *good* care! Do you know what this looks like on my record?"

"Did you see anything suspicious? Anyone suspicious?"

"This is absurd!" Mary Jane protested, ramrod straight and trying hard to keep her hands at her sides. Must have been tough not to have a clipboard or patient file to hide behind when she needed to show authority. She didn't even have glasses to wave around. "You'd better think a little harder about what you have to lose before you continue making accusations like this."

Timmie didn't even listen to her. She was focused instead on Gladys, who was still shaking her head as if it would help settle her suspicions and frustrations into a more identifiable pattern.

"I've gone over it a hundred times," the nurse said. "I can't figure it out. None of us can. It mostly happens on late shifts, but that's when most of our patients pass anyway."

"Clients," Mary Jane ground out.

*Die*, Timmie wanted to say. But it wasn't exactly the time to dip Gladys's toes in the reality bath.

Gladys was way beyond caring. "*Patients*. There isn't a pattern we can figure out. No one nurse who was on every time. There wasn't anything obvious we could point a finger to."

"And nobody asked you about it?"

"We've been told it's being looked into. It's not, is it?"

"Of course it is," Mary Jane insisted instinctively.

Timmie had had enough experience with middle management to know that Mary Jane wasn't going to admit anything in front of her staff. Besides, a good threat was always best made in private. If Ms. Arlington wasn't the murderer, then Timmie needed her acquiescence. If she was, Timmie needed her to feel pressured.

"Ms. Arlington," she said in the most supplicating tone she could manage, "could I talk to you alone for a minute? Please. I think it will help Alex."

Mary Jane took a couple of looks around and then nodded. Timmie followed her into Alice's room, where the bright yellow-and-blue coverlet was still spilled off the side of the bed from the frantic fight for Alice's flickering life.

Timmie had been in plenty of rooms in which patients had died. In some, she'd been able to feel a sense that somebody was still around, maybe dragging their heels before departure or just keeping an eye on things. Probably checking her procedures. Alice, evidently, hadn't been interested. The room was as empty as Timmie's bank account.

Mary Jane didn't bother to make either of them comfortable before Timmie shut the door. "I know this must make you nervous," she began, a hand up to corral a wisp of wayward hair. "With your father up here and all. I just want to assure you—"

"Something has to be done," Timmie said. Her heart was pounding and her hands were sweaty, and all she could think about was that she hoped Mary Jane didn't notice. "Ms. Arlington, I know what's going on here. The whole hospital knows. If the public finds out before it's stopped, Alex will be ruined."

Mary Jane did everything but shudder. She stood as straight as a deb, her hands at her sides, her breathing controlled. "You would only hurt Alex if you let this out," she accused. "You wouldn't do that."

Timmie raised an eyebrow. "And if I don't do something, I could be hurting my father."

"That's absurd! He's perfectly safe."

"How do you know that? I thought Alice was perfectly safe."

Mary Jane looked away, as if Timmie's argument were simply beneath her. "What did you want to ask?"

Timmie sucked in a slow breath. Organized her thoughts. She wasn't stupid enough to ask for what she already had, so she made a stab at what she suspected.

"We need to act, Ms. Arlington," Timmie insisted quietly. "Or it's going to happen again. You need to ask Alex to request a postmortem on Alice."

Mary Jane was already shaking her head. "I can't. He's busy. He isn't even in town."

"You mean you don't call him when he's out of town to tell him a patient died?"

Mary Jane couldn't quite look at her. "All you're doing is making trouble for yourself. You're making wild accusations that threaten the viability of this unit, and I won't have it."

Timmie didn't move. "I won't stop, Ms. Arlington."

Mary Jane closed her eyes. Timmie held her breath, because she couldn't manage anything more. Was Mary Jane simply protecting Alex, or was she protecting herself?

"I can't." The woman moaned. "I just can't."

"Then I'll do it."

That got Mary Jane's eyes open, and Timmie once again saw that instinctive fear. That protective reflex that made her wonder if Mary Jane wasn't just protecting Alex, but pretending she didn't suspect him.

Alex.

It couldn't be Alex. Timmie wouldn't let it.

So she asked the most difficult question she had ever asked in her life. "Do you think Alex is involved?"

"No!"

Too sudden, too certain. Way too frightened. Timmie wanted to vomit.

"Can you think of anyone else who it might be?" she asked instead, and realized that her fingers hurt. She looked down to see white knuckles from where she'd clamped her hands together around the hidden box.

"There isn't any problem," Mary Jane said, again too quickly. "But if there were, Alice's main nurse was Gladys. Or Trudy, or, uh, Penelope."

Ah, ever the administrator, Timmie thought with new disgust. When in doubt, jettison the faithful staff.

"May I talk to them?"

Mary Jane damn near sneered. "You don't need my permission for that. You'll just find out where they live and harass them there."

"And the postmortem."

Mary Jane blinked, looked away. "Maybe. I'll see."

Nothing definite. At least the seed was sown. "Bertha Worthmueller," Timmie said. "I think the hospital should give her a private-duty nurse for a few days. Maybe somebody from outside the hospital, just to be sure."

Mary Jane turned for the door. "Bertha is perfectly safe."

"There is one other thing," Timmie said, figuring this would be her last chance. "I'm sure you've already asked Mr. Landry about my trip into orbit the other day. I found out it was to keep me from sharing a directive I'd stumbled on. I just don't know why."

Mary Jane arched an eyebrow, once again the supervisor. "I'm not giving you information just so you can take it back to your lawyer."

"I'm not taking it anywhere. I just want to know if it has anything to do with this."

Mary Jane shook her head. "Certainly not. It was just a schedule for the next level of streamlining we need to implement to strengthen the hospital's financial future."

Streamlining. Read "downsizing." Layoffs. No wonder it was hot stuff. The staff found out early and all hell could break loose. Still not enough to ruin her car, Timmie thought.

"I don't suppose this stage includes the introduction of GerySys to the family, does it?" she asked, looking for a reaction.

The reaction was Timmie's, because Mary Jane just nodded briskly. "As a matter of fact, it does."

"You don't look upset about it."

"Why should I? It's a logical business decision. GerySys has the capital and we have the reputation."

It made Timmie even angrier. "What would Alex say?"

Mary Jane smiled, almost fondly. "If we're lucky, Alex will never lift his head from his workload long enough to figure it out. He doesn't understand finances, Ms. Leary. He shouldn't have to. But a unit like ours simply can't survive now without additional funding. It's as simple as that."

Go figure. Timmie clamped her evidence box under her arm and prepared to get the hell out of Dodge.

She didn't get out fast enough. She'd just made it out Alice's door when she heard skidding footsteps.

"Oh, Ms. Leary, there you are!"

Timmie looked up to see Tracy rush from her father's wing and slide to a halt in the unit doorway, looking almost as frazzled as the bunch on this end. Amazing what a person could block out of her receptors if she really tried. The minute Timmie saw Tracy, she heard what she knew had probably been going on for at least ten minutes over on the other hall.

"Where's my daughter? Timmie, help! Help me, Timmie!"

The evidence box became a football on a forty-yard run as Timmie took off toward the smell of popcorn and certain disaster.

He was backed into a corner like Frankenstein's monster facing the pitchforks. Except that the pitchforks were really upheld hands belonging to some nurses and more than one security guard.

"I'm sorry," Timmie gasped, skidding to the edge of the crowd. All up and down the aisle she could hear the anxious babble of fractious voices responding to the uproar.

Joe never looked her way. "Timmie! Where's my daughter?" he pleaded, striking out at the nearest security guard, a beefy kid named Dave who just ducked and held his ground. "They have her," he insisted, pleading, his eyes wet. "In Glen-Car. Look for her there, please?"

"Glen-Car?" one of the nurses asked at the back of the crowd. "Where's that? What's he talking about?"

Dave smiled, never taking his eyes off Timmie's father. "That poet he likes, Yeats. 'The Stolen Child,' isn't it, Joe? 'Come away, O human child! To the waters and the wild'? It's about fairies."

The nurse nodded, impressed. "No shit."

"Da!" Timmie called, shoving her way through. "Daddy, it's me! It's Timmie!"

It was the damn popcorn. She should have remembered that that was something else she'd rarely had at home for this same reason. He smelled it, boomeranged back to the great old days, and became frightened when he couldn't find the door into the bar.

He still couldn't. "'For the world's more full of weeping,'" he all but sang to Dave, as if explaining, tears trickling down his face, "'than you can understand.'"

Timmie carefully set down the coat-wrapped box with the county seal on it before approaching her father, hands lifted so he could see her better. Don't, she wanted to beg. Don't be wild and sad. Not tonight. I can't take it tonight.

"Da, I'm here," she pleaded. "I haven't gone off. I'm here."

He was too lost in his own fairy world to even hear. "Timmie, where are you? Help me! They won't let me out and I have a gig at nine!"

She lifted her hands to his clean-shaven, soft face. "Da, I'm here!"

He swiveled those watery blue eyes her way like a horse trying to escape fire and flinched back. "Where is she?" he pleaded, taking hold of her arms so tightly it hurt. "I can't find her. I . . . she'll be afraid, and I can't find her . . . "

"I'm here," Timmie pleaded back, suddenly tired to death of all this drama. She wanted to go home and crawl under her comforter, play with her daughter, chase a chameleon or two. She wanted, for once in her life, not to have this man on her conscience.

He looked straight through her. "I know she can't get home, please, please help me because she comes to the water and the wild . . . "

Well, at least it wasn't "Innisfree."

"Da, please, Da, it's Timmie, it's all right, I swear, shhhhh, come on now, Da, please," Timmie begged until she was chanting just like he was. Like they all were, the words mindless and meaningless and meant to be soothing.

Except that they weren't. They grated in her like ground glass until she was sure she was bleeding, and she ended up holding on to him as he crumpled into an untidy ball in the corner, sobbing because his daughter had never come home and he didn't know what to do.

In the end, Timmie made it back to her own daughter. She sent Cindy home after getting one more harangue about faithless asshole boyfriends, and then she crawled up into her bed and let Meghan do her homework on top of the aqua-and-pink duvet. And all the time she thought of gomer noises. The chanting, wailing, mindless repetition she could no longer stand. The morass her father was quickly sinking into, from which she couldn't save him. Near which she was so afraid to venture.

She must have fallen asleep, because the next thing she knew it was late and Meghan was curled up next to her, sound asleep in her play clothes. For a minute Timmie couldn't figure out what had woken her. Then the phone rang again and she jumped to answer it.

The alarm clock said 2:00. Only bad things happened at two in the morning, which meant that either her father had had a new crisis or the emergency department had a disaster on its hands.

"Hello?"

"Timmie?"

The voice was soft. So soft. Creepy. It made her shiver, even cocooned within down and her daughter's small warmth.

Timmie sucked in a breath to calm her racing heart. "Yes?"

"You're not alone, Timmie. I thought you should know that."

"Alone? What do you mean?"

"Your father . . ." The voice paused, but Timmie had already held her breath, not recognizing it. "He's such a special man. An awful lot of people in town love him. They can't stand to see what's happening to him any more than you can."

Not creepy. Hypnotic. Compelling. A snake that had slithered straight out of her subconscious to torture her. "Yes?"

"He used to be so strong. . . . Why, he could hush a room by just walking in, remember? He could bring the entire town to tears with just one song . . . a poem. Like the poem about the lions of the hills, you remember it?"

Timmie heard her voice grow smaller as the other voice took hold. A low voice, a soothing voice, a compelling voice in the dead of night. "Yes."

"'The lions of the hills are gone, and I am left alone—alone.' It's him, yes? Such a beautiful thing. It's so hard to see that light fade right before your eyes when you know how magnificent it once was."

Now her heart was bouncing around like a frog in a skillet. "Who is this? What do you want?"

"This just has to hurt him so much. Somebody like him, not even remembering his name, much less all those beautiful words he used to love so much. But I know you know that."

*I do. Jesus, I do.*

"It's torture, isn't it?"

*Yes.*

"What do you want?" she repeated, her voice a whisper.

It was so dark outside, no moon, no stars. The lights were off in the house, too, so that Timmie could see only shadows. Could hear only tickings and creakings and whisperings, as if the house were already haunted with her father's voice.

"What do you want?"

A soft sigh, like the wind. Like her own regret. "I just want to help."

"To help."

"To help you and Joe both. You have the power to help him, Timmie, do you know that? Only you. It would be so easy."

She couldn't breathe. She couldn't think. "I do?"

"So easy," the voice purred, sinking straight into her. "He deserves better than to be tied down and drugged, Timmie."

Don't ask me to answer, she all but begged. Don't.

"And you just have too much to deal with right now. You have to be tired. And you have to be wondering if you're really helping anybody after all with all those questions."

In all truth? Probably not. Timmie turned her head toward the window where the sky should have been, where trees should have stood out against a moon of some kind. There was just the faint reflection of her own face, moon pale in the darkness. As insubstantial as the voice on the phone.

"And?"

"And . . . I thought we could help each other out. You could just kind of leave this alone, and I could . . . well, your father could finally have some peace."

Timmie went perfectly still. She closed her eyes and held on to the phone. "If I just . . . stop. Right?"

"He's only going to get worse, Timmie. You know that."

She didn't answer. She couldn't. It didn't seem to matter.

"Tell you what," the voice said, its cadence even and soothing and sweet. "Why don't you take a day on it? Visit your dad. Think of what he'd want to do. You can get another call tomorrow night about this time if you have any questions. That would be all right, wouldn't it?"

"Yes. Yes, I think it would, if you promise to . . . uh, wait."

"Of course. I only want what's best for him and for you."

"And he wouldn't . . ."

"Suffer? No, of course not. That's the whole point, isn't it? Take your time. Just think of what you'd be doing for him, how easy it would finally be for him, how much you want him to finally have peace. Just think about that, Timmie."

Timmie didn't answer. She didn't even hang up the phone. She just lay there staring at the sky and shaking. She didn't call Micklind. She didn't call Murphy, which she should have.

She had twenty-four hours to decide.

Twenty-four hours.

Because the man on the phone hadn't just offered to make her a deal. He had offered to fulfill her most terrible wish.

# TWENTY TWENTY TWENTY

WHEN MURPHY STUMBLED INTO HIS HOUSE LATER THAT MORNING from his abbreviated run, the phone was ringing. He wasn't really in the mood to answer it, so he let it go. It refused to stop.

It rang while he brewed coffee and while he washed his face and while he opened the paper to see the front-page teaser about his article on Joe Leary. It stopped briefly and then began to ring again when he poured his coffee.

So he picked it up.

"Do you know what time it is?" he demanded.

"You've been out running," the soft voice retorted.

Instinctively Murphy hit the Record and Caller ID buttons. A woman, he thought, although he couldn't say why, or whether it was the same one. The voice was more muffled than the last time he'd heard it, deep in the night.

"I've been out limping," he corrected, sitting down at his table. "What do you want?"

"I . . . you . . . you need to *do* something."

Murphy sipped at his coffee. "You think I'm not doing anything?"

"No. If you were, it wouldn't still be happening."

Murphy stopped sipping and sat up straight. "What do you mean?"

"Last night. It's not going to stop, because nobody wants it to. It's only old people, after all. Well, nobody asked those old people, you know?"

"Yeah," he answered, his brain kicking painfully into gear. "I know. You say somebody else died last night? Who, do you know? Was it Bertha Worthmueller?"

There was a startled little sound and a pause. "Then you know."

"I may not be flashy," he said, "but I get the work done. Was it Bertha?"

"No. She's still alive. It was Alice Hampton, a newer patient, which doesn't make any sense. But ask Timmie Leary. She was there. She can tell you."

Leary, huh? Why hadn't she called him about it? What did she know, and what had she done about it?

"*You* tell me," he insisted. "Tell me what you know."

"No . . . I can't. Timmie can do it."

"Do you know who it is?"

Another, microscopic pause, more telling than the last. "No. I just know that somebody does, and it has to stop."

*Click.*

A new death. Another call from his mysterious angel, who most certainly did suspect who was responsible for the deaths but was too afraid to admit it. And, this time, a tape of the conversation and a phone number to boot. Murphy wrote it down, just to be sure, but figured with his luck it was probably a pay phone someplace.

He was going to have to talk to Leary. He didn't really want to. Not after what he'd forced out of her yesterday. He'd sat up most of the night staring at the pictures of his daughters, trying to decide if it was time to call them, and hadn't been able to come to any conclusions. He couldn't imagine how she'd spent her night. She knew too much, that little nurse did. She'd told him things about his own kids he'd successfully avoided for years, and he could have done without that for the rest of his life. He could just imagine what kind of night she'd spent.

So, why hadn't she called him about the latest death?

Murphy checked his watch and still came up with only a quarter after the crack of dawn. Leary was not a crack-of-dawn person. So he would call her after he showered and checked a couple of things, like who belonged to the phone number in his hand. And, maybe, checked on the girls. By then Leary should at least be communicative, if not any happier to see him.

He tried at nine and he tried at eleven, and then he called the hospital to find that she wasn't scheduled for work. He called his buddies at the *Post* and got the address of that phone number from the cross-street reference, to find that it belonged to a gas station pay phone. He called Barbara to find out that Timmie had asked the doctor to do some testing on one Alice Hampton, who was even now cooling her heels in the hospital morgue waiting for her primary physician to decide what to do with her mortal remains. The physician in question was due back from a gerontology conference that afternoon. Barbara couldn't say much more than that, since Leary had evidently decamped immediately after her request, and hadn't been heard from again.

Murphy was starting to get nervous. He called again and got the same damn answering machine. "Yeah, it's an answering machine. Live with it. Better yet, communicate with it. Beep."

The last two times he'd called, he'd left messages. As the clock edged toward noon, Murphy decided it would be just as easy to go over.

He was sure she was fine. Probably just working in the yard or something. Attending parents' day at school. Walking the lizard. It wouldn't hurt to check, though. He got there in record time and blamed it on the Porsche.

The house was quiet. A pretty place ringed in flowers with a porch that creaked right at the top step. He remembered that from the night he'd done a belly flop on Leary's floor. Amazing how different the outside and inside of that house were.

Nothing looked out of place, though. There weren't fire engines or worried neighbors. Just a pretty, tree-lined street where kids played in the afternoons. Slamming the door of his Porsche shut, Murphy trotted up the steps, still expecting Leary to appear any minute with a trowel or something in her hand.

He rang the doorbell and waited for an answer.

Nothing.

He could hear something inside, though. He leaned closer, trying to make it out. A flute? No, it wasn't as full-throated as a flute. Pretty, though. Soft and sweet. She must have a CD on, although where she'd gotten a recording of some wind instrument playing Barber's Adagio for Strings, he couldn't figure.

He rang again. And again, he got nothing.

This wasn't right. The back of his neck was itching, and he had the most overwhelming urge to walk away before he found something bad on the other side of that door. So he did what any self-respecting newsman would do. He tried the knob.

And just like in the movies, it opened.

"Leary?"

Nothing.

Somebody was in here. He could sense it. He was already holding his breath, and he wanted to tiptoe. The flute, or whatever, stopped. It had been coming from upstairs. There wasn't another sound in the house. No obvious signs of a struggle. The Nerf ball had been knocked off the line again, but Murphy imagined that happened a lot around here.

"Leary?" Gingerly, Murphy mounted the stairs.

Those creaked, too, which didn't help his heart rate any. Jesus, he hated walking into something like this. He'd walked in on one too many crime scenes, and in almost every one the victim had greeted him with wide eyes, as if still startled by what had happened.

"Leary? You up here?"

He got three fourths of the way up the stairs and saw her.

Alive. Sitting in the first bedroom on the left, on top of an old mahogany sleigh bed. Disheveled and pale, cross-legged and dressed in a pink sweat suit, a punk Buddha of the Flea Market.

"What the hell's wrong with you?" Murphy demanded, trying as hard as hell to calm his heart down. He was still half-expecting to see a gun-wielding madman forcibly keeping her in the room.

She didn't move. "I should have remembered to lock the door."

She was way too quiet. Her body language was all wrong. Tight, curled, her fingers tapping like a typist's against something in her lap. Murphy suspected she'd slept in that sweat suit, and at the foot of her bed sat a sealed brown evidence box and a phone that dangled a broken chord. This was going to be complicated, and he hadn't even had breakfast yet. He climbed the rest of the stairs and made for her room.

"What's wrong?" he asked.

"I'm out of practice," she said in an odd, small voice, her attention back on whatever she was mangling in her lap. "I can't remember the whole piece."

She was way, *way* too quiet.

Then Murphy saw what she'd been holding. A tin whistle. The kind of thing you saw the Chieftains play jigs and stuff on, all high, sharp notes that could shatter glass. She'd been playing that? She'd been playing Barber on that?

"You play that thing?" Murphy found himself asking.

"Maudlin, but appropriate, don't you think?"

"Aren't you supposed to play, like, 'MacNamara's Band' and stuff like that?"

She almost smiled. Lifted the thing to her mouth and spun off about thirty bars of the most complicated jig Murphy had ever heard. Then she dropped it back in her lap and went back to battering it.

Murphy decided it was wiser to stay where he was and leaned against the doorway where she wouldn't notice how uncomfortable she was making him. "Wanna tell me what's going on?"

She shrugged, still not facing him. "I'm just sitting here."

"You're not answering your calls."

She shrugged again, fingered the instrument. Made him even

more nervous. This just wasn't the Leary he'd come to know and fear.

"I saw your article on my father," she said. "You did a good job."

Murphy couldn't contain his surprise. "I didn't think you'd read it."

She nodded absently. "You were right. He really did make an impact on the town. On everybody he met, really. He's never known a stranger or had a dollar that didn't need to be in somebody else's pocket more. My mother always yelled at him because he spent his paychecks at the bars. The truth is, he never paid for two drinks in the same night. But he never said no if a person needed help."

"I'm just sorry I didn't know him before," Murphy said.

Unbelievably, she smiled. She smiled fondly, as if they'd never had the conversation the day before. "You would have loved him," she admitted. "I probably wouldn't have been able to pry you two out of the saloon for a month."

Murphy was itching again. He had the most insane urge to look over his shoulder, as if the real conversation were going on right behind him. He sure couldn't figure this one out. So he lobbed a test missile.

"I heard we have another set of statistics," he said.

She started a little, as if she'd come in contact with a live wire. Then she just tightened up a little more. "Maybe," she said. "Maybe not. After all, like everybody said, she was old and she had Alzheimer's. Maybe it was just her time to go."

Murphy blinked in surprise. "You believe that?"

She looked out the window, then back at her hands. "Ah, who knows? I think it's one of the great conceits of the modern world that so many people know just what other people need or want or believe. I don't think I want to do that anymore."

Now he knew he was nervous. "You don't."

She shook her head. "My mother does that, and she doesn't have any friends left. Only dependents."

"And you think that's what this is all about."

Another shrug. Another silence.

"I will tell you one thing I've figured out," she said as if continuing a thought. "An awful lot of people are trying to cover up something they haven't figured out yet. They think maybe patients are being murdered in their geriatric center, but they don't want to know for sure. Landry because it would hurt the hospital. Mary Jane because it would hurt Alex. Davies because it would hurt research, and Van Adder because it might interfere with his towing business. Oh, and the nurses up in the nursing care wing because it could hurt their reputations as good nurses. You know what I haven't heard as a reason yet, Murphy?"

"What's that?"

She looked at him, and he saw what she'd been hiding. Tight, old eyes that glittered with shame. "Those patients. Not one person is doing what they're doing because they think maybe they're helping those poor little old people." She sucked in a shaky breath. Shook her head. "Maybe if *one* person . . . "

She shook her head again, uncrossed her legs. Climbed out of bed, as if the words demanded action.

"Leary?"

"It's a question we all ask," she explained, standing there looking out her window into the trees, her hands cradling that tin whistle as if it were a relic. "What's best for the poor old gomers we have to take care of all the time. You know, just how hard should we fight to save them? When does it stop being sensible and become obscene instead? I could understand if any one of the people who's covering this up had said they were doing it because deep in their hearts they really believed it was better for those old people. Because they really did think whoever's doing this was giving them peace. A chance to be rid of all of us, ya know?"

He'd thought it when he'd finally sat down with Joe Leary. "Yeah. I know."

"But not one person really even thought about it. Not one." She turned on him, her eyes accusing. "Not even me. And that's just the most enlightening thing of all."'

She was trembling. Murphy wasn't even sure she knew it, but

he could see it in her hands and along her arms. She looked like she was going to break, those big blue eyes of hers bleaker than any survivor's waiting at a mine shaft. And Murphy didn't know what to do about it.

"What happened, Leary?" he asked.

She laughed. "Happened?" She hesitated a heartbeat, as if battling something. When she turned away from him, Murphy had the most unholy feeling she'd lost. "Nothing happened. Nothing at all."

This wasn't helping his peace of mind.

"All right," he said. "Let's try this. What's in the box?"

She didn't move. "Nothing."

"You just developed a fetish for evidence boxes."

"Uh-huh."

Murphy had been able to weasel the truth out of four embezzling senators, a bomb-hiding revolutionary, and several dozen reticent whistle-blowers. He stood at the edge of Leary's room and didn't have a clue what to say next.

"And you have nothing to say about this Alice Hampton, or whoever, who died last night."

She tensed like an animal scenting predators. "Not right now."

"Then when?"

"I don't know. Tomorrow . . . I think, tomorrow. You might want to take today off, too. Go see a movie or something."

"Are you sure it can wait?"

Not a breath of movement.

"Leary?"

She never turned around. Just shook her head. And Murphy, not knowing what else to do, turned around to leave. He'd made it all the way down the steps before he heard movement behind him.

"Murphy?"

He stopped. She was standing at the top of the stairs, her face in shadow, her hands tight around that damn sliver of tin.

"What?"

It took her a minute to speak, and when she did, she sounded scared. "Would you come back later tonight?"

"Why, Leary? What's going to happen?"

She lifted her head a little, and almost smiled. "You mean you don't believe I just want some mindless sex?"

"Not really."

"Please." Murphy heard desperation and couldn't believe it. "Come over about midnight. I think I'm going to need some help."

Murphy knew something substantial was happening here. He just wished like hell somebody'd tell him what it was.

"I'll be here." He was all set to walk out when he remembered at least one of the reasons he'd intended to come over here in the first place. "One thing. I got another call from my whisperer this morning. It's a woman. And she called from a service station. Any ideas?"

"A service station?"

"Yeah. Mike's Mobile. Mean anything?"

And here he'd thought she sounded bad before. This time when she spoke, she sounded as if she were going to die. "Yeah," she said. "It does."

"And?"

"Tomorrow. We'll talk about it tomorrow."

Leary just turned back to her room, which left Murphy nothing better to do than leave. He made it all the way out the door this time. When he closed it behind him, though, he couldn't shake the feeling that he'd just run away.

Timmie spent the rest of the day right where she was. Far away from the phone, far away from her friends, as far from her father as she could manage. She listened to the phone ring half a dozen more times and didn't move an inch to answer it. She thought about calling Murphy back more than once. She didn't. She didn't do anything, because there was just nothing she could manage to do right now.

At three the door opened again and Meghan clomped in. "Mom!" she yelled. "Hey, Mom! I'm home! I have the mail! And Mr. Mattie's here!"

Timmie wasn't ready for Meghan. She definitely wasn't ready

for the Reverend Walter with his sweet, Christian heart and old, old eyes. He'd see right through her. He'd know exactly what she'd been thinking ever since the moment that voice on the phone had offered to solve all her problems. And then he'd forgive her, and Timmie really wasn't ready for that.

So she climbed out of bed and walked to the head of the stairs. Down below, standing square and tall and strong, just like a soldier of God should, Walter took up the entire doorway.

"Timmie? Brought your baby home."

"Thanks, Walter."

Walter leaned over a little so he could see Timmie better as Meghan bounded up the stairs with a handful of bills and one manila envelope in her hand. An envelope from Conrad. Timmie wasn't sure how she could feel worse. She dropped it on the floor where it couldn't hurt her and hugged her baby. It wasn't until Meghan had galloped back down to the kitchen for cookies that Timmie realized that Walter still stood at the bottom of the steps.

"My pleasure," he rumbled in a soothing baritone Timmie loved. "She's a treasure. How much longer you think I'm gonna need to keep an eye on the children?"

No longer, she wanted to say. It's all over. The children will be safe, I'll be able to sleep again, and my father will be . . . safe. Far away from me and my mother and anybody else who can't remember how wonderful he could be.

"I'm not sure," she said instead, feeling it in her chest. In her stomach. In the tense ache of her hands where they were clenching that damn tin whistle. "Do you mind?"

The reverend shook his head. "Not if it means you can stop this evil with a clear mind. I'm happy to do it." When Timmie couldn't seem to manage an answer, he frowned, a polite man. "Are you all right, Timothy Ann?"

Stupid question. She needed to confess, but Walter wasn't a priest. She needed to act, but she was frozen. She needed to believe that whatever she ended up doing tonight, it would be the right thing. That it was all right that she hadn't told her caller no last night.

She needed to believe that she'd hesitated only because she couldn't stand to see her father hurt anymore, and she couldn't quite do that. Which didn't leave her with much.

"I'm fine, Walter. Just fine."

Walter's nod was slow. "All right, then. I'll see you tomorrow."

Timmie meant to tell him to tell Mattie to stay home. She didn't quite manage that, either. So twenty minutes later to the minute, the front door crashed open and Mattie, Ellen, and Cindy marched into the house. Timmie waited for them on the top step.

"You are not all right," Mattie accused from the bottom of the stairs.

Timmie didn't move. "Go away, Mattie," she said softly. "I'll call you tomorrow."

Mattie straightened like a shot. "I will not. And you'll tell me now."

"Mom?" Meghan had heard the noise and run out of the back room where the single television lived. Then she spotted the trio, who were still trying to stare Timmie down, and frowned herself. "Mr. Mattie went home already," she said. "Didn't he get there?"

"He did, honey," Mattie said without looking at her. "Thank you. I just need to talk to your mama right now, okay?"

Meghan looked at Mattie. She leaned around the banister to where she could see Timmie and checked her out. Timmie smiled.

"It's okay, baby. It's just work stuff."

So she was lying to everybody now. How pleasant. The minute Meghan walked back in to her after-school treat and TV, Timmie climbed to her feet and walked back into her room. Inevitably, the three women followed.

"You look terrible," Cindy blurted out. "What can we do?"

Timmie sat back up on her bed. "You can tell Walter not to worry about me. Everything's fine." Even she heard the lie in that one.

Mattie came to stand over her like a mother about to feel her forehead for a fever. "We're not going," she said softly. "So spill it."

She couldn't. Not now. Not here. Certainly not with an audience, especially after what Murphy had told her.

"It's nothing," she said. "I promise." And then she lied some more. "I got served again by Jason this morning, and I'm just feeling sorry for myself."

"Served?" Ellen asked. "What does the lawyer say?"

Timmie tried hard to sound offhanded. "That this one may stick. He's going after Dad's house, since it was in my name all along. After all, we were divorced in a community property state."

The three of them started choking as if somebody'd let off a smoke bomb.

"You joking!" Mattie accused.

Not wanting to compound her time in purgatory now that she was certainly destined for hell, Timmie said nothing.

Cindy immediately turned a bright shade of red. "Well, that asshole! It just figures. I swear, you give 'em an inch and they want to take your house! What can we do?"

"Nothing. I told you. I just need to sulk a little."

Cindy shook her head. "I'll stay. It's the least I can do."

"No." Timmie was sure she said it too quickly. Only Ellen looked her way.

"How about if Meghan comes to my house," Ellen offered. "My kids would be tickled. Besides, you don't want her here when you're this upset with her daddy. She wouldn't understand."

"I'll stay with her," Cindy offered. "I'm even beginning to like that miniature handbag she feeds."

"We'll work it out together," Mattie decided, eyes unwaveringly on Timmie. "Why don't you two go down and see if she'd like McDonald's?"

"We should stay," Cindy protested.

Timmie almost managed a smile. "Thanks anyway. Really. I just want time off."

The two of them eventually went, which left Mattie, who was neither as polite as Walter nor as passive as Ellen. "You gonna tell me the truth?"

Timmie could barely stand to look at her. "Not today."

Mattie just stood there, a seething energy behind sharp brown eyes. "You know, this may be a real unpleasant shock to you, girlfriend, but we do give a shit about you."

After everything, that was the thing that brought Timmie closest to tears. Only one other person in her life had offered unconditional support, and she'd just been contemplating killing him.

"Thank you, Mattie," she said anyway. "I know. And it'll be okay, I promise."

Another lie. This one easier to pass, because it was the one she most wanted to believe.

At least it soothed Mattie a little. With only a few more protests, she guided the flock to the door and left Meghan a moment with her mom.

Timmie sat on the edge of the bed and pulled Megs into her arms, reptile cage and all. "I'm sorry this has been so crazy for you, baby. Do you know I love you?"

"Yes." Not as certain-sounding as Timmie would have wanted.

So Timmie hugged tighter. "I'm not going anywhere, Megs. Neither are you. But there's just a lot going on that you shouldn't have to worry about, so Mattie and Ellen are helping me make it easier on you. And the sooner I get this all resolved, the sooner we can really settle down and be country mouses."

Meghan looked up at Timmie, suddenly very hesitant. "You mean it?"

Timmie gave a brief thought to Traumawoman and then waved good-bye. "Yes, Meghan. I mean it. We're staying right here where you can see shooting stars and feed apples to Patty's horse. And when things settle down, maybe you and I can really be country mouses. Go camping or fishing or something. All by ourselves."

Meghan wrinkled her nose. "I hate fish. Besides, we can't go anyplace. There's Grandda."

Timmie was very proud of the fact that she didn't give herself away. "I know all about Grandda, honey. Don't forget, I met him a long time before you did."

"Okay, Mom. I'll see you tomorrow."

Timmie held her close. "Tomorrow, baby. Then everything will be fine."

That was, if she could get through tonight.

# TWENTY-ONE

"YOU HAVEN'T BEEN TO SEE YOUR FATHER TODAY."

The voice was just as soft. Just as sinuous, a sibilant snake of temptation. Just the sound of it made Timmie's palms sweat.

"How do you know?" she asked, not daring to look over to where Murphy was listening in on the kitchen line.

"He didn't have a good day, I'm afraid. Not that he's sick, of course. He has the heart of a fifteen-year-old. But he's frightened, yes? He's frightened all the time now."

Timmie sucked in a breath. Closed her eyes and stopped the monologue cold. "No."

She was met by silence.

"Thank you for the offer," she said. "I know you only had his best wishes at heart. But I can't accept it."

She should get him to indict himself, she knew. She couldn't think that well. She couldn't even stay on the phone that long.

"Are you sure, Timmie? This is really what you want?"

No. She wasn't sure. If she'd been sure she would have spent the day ripping through this miserable excuse for a town finding out who was trying to coerce her into compliance instead of just sitting in the lotus position like a comatose yoga teacher.

"And just so you know," she said, eyes still closed so she did this all on her own. "You're not going to kill any more people in that unit, and you're definitely not killing my father. I won't let you."

"How could you say that about me? I'm just trying to help."

"Oh, I know. But I don't think anybody wants your help anymore. Good-bye."

And that, after what she'd dreaded all day, was that. No confrontations, no protestations, no huge emotional rock rolling down on her head. She felt a little calmer, kind of like the moment she'd finally filed for divorce. The decision wasn't easy, but the uncertainty was over. At least until the next time somebody made the same offer when her father was even more frightened and old.

"So that's what that was all about," Murphy said quietly from the kitchen doorway.

Timmie didn't bother to look at him. "I appreciate your coming over to witness this, just in case there was a question."

"I also got the caller number," he said. "You want to know what it is?"

"No."

At least Murphy wasn't asking for explanations or demanding that Timmie share her reactions with him. Hell, he hadn't even told her that what she'd done was the right thing to do.

Probably why she'd asked him to be here instead of her friends. The last thing she needed right now was sympathy and understanding.

Murphy didn't look in the least sympathetic. He looked avid. "555-1230. Ring any bells?"

Timmie rubbed hard at her tired eyes. "Yeah. It's a hospital extension. Not a big surprise, I guess."

Almost a relief, really. She'd sure rather it be the hospital than quite a few of the private numbers she knew in town. Murphy reached around her to pick up the old black phone. "I take it you don't know just which hospital extension?"

Timmie grabbed the phone right out of his hand. "How about I do this?" she asked with a tight little smile. "I think it's safer."

Murphy almost slipped and let a flash of compassion through that wry expression. Timmie turned away just in time to miss it.

"Go right ahead," he said, his voice brisk and businesslike. "Just remember. I can find out myself whenever I want."

"I know you can, Murphy," she said, dialing the switchboard. "I just like to know first. It's a fault of mine."

"Then I guess that means we can't live together," Murphy said easily. "We'd always be fighting for the paper in the morning."

"God, Murphy," she protested. "Don't even suggest it. I have enough on my mind right now without you insulting me."

He chuckled. Timmie wanted to thank him. She didn't. She waited for the night operator to pick up. An ancient, Marlboro-puffing, Southern lady with the basal metabolism of a land tortoise, the operator had been known to take six rings to pick up the red phone that only called in code blues.

"The voice was familiar," Murphy was saying to himself.

"This is Memorial Medical Center," the sixty-year-old voice drawled in Timmie's other ear. "How may I direct your call?"

"Ginny?" Timmie asked at three times the speed. "This is Timmie Leary from the ER, and I can't find my listings. What extension is 1230?"

"Timmie?" Ginny echoed, delighted. "How are you, honey? How's your daddy? I got over to see him t'other day. He's just so sweet."

"He's fine, Ginny," Timmie said, twitching with the delay. Ginny always did this to her, like automatic doors opening too slowly. "What's the number?"

"Well, I can connect you, sugar," she offered, "but it wouldn't do you any good. Nobody's up there this time of night."

Nobody who wanted to be noticed anyway. "Where is it?" Timmie asked anyway.

"Well, I figured you might know, your daddy being in and all."

"It's late. I forgot."

"It's Dr. Raymond's office, honey. Why don't you call back tomorrow? I heard he was out of town tonight anyway."

Timmie white-knuckled the phone, trying to maintain her composure. "Thanks. I'll do that."

She hung up to find Murphy watching her with quite a bit less objectivity than he had had a minute before. "So, you don't have to call your friend after all?" he asked.

"It's not him," she insisted.

"Was it his office?"

"Yes."

"How many people would have the keys?"

Timmie snorted. "This is a hospital we're talking about," she reminded him. "Not a bank. Half the administrative staff, most of housekeeping, and all of security. Where would you like to start?"

"Do you think we need to make sure nobody's trying to get to Joe after all?"

Timmie frowned. "I don't know. If the offer is to kill him, would the threat be to kill him, too?"

"If you didn't want him dead."

This was way too complicated. And Timmie wasn't about to give Murphy all the truth just because he'd kept his mouth shut. So she dialed the phone and got her dad's night nurse.

"Hi, Timmie," the nurse chirped. "We've been trying to get you all day. Everything okay?"

"Fine. How about my dad?" she asked, shoving the guilt aside for a more convenient time.

"Well, that's it. We talked to Dr. Raymond, and he changed your dad's Prozac dose. I think it's going to make a world of difference. He's already not nearly as afraid now. And the best part is, he's been asleep since nine. How about that?"

Timmie squeezed her eyes shut. "Yeah, how about that? Has anybody been by to see him tonight?"

"Good heavens, no. Nobody comes in here late at night."

"I need a favor, Cathy," she said, praying she was asking the right person. "I need to make sure you don't let anybody in that room but me till I get there and talk to you. Not even Dr. Raymond."

There was a polite pause of disbelief. "This doesn't have to do with what might be happening over on five, does it?"

"Yes."

"He wouldn't do that."

"I know. But it's safer for him if he isn't even considered, ya know?"

"Sure."

She didn't. Timmie could hear it in her voice. But Cathy would stand guard anyway, over both her father and her father's doctor.

"Okay," Timmie said, hanging up. "What next?"

"Call Raymond. See if he's home."

Timmie did notice that at least Murphy wasn't calling Alex golden boy anymore. She should thank him for that, anyway. She spun around as if Murphy's suggestion didn't scare the hell out of her. "Nope. I've been in the house all day. Let's go check on Dad."

"I suppose you want me to drive."

"Only if you want to find out what's going on."

"There's one other thing you might want to know before going over there," he said, not moving, his expression not quite as flippant as Timmie might have expected. It pretty much stopped her.

"The results on Alice Hampton's blood tests," he said.

Timmie guessed she should have known. "So spill it," she said. "I can tell you're dying to tell me."

"Barb said that the old lady's dij level was way high. That mean anything to you?"

At least he had Timmie thinking back along the lines of problem solving. Much less traumatic than responsibility and remorse. "Digitoxin," she said. "It's the generic name for Digoxin, which is a heart medication she was on. Great stuff for old hearts, but lethal as hell if you get too much. It's from the foxglove plant, which is one of the most toxic poisons around."

"Well, Barb thinks that's what probably killed her. Since she evidently wasn't sick first, Barb thinks she got it fast."

And since Alice had had only oral Digoxin in her locked nurse server, the dose she'd gotten had obviously either been deliberately pulled from stock and shoved in by Gladys fifteen or twenty minutes before the cardiac arrest, or substituted for one of the IV push medications Alice already had stocked in her nurse server, which meant that Gladys would have given it without realizing it.

Which led to two conclusions. If Gladys hadn't intentionally killed Alice, which from her reaction, Timmie didn't think she had, then anybody in the hospital with a key to the nurse server could have substituted those drugs any time in the days preceding old Alice's death. The field was wide open.

And if the killer thought nobody'd notice, maybe he or she had left fingerprints on the vials that sat in the evidence box Timmie had upstairs this very minute.

If this ever went to trial, the only way to keep the findings on those medications valid was to protect the chain of evidence. Which meant Timmie had to have that thing in sight until she handed it off to Conrad like a forensics baton.

She hoped Murphy wasn't waiting for an answer. She headed up the stairs instead.

Five minutes later, the evidence box tucked under her arm, Timmie jumped the bottom three stairs and headed for the front door. "Let's go," she said. "I have a chart to read and an old man to visit."

The only way to enter the hospital at that hour of the night was through the ER. Fortunately, only the secretary was sitting at the triage desk, and she just waved, perfectly comfortable with seeing staff wandering around at odd hours. Timmie guided Murphy past her and through the maze that led to Restcrest.

She stopped by her dad's room first. True to her word, Cathy was lounging in a beanbag chair doing her charting near the memory case that held Cardinals and Clancy Brothers. She smiled benignly when she saw Timmie.

"Quiet as a church," she said.

"Nobody's been by?"

"Nope."

Murphy waited outside while Timmie, needing visual confirmation that her father was still okay, crept into his room.

He was sound asleep. Flung out across the bed as if he'd just fallen there after a hard night playing rebel songs, he snored like a fighter. Timmie couldn't help but smile, kind of the way she did when she watched Meghan sleep. Somehow all the troubles and turmoil eased when their eyes closed, and only the softness remained.

He was soft. Always had been. But it had taken Timmie a long time to figure it out. She'd always thought of him as larger than life. Mountains and thunderstorms, when he was in the mood. Now that she was an adult and he was old, he should have looked smaller, shrunken with the decline of his power. He still looked massive to her. Untamed, unquieted, his only concession to the disease that ravaged that quixotic brain of his the sudden, terrifying detours that sent his thoughts skidding off into space. He was still the man who'd held her above the world to see Bob Gibson and Timmie McCarver and Mike Shannon riding through downtown St. Louis in flashy convertibles and World Series rings. He was the man who insisted, no matter what her mother said, that Timmie was magic. He was the man who would forget her for hours while singing in the pub and then, suddenly, lift her in his arms and proclaim her his fairy child.

God, she wanted him back. Every drunken, wild word. Every silly generosity. She wanted to sit at his knee again and listen to him weave his words into living things and feed on the delight in his audiences' eyes.

She wanted him to never be afraid or lost again.

She'd known since she was five years old that her father was really her responsibility. It was only since the moment she'd been given the chance to permanently hand that responsibility off that she'd accepted it.

"Do not go gentle, Da," she said, hoping that someday soon she'd really mean it. And then she turned around and walked away before the doubts could creep back in.

She didn't even make it to the door. Just the sound of her voice, evidently, was enough to call him back tonight.

"Timmie?"

Timmie all but held her breath. "Yes, Da?"

He smiled. A beatific smile that Timmie hadn't seen in months. "I'm sorry, sweetheart," he said, reaching out for her hand

She gave it to him, even less sure of herself. He knew it was her. The contact was there, that indefinable something in his eyes that clicked so rarely now, and Timmie knew she had him back.

"What for, Da?"

His smile widened. Damn near glowed, so that Timmie was sure that even Murphy saw it and smiled back. "You're such a good daughter . . . you always have been . . . but . . . did you know there's a bird on your shoulder?"

And damn it if she didn't look.

Timmie smiled until he went back to sleep. Then she walked out the door, sat down in one of the chairs, and burst out laughing. Murphy would probably tell her she was an idiot, but she considered it a sign from God that she really had done the right thing. Which made her laugh harder, until there were tears in her eyes and the nurse started casting nervous little looks at her.

"Feeling better, Leary?" Murphy asked dryly.

Timmie wiped her eyes and laughed some more. God, it felt so good. A cliché, but like water in the desert. She'd been parched for it. "That's why he has to hang around," she said. "Nobody else in this town is as nuts."

Murphy snorted. "I wouldn't put any bets on it."

"Okay, they may be nuts. But they're not as much fun."

He nodded. "You got me there."

It took a second, but Timmie pulled herself together again. Then she got to her feet, straightened herself, and reclaimed her box. "All right, kids. Let's kick some angel-of-death butt."

Amazingly enough, Cathy jumped to her feet as if Timmie had just called the troops to order. "Thank heavens. What can we do?"

So Timmie told her. And then, trailing Murphy behind like an aide de camp, she headed over to find out just what she could about Alice Hampton's death.

It wasn't Gladys who was staffing unit five this late at night, but her compatriot Penelope, a softer, rounder woman with mocha skin, grandma's eyes, and a slow walk, who couldn't quite keep her gaze away from the rectangular box under Timmie's arm.

"You the one went up against Ms. Arlington, aren't you?" she asked Timmie when she'd introduced herself. "Gladys told us."

"Do you know if Alice's chart is still here?" Timmie asked, shifting the box against her hip like a baby.

"Sure. We kinda haven't been able to find it as fast as the review committee wanted. 'Specially since Dr. Raymond hasn't seen it yet, and since Gladys said you might want to take a look at it."

She seemed to glide over to the wall shelves, where all the research books sat, and reached behind the *PDR* and *Merck*'s to pull out a thick wad of paperwork in a familiar manila folder. Timmie smiled her thanks. Penelope's answering smile was much brighter and more telling. Another big fan of Mary Jane's. What a surprise.

"You really don't have any suspects in mind?" Timmie couldn't help but ask.

Penelope shook her head in frustration. "Weird, isn't it? Most times you know damn well who's the problem."

From the list Timmie had gotten from Conrad, absolutely true. Taking half an hour to skim it while waiting for her call, she'd been amazed at the suspects everybody had fingered for possible serial murderer in their hospital and nobody had been able to reel in. It had been rarer that no suspect was named than vice versa. Which was why Timmie still thought that whatever was happening at Memorial was a conspiracy rather than a lone act. Lone actors tended to get recognized in hospitals. At least by the nurses.

"You haven't seen Dr. Raymond tonight?" Timmie asked as she sat down and began flipping through the chart.

"No. He's not due back till tomorrow."

"Seen anybody interesting?" Murphy asked.

Penelope's eyes widened. "On nights? In an old folks home? Who you expect, honey, Madonna?"

Timmie took that as a no and concentrated on her reading.

Around her the patients rustled and whimpered and snored. The lights were dim, with the occasional monitor glowing green in the dark and IV pumps whirring in tidal syncopation.

Timmie had always hated places like this. Too quiet, too final

Much too real. For the first time Timmie could remember, though, the sights and sounds calmed her. It was as if she were finally seeing how this place was choreographed to soothe the end-stage patients toward sleep. Toward rest and peace and finality. They'd had their fireworks. It was time to shut off the lights and ease away.

"Here," Timmie said, pointing to the medication schedule. "Gladys bolused her with eighty of Lasix ten minutes before the arrest."

"Alice had bad kidneys," Penelope said. "We'd been upping the dose for a while. That couldn't'a killed her, though. She hadn't even had a chance to make pee yet."

"Not Lasix," Timmie said with a considering look at her evidence box. "Dij. I'm hoping there's a Lasix multidose vial in there that's chock-full of Digoxin. And since Lasix comes 10 milligrams a cc, that would make 8 ccs of Lasix. Make that 250 micrograms of Digoxin per cc instead, and that means Gladys ended up bolusing Alice with 2000 micrograms of Digoxin, which is about eight times the loading dose. . . . And here's Alice's dij levels at 1.85, which means she was bumping right at the top of therapeutic anyway . . . "

Penelope looked appalled. "It would have dropped her like a rock. Oh, my God, that poor thing."

"Not a word," Timmie warned. "Not till we've proved this."

"Whatever you need," she said, her placid eyes sparking sudden rage. "Nobody does that to my little old people."

Timmie almost cried. She felt like Lot trying to find one just man, and actually succeeding with three seconds to brimstone. "Thank you, Penelope. We'll do it. Now, if you don't mind, I'm going to do some perfectly illegal copying of this chart before anybody with less altruistic objectives can get hold of it."

"It's not Dr. Raymond," Penelope insisted.

Timmie smiled. "I know. But it's somebody."

Timmie copied the pertinent sheets and passed them to Murphy, who tucked them in the inside pocket of a twin of that ratty jacket he always wore. Then it was time to check for possible surprise visitors. Since the only way they could have gotten in was the same way Timmie and Murphy had gotten in, they both headed back to the ER.

The secretary was no longer sitting in the triage area by the time Timmie and Murphy made it back there. Instead, Ellen and Cindy were perched on the desk, clad in identical hospital greens, their backs to the front doors. A sure sign that the place was empty. Not only that, the lights were down and the monitors off, leaving the place looking spectral.

Timmie and Murphy had almost reached the desk before either of the nurses looked up. "What are you doing here?" Cindy asked.

Perched next to her, Ellen straightened like a shot. "Timmie, what's wrong? Are you okay? Is it your daddy?"

"I'm fine," Timmie assured them. "I was just up seeing my dad. Why are you still here, Cindy? Weren't you on evenings?"

Cindy shrugged, her attention torn between Timmie and Murphy. "Just visiting. You know me."

Timmie did, actually. Cindy rarely went home right after her shifts, much preferring to stay with the staff than face her apartment. It was why she showed up at friends' houses so much.

Actually, once Timmie had thought enough to realize she was going to have to stop by the ER, she'd counted on Cindy's habits. That way she could kill two birds with one stone. Or two phone calls with one question.

"You don't see your dad this late," Ellen all but accused.

Oh, well. It was as good a time as any. Never would have been better, but Murphy had raised a question that needed answering.

"I got a phone call tonight," Timmie said, leaning against the open doorway into the desk area, the box still at her hip and Murphy standing guard at her back. "Somebody offered to kill my father if I'd just stop investigating the murders up in Restcrest."

Well, she'd been hoping for a reaction. She got it in stereo. Ellen blanched and Cindy gaped.

"He wouldn't do that!" Ellen protested.

"Of course he would," Cindy immediately disagreed.

"Who wouldn't do that?" Timmie asked, and Ellen paled even more.

It took her a moment longer to actually speak, and by then she looked like she was going to faint. Timmie just waited her out.

"I'm sorry," Ellen all but whispered, shooting Murphy a frightened glance. "I did what I could."

Timmie wanted to hit her. Actually, she just wanted to cry. "You called Murphy to warn him about what was going on."

Cindy was staring now. "*I* called," she protested.

Ellen answered as if she hadn't even heard. "I didn't know what else to do. You saw Alice die. You saw how sudden it was. She wasn't even sick! That's been happening all summer, Timmie. What could I do?"

Timmie struggled to hang on to her respect for Ellen, who hadn't had the courage to help her patients any more, in the end, than she had herself. "Call the police?"

Ellen shook her head, a frightened, ineffectual woman. "Do you know what would have happened? I would have been fired from the only hospital in town. I had to raise my children."

"You didn't even tell anybody until a couple of weeks ago."

"*I* called him!" Cindy insisted. "Because I knew who it was."

Timmie didn't even look her way. "Who?"

"Landry, of course. He's a lying, cheating, money-hungry piece of shit who'd do anything to get his way!"

Well, at least she hadn't called him a nigger. Timmie couldn't help noticing that her fury was out of proportion to the discussion they were having.

"Cheating?" she asked.

Cindy's eyes welled with tears of distress. "I hate him."

"And Mary Jane?" she asked, remembering the recent accusation.

Cindy didn't say a word, just glared. Oh, good Lord, Timmie thought. She needed a scorecard. Praying for patience, she turned back to Ellen, who at least made sense.

"You're my friend," she said. "Why couldn't you come to me?"

"Because you love him."

Timmie stopped, open-mouthed. "I love who?"

Ellen couldn't look at her anymore. "I don't have proof," she protested. "Not really."

Timmie's stomach had just hit her shoes. "Alex?" she all but shrilled. "You think *Alex* is doing this?"

"It's Landry," Cindy insisted on a whine.

"It is not Landry," Timmie informed her. "He hasn't been here long enough."

"Well, it sure as hell isn't Alex!" Cindy insisted. "I would have been able to tell."

"How's that?" Murphy asked, whether Timmie wanted him to or not.

"Because I worked in a hospital where this happened before. Alex just isn't the type."

"You did?" Murphy asked.

"In Chicago, before John died."

"We'll compare notes later," Timmie suggested, knowing that the very last thing she needed right now was Cindy one-upping the situation they were facing. "Ellen, why did you think it was Alex?"

"He and Dr. Davies talked about how badly they needed the material for research. He always seemed right there when one of his people passed."

"He's always there anyway," Cindy insisted.

"Was he here tonight?" Timmie asked.

Both of them looked at each other. "No. Why?"

"Because whoever called me, called me from here."

"I saw Landry earlier, by the elevators," Cindy insisted. "He was wearing a black sweat suit."

"Uh-huh. Thanks."

Timmie was ready to head down the hall toward the elevators to blow that theory out of the water when Ellen grabbed her arm. Timmie turned on her friend, still angry with the deception.

"I'm sorry," Ellen said. "I'm just not as strong as you are, Timmie. I tried."

Timmie almost laughed, kind of the way Barb had when she'd discovered her ex-husband on her treatment table. Sometimes it was the only thing you could do. Timmie was blaming Ellen for doing exactly what she'd spent the day wishing she could have done

"It's okay, Ellen," she said as calmly as she could. "We know now. And whatever's going on, we'll stop it."

Ellen smiled.

Cindy frowned. "I still say it's Landry."

Timmie didn't listen, though. She was already on her way to the executive suites.

"Boy," Murphy said as they walked. "Once you get going you don't waste time, do you?"

"Shut up, Murphy."

"There's just one question you haven't answered tonight."

"What's that?"

"Who do *you* think offered to kill your father for you?"

# TWENTY-TWO

Barb started calling damn near at dawn. "What's going on?" she asked. "I would have been over there but I was stuck pulling a double shift in the city. Murphy said he was handling it."

"He said that, did he?" Timmie asked, half-asleep at her kitchen table.

"He didn't think you wanted to be bothered. Now, what the hell is going on?"

Timmie stared into her coffee without much seeing it. "How about I give you the *Reader's Digest* version?"

Even that took fifteen minutes.

"Well, was it Landry?" Barb demanded when she'd finished.

"Beats me. Nobody saw him but Cindy."

"Oh, great. The ideal witness. She probably swore she saw him with Elvis. Okay, what else is going on?"

"Conrad's coming in this morning to pick up the box with Alice's meds. I think I'm going to miss it. It's become kind of a mute but tasteful pet, you know?"

"Only you would think a chameleon is too noisy. I've been keeping tabs on the official game of hot potato they're playing with Alice's earthly remains. Van Adder refuses to consider it as one of his cases. Alex doesn't want to release her until questions about that dij level have been answered. It was 6.7, by the way."

Timmie whistled. "Considering how slow her system was, imagine how much higher it could have gotten if she just hadn't croaked."

There was a small silence. "You're a bit more chipper than the last time I talked to you."

Timmie thought about it a minute. "I guess I am."

"How's your dad?"

She considered the question and realized she could answer it almost free of guilt. Was this all it took to free yourself of that kind of turmoil? Turn down one murder-for-hire offer? Maybe she could share this with other Alzheimer's children.

"He's okay," she said, and damn near meant it.

Barb sounded as if she were smiling. "Good. Now, how can we prove who called you?"

"How the hell do I know? Nobody saw him but Cindy, he called from Alex's office, which was locked tight when we got there, and I couldn't identify his voice again if my life depended on it."

"Fingerprints?"

"I'll suggest it to Micklind, but who says he'll be allowed to investigate? We don't have the tape with the offer on it. Besides, what do you bet Landry has the perfect alibi?"

Barb snorted in disgust. "This stuff sure looks a lot easier when they do it in the movies. Well, what about Ginny?"

"Ginny? The night operator Ginny?"

"Sure. Anybody using the doctors' lot has to punch in with his ID card. When they do, their name flashes up on the night operator's board in case she has to page them."

Timmie almost couldn't breathe. "And the administrators park in the doctors' lot?"

"You think they're gonna park with the peons? Tell you what. I'll get Ginny's number and call her."

"You get the number. I'll call. I need to know more than you do."

Ten minutes later, a sleepy but agreeable Ginny was on the phone. "Honey, what can ole Ginny do for you?"

Timmie worked very hard to keep her tone level. "Last night when I called you about Dr. Raymond's phone number?"

"Sure, sugar."

"About that time, did you notice anybody check in from the doctors' lot?"

Ginny thought about it for almost five minutes longer than Timmie could tolerate. "Couple o' OBs," she said. "We had twins this mornin', didya know?"

"No, I didn't. Anybody else?"

"You want somebody in particular?"

"Mr. Landry?"

"Aw, heck no, sugar. I woulda remembered. Last time I saw him here on nights he pulled a surprise inspection, got four people fired. He wasn't here."

"How 'bout Dr. Raymond?"

"No. Like I told you. He's been away. In fact, I saw Miss Arlington heading out to pick him up at the airport. Evidently somebody's borrowing his car."

Then he hadn't been home. He had an alibi. He was safe.

At least for that. Timmie let out her breath. She'd have her talk with him when he came to pick up the car she hadn't even used.

"But that other doctor was there," Ginny said, grabbing Timmie's attention.

Timmie gulped. "Other doctor?"

"Sure. I noticed because I didn't see his name on the board. But I saw him at the elevators about two, and I thought, why, that's the second time I've seen him in two days. You know?"

Timmie held her breath. "Who, Ginny?"

"Why, Dr. Raymond's partner. Dr. Davies?"

Timmie was still sitting in the same place ten minutes later when the doorbell rang. She almost didn't get up to answer it.

Davies had offered to kill her father? Davies was their angel of death? Timmie didn't know how to feel about that. She didn't know him well enough to feel disappointment or anger. She just wanted to know how this affected Alex. How it was going to affect the unit. She wanted to know how they were going to prove it.

The doorbell rang again. Timmie held off answering it until she made a quick call to Murphy, who wasn't there. She left the message on his machine.

"Get everything you can on Dr. Davies. I think he was the one who called me. Call me at work this afternoon."

By the time Timmie reached the front hallway, the jabs on her bell were starting to sound frantic. She thought to look through the glass in the door, and then remembered she hadn't replaced it yet. So she checked through the window and got the third or fourth surprise of her day. Talk about her work coming to her. She yanked the door open so fast her guest took a surprised step back.

"Alex," she greeted him. "Come in. You and I have to talk."

He didn't know. Timmie just couldn't believe it, even seeing the reaction set in on his lovely golden features when she told him what was happening up in his beloved unit. He really didn't comprehend the fact that those lovely old people who were dying in Restcrest weren't just filling a heavenly transportation quota.

"How could you not figure this out?" Timmie demanded, suddenly furious. "Everybody in town knows but you. And it's your unit!"

Alex Raymond sat in stunned silence on her couch. "You have to be imagining this, Timmie."

Timmie was pacing. She'd had her fill of sitting in one place for a lifetime, evidently, because suddenly she couldn't hold still. "Am I?" she asked. "Then I imagined Daniel Murphy being beaten half to death to get him to stop investigating. I imagined somebody phoning me last night who might be your partner, offering to kill my father if I'd just shut up and leave everything be. Hell, Alex, I must have imagined Victor Adkins being murdered because he believed Charlie Cleveland when he said his father had been murdered. Charlie came to you and you didn't even listen to him!"

Alex paled. Clasped his hands together. Bent his head. Timmie thought he was praying. He wasn't. He was just frozen.

"What did *you* think those patients were dying of?" she asked.

He didn't budge. "They were frail. They were sick. It wasn't such a surprise, Timmie."

"It was an answer to a prayer, Alex," she accused, having recited a similar version herself more than once. "It was an answer to a lot of prayers."

And it was just easier to pretend it was all okay.

God, she'd lived with that one most of her life. She just couldn't do it anymore. Not simply because her father had been threatened. Because she'd almost been seduced into killing him for her own comfort.

"There's something I don't understand, Alex," she said, standing before him. That forced a laugh from her, a short, sharp sound that made him flinch. "Hell, there are a *lot* of things I don't understand. But one thing in particular. I don't know Davies from Adam. And yet, he knew me. He knew my dad. He said things . . ." She stopped for a second, pulled herself up straight, as if that could help her reassert control. "He talked about my dad like he'd known him his whole life, Alex. How could he do that?"

Alex looked up at her, his face ashen and still. His smile, when it came, was wistful, just like it always was when he discussed her dad. "Peter Davies is my partner, Timmie. And your dad . . . well, you know how I feel about your dad. I talk about him all the time. . . ." He shook his head, tentative acceptance of Timmie's words dying. "It couldn't have been Peter. It simply couldn't. And he is *not* committing euthanasia just to get research material. I mean, my God, what kind of man do you think he is?"

"You need to find out," Timmie said, and saw him flinch again.

She guessed Alex figured that Alzheimer's was enough reality for him in this lifetime. If he paid his dues to reality there, maybe he wouldn't have to set his feet in it anywhere else.

Well, Timmie waded hip deep in reality every time she set foot in an ER. But reality also waited outside those doors for her, just like it did for everyone else. Everyone else who wasn't Joe Leary or Alex Raymond, evidently.

"Help me, Alex," she said. "Protect the people you've spent your whole life trying to help."

If it were any other situation, any other threat, she would have asked him to think of his mother. She would have asked him whether he would have wanted to put his mother in this kind of peril, simply because she was ill. But she'd walked much too close to that truth to offer it up now.

He was shaking his head again. "There has to be some other explanation."

"Then help me find it. Order a postmortem on Alice Hampton. Go back through those other charts with a fine-toothed comb. Call the police and demand an investigation. Raise holy hell before somebody else does and blames you and the unit."

Still, unbelievably, he just sat there. Just as Timmie had done only yesterday, which meant she couldn't really blame him just because she was finally ready to act. She *could* blame him for being deliberately blind, but that wouldn't help.

"Let me think," he begged, rubbing at his eyes with the heels of his hands. "I need to think."

"If that's what you need to do," Timmie conceded. "But I can't wait."

She didn't. Even before Alex made it all the way out the front door, she was on the phone to Micklind. By the time Timmie went in to work at three, she had assurances that Conrad was hard at work sending the medicines in her box through both his gas chromatograph/mass spectrometer and his fingerprint techs, Ginny was making a statement to Murphy about Dr. Davies, and Detective Micklind was pressuring his chief to open a case investigating the strange death of Alice Hampton.

Which left Timmie with the big question of what Alex was going to do. She never got the chance to find out. Twenty minutes after she arrived at work, the area had its first full-fledged ice storm of the year, which inevitably signaled the kickoff of the Puckett County TraumaFest.

* * *

Murphy realized what was happening to the roads when he made the last turn onto Charlie Cleveland's street and slid sideways into a mailbox. The mailbox, one of those craft-show specials that looked like a barn on a milk can, tilted over. The Porsche stopped, without noticeable injury. Murphy cursed himself blue. Then after pulling the mailbox upright, he left the car at the side of the street and slid the rest of the way downhill to Charlie's house.

He'd spent the first two hours of the afternoon getting a five-minute statement from the hospital night operator who had seen Peter Davies wandering around the hospital two nights in a row, when he had no reason to. The operator had said he'd been mumbling to himself, a man intent on a mission.

Or a man terrified of an outcome.

Murphy had followed the talk with the operator with a call to his friend at the *Post* about the state of Peter Davies's research.

"Fine," he'd said, punching up names on his computer, which was even more ancient than Murphy's. "Getting a lot of notoriety. Matter of fact, he's in the final running for a huge health department grant that could set him up into the next century."

"He is, huh?"

"Yeah. Finalists' names came out this week."

"When do they decide?"

"Next couple of weeks. I've had four calls from the Price PR department in the last two days about it, and the health and leisure editor's three up on me."

Which meant that Davies might well have had an impulse to quiet things down the last few days or so. Tough to convince a government agency that you're working for the welfare of patients you're killing to get their brains.

But if Davies had just been informed in the last week about the finalists' position, would he have had as much reason before to kill people off, raw material or no? Murphy had sat and talked with the guy, and he wasn't convinced that murder was his standard MO for getting his material. And an offer made out of desperation was a lot different than one made during the course of a regular working day.

Davies was gifted, no question. Dedicated, focused, probably brilliant. Definitely a geek with clusters. But a man who didn't just murder people, but made their relatives take part in it? Murphy couldn't quite see it.

Which was why he'd decided to visit Charlie Cleveland.

"Well, hi there, Mr. Murphy," the gray man greeted him when he opened the door to Murphy's knock. "Awful day outside, isn't it?"

"It is, Mr. Cleveland," Murphy agreed. He'd traded in his standard uniform for the turtleneck, leather jacket, and combat boots he'd used for some of his more mobile assignments, and he was still wet and miserable. "Mind if I come in?"

Mr. Cleveland cast a careful look over his shoulder. He wasn't reading the paper this time, but his half glasses were pushed up to the top of his head as if he'd been working at something. Behind him, Murphy could hear the chatter of a television.

"It's important," Murphy insisted gently. "The woman who was here with me before got a call very much like yours, and we taped it. I need to know if you recognize the voice."

Mr. Cleveland said not another word. He just pushed open the storm door and stepped aside.

And then reinforced Murphy's suspicions ten minutes later, after he'd heard the tape.

"That's not him."

Mrs. Cleveland stood in the doorway to the kitchen, as if distance could protect her from her husband's admissions. She was as tidy and unremarkable as Mr. Cleveland, with helmet-permed steel-gray hair and the kind of housedress Sears sold. She was frowning, but Murphy had the feeling she wasn't given to it.

"You're sure?" Murphy asked her husband.

Mr. Cleveland nodded emphatically. "The person who called me didn't have as deep a voice as this. Also didn't sound quite so . . . unsettling."

"Are you saying it wasn't a man?"

Mr. Cleveland blinked. "I'm not saying that at all. It could have been either. I just know it wasn't *this* voice."

Murphy nodded and pocketed his tape recorder. "Thank you."

"Something else," Mr. Cleveland said, sliding those glasses back onto his nose as if making a statement. At the kitchen door, Mrs. Cleveland deliberately turned away. "Remember we talked about people possibly donating to Restcrest?"

Murphy had been about to get to his feet. "Yes?"

Mr. Cleveland nodded without emotion. "I thought I'd ask myself. Seemed to make more sense that way."

"Yes, sir?"

The man nodded now, his fingers tapping against gray serge pants legs. "So far I've talked to five people in town who had parents there. All five made donations. Also asked for donations in lieu of flowers, if you know what I mean."

"Yes, sir, I do."

He nodded again. Tapped his leg as if putting in the final punctuation. "At least five of them."

Murphy got to his feet. No wonder none of them had wanted to talk to him. "Thank you, Mr. Cleveland. I'm sorry we had to put you through this."

When Mr. Cleveland looked up to answer, Murphy saw the tears in his eyes. But the man couldn't manage an answer after all. He just shook his head, and Murphy showed himself out.

Timmie got a call from Murphy at five, but she was busy helping to put pins in a femur fractured in a motorcycle accident. She told the tech to tell Murphy she'd call him later. She never got around to it.

By six she'd increased her take to seven various injured limbs, a brace of back pains, and a gunshot wound of the lower leg, and by seven, she was triaging a busload of high school athletes who'd run right through the front window of a Stop & Shop, where a gaggle of senior citizens had been making a run on toilet paper, bread, and milk to get them through the storm.

"How do you do that?" Ron asked as she shuffled carts and redirected doctors.

Timmie didn't even bother to look up. One of the kids had a

head injury. One of the seniors was dead, and thirty other people needed to be seen. "Experience," she said. "Triage isn't any tougher than air traffic control."

"Planes don't scream at you if they have to wait."

"That's because pilots understand that the one with the least fuel lands first."

"Then why are you getting involved with that stuff at Restcrest?"

Timmie stopped dead in the middle of the hall. "What do you mean?"

Ron shrugged, even as he handed her three more charts. "Those gomers aren't low on fuel. They don't have any fuel. Wouldn't it be kinder to just let them die?"

This wasn't the conversation to be having in the middle of a minor disaster. Timmie triaged three more kids to waiting and intercepted a set of hysterical parents trying to find their son.

"Do you know *why* those old people are being murdered?" Timmie asked Ron.

"To put them out of their misery."

"You're sure."

He took a second to gather paperwork. When he answered, he couldn't quite look at her. "No."

"That's why it needs to be stopped. Last I heard, even in places with right-to-die laws, only the patient can ask. Those little old people didn't ask."

He still wouldn't face her. "Not everybody's gonna feel that way. Especially when you could end up ruining the hospital."

Which meant that Timmie's problems undoubtedly wouldn't be over once she got her answers. A pleasant thought. After all, maybe she'd had to be on constant alert when she worked in L.A., but she'd never had to protect her back from her fellow workers.

"Everybody should have thought of that when this was a little problem," she said, turning back to work.

By nine, the noise level was deafening, and Timmie was feeding ipecac to a toddler who'd thought birth control pills were Pez.

"Timmie Leary, Dr. Jones, line one. Timmie Leary . . . "

Timmie handed the barf basin to the anxious mother and jogged to the door.

"Hello?"

"*Cara mia*, it sounds like a madhouse there. Let me take you away from all that and make you a happy woman."

Timmie stripped off her gloves as she checked to see who was within earshot. Only Mattie, and she was busy trying to explain to a private doc how his forty-six-year-old patient had ended up with his tongue stuck to a post.

"Conrad, *mi amore*," she crooned in the receiver. "You give me the answer I want, you'll make me a delirious woman."

"How could I not?" he demanded. "When you give me gold, I have no need for alchemy."

Timmie caught her breath. "I was right?"

"Unless you prefer to find your digitoxin in a bottle marked Lasix. This poor grandmother either needs to contact the law offices of Brown and Cruppen or the district attorney."

Timmie found herself in a chair without realizing how she got there. "My God. We have proof."

"But not an identity."

"No prints?" she asked.

"One partial index and thumb only. What do you think our chances are they're our perpetrator's?"

Timmie sighed. "None. With all the people who've handled that vial, there should have been dozens of overlapping prints. Our man must have wiped them all off. They'll be Gladys's for sure."

"Our man?"

"That's the current thinking."

"What else can I do?"

"I'll let you know. *Grazie*, Conrad. I'd kiss you full on the lips if you were here."

"I can make it in half an hour," he promised. "Fifteen minutes if I commandeer a helicopter."

Timmie laughed. "Would that I could, *caro*. But I'm up to my armpits in alligators. Maybe later."

"*Ciao*, then, *bambino*. And Timmie, my heart? Take care. There's somebody bad in your hospital."

And he didn't even know about her friends.

Timmie took a second to call Murphy, but his line was out of order. Evidently the ice had started taking its toll on the utilities in the area. Thank God her dad was safe next door.

Considering the conversations she kept having, though, it wouldn't hurt just to make sure.

Cathy was on, and reported that all was well, vigilance high, her father safe and happy as he entertained his cadre of caregivers with a one-man Eugene O'Neill retrospective. Timmie truly hoped so. She figured she could take care of herself, and Walter had Meghan safely tucked away at his house. But Joe was vulnerable. Especially now that Timmie had made him so.

"New patient to room five," the intercom droned.

Timmie looked up. Her room. She was about to get to her feet when she heard it. A high, wavering whine. Gomer noise. She damn near sat right back down. Was this divine retribution or staff retribution, she wondered? She didn't ask, just walked in to where the patient waited, skeletal and unshaven and vacant-eyed.

Mattie located her there twenty minutes later. "Girl named Gladys on the phone for you. Somethin' about pharmacy?"

Timmie looked up from the mountain of towels and sheets she was bundling up. The first thing she'd had to do for her patient was wash him, top to bottom, because no one had. For a long time.

Mattie scowled. "You bein' punished, ya know."

Timmie finished stuffing sheets into the contaminated bag and closed it. "I was thinking that same thing."

"But then, I always seem to get Sheena, Queen of the Jungle. She 'cross the hall."

Timmie stretched and headed for the phone. "Sheena, huh? Is she as pretty as they say?"

Gladys huffed. "Only if you like chest hair and Adam's apples."

At least Timmie could laugh about that. Dumping the bag outside her patient's door, she reached for the phone. "Hello?"

"Timmie? You wanted to know about Alice's medications?"

"Yes, Gladys."

While she talked, Timmie leaned around to catch sight of Sheena, who at six foot plus was swathed in what looked like a fake leopard-fur rug, long black wig, and red stiletto heels. Obviously for stealthy jungle attack, Timmie thought.

"Well, I talked to my pharmacy tech this afternoon," Gladys anxiously informed her. "The one who always services us?"

"Uh-huh."

Timmie had also just noticed that Sheena evidently never traveled without her jungle cats. These were stuffed and moth-eaten and moldy, piled on the cart behind her like dirty blankets.

". . . changed just that afternoon."

Well, that yanked Timmie back from the ozone layer. "I'm sorry, Gladys. What?"

"The meds in that nurse server. The pharmacy tech had just restocked them the afternoon Alice died. Right about two o'clock."

She had Timmie's undivided attention. "What about the Lasix, Gladys?" Timmie asked, hopping onto the desk to focus on the situation at hand. "Does she remember that Lasix multivial?"

"That's just it. She restocked the Lasix at two, because Alice was out. She put in four multidose vials. So the Lasix was only in that nurse server from two until five, when I gave it."

Timmie forgot Sheena completely. "Which means that only a limited number of people could have switched it."

"Yes."

"Was Dr. Davies in that afternoon?"

"Dr. Davies? Sure, but . . ." Her voice started out sounding confused and wound up outraged. "Dr. Davies?"

"Okay, let's try this. Write down all the people you know were there for sure. You and the day crew. Okay?"

"Okay, but it can't have been—"

When the first person screamed, Timmie looked up. When it was followed by a growl of outrage that sounded a lot like "Don't fuck with me!" she damn near forgot Gladys altogether.

Sheena had escaped her lair. She'd also escaped her clothing which just proved that that Adam's apple wasn't an illusion. Sheena had run off with Tarzan's equipment. She'd also broken out a defibrillator, and was brandishing the paddles at one of the techs. Unfortunately, they were charged and blinking, ready to discharge.

"Gladys?" Timmie asked. "I'll call you back."

Timmie hopped off the desk, and Sheena turned his attention to her. "These are deadly," he threatened, "and I'm not afraid to use them. Now, I want out of here."

Fighting hard not to give in to a silly grin, Timmie shrugged good-naturedly and pulled the tech out of the way. "Sure. What the hell? Have a ball."

"You crazy?" Mattie demanded behind her.

"Nah," Timmie assured her under her breath. "That's not the Fry Daddy he has, just the Fry Baby. Doesn't have as much battery power. He'll run out of juice in half a block."

"By then he could roast a sheep with those things."

"He'll freeze his own little weasel long before that."

"Timmie Leary, line one. Mr. Murphy. Timmie Leary!"

Eyeing the large, hairy, naked man who was holding the crash cart hostage, Timmie sighed. "Tell him I'll call him back."

And then, like the second float in the National Cardioversion Day parade, Timmie followed Sheena out the door.

Timmie didn't think she'd laughed this much in weeks. She and Mattie were sliding around the sidewalk on the way to her house like Sheena hitting the driveway with a loaded crash cart. After the evening they'd just survived, they'd decided it would be pushing their luck to try and get to Mattie's, so they'd called the Rev, whose phone still worked, to tell him to meet them at Timmie's the next morning. Then, like mountain climbers without pitons, they had slithered all five blocks to Timmie's house.

The storm had stopped after depositing some four inches of ice across the western third of Missouri. Trees glittered and glistened, bushes hung over like old men, and electrical wires spat sparks and snaked across the gleaming streets from where they'd simply broken under the weight of the ice. Half the town was without power, and the rest without salt or traction on the steep, winding streets. The city lights reflected in a low, gray sky, and the world shimmered. It was a beauty Timmie had all but forgotten out on the coast. It was a cold that soaked right through her jacket.

"I will never forget the look on your face when Sheena walked out of that room without his fur," Mattie chortled.

"He had his fur," Timmie disagreed, wiping tears away. "He just forgot his clothes."

Mattie's laugh was high and shrill. "Girl, you know we never gonna get over havin' our defibrillator kidnapped."

Timmie laughed even harder and almost landed right on her butt. "I could already envision its picture on the side of a milk carton. Holding today's paper in its little paddles . . ."

Mattie smacked her on the head. "Stop it! I thought you was crazy when you let him go outside. But, girl, the minute he hit that ice, he turned that crash cart into a bobsled."

"Woulda made a helluva run, too, if he hadn't broadsided that ambulance at the bottom of the hill." Timmie pulled her key out and blew on her cold, chapped fingers. "Be careful of the steps. I haven't salted any better than the county."

They clung to each other and the ice-slick porch posts to keep themselves upright. Timmie strode over the creaky step and pulled open her screen door.

"You get some answers about your old people tonight?" Mattie asked.

Timmie smiled almost benevolently. "I did. I see a light at the end of the tunnel, and this time it isn't a freight train."

Not a freight train. A superliner that smacked Timmie full in the face when she opened the door to her house and realized that her lights were on.

"Get out," she instinctively urged, hand back against Mattie.

"What?"

She hadn't left her lights on before leaving. She hadn't let anybody in her house. But somebody was there.

"What . . ."

Timmie stopped pushing. She'd just caught sight of the wall.

Her grandmother's cabbage rose wallpaper, spattered in gore.

"No. Oh, no."

Her first thought was that her father had gotten here. Sneaked out of Restcrest while she was busy with normal mayhem and completed his attempt to blow his brains out with that huge old .45 she'd hidden high in the front hall closet.

"Timmie?" Mattie, right behind her, didn't see it yet. She didn't hear the sudden, startled thudding of Timmie's adrenaline- stoked heart. No emergency room nurse could mistake the smell, though. Sweet, cloying, coppery. The smell of tissue and blood and destruction.

"Oh, Jesus . . . "

Timmie saw feet in tasseled loafers. Gray pin-striped pants. Long legs. She couldn't move. She couldn't look.

She couldn't stop.

His brains and his blood were spattered on her wall. His body lay across her living room floor where it had fallen, his pants dark with urine, his eyes wide and sightless, the right side of his head simply gone. And lying just beyond the reach of his right hand, her father's old .45

"Oh, my dear sweet Jesus," Mattie whispered in sick dismay. "Timmie, who is that?"

Timmie choked. She tried to suck in a breath and sobbed instead. "Jason. My ex-husband."

# TWENTY-THREE

"WHAT AM I GOING TO TELL MEGHAN?" TIMMIE ASKED NO one in particular.

In a room packed to the ceiling with police, evidence technicians, and paramedics, no one thought to answer. So Timmie didn't bother to ask again.

Jason was dead. Jason, who had been the focus and fuel of her life for the last ten years. The man Timmie had attracted, loved, loathed, left, and tried to survive, who had gone from designing her engagement ring to selling it for cocaine. Lying on her floor, his wide blue eyes still seeming to accuse her of her failings, as if she should have been here to prevent this somehow.

His wide blue eyes that had been so perfectly reborn in Meghan. Who didn't know. Who slept at Mattie's, still expecting her father to sweep back into her life and reclaim the family he'd thrown away. Well, he'd sure as hell swept back into their lives.

"Here, baby," Mattie crooned, easing into the chair next to Timmie's. She had a jelly glass in her hand half filled with something amber, the smell of which Timmie could have recognized at forty yards. The two of them had taken up position at the far edge of the dining room, as far away from Jason as they could get while a photographer snapped pictures and the transport crew leaned against the stairs, waiting their turn.

"Where'd you get that?" Timmie asked, not bothering to take the glass.

"At the back of your kitchen cabinet. Come on."

Timmie shook her head. "I thought I'd found all his bottles. Thanks, Mattie, but I don't drink."

"Neither do I," Mattie reminded her. "This is shock medicine. Goes down easier'n Thorazine and don't leave you so fuzzy."

Timmie took it to make Mattie feel better. "What am I gonna tell Meghan?"

Mattie sighed like the mother she was. "I don't know, baby. Let's ask Walter later. Now, drink that."

Timmie just nodded, her attention on the movements of Micklind and his crew where they worked in her living room. They were measuring, comparing, nodding to each other. Pointing to the gun, to the blood-spatter pattern on her wall, to Jason's feet.

Timmie wondered vaguely why Murphy hadn't found his way here yet. Wasn't he the one with the legendary nose for news? Couldn't he see the strobes all the way across town? Didn't he know she needed his good sense right now?

Timmie vaguely noticed a commotion at the door and looked up. It was only Van Adder. Evidently rousted from bed, he hadn't bothered to button his Mobil shirt over his pajama top and jeans. He caught sight of her at about the same time. "You know what this is probably doing to your daddy?"

Timmie damn near laughed. Even if her father had been in mental attendance, he probably wouldn't have thought much more than that it served Jason right. Joe Leary had not had the time of day for Jason Parker.

"So, what's she gotten herself involved in now?" Timmie could hear Van Adder ask Micklind.

Mattie just about bolted to her feet. Timmie held her back. "He's on the board of the hospital," she reminded her friend.

"I don't care if he the only man on earth can give me a job," Mattie declared. "He got no right!"

"Ah, see, that's the funny part," Timmie assured her with a pat to her knee. "I could care less. He's a fat, lazy, white racist who can't tell his putz from a peashooter. We'll get him."

There was another disturbance by the door, and Timmie thought maybe this time it was sure to be Murphy. It wasn't. It was Cindy.

"Timmie?" she yelled, shoving cops out of the way to get to her. "Timmie, are you all right?"

Timmie just sighed. Cindy spotted her and threaded her way through the crowd in the living room. No wonder the cops had stopped her. She was dressed in what looked like cowboy drag tonight. Rhinestones and Lycra and snakeskin boots. Blue eyeliner and earrings that hung almost to her shoulders. She wasted no more than a second reacting to what was on the floor, then headed straight for where Mattie and Timmie sat in the corner.

"My God," she said, crouching at their feet. "What happened?"

"Whatchyou doin' here, girl?" Mattie demanded. "Don't you know it's damn near two in the mornin'?"

"I was on my way home from a date, and saw all the lights over here. God, I thought the house was on fire." She laid a metallic blue-nailed hand on Timmie's knee. "Are you okay?"

Stupid question. "Yeah. Just trying to figure it out."

Cindy just kept patting. Recognizing the anxiety to help in Cindy's eyes, Timmie managed a vague smile. It wasn't Cindy's fault, after all, that she reminded Timmie so much of her less favorite sister.

"You want to tell me?" Cindy asked, her attention straying to where Micklind was regaining his feet after closely inspecting something on the floor.

"It's her ex-husband," Mattie said simply.

Cindy's eyes widened almost comically. "You're kidding. Oh, my God, Timmie, you said he should be next. You didn't . . . "

Mattie glared. "No, she didn't. He did."

Cindy let her breath out in a rush. "Oh, Timmie, I'm so sorry.

You know I'll do anything I can to help. After all, I know . . . I mean . . . "

Timmie ignored her. She couldn't quite look away from that gun on her floor. That gun that had been hidden away in her closet behind the fireman's hat. She remembered telling somebody where. She just couldn't remember who.

"What are you going to do?" Cindy asked, pulling over a third chair and planting herself on it. "What can I do to help?"

Timmie shook her head. "I don't know."

She had to call Murphy. Past that one thought, she couldn't come up with a damn thing except the fact that when the sun came up she was going to have to try and explain all this to her daughter.

"What can you tell me?" Micklind asked in a soft voice.

Timmie hadn't even noticed him approach. It seemed that Mattie had lent him her chair, though, and he perched on it like a third-string player on an empty bench.

"I can't tell you much of anything," she admitted. "Do you have a time of death yet?"

He shrugged, doing his best to stay physically between her and Van Adder, who was rattling around her house like a master reminding the rabble of just how the craft was practiced. "Nope. But with rigor and livor, I'd say he's been in the same position about four hours now. He died where he's lying."

"And nobody heard anything?"

"One neighbor did, but she thought it was backfire down the street. She didn't investigate." Micklind paused a second, his attention caught by the flash of Cindy's attire. "You are?"

Leave it to Cindy to already show tears. "Cindy Dunn. I'm a friend of Timmie's, so don't even think I'm going to leave. My husband was a cop, after all."

As if that explained everything.

"Don't go there, girl," Mattie suggested sternly.

Cindy just lifted her eyes heavenward and hushed. Micklind watched her for a second longer, then returned his attention to Timmie.

"What can you tell me?" he asked.

Timmie rubbed at exhausted eyes. "Four hours," she said. "I was chasing the Sheena bobsled team."

Micklind blinked. "Pardon?"

She shook her head. "I was at work. Got there at three. Lots of witnesses."

"I'm one of them," Mattie said.

The cop raised an eyebrow at Timmie. "You telling me you should be considered a suspect?"

Timmie smiled sourly. "I seem to remember telling you I had something like this in mind. And that is my gun. My dad's, anyway."

"You *what*?" Cindy demanded.

Micklind didn't spend more than another look on her. "This Jason Parker was your ex-husband. That correct?"

Timmie couldn't take her eyes off those shiny loafers on her floor. "I haven't seen him in almost two years."

"Until tonight."

"He's called a few times. Said he was in town. This is the first time he's made an appearance."

"He seem depressed or having trouble with alcohol or drugs?"

"I don't know."

Mattie leaned forward. "There was that message he left on you answerin' machine 'bout makin' you know how much you hurt him."

Timmie couldn't seem to do much more than stare at her.

Mattie grimaced. "Barb told me. She was so mad about it."

Cindy nodded. "Yeah, I was there, too. We just figured he was talking about taking you back to court, though."

Timmie frowned, wondering what else her friends had all shared. Guilty all over again at the thought that she was angry, when they just wanted to help. Hell, she talked as much about each of them with the others as they probably did about her.

Micklind just jotted down notes. "I'll check up on it. I don't think it'll go much farther than this, though. He's got tattooing and gunshot residue on the right temple. No signs of a struggle, gun within reach of his hand. We'll probably find blowback on his shirtsleeve and his prints on the weapon. Which means that it looks like he broke into your house to commit suicide where you'd find him."

"It does look like that, doesn't it?" she said, and finally took a sip of the whiskey, so that it would burn all the way down to her stomach and help her focus.

Micklind had been all set to go back to his notes. Instead, he refocused on her. "But?"

Her smile was neither pleasant nor amused. "But nobody broke into my house, and my ex-husband didn't shoot himself."

"Don't you tell him anything," Cindy insisted sharply.

Micklind ignored her. "What makes you say that?" he asked Timmie.

Timmie didn't bother to point to the obscene decoration on her wall. "Look at the blood-spatter pattern. Jason is six feet one. That pattern isn't tall enough, and the trajectory is upward, so he was definitely below it when the gun was fired. He wasn't standing up when he died."

Now everybody looked. "So he was kneeling," Cindy said. "Why couldn't he kneel to shoot himself?"

"If he knelt down to shoot himself," Timmie said, "wouldn't he have fallen forward or on his side? He's on his back with his feet stretched out in front of him. I just don't think that's possible."

Van Adder heard her and laughed. "Oh, that's right, Mick. You haven't heard. Miss Leary here is a forensic nurse. She's going to tell us our jobs now. What else do you want to tell us, Ms. Leary? You getting vibes, are you? Messages from the dead?"

Timmie watched as the evidence tech reached down to lift the gun from where it lay, just beyond Jason's outstretched right hand. "Well, there is one other thing," she said.

"And that is?"

She didn't look at Van Adder. She didn't look at Micklind or her friends. "My ex-husband was left-handed."

Murphy hadn't intended to walk to Timmie's house. But then, he hadn't intended to leave his Porsche across the street from Charlie

Cleveland's, either. The ice should have cleared with the sun. Somehow, though, in this particular part of the world, the temperature didn't seem to rise in the morning. Which meant that the ice stayed right where it was, and with it, his car.

So he walked. Three miles. Just to tell Timmie that they still had more than one suspect, and Murphy's favorite was still the golden boy. At least that was what he'd set out to do. All plans changed when he got to her street and saw the crime scene tape. Murphy began to run and ended up sliding halfway down the damn street on his ass.

"What happened?" he demanded of the neighbors who had clustered next door to drink coffee and consider the empty house that was decorated like a Christmas package with shiny yellow ribbon.

One older lady in curlers and moth-eaten mink turned to him with an avid smile badly disguised as concern. "Do you know Timmie? Isn't it terrible? You don't think she'd kill her husband, do you?"

Five minutes later, Murphy was skidding down the street toward Mattie's.

"You out exercising, or you need a lift?"

Too focused on forward momentum, Murphy hadn't even noticed the nondescript Caprice pull up alongside him. But there, leaning across the passenger seat, was the redoubtable Micklind.

"You wouldn't be heading to the Wilson house, would you?" Murphy asked.

Micklind unlatched the door and pushed it open. "You heard, did you?"

"I saw," Murphy said, climbing in. "What the hell happened?"

Murphy had to wait for his answer until Micklind had navigated two turns and a fairly steep street, which he did in first gear.

"Your friend thinks her husband was murdered. I was all set to call it a flashy suicide and go home, when Ms. Leary informed me that the victim couldn't have committed the act himself, and proceeded to point out why." Micklind actually smiled. "To the great chagrin of the coroner, I might add. He doesn't like her much, did you know that?"

"It's okay. She doesn't like him much, either. She a suspect?"

"Hard to be unless she contracted it out, which I doubt she'd go to the trouble of doing and then ruin it by telling us all it was murder. She also has a pretty good alibi for the time. Seems she participated in the Ice Capades at the Med Center in front of about fifty patients and the entire staff."

"Could she have been the intended target?" Murphy asked. "She hasn't been quiet about what's been going on."

"I'd stay close to her if you can," Micklind said. "You can bet nobody's authorized me to. They still want me to bring her in."

"Who do *you* think did it?"

"Well, now, that's the question, isn't it?"

The Wilson house was a tiny white cottage situated on the same property as the similarly clapboarded Hill of Zion A.M.E. Church. Kids of just about all colors spilled off the porch in noisy confusion, and the driveway was clogged with vans, all bearing the church's logo in neon purple. Murphy couldn't imagine Leary finding any peace and quiet here after what must have happened last night. But then, Murphy wasn't a big-happy-family kind of guy. He hadn't figured Leary to be, either.

They were met at the door by a man the size of one of those vans, who had a stillness about him that connected him with the church next door. "I'm Walter Wilson," he introduced himself, opening the door to Micklind's badge. "Mattie's husband. I imagine you're here to talk to Timmie."

He led them through what there was of the tiny house to where Mattie stood guard at one of the back bedrooms.

"You go on in, have something to eat," was all she said as she stood there, arms akimbo over an impressive chest and beneath a more impressive scowl. "She be out in a minute."

As he turned to go, Murphy caught a peek in the room and saw why. Leary was seated in an old rocker by the window with her little girl in her arms. The two of them were rocking together, heads close, arms wrapped around each other, Leary humming quietly.

The little girl was sobbing herself to sleep. Murphy backed right out and got himself some food he didn't want.

It took Leary more than half an hour to come out of that bedroom. Murphy and Micklind waited in the kitchen with Mattie and her husband, who spent the time wasting their curiosity on Micklind.

"How's my baby?" Mattie asked when Leary showed up.

Timmie looked older than death. "She's had better days."

"At least he didn't do this to himself," Walter said in that quiet voice of his.

"Yeah," Timmie retorted, "but somebody did." Which was about when she noticed that Murphy was standing not ten feet away, munching on coffee cake. "Where were you last night?" she demanded. "I kept expecting you to walk in right behind Cindy."

"I missed this one, I'm afraid. You okay?"

She grimaced. "Oh, sure. I love funerals. I was just saying the other day that I was still short one for my quota. These things happen in threes, ya know. Guess the town is safe for a while."

"*That's* where I recognized her from," Micklind said to himself with a little nod. "I kept seeing her at funerals. I wondered."

"Who?" Murphy asked.

"Has to be Cindy," Mattie retorted.

Timmie's grin was halfhearted at best. "I can't tell you how grateful I am you took us in, Walter. It saved me from hearing how hard it was on her when her husband died."

"Even though he didn't kill himself," Mattie added.

Timmie raised a finger. "He didn't *look* like he killed himself. Even she should be able to get that distinction."

"She has a dead husband, too?" Micklind asked. "What is this, an epidemic?"

"Come to think of it, he was murdered, too," Timmie said, but held her hand up the minute Micklind started looking interested. "It was investigated three years ago. You might have known him. He was a Chicago cop, died on duty. Named John Dunn?"

Micklind considered it. "Three years ago?" he asked, then shook his head. "Doesn't ring a bell. Says something about this job that I can't remember a copper I taped my badge for, doesn't it?"

"If he was anything like Cindy, he probably wasn't that great a cop," Timmie said.

Mattie harrumphed. "Probably shot hisself by accident."

"Mattie Lou Washington Wilson," Walter chastised in his soft voice. "Cindy is your friend."

Timmie felt properly chastised. Mattie flashed her husband a grin the size of a dinner plate. "Which is why nobody but me can talk 'bout her that way."

Walter's chagrined smile said it all.

"Would you mind answering some questions about what happened last night?" Micklind asked Timmie, his voice almost as quiet as Walter's.

Timmie leaned against the counter next to Mattie as if settling in. "I can't say I'd be happy to, but I will."

"Have you had a chance to think about it?"

"Hard to do anything else."

"Y'all want us to leave you alone?" Walter asked.

"She does not," Mattie said, wrapping a protective arm around Timmie's shoulder.

Timmie smiled and rubbed at her chest. "Doesn't matter. This is all gonna have to be said sooner or later."

Micklind didn't bother with tact. "Do you think your husband was just at the wrong place at the wrong time?" he asked.

Timmie sipped her coffee. She looked tired, Murphy thought. Wrung out and hung to dry. But at least the life in her eyes didn't look like it was going to blink out. This was going to be tough, but it wasn't going to break her like that call about her father almost had.

"They doing Jason's autopsy this morning?" she asked.

Micklind nodded. "The St. Charles ME's doing it."

She nodded, contemplated her coffee. "Good. Conrad's already been helping me." Then she just stopped. "God, Jason would be so furious at the mess. He was such a tidy man."

"Do you know why he was at the house?"

"Last night? No. He was in town to see Meghan. To harass me. He'd already served me with one court order."

"Two," Mattie offered. "Remember?"

Timmie's smile was sad. "No, hon. I lied to you guys about that. It was an easy reason to give you for why I was so nuts."

Mattie frowned. "But we all thought—"

"We'll talk about it later, Mattie. Okay?"

Mattie just patted and hushed, probably like she had to Timmie's little girl.

"If he wasn't supposed to be at your house," Micklind said, "could you have been the target and he just got in the way?"

Murphy saw Timmie suck in a breath and Mattie squeeze more tightly.

"Or maybe they set Jason up, knowing you'd be at work," Mattie offered. "Then maybe they'd try and pin it on you."

For a few seconds, there was dead silence in the kitchen. Then, unbelievably, Timmie shook her head. "See, that's where I'm having trouble with all this."

"What do you mean?"

She just sat there for a second, focused on her coffee as if divining answers in it. "Well, if I'd kept my mouth shut about Jason's left hand, everybody else would have closed it as a suicide. Am I right?"

Micklind nodded. Murphy just waited her out.

"Then, why do it that way? Everybody in town knows I hated the guy. Heck, I publicly expressed my desire to kill him . . . to a cop, no less. Why not make it look like murder and pin it on me?"

"Because nine out of ten women in that situation probably would have just kept their mouths shut," Micklind said. "If you'd followed suit, whoever did this would have had you in the ten ring on the blackmail target."

"But everybody knows about the deaths at the hospital now."

"They don't know who's doing it."

Timmie leaned against Mattie as if her friend could shield her. "What if I said I didn't want to know, either?" she asked miserably.

Micklind offered no comfort. "I think it's too late. Whoever's doing this is feeling cornered, and you're the one they're coming after."

# TWENTY-FOUR

Timmie had definitely had enough of funerals. Especially when it was her turn to ride in the limo with the in-laws she hadn't seen in almost five years. It probably could have been a lot worse. Jason's parents were so shaken by the death of their only child that they couldn't find it in their hearts to lay blame anywhere near Timmie's feet. They also clung to their granddaughter with a sort of fragile desperation that actually helped Meghan get through it.

The SSS had all caravaned up to be there. Murphy was there along with Micklind as the line of mourners who owed or loved Jason's parents trudged through the slush to the stone building Catholic Cemeteries used for their grave-site services in St. Louis. No more standing out in the biting wind, staring at your loved one's mortal remains perched over a rectangle of empty air. No long wait while the casket creaked its way into the ground. No chance for the bereaved to fling themselves into the grave, alongside the loved one. Evidently the archdiocese had decided that the pile of fresh dirt next to the flapping tents was just a little too real for a grieving family.

Timmie wanted the dirt. She wanted the hole and the wind and the specter of gravediggers waiting in the shadows to make what they were doing real. To give that awful scene in her living room proper closure. This way it all ended with a few careful words echoing from cold stone and finished with a brisk request to return to cars so the next grieving line could pull up. She hated it.

But then, she hated the whole ritual. The stiff discomfort of survivors, the sloppy disbelief of parents who'd survived the son unto whom they'd entrusted all their earthly dreams. The hollow confusion of the little girl who couldn't quite believe her father wouldn't come through the door smiling just one more time.

They should have been burying Timmie's father, not Meghan's. They could have at least done that with gusto, sharing wild stories and wilder songs over aged whiskey and sandwiches. But there hadn't been enough of Jason to toast. So they'd all filed quietly out and reassembled at the Parkers' tasteful colonial in the heart of Ladue, where everyone but Timmie studiously avoided the fact that Jason had been murdered for no apparent reason.

"You didn't tell me he was a child of privilege," Murphy said to her as they stood near the living room door.

Ladue was the Bel Air of St. Louis, where the obscenely wealthy rubbed elbows with the simply respectably wealthy over dinner parties on manicured lawns and old brick patios, and a former mayor had once gone all the way to the Supreme Court to try and keep political signs from marring pristine front yards.

"He was a spoiled child of privilege," Timmie amended, watching her in-laws cruise the rooms. "This isn't exactly the Wilsons' house, is it?"

"You grow up in a place like this?"

"Nah. Jason and I met in college, where it was romantic to ignore financial disparity. It might have worked if Jason hadn't inherited his father's acquisition gene and his mother's knack for habit-forming behavior. I was a caregiver, first, last, and always."

And Betty and Jason Senior, whom Timmie had so wanted to love her, had settled for her instead. She hoped they'd end up offering more to Meghan, because Meghan needed it much, much more.

"Is Micklind still here?" she asked Murphy, sipping her mineral water.

Murphy's smile was grim. "Since he drove me, he said he couldn't go home till I did. I think he's just here for the food."

Timmie laughed. "Hell, *I'm* just here for the food."

A tidy little family of four in Lord and Taylor's best paused a moment to press cheeks and murmur something trivial about Jason's life and death before moving on. Timmie sighed and leaned against the wall. "So, what's been happening on the investigation front?"

Murphy sipped his water as if it were a couple of fingers of neat scotch. "You already have a homicide officer attending your ex-husband's funeral. Don't you think you might want to put this off for a while?"

"It gives me purpose, Murphy."

"It's gonna give you a homicide file of your own, if you're not careful. Word's out around the hospital who's been making waves, which means Micklind's right. You're asking to be target *du jour*, and Walter and I can only watch you so much."

She grinned at him, wanting very much for him to ease the pressure. "Worried about me, Murphy?"

"You bet." He looked away. "Nobody else in this state's even let me suggest meaningless sex."

Timmie was stunned by Murphy's reaction. No one else noticed because Murphy responded in millimeters. But Timmie saw the flash of anger that had escaped into those lazy eyes. She heard the hitch in his easy answer. She wanted him to be funny for her. Not to be afraid for her.

"Humor me, Murph," she all but begged, and he regained control.

"That guy who looks like Truman Capote and sounds like Father Guido Sarducci . . ." he offered.

She nodded. "Conrad."

Murphy nodded back. "Finished the post on your ex. Said there wasn't anything to see except the gunshot wound, which means he didn't put up a fight, and alcohol both in his bloodstream and stomach, which means he'd probably had something to drink at your house and then been capped."

"My house?" she echoed. "There isn't any alcohol in my house."

But there had been. Mattie had found it at the back of her cabinet, where Timmie could have sworn it couldn't have been.

"Alcohol," she mused, thinking of another death. One in which the victim had been anesthetized. "Much?"

"Probably one to two drinks."

"Which isn't even enough for Jason to notice," Timmie mused, rotating her glass so that the ice clinked. "If you were trying to get somebody in a position to inflict a close-range gunshot wound to the head, how would you hold him still?"

Unfortunately, more than one person heard. Timmie just smiled politely and lowered her voice. "How about a Mickey Finn?"

Murphy turned her way. "Chloral hydrate and alcohol? It'd certainly work. The question still is, who did it?"

"I don't know. Somebody not given to violence, I think."

Murphy squinted at her. "Why say that?"

"Because all the murders have been committed at a polite distance. As if the perpetrator couldn't stand the idea of seeing the victim in pain, or didn't want to be close enough to bear responsibility."

"You don't think a close-range gunshot wound is close enough?"

Timmie shook her head. "Not if he's unconscious. That seriously lowers the personal contact factor."

"Like shoving drugs in the line of a snoozing patient."

"Almost exactly."

"Which would certainly cover your crowd at the hospital."

"Access, method, and motive aplenty." Timmie sighed. "I think I was right. It's everybody."

They thought about it for a moment as a couple lighted next to them long enough to commiserate and comment on Jason's pretty daughter.

"Well," Murphy said, watching them go, "we know that the only person Davies offered to kill was your father."

Timmie leaned back against the wall, rubbed her eyes. Slugged down some water. "Have they questioned him?"

"Who, Davies? Oh, yeah. Micklind says he admitted to making the offer to you, but he swears he wouldn't have been able to go through with it. And he swears that was his only involvement. Says he got the idea from hearing Mr. Cleveland rant about his mother."

"Uh-huh."

"They also got the fingerprints off Alice Hampton's vial. Her nurse's, just like you said. The old gal died of a massive digitoxin overdose, also like you said." He sipped a second, watched the crowd.

Timmie opened her eyes again, hopeful. "And the floor nurse said Davies was there around the time we think the medication was switched. I'm telling you, he's looking better and better."

"Is there any reason it couldn't be more than one murderer, just like we thought?" Murphy asked. "Maybe Mary Jane's helping out. She and Davies. Or she and Raymond. After all, Mr. Cleveland couldn't swear the other caller was a man."

"Or Mary Jane and Alex and Davies and all the floor nurses. Or all the floor nurses and Ellen and Cindy and me, because the three of us have been up there, too. Gladys said that the same nurse didn't take care of all the patients who died, so maybe we were working in shifts."

"Could it be?" he asked.

Timmie wanted to laugh. She didn't quite make it. "I don't know," she said. "I don't know anything anymore."

Except for one thing. Just as much as Murphy had wanted Alex to be responsible, Timmie wanted it to be Davies. Davies, whom she didn't know. Who couldn't disappoint her or hurt her by being selfish and shortsighted and cowardly. Davies, who could kill anybody in town he wanted without making it a personal thing.

"There's something else to consider," Murphy said. "I can see Victor being killed to keep him quiet. I can see Jason being a warning or a mistake. But what about the other murder?"

The fact that it took Timmie so long to make the obvious connection betrayed just how badly Jason's murder had affected her. The fact that she'd been progressively forgetting it over the last couple of weeks betrayed how bizarre this whole deal had gotten.

Timmie had to follow Murphy's line of sight to where Ellen was saying her good-byes to her hosts to remember what had gotten her involved in the first place.

"Oh, God," she murmured, her stomach sliding. "I completely forgot."

Murphy nodded. "Why kill Billy?"

For a moment, the two of them couldn't seem to do much more than stare. "Could that have scared Ellen enough to keep her mouth shut?" Murphy finally asked.

"You mean, was it a message to her?" Timmie shook her head. "It's another one of those perception problems. I'm the only one in the known universe who thinks Billy Mayfield was murdered. And if it was to scare Ellen, don't you think she might have said something when she finally told us she'd been calling you? And if Billy was a present for keeping her mouth shut, why open it?"

"She only opened it surreptitiously. And don't forget, Cindy claims she was the one who called."

Timmie sighed. "Cindy would take credit for the invention of CPR if she could figure out how. No, I think I'd like to talk to Ellen before she leaves."

Murphy followed her across to where Cindy was helping Ellen pull on her coat.

"Ellen," Timmie greeted her friend. "I need to ask you an important question."

One sleeve still only half on, Ellen stopped dead. "Of course, honey. What is it?"

"Has anybody threatened you to keep your mouth shut about Restcrest?"

Ellen didn't so much as blink. "No, they haven't. I have to admit I've been living in mortal fear, waiting for somebody to figure out what I was doing. But nobody did."

"Me, either," Cindy said. "You don't believe me, but I did call, too. I wanted to help."

"Why do you ask that now?" Ellen asked.

Leave it to Murphy to cut through etiquette. "Nobody offered to get your ex-husband permanently out of your hair if you'd just keep quiet, did they?"

Ellen opened her mouth. She dropped her arm, dragging her coat on the ground. She paled so badly Timmie thought she was going to have to pick her up.

"What are you talking about?"

Timmie couldn't manage an answer. Neither, evidently, could anyone else. Ellen came up with it anyway. Her mouth closed, then opened again for another abortive attempt at speech. Her eyes filled with tears.

"I'm going home now," she said in a hush. "I don't think I want to hear about this anymore."

The worst part of the conversation was that when Timmie watched Ellen sweep out the door, she couldn't decide whether Ellen's reaction had been one of surprise, relief, or shame.

And then, inevitably, Cindy added her two cents' worth. "You just don't get it, do you?" she demanded, bristling and teary.

Timmie was still watching Ellen. "Get what, Cindy?"

Cindy was shaking her head, quivering with fury. "You think this is what, a game? She's your friend. She's just starting to feel better now that that asshole's dead, and you blame her for it? What's wrong with you?"

"That asshole was murdered, Cindy."

"And, so what? You think it's the same person who killed Jason? I'd say you shouldn't get mad. You should say thank you. *I* sure would."

And then she stalked off, too.

"Well, that was a success," Murphy said.

Timmie didn't say anything. She was too busy regretting her impulse. Thinking how it had ended.

Wondering, suddenly, about what Cindy had said.

"Murphy?"

He scowled at her. "I don't think I like that look."

Timmie didn't answer. She just walked through the thinning ranks of mourners until she reached a quiet corner back in the Florida room, where potted palms defied the frost outside.

She should have thought of it before. She might have if she wasn't still dreaming of trying to wash her husband's blood off her hands.

"Leary?" Murphy asked, close by.

Timmie kept looking out the window into a yard that had managed to maintain its elegant tailoring after the ice storm of the decade. "What if we've had it backward?" she asked.

"Backward? Is this going to make me itch?"

Timmie looked down to her glass, but she was out of water. As if that would help. "Well, think about it. If we use the theory we've been working on, Billy's murder doesn't fit."

"Not that we know of right now," he amended.

Timmie almost closed her eyes to better focus on imperfect logic. "Think about what Cindy just said, Murphy. I should be thankful. Well, if you think about it on the surface, I should. So should Ellen and Barb. And every family who buried an old relative." She opened her eyes, turned on him. "What do all those murders have in common?" she asked. "Billy Mayfield was abusive. He stopped hurting Ellen and the kids when he died. Victor was not just fooling around, he was going to try and sue Barb blind. Barb doesn't have to worry about that or his white-trash girlfriends hurting her little girls anymore. Each and every relative of those Restcrest patients was going broke trying to take care of their loved ones. They've been saved from that."

"And you have the insurance policy."

Timmie blinked. "I have what?"

Murphy squinted, as if testing her honesty. "Your ex-husband's insurance. You won't have to worry about affording your father's care anymore."

Now it was Timmie who opened her mouth without effect. Suddenly she couldn't breathe. She just kept staring at Murphy, waiting for him to laugh. "Murphy," she finally said. "What the hell are you talking about?"

Murphy's eyebrows slid up fast. "You can't tell me you don't know. I heard it from Micklind during the funeral mass. He said he heard it from one of your friends."

It took her a second to find her voice. A second or two more to have the courage to ask, "How much?"

Murphy was getting as quiet as she. "Quarter million?"

Timmie thought she was going to pass out, and not just from surprise. "He canceled that policy. I swear he did. He *had* to. He hated me!"

Heads were turning. Timmie barely noticed. She couldn't seem to look away from Murphy, who was, oddly, smiling. "He didn't hate his daughter."

Timmie should have said something. She couldn't quite manage it. Instead, she found herself stalking through an untidy cluster of mourners to get to Micklind, who was quietly standing with his back to the dining room wall, watching the crowd.

"Where did you hear about this fictitious life insurance policy?" Timmie demanded without preamble.

Micklind didn't react. "Not fictitious. And impressive enough to almost make me reconsider that alibi of yours. I heard about it from your friend over there."

Timmie turned to see him point at Mattie. She headed that way, trailing Murphy as she walked.

"Where did you hear about this life insurance policy?" she asked her friend, her hold on her glass tight enough to leave dents.

Mattie smiled, then frowned, then cast looks at both Murphy and Micklind. "From Barb."

Timmie repeated the pattern, now trailing Mattie behind as well. They all saved time, though, because Barb was standing by the front window with a predictably crying Cindy.

"Cindy," Barb answered when asked.

Cindy looked up, eyes red-rimmed and watery. "But his parents told me," she said. "Yesterday, at the wake."

At least they all didn't follow Timmie in when she confronted her ex-in-laws.

"But we naturally thought you knew," Betty Parker said in her perfectly modulated voice, the only hint of real grief tucked way at the back of her eyes. "Actually, we paid the premiums for him while he was . . . well, so uncertain of everything. He paid us back, though. Every penny. And, of course, his will was never changed. You're still executor for Meghan, who gets everything else he has." She shook her head apologetically. "But we thought you knew, dear."

Timmie couldn't do much more than shake her head. "No. And you told my friend Cindy about it yesterday?"

"We talked about it, I guess. Yes. People should know that Jason would never really desert you or Meghan, you see? I talked to Jason the night before . . . the night before it happened, and he wanted me to know that he'd talked to you. That he was going to see you. I thought . . . I hoped . . ."

Timmie nodded, mute with shock. She had lived a long time on self-righteous indignation. It was just too much to ingest the concept that Jason had been trying to grab her security with one hand and hand it back with the other.

"Which meant that his death really was a benefit to me," Timmie finally managed to admit to Murphy fifteen minutes later as the two of them stood with Micklind and Mattie in the Florida room. "Is it possible that this isn't about Restcrest after all?"

Mattie just kept shaking her head. "This is all way beyond this poor girl's head."

"If it's not about Restcrest, what's it about?" Murphy asked.

Timmie wished like hell she hadn't heard about the insurance policy. The will that would see her daughter safely educated and raised, when Timmie had been worried about affording peanut butter and jelly. It was confusing her, distracting her from the original question.

"We've been working on the assumpton that Victor was killed to keep him quiet about Restcrest," she said. "That Jason was a threat to me. What if they were just part of the same pattern? A mercy killer who's just moving a little wider than the hospital."

"You really don't think that your husband's murder was a threat to you?" Micklind demanded.

Timmie was having trouble breathing again. "No," she said. "I think it was a gift. So, what the hell does that mean?"

Two hours later Timmie drove home with Mattie, but without Meghan. Betty and Jason, their eyes brittle with weary grief, had begged Timmie to let her daughter stay with them for a couple of days, and Timmie, seeing the matching need in Meghan, had said yes.

"Are you okay that I'm staying, Mom?" Meghan had asked, her arms around Timmie's neck.

Timmie squeezed hard, inhaling her daughter's scent. "No," she admitted. "I'm selfish. I always want you with me. But I bet Gram and Gramps would like to tell you stories about your daddy when he was little like you. And I'd really like you to hear them."

Meghan pulled back. "You mean it? You're not just being nice because Cindy blabbed about that insurance thing with Gram before Ellen said it was okay?"

"Nah. I'm being nice 'cause I'm nice. Now, I have to go, or Renfield doesn't get any flies."

"Stay with Mattie," Meghan insisted.

"I will, baby. I'll call you tonight."

Timmie stayed with Mattie. In truth, she couldn't imagine how she was going to live in her own house again after what had happened. Micklind had pointed her to a company that actually cleaned up the kind of mess they'd left in the living room, but the afterimage tended to linger a lot longer than the stains, like a bad smell caught in upholstery.

The problem was that Timmie couldn't imagine staying at Mattie's, either. Not that she didn't love Mattie and Walter and the six kids of various ages who were tucked into every nook and cranny of that tiny house. But no matter how much Mattie and Walter insisted Timmie wasn't in the way, she knew she was. So she went back to work the next afternoon and actually sighed with relief at the relative quiet.

She also had the chance to sit with her dad, who really had settled down some on the new dosage of medication.

"When are they going to come question us?" one of the nurses asked Timmie.

Timmie blinked up at her. "I'm sorry?"

"The police. We know they're going to crucify this place. Word is, the media's already preparing the skewer. It isn't fair, you know."

Timmie got to her feet. "They haven't been by yet?"

The nurse stiffened in renewed outrage. "This is a good place," she insisted. "You don't think they're dismantling it fast enough?"

Timmie straightened herself, tired of being batted back and forth like a shuttlecock between all the special interests in this town. "This isn't a good place," she said in her most quelling voice. "This is a great place. Which is why at least one person should have had the balls to stop what was going on, because you can't tell me that not one of you knew it was happening."

"Last of the idealists, my Timmie," her father suddenly said.

Both nurses glared at him for a minute. Then Timmie decided to take it outside where she couldn't rile him.

Too late. By the time she reached the middle hallway, he was singing the first words of "The Patriot Game," a lovely song about idealism gone bad. The other nurse was fortunate enough not to be familiar with it.

"You know, of course, that two of the nurses on unit five are getting pink-slipped."

All right. She had Timmie there. "Why?"

"Because they didn't report the possible problem."

"Of course they did. Nobody did anything."

Another glare, hands on hips. Nurse's sign language for "Well, no shit."

Timmie shook her head. "Doesn't it just fuckin' figure. Okay, I have contacts in the press. Let's see what we can do. In the meantime, help the police, okay? If you don't, this whole place could go up in flames."

She didn't bother to wait for an answer. Just stalked over to unit five to find Gladys finishing paperwork in her civvies.

"What happened?" Timmie demanded, grabbing a seat next to

her. Another nurse, who was dressed for work in her best white polyester, made it a point to ignore Timmie as she walked by.

"What do you think happened?" Gladys asked quietly, never once raising her eyes from her task. "The shit rolled downhill, and I happened to be standing at the bottom."

Timmie almost smiled. She hadn't thought Gladys had it in her. "What reason were you given for being let go?"

"Poor performance. Lack of faith by the families. Typical bullshit. My last review, which was rated exceptional, evidently doesn't count. The next thing we probably need to address in this facility is a union."

"One thing at a time. Did they fire you before or after you talked to the police?"

That got Gladys's attention. "I haven't talked to the police."

Timmie wanted to curse. Wouldn't do either of them any good. "Guy named Micklind hasn't been by?"

Gladys shook her head. "Amazing what power in the right places can prevent."

"It can't prevent it forever. You remember that list I asked you for of anybody who could have gotten at that vial of Lasix?"

"Of course I do. I've been carrying it around ever since you asked for it, waiting for the police to take it."

Timmie decided that now wasn't the appropriate time to remind Gladys that the phone worked two ways. "You haven't said anything to Dr. Davies?"

Gladys shook her head. "I told you. It couldn't be him."

"But you said he was here."

"He was here for a half hour, from two-thirty to three, and he spent the whole time in Mr. DiAngelo's room doing a cut-down. I know, because I was the one who helped him. I hadn't clocked in yet, but the day nurse asked me if I'd give him a hand. So I did."

Timmie fought the urge to argue. "And he couldn't have gotten near Alice's nurse server without you knowing it."

"Heck, no. We had to call him in from a meeting he'd been attending. He ran in, did the job, and ran out. I saw him the whole time. Besides, he would have had to get access to a key sometime or another, and he's never involved enough to do that. Heck, I'm not even so sure he knows where a nurse server is. He's not exactly your hands-on kind of guy, you know? The only reason he came in that day was because Dr. Raymond was out of town."

"Dr. Raymond could get a key?"

"Sure. But he wasn't here. But the point is, Dr. Davies just didn't have access to that nurse server while he was here."

Timmie tried any way she could think of to make him suspect, and couldn't. "What about Ms. Arlington?"

Another shake of the head. "Nope."

Timmie's hopes died a painful death. "You're sure."

"Believe me. We know when she's around. I called her in from an all-day function when Alice coded."

Timmie wasn't going to be able to stand much more. "You have the whole list?" she asked.

Gladys reached for her purse where it sat, next to her chair. "Sure. It's not very long, though. Shorter when you think of how tough it is to get one of our keys. Maybe they're free with them in other parts of the hospital, but we're real careful of our old people. Especially since we've figured out what's been going on."

Gladys had made her list on the back of a preprinted prescription form one of the pharmaceutical companies passed out. Oddly enough, for Lasix. Timmie wondered if she'd noticed, but she'd never pegged Gladys for an irony kind of girl.

She'd been right. The list was short. Six people, including Davies and Gladys herself. Timmie noted them, then the pharmacy tech. Another nurse's name she didn't recognize. And then, two names that sucked away her breath.

"You're sure about these?" she asked.

Gladys looked. "Sure. When Mr. DiAngelo got really sick, we needed extra help. They were really sweet about it."

Timmie kept staring at the list. Kept willing the names to change. Kept waiting to feel surprised to see them in the center ring of the suspects' target.

"And they could have had access to the key."

"Yes. The only person any of us can vouch a hundred percent

for is Dr. Davies. The rest of us were coming and going. Mr. DiAngelo was pretty sick, and his family was really worried about him. We ended up sending him through the ER and upstairs to the unit."

Timmie nodded, still trying to figure a way out. "Thank you."

"By the way," Gladys said, hand on Timmie's arm. "I'm sorry about your husband. That was a terrible thing."

Timmie barely heard her. "Thank you. It's harder on my daughter, of course. Jason and I really hadn't been together for about three years."

Gladys nodded, went back to her work. "Well, at least you were lucky enough to have an ex who was still thinking of you. I can't imagine my ex-husband leaving me money."

Timmie had been all ready to stand up. Gladys's words took the stuffing right out of her knees. "How'd you know that?" she asked with far more fatalism than astonishment.

Gladys literally flinched. "I'm sorry. I thought it was common knowledge."

"How'd you know?"

"One of your friends told me."

"When?"

Gladys was all set to throw off an answer. One look at Timmie's face seemed to change her mind. Timmie could actually see her considering. "Well, I don't know. I do remember that I already knew when I heard about his death, and that news was around the morning after he died."

All those old clichés were true. Time really did seem to slow when the mind suffered a shock. Timmie swore she could suddenly smell the tube feeding the other nurse had opened down the hall. She could hear half a dozen monitors blipping in syncopation. She remembered just what Meghan had said about how she'd seen the insurance information passed, and what every one of her friends had told her.

"You knew before he died," she said very carefully.

Gladys blinked. "I guess I did."

"And you don't remember which of my friends told you."

She thought about it. "Well, I'd probably have to say it was one of those two, although I couldn't tell you which, which I guess is silly. It's not like they look alike or anything, but I can't remember."

Those two.

The names on Timmie's list. Her two friends, who would have had access and availability to the nurse server where Alice Hampton's Lasix had been magically transformed into digitoxin.

Timmie took another look at Gladys's precise, schoolmarm handwriting. At the last two lines, which read:

From the ER—Dr. Adkins
From the ER—Ellen

"Barb," she said, praying for deliverance. "The—"

"Big woman," Gladys said with a nod. "The doctor. She's tough to mistake."

"And Ellen."

"Smaller, had that husband who hit her, who died."

Timmie nodded. She kept looking at those names, and all she could think of was that she'd been right. They'd been looking at it from the wrong side all along. The husbands hadn't been killed to cover up the old people. They'd been killed just like the old people.

And one of her friends had done it.

# TWENTY-FIVE

WHAT DID SHE DO NOW? DID SHE CALL MURPHY? DID SHE CALL Micklind? Did she confront her friends, who were almost all downstairs working the shift?

It made such terrible sense all of a sudden. Mercy killings, all of them. Even Victor, turned into ashes in the space of fifteen minutes, asleep the whole time. Polite, almost reluctant murders, which seemed to escalate as the pressure around them built.

How had the hospital murders begun, she wondered? As wish fulfillment? As a favor? As a simple failure of patience and hope?

It didn't matter now. What mattered was that they had to stop, and Timmie was probably the one who was going to have to do it. She was going to have to turn in one of her friends, because one of them was certainly killing people.

She actually managed to walk back into the ER and work another half hour before giving in to the inevitable and telling everyone she had to go home sick. Everyone understood. Mattie wanted to drive her home. Timmie shook her head and called Murphy instead.

Murphy, who was safe. Murphy, who might not understand, but at least would respect her distance. Murphy, who would help her convict one of the charter members of the SSS of murder.

Tucked behind a closed lounge door, Timmie briefly told him what she'd discovered. She asked him to meet her at her house, and then collected her coat and purse.

"You're sure you're okay," Mattie said with an anxious frown when Timmie reached the front desk.

Mattie wasn't the only one there. Cindy waited, and Ellen and Barb. The inner circle of the SSS. Timmie gave her audience a chagrined smile. "I'm sorry. I misjudged my stamina."

Timmie could tell that Mattie didn't completely believe her. It didn't matter. She'd support her no matter what, which was just about what Timmie could handle right now.

Of course, Cindy was still pissed about what had happened the day before. Just as Timmie passed beyond earshot, she could be heard saying, "Stamina, my ass. When my husband died, I went back to work the next day. And I loved him."

For some reason, that was the last straw. Timmie spun on her heel and nailed Cindy with a glare. "You know it's funny you should mention John," she snapped, walking right back up to her. "We were talking about him the other day, weren't we, Mattie? He was shot, what, three years ago? In Chicago?"

"You know he was."

Cindy was beginning to look hurt. Timmie shrugged, furious enough at what she had to do that she felt like kicking dogs. And since Timmie knew she was probably going to have to admit that Cindy wasn't the one lying about making those warning phone calls, she kicked her instead.

"Well, that's the funny thing," she said, feeling like a heel and unable to stop. "See, Detective Micklind is an old Chicago cop. And he can't remember a John Dunn getting shot three years ago. His name was Dunn, wasn't it? You didn't change your name back just because he died?"

Now everybody was staring. Cindy looked as if she were going to vomit. "No. I never changed it in the first place. You think I wanted to go through life with a name like Cindy Skorcezy? It sounds like a Polish sedan." Finally, she teared up, straightening like Jackie Kennedy boarding the plane. "His name was John Skorcezy. Sergeant John Stanislaus Skorcezy, born in Chicago on July 12, 1959, badge number 23548, social security number 270-23-2122. He died in my arms of a gunshot wound to the head. Happy?"

"Yeah, I guess so. Now Murphy can look up the right name. He wanted to read the story himself."

The minute Timmie said it she wanted to take it back. It was a small, ugly thing to say, and she knew better. Forget what Mattie or Walter would have said. Her father would have blistered her butt until she couldn't sit down. Especially since the name had rung a bell. She had heard of Skorcezy. She'd probably seen the human interest story with the picture of his young wife holding his bloody body in her arms on a downtown street. But somehow, she just couldn't admit it. So she ignored Mattie's stunned silence and Ellen's wide eyes and just walked out the door.

Murphy didn't show up for close to an hour. By that time Timmie had already been inside the house and retrieved her evidence. She sat with it in a paper bag on her front porch, shivering and watching the sky darken.

It had been where Mattie had said it would be, in the kitchen cabinet next to her sink, right where anybody not familiar with her house would expect it. A half-empty quart of C and G bourbon. Choke and Gag, her dad had always called it. The cheap stuff. Exactly the brand of bourbon she'd cleaned out of the house by the shopping cartful when she'd first moved in. And now it was back, and just in time for Jason to drink it in the final moments before being shot to death.

"You look like a kid wanting to run away from home," Murphy said to her in greeting when he stepped out of his car.

Timmie was shivering where she sat, the impulse of the original idea long since dead. It would have been wiser to wait inside with her find, but there was still an obscene Rorschach splotch on the living room wall, and Timmie didn't want to spend time with it.

"I need to take this to Micklind," she said. "Do you mind?"

He didn't move from where he leaned, with one elbow on his open door and the other on his roof. "Nope. He said he'd meet us there."

Timmie just nodded her head.

"We can go any time."

She looked over at him. "You still interested in that mindless sex, Murphy?"

Timmie would have thought he'd look more enthusiastic. "I'm always interested in mindless sex, Leary. You serious, or you just looking to warm up a little?"

She sighed. "I don't know."

"Well, while I highly recommend it, I suppose I should warn you that it does nothing to ease the guilt of turning a friend in to the police."

Oddly enough, that made her grin. "Romantic."

He really did look like an old beaten rug, especially in this light. But he didn't carry any baggage with him. At least none Timmie would have to help tote if she decided to just enjoy his wry smile and sly eyes for a while.

"Did you tell Micklind what I think?" she asked, climbing to her feet with all the grace and enthusiasm of a septuagenarian.

"Nope. Figured you could do that. I did have him run your friends for wants and warrants, though. He came up empty."

Timmie shook her head. "There's got to be some kind of record. Serial killers who are this adept at murder have had practice." Hefting the bag in her arms, she walked to Murphy's car. "There's a trail somewhere."

"You sure it's one of them?"

"Nope," she lied. "I just have a sinking feeling." They both climbed in, and Murphy started the engine. "Anybody could have killed those old people, but only somebody who knew about Jason could have killed him. And only the SSS knew about Jason."

"All of the SSS?"

"The way we share information, it wouldn't have taken long. Just look how fast that insurance news made the rounds."

"But you said there were only two names on the list that nurse gave you."

Timmie stared out at the houses on her block as Murphy backed the car out and headed down the hill. "I did, didn't I?"

"Well, if it's Ellen, why would she call the murders in?"

Timmie rubbed at her eyes. "How the hell do I know? How do we know she really did call? What if it really was Cindy?"

"I don't suppose you thought to ask each of them where they made their calls from."

"I thought of it. I couldn't quite motivate myself to do it."

"You're going to have to, Leary."

She gave a sour laugh. "They're my friends, for God's sake. I still can't believe they'd be capable of mercy killing, much less first-degree arson. Any of them."

"There's something else to consider," he said. "How did Jason end up at your house with a murderer while you were at work?"

Timmie clutched more tightly to the bottle in her arms. "I didn't arrange it, if that's what you mean." She paused, sighed. "At least I don't think I did. I don't really trust my judgment anymore."

"You still don't think it could have been gold . . . uh, Raymond? He's pretty close with your friends, and I can damn well bet he'd have plenty of reason to make you happy."

"He couldn't have killed Alice Hampton. The more I think about this, the more I see one mind. Passive, nonconfrontational, intelligent enough to plan it and get away with it for so long."

"Those mercy killings were so tough?"

"The nurses up there knew exactly what was going on. They just couldn't manage to stop it or catch who was doing it. Which reminds me, I have an exposé article for you on the administration that's firing the nurses who tried to report a series of murders on their Alzheimer's unit."

Murphy scowled. "I'll give it to Sherilee. It's just the kind of shit she's looking for."

"You don't want it? It's a natural follow-up to a Pulitzer winner like this."

"I'm not sure I'll still be around. All this action's made me realize that I haven't escaped from anything here. So what's the point of staying?"

Timmie looked over, disappointed and relieved at the same time. The passing streetlights, flickering to life in the dusk, silhouetted Murphy's sharp features. His hair was still shaggy, his chin rough from inattention. His eyes were sharper than ever, capable of ferreting out truth from the most innocuous expression. Those eyes were the only real reminder Timmie still had of the life she'd lived until a few months ago.

"I'm going to miss you," she said, and found that she meant it.

Murphy gave her a fleeting look that bordered on wistful. "You could always come along."

Timmie felt even more ambivalent. Just as melancholy, as if they were already standing at the door. "Thanks for the offer, even though I know you wouldn't have made it if I could have gone."

Murphy laughed. "Actually," he said, sounding as surprised as she, "I think I would have."

Timmie couldn't even manage a pithy comeback.

"You really want to stay here?" Murphy asked.

Timmie smiled. "Believe it or not, yeah. I kind of do. It'll be good for Dad, good for Megs, and if I need action, St. Louis isn't so far away."

He took just long enough to pull into the police station parking lot before closing the conversation. "The invitation stays open," he said, turning her way.

Close, a handsbreadth away in this little sports car. Smiling as if he meant it. Timmie smiled back the same way. "Not without that meaningless sex, it doesn't. I'm going to get something out of this relationship besides computer access if it kills me."

He laughed. She laughed. He bent over his stick shift, wrapped a calloused hand around the back of her neck, and pulled her close for a kiss. Timmie tasted tobacco on him. She smelled soap and leather and cold air. She knew for sure that sex with Murphy would be hot and fun and frivolous, and that Murphy would end up being a good friend. She missed him even before he was gone.

* * *

"I only accept gifts of alcohol at Christmas," Micklind said when they showed him what was in the bag.

Timmie wasn't in the mood for games. "If we're really lucky, we'll get at least a couple sets of prints off this. Especially if our murderer thought I wouldn't notice an extra bottle of bourbon in the house."

Micklind finally looked interested. "Anyone who'd ever spent time with your dad might make that mistake. I'll get 'em pulled. Anything else?"

Timmie sucked in a steadying breath. "Yeah. Sit down."

Twenty minutes later Micklind had all the information Timmie had, and Timmie learned that Alex hadn't been at the funeral because he'd been in interrogation, the cops had just searched Jason's motel room and come up with nothing of import but Timmie's phone number, and they were still waiting for phone records to see who else he might have called while he'd been in town. Timmie had also suggested they carry certain pictures to the motel and see if Jason had been seen in the company of any of the SSS. They'd been right. Jason's death had been no chance.

"And you're sure there wasn't any kind of history on the names I gave you?" she asked Micklind.

"Nothing more than traffic violations and the disorderly conduct we hit Dr. Adkins with when she tried to run over Vic's girlfriend once. One suspicious loitering, but that wasn't much."

"Suspicious loitering?" Timmie echoed. "Who, Cindy?"

"No. Ellen Mayfield."

"Ellen? Against who? Why the hell would Ellen loiter, suspiciously or otherwise?"

Micklind threw his hands up. "It didn't rate a big note in the file. I don't see it as practice for the big one, you know?"

"But you'll check."

"I'll check," he assured her. "Give us more time and we might be able to pull down work histories and stuff, but not tonight."

Murphy resettled in his chair, as antsy as Timmie. "Ms. Leary believes that whoever's doing this probably has a pattern already, or they wouldn't be this effective. Any way we could fire up

VICAP or NCIC to see if there's a matching pattern anywhere?"

VICAP. Timmie almost leaped straight to her feet. "Oh, shit."

Micklind damn near reached for his gun. "Problem?"

But she was grinning. "You don't need to go through the computers. Conrad already did it for me."

Now both men were paying attention. "He did?" Murphy asked. "What did he come up with?"

"Nothing that made sense when I read through it before. But I have the printout at my house. We can look at it again."

A uniform tapped on Micklind's open door and leaned in. "Sarge, that nurse is in interrogation one for you."

Micklind scowled and climbed ponderously to his feet. "We only have one interrogation room, Bradley."

Bradley didn't smile. "Yes, Sarge."

"And here," he said, lifting the brown bag. "Have this bottle dusted ASAP. Carefully, Bradley."

"Yes, Sarge." He accepted the bag as if it held the grail and proceeded with it from the room.

Micklind shook his head at the young officer and then turned back to Timmie and Murphy, who were also on their feet. "We finally got the time to interview the unit nurses. Did you know the hospital already fired two of them?"

"Something I plan to help rectify," Timmie vowed.

Another uniform leaned in. "Those phone records are coming in."

Timmie almost sat back down. Micklind gave her one of his almost visible smiles. "You were going to check patterns you might recognize better than I would. I'll call if I find anything interesting here. All right?"

She glowered. "It'll have to be, won't it?"

Micklind pulled his jacket off his chair and slipped into it. "Oh, just for curiosity's sake, didn't you say that Chicago cop's name was John Dunn? I couldn't find a record of him anywhere. You sure he was a Chicago cop?"

Oh, good. Frustration *and* shame. "My mistake," Timmie admitted. "Evidently it wasn't Dunn. It was Skorcezy with a 'z'.

Sergeant John Stanislaus Skorcezy, born in Chicago 1959, badge number 23548. He has a social security number, too, but I can't remember it. Cindy said he died in her arms."

Out of habit, Micklind jotted as Timmie talked. "You sure he was a sergeant?" he asked. "His badge number's wrong."

Timmie shrugged. "That's what Cindy gave me. But then Cindy also said she dated my fireman."

This time both of the men stared at her.

"Probably gave me his patrol badge," Micklind finally said. "Those are the only badges with five numbers."

Timmie raised her eyes. "Which meant he was probably a patrolman."

"I don't want to keep this nurse waiting. I may dig a little more later. Thanks for coming in."

"And you'll keep me apprised," Timmie said.

Micklind did smile this time. "Yes, ma'am, I will."

The last place Timmie wanted to return to tonight was her house. That was where she went, though, Murphy in tow. This time she didn't bother to turn on the lights. Only the fluorescent in the kitchen, which was plenty of light to find her mail. She couldn't believe she'd forgotten about the list of mercy killing cases Conrad had sent. She also wasn't all that sure it would help. But any port in a storm.

Besides, she hated having to wait for Micklind to chew his information before spitting it out. She was close; she could feel it. And trauma nurses were not paid for their patience. So she did one more thing.

Without bothering to ask Murphy, she grabbed the phone and dialed information for the number to the Red Roof Inn.

"Red Roof Inn, how may I direct your call?" the nasal, asthmatic operator asked in a rush.

"I'm sorry to bother you," Timmie said, greeting her in her best let's-both-solve-a-big-problem voice. "You had a guest there by the name of Jason Parker?"

Pause. "Maybe."

Timmie smiled. "I'm Mrs. Parker. His wife. I wanted to ask about his bill."

"Oh, ma'am . . . oh, I . . ."

"I know what happened," she said mournfully. "It's only been today that the police were finally able to tell me where he was staying. I . . . well, they gave me his effects, but I've been concerned about his bill. Jason simply never left a bill unpaid."

"Well, there was his credit card . . ."

"Which the company probably froze at his death. I thought if you didn't mind I'd just come by and settle it for you. For . . . Jason."

"Why, uh, thank you. We had to charge him till today, you know. And I'm sure . . . I don't mean to . . ."

"I'll be there in fifteen minutes," Timmie said.

"Those bills always list any phone number that's called and charged to the room," she explained to Murphy as she hung up the phone. When he didn't move, she frowned at him. "Somebody knew Jason was coming to my house. And Jason didn't know anybody in town but me. Don't you think that's a problem worth exploring?"

"The police are looking at the same information right now."

She stopped him with a look. "These are my friends. And once upon a time, Jason was my husband. I need to know."

Murphy just turned for the door. Grabbing the brown manila envelope that had been sitting beneath her toaster, Timmie followed. "I'll read this on the way over."

She tried her best to read by the overhead light, but Murphy's driving made her nauseated. Besides, Conrad's printer must have shared shelf space with the first Fortran computer. The information he'd sent her had been printed on nine dot with what looked for all the world like disappearing ink.

By the time they pulled into the parking lot, she'd only made it through three cases, and not one of them helped. Supermen syndromes all, with possible suspects the authorities simply hadn't been able to nail yet. All men.

The desk clerk was fifty-five and counting on the lottery to save her. Until then, she moved as little as possible and thought even less.

"I'm not sure . . ." she hesitated at Timmie's repeated request, fingers twined in stringy yellow hair. "Jo talked to you before."

"I understand," Timmie commiserated, pulling out her wallet and flipping out driver's license, credit card, and the only picture she had left of the family she'd once had. She'd almost cut Jason out of the pose, leaving just her and Megs, but Meghan would have noticed. Now she was glad she hadn't. "Did you get the chance to meet my husband?" she asked in her best grief-stricken voice.

"Yeah."

Timmie nodded and pushed forward her identification. "You see?" she said. "My name is Timothy Ann Leary-Parker. Here's my ID, and my picture with my husband and daughter."

"I'm still not sure I should allow you to do this. It could be illegal . . . *Timothy?*"

Timmie came very close to grabbing the woman by the shirt. "You're not sure that your company would want their bill paid? I'm a little confused. Why not?"

That stumped her.

Murphy leaned over Timmie's shoulder and peered at the picture on her license. "Good grief, what color is that?"

Timmie squinted herself. "Uh, sunrise orange. It was all the rage at USC that summer."

He just shook his head. "Your name really is Leary-Parker."

Timmie scowled at him. "Well, yeah. If you'll remember, I did my best to introduce myself that way. But since nobody listens, I just gave up. So I'm back to just Timmie Leary."

Didn't it just figure that that was what finally brought the clerk to life. "Leary?" she asked, brightening in that all-too-familiar way. "You aren't Joe Leary's daughter, are you?"

Timmie brightened right back. "Why, yes. You know him?"

The woman laughed like a seal. "You kiddin'? I seen him down at the RiverRat Tavern all the time. He used ta sing and shit. 'I will go and I will go, and I will go now to Englishfree.' "

Well, that was an interpretation Timmie hadn't heard before.

"That's it exactly," she agreed.

Another laugh, and Timmie had the bill in her hand along with the printout of phone numbers and dirty movies Jason had rented while waiting to see his daughter.

"I don't suppose you know—"

"If there was any women here with him?" The woman shook her head. "No."

Timmie blinked. "How'd you know I was going to ask that?"

She got another seal bark. "You kiddin'? The only question I get more'n that is 'Where's the condom machine, honey?' "

Timmie was proud of herself. She at least waited until she got back to the car before she read the bill. She didn't even notice Murphy start the car and back out of the lot. She was too focused on the long list of numbers in her hand.

His parents, his parents, his accountant, his lawyer. Even after all this time, Timmie knew that damn number by heart. St. Louis old money making the link with Los Angeles greed and seeing her straight to the streets.

She knew which numbers she didn't want to see on the list. And she didn't. Ellen's wasn't there. Neither was Barb's, Mattie's, Alex's, or Cindy's. But there was one number she saw more than once.

She got to the end and read it again. It still didn't make sense.

"I need to call Meghan," she said. "Can we—?"

Then she looked up to see that they were already in the parking lot of the *Puckett Independent*. The car engine was off and Murphy was lighting a cigarette one-handed as he scanned Conrad's computer printout.

"We going in?" she asked.

"In a second. Sherilee doesn't like smoke in there. What'd you find?"

She looked back down at her list. "Me. I'm the culprit again."

Murphy didn't bother to look over. "No kidding. You wanna just head over to the station now, or are you going to make a run for it?"

Timmie looked back at the list. At the dates and times. "I wasn't at the house when he called. I couldn't have been. But he told his mother he'd talked to me."

"Who else could he have talked to?"

"Exactly."

And then, she began counting backward from today and tried to remember just what had been going on at about four-thirty in the afternoon.

"Oh, my . . ." Timmie sat up straighter. Counted again so she didn't get it wrong. Laughed, because it was the only thing she could think to do. "No, that can't be right."

"What?"

Timmie stared at the corrugated metal wall of the building, with its oak and brass nameplate pulled from the original brick Victorian presses when they'd moved to escape the '93 flood. She looked over at Murphy, but he had his nose in that printout. It didn't matter. She had the answer she didn't want, and she still didn't want it.

Next to her, Murphy abruptly stiffened. "Bingo."

Timmie didn't hear him. She was trying to decide who to call first, Gladys or Barb. She was wondering how she could get information more quickly than Micklind. She was wondering how she was going to feel about this when the truth finally sank in.

"I bet you know who it is," Murphy said suddenly.

Timmie looked over to see that avid gleam in his eye and nodded, still trying her damnedest to believe it. "I do."

"Me, too."

Finally, Timmie heard him. "I know," she said, and began to believe it.

Even so, Murphy pointed to the tenth case Conrad had copied for her. A possible angel of death stalking the halls of a VA hospital in Joliet, Illinois. "Ring a bell?" he asked.

Murphy did not want to be put on hold. Not when he had dynamite in his hand. Nitro. Plutonium. It was so damn easy. So obvious, according to his cohort in crime, who was even now finishing a call to her mother-in-law.

All Murphy could do was wait for Micklind to get his ass back out of that interrogation room that was going to prove useless, and get on the damn phone.

"What?" Micklind asked by way of greeting.

Murphy stubbed out the cigarette he'd brought in anyway and leaned over his printout. "That nurse Gladys still down there?"

"Yeah. She couldn't tell me much."

"Well, ask her this. Ask her how Ellen's husband died."

"What?"

"Ask her how Ellen's husband died. Trust me."

Micklind grunted and put Murphy back on hold. Next to him, Timmie was smiling and discussing green flies and chameleons, which Murphy figured meant she was talking to her daughter. He should call his. When this was over. When he decided what to do. After he'd had his meaningless sex with Leary and recovered his breath.

He lit another cigarette while he waited. He thought how refreshing a stiff drink would be right now. How he'd never really celebrated an exclusive story without at least a bottle of something flammable, if not combustible. He sucked hard on the cigarette and focused on winning instead.

"Murphy?" It was Micklind, and he sounded downright stunned. "Guess what I found out?"

Murphy smiled like a pirate. "Her husband was killed in the line of duty in Chicago."

It sounded like Micklind was smoking, too. Might as well. This was even better than good sex. "This Gladys apologized for the mix-up. She said she always got those two mixed up, since they were so much alike and they were both widows. How'd you figure it out?"

"Leary figured out from a phone bill that her husband had been conversing with someone at her house when she wasn't home. There's only one other person who was definitely in the house at four-thirty P.M. two days before Jason Parker's death, when he made his last call. I also got some great information for you—"

"Actually, so did I. That's what took me so long. I got the information on that Cindy's husband's death. Turns out he didn't."

"Didn't what? Die?"

"Die? He didn't even exist. There was no such cop as John Skorcezy. Hell, there wasn't even a man from Chicago named John Skorcezy. I went ahead and asked right after you left. The information just came up."

"Actually," Murphy said, "there might not have been a John Skorcezy, but there was a Stanislaus Skorcezy. He was the first patient to die in a series of fifteen murders that took place almost four years ago in Joliet, Illinois. They had a suspect, but failed to indict for lack of evidence."

"Don't tell me. Cindy Dunn."

"Not exactly. Cindy Skorcezy. Stanislaus's daughter."

Silence. "She was a nurse at her father's hospital?"

"She was a nurse. Just not there."

"Jesus." Murphy waited, but it took Micklind a minute to catch his breath. Murphy didn't blame him. "We're waiting for the AFIS results on those prints, but I bet it's a clean match. Does Timmie know where this Cindy might be?"

"Hey, Leary," Murphy said. "Can you find Cindy? Micklind wants to talk to her."

Timmie was just hanging up the phone. "Cindy told Meghan not to tell me her daddy had called. Said it was going to be a surprise for me." She shook her head, her eyes tight and troubled. "She was at work. Let me check."

She dialed, greeted, waited.

". . . how long does she have left for lunch . . . no, I'm not going to insult her again, Ellen. I'm going to apologize. Is that okay?"

"I think the suspect is working her shift at the hospital," Murphy interpreted for the cop. "She is, however, on lunch break."

Micklind snorted. "It's damn near nine. You'd think she was a cop."

Murphy was grinning when he caught the sudden consternation in Timmie's voice. "What do you *mean* they can't find him? She was suddenly on point, bristling with annoyance and impatience. "Thanks, Ellen. I'll call them right now."

"Problems?" he asked when she hung up.

"My father." She punched buttons as if they needed punishment. "He's wandered off the floor. They wonder if I wouldn't come in and help them *look* for him. I don't think I'm paying all this money to have them misplace him, for God's sake."

"He's not in any danger, is he?"

"No. He has an electric alert anklet that will sound like a dive Klaxon if he so much as wanders into the regular hospital. He's probably hiding in some old woman's closet pretending her husband is due home . . . Hello?"

That call took three minutes, four monosyllabic responses, and one promise. By the time Timmie hung up the phone, Murphy was on his feet, both phone bill and printout in hand. "Need a ride?"

She scowled. "Yes. What is Micklind going to do about Cindy?" That gave her pause. She stopped, laughed an odd, mirthless bark of surprise, shook her head. "My God. Cindy."

"He'll pick her up at work. Which probably means you should go in the back door when you go see your dad. I'll drop you off and take this over to Micklind. Call me there when you need a ride."

She kept shaking her head. "*Cindy*. And here we thought she was all talk."

Murphy dropped her off at the Restcrest entrance and headed back out of the campus again. It was a pretty night, if you liked winter. The sky was clear and black and brisk, with a few stars peeking past the city lights and the moon hanging parchment yellow over the hospital. Everything held still in the darkness beyond the orange glow of the parking lot lights.

Murphy had just hit his blinker to turn left off the southern exit of the hospital when he noticed the car that had stopped at the sign. Must be an out-of-towner, was his first thought. Missourians tended to consider stop signs as suggestions rather than orders. As long as they hit their lowest gear and at least pulled their foot off the gas, they considered themselves to be making a legal stop. Which was why this guy looked so odd sitting there.

Maybe he was trying to see past the stand of trees at the edge of the lane. Whatever it was, something was confusing this poor white-haired guy sitting there in his sedan.

White hair.

Throwing his car into neutral and yanking on the brake, Murphy leaned forward to get a better look. He hit his high beams and watched them glint off that singular mane. Murphy saw the guy look around, as if seeking something. He saw, to his astonishment, that he was in his pajamas.

And he knew without a doubt who it was.

Restcrest was mounting an indoor search party, and somehow Joe Leary had made a clean break as far as the nearest auto. Now that he had it, though, he had obviously forgotten what to do with it.

Murphy climbed out of the car as quickly as possible and headed for the sedan.

"Joe? Joe, you okay?"

He hadn't gotten as far as figuring out what he was going to do with him. He just knew that this poor old geezer was shaking like a malaria patient and getting alarmingly blue around the lips. And he was singing . . . what? It was familiar.

"Joe, remember me? My name's Murphy." He leaned a hand against the door. "I think maybe you need to come with me, bud."

"Magic Bus." That was what it was. Murphy wanted to laugh. Joe Leary was sitting in a stolen car at nine at night in his pj's singing "Magic Bus," and there wasn't anybody around to witness it.

" 'Hey, Joe,' " he crooned, trying to get the guy's attention and thinking that it was the wrong song. "How the hell'd you get here?"

Murphy was leaning over far enough to see that Joe was barefoot. Joe turned, saw Murphy, and then looked up. Murphy was already bent over to get hold of Joe's arm. By the time he heard what Joe saw, he was too off-balance to protect himself. Murphy spun around in time to catch the impression of wood grain.

Oh, hell, was all he could think of as the bat cracked against his head and sent him slamming against the car. What a stupid jerk to fall for that one. And then the gravel bit into his cheek and he felt his legs go numb.

# TWENTY-SIX

TWENTY-SIX
TWENTY-SIX

TIMMIE WAS STARTING TO GET FRANTIC. THEY'D COMBED EVERY inch of Restcrest, and still there had been no sign of her father. Hospital security had been notified along with the police. They'd even called Alex, who, for once, hadn't answered. It didn't matter. With the temperature outside hovering in the teens, they didn't have time to wait.

"He was just in the main room enjoying a snack," Cathy kept protesting. "He couldn't possibly have wandered away."

Timmie wasn't in the mood for mercy. "My father could have been in New York by the time you had the first call into the police."

"They're going to get the dogs," the nurse promised.

And then they found the ankle bracelet that was supposed to keep her father safe. It had been sliced through with a dull knife—probably taken from the snack areas—and left by the side entrance. Timmie didn't wait any longer for the police or dogs or angel hordes. She shrugged into her coat and ran toward the ER.

Maybe if it wasn't busy she could get some help there. God knew the hospital was ready enough to turf the ER staff up to work Restcrest. Maybe they could also be used to help rectify its mistakes.

"Code blue, emergency room four. Code blue."

Timmie wanted to cry. There went most of her staff.

"Trauma code blue, emergency room one."

This wasn't just bad luck. It was a conspiracy. Well, at least she wouldn't have to face Cindy. Micklind should have carted her off at least an hour ago. And with any luck, at least one of the codes would be for show and only last a few minutes. Then Timmie could grab the extras. One extra. A tech with a flashlight. She didn't care.

She knew she was screwed when she spotted Ellen running down the work lane in full flight, tears streaming down her face.

Timmie tried to match her stride. "I need help, Ellen . . . "

Ellen stopped on a dime and pivoted. "No, Timmie. I don't have time right now. We're short-staffed, and now this. This!"

She waved her hand toward the room behind her, where the non-trauma code was in full swing, but Timmie didn't notice. "I'm sorry. I didn't mean for it to come down like this. Have the police been here already?"

"The police? Why would they be here? Has something happened to Cindy?"

Timmie lost track of all the mayhem around them. "Happened? Haven't they picked her up?"

"Picked her up? Of course not. She walked out of here right after you hurt her, and we haven't seen her since."

Oh, God. Oh, no.

"Ellen—"

Ellen flashed an unheard-of rage. "I can't right now, Timmie. Don't you see we're busy?"

"But my dad's missing. And Cindy's missing. And nobody can find Alex."

Somehow that brought Ellen to a halt. "Find him? You don't need to find him. He's right there."

She pointed to that room again, and Timmie finally saw. Standing in the far corner, her eyes swollen and red, her hands wrung together like socks in a spin cycle, her voice a low moan of grief. Mary Jane Arlington. Next to her, Barb was slipping paddles back into the defibrillator, Mattie was yanking off gray slacks, and one of the techs was lubricating an Ewald tube.

"Okay," Barb was saying. "We've got a rhythm. Now get me some dopamine, and where the fuck's the Narcan?"

"Narcan?" Timmie asked for no apparent reason. She knew damn well what Narcan was the specific treatment for.

"Mary Jane found him in his office," Ellen all but accused. "He overdosed."

And then she just spun away and ran into the room, leaving Timmie behind to stare at Alex Raymond's naked feet like a witness at a roadside accident.

She didn't have time for this. Her father was out there someplace freezing to death, or worse. Cindy was missing. Alex was a big boy who should be able to handle his mistakes like an adult.

Which, of course, was why everybody in this town, including her, had spent so much time protecting him from reality.

Timmie wasn't going to be able to tolerate much more of this reality shit herself before she caved in like a tree house full of termites. She had to call Murphy. She had to call Micklind. She had to get the hell out of here before it dawned on her just why Alex Raymond had tried to kill himself.

"Hey, man," one of the paramedics was saying to a member of the other team as they restocked. "I'm sorry I almost sideswiped you. I didn't see that Porsche sitting there till the last minute."

"Jesus, no kidding," the other guy said with a shake of his head. "Can you believe somebody'd leave a classic like that just sitting there in the driveway with its lights out?"

Timmie turned to them. "Porsche?"

They nodded in unison. "Eighty-eight candy-apple-red Cabriolet."

This was impossible. How could this possibly get worse?

Timmie was a trauma nurse. She knew damn well how it could get worse. "You didn't see anybody inside?" she asked, her hands clutched as tightly as Mary Jane's.

"Not a soul. I told your security guys. Guess they'll tow it."

Timmie didn't even bother to say good-bye. She just ran for

the phone and tried her damnedest to remember the number for the police department. She finally settled for the operator, who kindly suggested 911. It took Timmie precious moments to convince her that that wouldn't work. By the time she finally got Micklind on the phone, she could hardly think.

"Detective Sergeant Micklind."

Timmie almost wept with relief. "This is Timmie Leary. Did you pick up Cindy Dunn yet? Have you seen Murphy? Do you know my father's missing?"

"Whoa, slow down. Again."

She repeated herself. "I just don't think it's a coincidence that Murphy, my father, and Cindy are all missing at the same time. Do you?"

There was a pause. A small sound of impatience. "I really don't need this tonight."

"I don't need this *ever*! What are we going to do?"

"Timmie Leary, outside call, line six. Timmie Leary."

That was the hospital operator, paging. Timmie's heart jumped. "Hold on." She hit the Hold button and dialed the outside line.

"This is Timmie Leary." She was so frightened her voice sounded like she'd been sucking helium.

Her caller whispered, "I want to say thank you."

Just from listening, she knew. It could sound like a man or a woman. Low, soft, anonymous. But it wasn't anonymous to Timmie.

"Cindy?" she asked, hanging on to that phone as if it would help her hang on to Cindy herself. "I'm sorry about what I said. I've just been so upset lately. Can we talk about it?"

"No," Cindy said quietly. "We can't. I'm tired of trying to be your friend. After everything I've done for you, you turn on me like that. I don't deserve that kind of treatment."

"You're right. You don't—"

"Listen to me. Listen to *me*. You think you're so smart. You think you know everything. Well, figure this out, forensic nurse. Who do you save first?"

"What?"

"No, that's a triage question, isn't it? Well, you're so sure you know better than anybody else which patient deserves all your attention. I collected a puzzle for you tonight. I was just going to stop and get any able-bodied person to make it fair, but I got a bonus. I got your friend the reporter. And I got your father. Now, who do you save first?"

God, she couldn't breathe. She needed to let Micklind know. She needed to alert somebody here.

Nobody here was paying attention. They were hovering over Alex, or ricocheting around the trauma room like racquetballs. There was nothing she could do but hold on and wait for the rest.

"Here's the clue," Cindy said, as if asked. "What are some of the other uses for fabric softener sheets? You have five minutes to answer, Timmie. After that it'll be too late."

*Click.*

Fabric softener. Fabric . . .

Timmie punched the Hold button. "Micklind, are you there?"

"Yeah, what the hell . . . ?"

"My house! They're at my house, and she's going to set it on fire!"

Timmie didn't even wait to hear him yell "Shit!" and hang up. She just ran.

There was a car in her driveway. A nondescript Japanese sedan she'd never seen before tucked back in the shadows by the garage. Lights were on all across the first floor. The second floor remained dark. Timmie knew the police would be coming soon. She also knew she couldn't wait. Cindy was going to start dropping lighted sheets of fabric softener all over the piles and mountains of flammables in those rooms until her house, her grandfather's and great-grandfather's house, was a conflagration of old memories.

If that was all Cindy intended to do, Timmie could live with it. But Timmie knew with dead certainty that she fully intended to take her father and Murphy along for the ride.

*Who do you save first?*

No, Daddy. No.

Timmie knew it was probably pointless, but she walked around the back of her house to get in. No creaky step for her. She pulled open the creaky screen door to the kitchen instead, counting on the fact that Cindy had unlocked the way in.

She had.

Timmie could hear the refrigerator humming. She could hear the clock ticking in the living room. Overhead the fluorescent light flickered, and the window that lit her sun catchers had disappeared into a rectangle of night. The house seemed so still. Sleeping, as if it were just lying dormant. Timmie knew better. Carefully avoiding the spots that would groan, she tiptoed across the floor, all the while conscious of how much time she was using up. Measuring her breathing, her movements, by the ticking of that clock. Keeping perfectly quiet, she leaned around the doorway to see into the dining room.

Nothing.

No bodies, no Cindy, no fire.

No, not quite nothing. Standing there in the stale air of an empty house, Timmie caught the first whiff of a familiar odor. Not much. But then, not much was needed. All Cindy had to do was drop a couple of fabric softener sheets into a pool of brand-new bourbon, and this place would go up like bananas Foster.

Where was her father? Where was Murphy? How long did Timmie have before Cindy started flicking her Bic?

And most important, what could she do to stop her?

Timmie had no gun. They'd taken that away with Jason. She had no pepper spray or dogs. She did, however, have a lifetime batting average of .310. Timmie turned toward the front door for her weapon and suffered her latest shock. It was gone. Her best Louisville slugger, autographed by Stan "the Man" Musial himself. And damn it if Timmie wasn't sure she knew exactly who'd walked off with it.

Somehow, that settled her. If there was one thing a trauma nurse was, it was resourceful. And Traumawoman was resource itself. Holding her breath against discovery, Timmie crept back into her father's room and raided his memory closet. Well, if she couldn't have Stan the Man, she could at least have Marty Marion.

"You might as well come on down," she said into the echoing rooms. "The police will be here in a minute."

Cindy's voice floated, disembodied, down the stairs. "I know."

Timmie thought she could hear distant sirens already, but that might have just been wishful thinking.

"Where are they?" she asked.

Cindy laughed, and the sound bounced down the stairs. "That's for you to find out. You're so damn smart."

Timmie rubbed the back of her neck and choked up again. "All right, then, how about this. Why?"

There was a long pause upstairs. A breathy sound that might have been a sigh. "I just wanted to help," she said.

"By killing gomers?"

"That was Landry's fault," she insisted, suddenly petulant. "That son of a bitch. I loved him!"

"He wasn't even here when you started killing those old people, Cindy."

"Well, all right, that was Alex."

"Alex asked you to kill his patients for him?"

"He couldn't do that. But he told me how much they were going to cost the unit. How tough it was going to be to make ends meet for a third time. How worried he was about it."

"He told you that?"

"Yes! I was there for him a long time before you were."

By now, Timmie knew better. But now wasn't the time to argue.

"And you called Murphy so that Landry would get into trouble? Or did you just kill Alice to cost him all that money?"

Silence. "I told you. He was using me."

"What about your father, Cindy? Who asked you to kill him?"

There was a shuffling sound. A familiar clicking that sent ice skittering through Timmie's veins. "You could have at least thanked me," Cindy said, her voice small and sad. And then she tossed the first of the softener sheets straight down the stairwell.

Timmie screamed and ran, but it was too late. Cindy had

dripped the bourbon down the side of the staircase, and it caught like a gas trail. As Timmie grabbed a bolt of fabric to beat it out, Cindy dropped another. And another. She walked right down the steps, floating sheets over the side of the railing like flash paper flowers.

Timmie gave up on the fabric. Paper had started to catch. The curtains were no more than a few feet away, and they were old. The pool of bourbon seemed to reach back under the hall closet door, where all her father's business papers had been kept. It was already too late. And Cindy, dropping sheets, was smiling.

Timmie leaped for her. Cindy clambered away, dropping another sheet she'd lit from the shiny silver Zippo in her hand. The paper caught fast, the smell acrid and thick, the flames licking upward toward old wood.

"It's too late," Cindy chanted, pulling another sheet free. "Which one do you save? You really gonna let Mister Murphy die just because you can't say good-bye to your father?"

"Cindy, stop it now," Timmie begged, crowding her back toward the stairs. "Help me get them out."

Cindy lifted the sheet high, flicked the lighter so that the flame shuddered in the depths of her dark eyes. "You still don't get it," she said. "I just wanted to be your friend."

And then she lit the sheet.

She was going to toss the thing right at Timmie. Timmie never let her. Winding up like she was going for the left field corner, she swung the bat straight at Cindy's arms.

Cindy didn't see the bat until the last minute. Her eyes popped. She dropped the lighter, threw up her hands. Caught the bat mid-forearm and screamed as her bones crunched.

Timmie didn't even wait to see what Cindy was going to do. She dove for the lighter, which was skating across the floor toward another pile of papers. Grabbing it, she scrambled back to her feet and shoved the shrilling Cindy aside to get up the stairs.

The stairs were already involved. Flames licked around the edges like logs on a hearth, and the smoke roiled up toward the second floor as if it were a chimney. Timmie choked and blinked, blinded by the sudden heat. She heard a terrible scream from below her and knew that Cindy had been caught by her own trap. But it was too late to worry about Cindy now.

Who do you save first?

It depended on who she found first.

Her bedroom was empty. Timmie searched her bed, under her bed, around the floor, into the closet. The smoke was getting too thick to see, and she was crawling.

"Daddy! Murphy, where the hell are you?"

On her hands and knees, pulling her shirt up over her nose and mouth, squinting through inky, oily blackness, the fire below moaning with delight. It was too fast, let loose in a house made for a holocaust.

"Daddy!"

She scooted into Meghan's room. Crouched lower. Heard the sirens and couldn't wait. She didn't even realize she still had the bat in her hand until it bumped into something. Something soft. Something big.

She had to bend close to recognize him. Silvery hair, soft blue eyes. Hands tied with the same duct tape that closed his mouth. She almost sobbed with relief. She almost dragged him out without looking for Murphy.

Murphy was four feet farther back. Wedged into a closet, unconscious. Taped and silent and sticky with congealing blood. Impossible to move easily, which was probably the point.

Who do you save first, smartass?

Timmie sobbed with frustration. She looked back to her father, who was calmly watching her, as if he knew that, like always, she'd take care of him. She looked at Murphy, who couldn't help himself at all. She heard the crash of something caving in downstairs and scooted over to untape her father.

"You have to get yourself out, Da," she said in between coughs. "Hold on to Murphy's leg and I'll guide you out."

He smiled. "Okay, honey."

She turned back and grabbed Murphy by the shoulders. Her lungs were bursting. Pinpoints of light danced in front of her eyes. She couldn't breathe. She couldn't think. If she stopped to worry about it, all three of them would be dead. She yanked on Murphy until she thought she was going to die, and finally felt his dead weight inch across the floor.

"Now, hold on, Da!" she yelled.

Joe took hold of Murphy's ankle and scooted right along with her. Timmie backed toward the door. She could really hear the fire now. Not the wood popping or the joints groaning. The fire. Hungry, primal, ferocious. Howling and cackling with glee, seething with power. Snapping at her like prey on a veldt. And softly, like psychotic counterpoint, her father, singing.

"'They asked me how I knew ... my true love was tru-u-u-u-e ...'"

"Smoke Gets in Your Eyes." Could he pick 'em or what? Timmie tried to laugh and ended up choking instead. She kept moving long past the moment she could see. Past the moment she could breathe. She finally got to a window over the back porch and punched it out.

The fire roared below. Timmie could barely make out strobes shuddering against the next house. She heard engines and pumps and voices. Not soon enough. She had to get these two out.

She looked back to guide her father on and realized he was gone. Somewhere along the hallway, he'd let go of Murphy, and she hadn't noticed. Timmie hesitated for only a second. And then, because of who she was, how she was trained, she acted. She triaged, and saved the person who had the best chance of surviving.

Breaking out as much glass as she could, Timmie pulled Murphy out onto the roof. It still held, and a pair of firefighters were just setting up to get a ladder to it. If the fire didn't reach them in the next minute, Murphy would be okay.

Timmie could hear the chaos below and knew it wouldn't be long before the entire house just folded in on itself. She turned away from the man she'd just broken her back pulling out.

"Hey, what are you doing?" the fireman yelled.

At the front of the house, two windows exploded, and the fire claimed the roof. Sucking in a few lungsful of clean air, Timmie climbed back into the window and went to save her father.

# EPILOGUE

MURPHY HATED HOSPITALS. IT WAS BAD ENOUGH SPENDING enough time in one to get a story. But that was nothing to actually being stuck in one as a patient. Especially now that he was feeling better.

Well, less dead. He could at least talk now that they'd taken that damn tube out, and he could breathe without coughing up chunks of what looked like coal. His head didn't feel like it was going to fall off, and he could successfully count raised fingers three times out of four. Even with the cast on his arm and the stitches all across his back from where Leary had dragged him over a broken window to get him out of that house, he didn't feel nearly as bad as he knew he should. He was just restless.

Sherilee had been in. She'd helped him finish the piece on the town that had covered up a serial killer. She'd also cracked a bottle of sparkling grape juice for the third Pulitzer she was sure it was going to earn. Murphy drank his juice, wished like hell for the real stuff, and smiled like a good boy. He put up with visits from Mattie, Walter, Barb, and Ellen, who seemed committed to dispensing only innocuous news. He even sat through the dressing down he'd been handed by the police detective who'd had to break into his Porsche to get it out of the path of careening ambulances.

But Murphy didn't want to talk to any of them. None of them knew what it felt like to be immobilized. None of them realized why he had to leave.

He heard her coming all the way down the hall. She was shuffling on feet still raw from where her rubber-soled tennis shoes had melted in the heat. She looked even worse than Murphy, her eyebrows gone and her face peeling like a bad sunburn. Her hair had been singed almost to the roots. She had her burned and lacerated hands wrapped in big, protective mitts to cushion them, and she had a set of stitches on her butt that matched the ones on Murphy's back. All in all, a pitiful sight. Murphy would have felt sorry for her, except that of any of the crowd who'd stopped by to see him, she seemed the most content.

Today that contentment was a little fragile, so Murphy took it upon himself to be the entertainer.

"When am I getting out of here?" he demanded, his throat still gravelly from smoke inhalation.

"I don't know when you're going home," Timmie said, easing into his armchair. "I'm not in charge. Of anything. Ever again."

"Don't be ridiculous," Murphy retorted, trying to find a more comfortable position and just making himself dizzy. "I heard you're going to be the coroner."

"Bite your tongue."

"You mean you don't want to know how people die?"

"Not as long as I live."

"But you got Van Adder disgraced. You got Landry fired, that security guard brought up on charges, and GerySys outbid by a reputable firm that will co-op Restcrest to financial security. Hell, you even got all those nurses rehired."

"No I didn't," she said. "You did. I just got my house burned down."

"And got Davies off with a warning."

"He didn't mean it."

Murphy could tell from her eyes how much he hadn't meant it.

Not something to argue about, though. He closed his eyes and leaned back against his pillow. "You been checking up on everybody today?"

He could hear her unsuccessfully try to scratch one hand with the other. "Uh-huh."

"How's your buddy?"

Timmie sighed. "Alex? They moved him out of ICU right before they moved you."

"He'll be okay?"

"Yeah, I guess." Timmie's laugh sounded as sore as Murphy's chest. "Isn't it funny how you don't realize who the stronger person is?"

Murphy opened his eyes. "What do you mean?"

She shrugged, her eyes looking bruised and introspective. "I always thought Alex would save me from my dad's weaknesses. And here it's my dad who was the survivor, not Alex."

"Alex will be okay as long as he has his cause."

"And an entire town to protect him from reality."

"Aren't there days when you'd like a little protection?"

"There are days when I'd like somebody to wipe my nose and schedule my naps. And when that happens, I usually end up homeless, hospitalized, and trying to figure out what happened."

"Nobody's gonna figure that out any better than they'll figure out Cindy."

Leary waved him off. "Oh, hell, Cindy's easy. She wanted to be someone. She wanted to mean something to someone. It's what we all do."

Murphy could do no more than shake his head. "You decided all this while she was chasing you around with a lighter, did you?"

"No. When she told me she'd just been trying to help. I feel sorry for her."

Murphy found himself gaping. "She's dead because she tried to kill us all, Leary. I'm afraid that doesn't inspire compassion here."

"She tried to get us to love her, Murphy. She just didn't know how."

He was back to shaking his head. "I guess that's why I'm a reporter and you're a nurse."

"Not just a nurse," she said with a secret smile. "Trauma-woman."

"Uh-huh. How's your dad?"

That cost her the smile. "I don't know yet. He's hanging in there."

Murphy sat up straighter. Barb had at least filled him in on that department. "They haven't put him on life support?"

Timmie shook her head. "I won't let them. If he lives, he has to decide to do it on his own. I'm not stacking the deck just so he has a heartbeat."

"You're sure about that?"

Timmie spent a moment considering the mitts on her hands. Murphy could see the memories taking her back to moments he knew nothing about. He'd heard about them from the police, of course, and the fire crews who had stopped by to visit their two miracles. She'd done the impossible, and then crawled back in to do it again, even as the house had fallen in around her. And then, with her six-foot four-inch father draped across her back like a winter coat, she'd made it all the way to the window before the floor had given way. Only quick hands and strong firemen had saved either of them.

Murphy knew that the hospital was putting her up for a lifesaving award. He knew that damn near every person in Puckett was praying that Joe Leary didn't die after his daughter had fought so hard to save him. He suspected that Timmie didn't agree.

"I'm not going to make Daddy live just because I feel guilty," she finally said, lifting clear blue eyes his way. "I'm not going to let him die for the same reason. It's time for nature to take over. If he lives, we'll do the best we can. If he doesn't, we'll toast him like the rare character he was, and then we'll go on. It's not my decision to make."

"And after that?"

"Right now I'm just trying to find a place to live." Then she smiled, her expression suddenly clear. "At least I don't have to worry about cleaning all those newspapers out of the living room."

"My apartment's going to be available soon."

A little of that light died. "How soon?"

"I have a tentative offer from the *Philadelphia Inquirer* I thought I'd check out. In a couple of weeks, maybe."

She nodded. "And the rest?"

Murphy thought of that sparkling grape juice he'd resented so much. "I guess we'll see."

Timmie nodded, smiled, went back to staring at her hands. "Well, then, how about that meaningless sex?"

Murphy laughed so hard he started coughing again. "Now?"

She laughed back, and the two of them sounded like a tuberculosis ward. "You name the time, I'll name the place."

"When those things are off your hands."

She nodded. "Deal."

They smiled, content with the deal. Anticipating the rewards. Regretting the loss.

"Not a deal," Murphy said. "A date."

When he fell asleep a few hours later, he found himself smiling.

"You should be asleep."

Timmie looked up from where her father was resting to see the night nurse hovering at the edge of the door.

"I couldn't," she admitted. "Hospitals are as restful as hockey rinks."

The nurse smiled. "He's been sleeping pretty well tonight."

Timmie nodded and went back to watching her father's face. It looked tired, yellow. He was finally beginning to look small. There was an re-breather over his nose and mouth, and a couple of IVs in his arm. His chest rattled, and his urine was scant and dark. Not enough to kill him unless he decided it was time to go. He evidently hadn't come to that crossroads yet.

"He been singing at all?"

"Actually, yes," the nurse said, stepping in. "He's been humming. And whispering about women."

Timmie turned her head. "Women?"

"Yeah. I don't know who it is, but he keeps talking about 'she this and she that,' you know?"

Timmie smiled. "Not she, like ladies. Sidhe, like leprechauns. He's talking to the fairy folk."

The unit was hushed at this hour of the morning, shadowy and unfamiliar. The sun was setting up to breach the horizon, and birds chattered in the bare trees outside the window.

Daybreak. The most superstitious time of the day, when light returned, when shadows and nightmares fell away, when reality reasserted its hold on a primal mind.

When the veil grew stronger, the fairies slipped into the darkness, and humans were given permission to hope.

Timmie clasped her father's hand between hers and thought how huge it was. How all-encompassing. He was a hell of a man. Lousy husband, uncertain father, titanic drunk. Dear, whimsical, infuriating friend.

She wanted so badly to recite Dylan Thomas to him. To beg him to stay. But it wasn't her place anymore. He'd choose to stay or go as he wanted. As he needed. And she'd just wait here by his side until he decided.

"Timmie . . . "

She straightened at the sound of his voice. "Well, good morning, Da, how are you?"

He struggled to get his eyes open even halfway. They were still red and swollen and tender, his face raw. "Timmie . . . "

Timmie was pulling the re-breather free so she could hear him better when the nurse walked back in. "Mr. Leary!" she yelled in a patented old-persons-and-foreign-tourists voice. "HOW . . . ARE . . . YOU?"

Timmie's dad flinched and closed his eyes. "Hush, woman."

Timmie held on tighter, felt a flutter of a response in his hand. "How you feeling, Da?"

"Like . . . crap. Who hit me?"

"O'Doole."

The nurse glared, but Timmie knew better. Her father didn't

have the strength to unravel the last few days. Let him nod in peace.

"Ah . . . he's got a mean left, that one."

"Yep."

"Timmie?"

"Yes, Da."

"Am I going to die?"

She sucked in a breath. "I don't know, Da. Are you?"

It took him a minute to work up the energy. "Don't know. If I do, though . . ." Timmie leaned closer, and he nodded, that quick, wry quirk his father had taught him. "I gave it a good pull, didn't I, girl?"

Timmie couldn't say she was surprised at all by the tears that splashed against her hands. "Yeah, Da. You did that."

He nodded again.

Behind Timmie, the nurse snuffled like a horse. " 'I will arise and go now, and I will go to Innisfree,' " she intoned, as if she were viewing a saint.

Joe Leary turned toward his daughter. "Timmie . . . "

"Yes, Da."

"Will you tell me . . . why people are always saying that to me?"

Timmie could hardly stop laughing. "It's from 'The Lake Isle of Innisfree,' Da, by Yeats. It's your favorite poem."

That got his eyes wide open. "Aw, Jesus, who said that? Do you know how tired I am of hearing that damn thing?"

Timmie laughed until the sun came up and the fairies fled into the darkness.